Printed in Australia

Cover and internal design by Shawline Publishing Group Pty Ltd

Images in this book are copyright approved for Shawline Publishing Group Pty Ltd

Illustrations within this book are copyright approved for Shawline Publishing Group Pty Ltd

First printing: February 2024

Shawline Publishing Group Pty Ltd

www.shawlinepublishing.com.au

Paperback ISBN 978-1-9231-0125-8

eBook ISBN 978-1-9231-0126-5

Distributed by Shawline Distribution and Lightning Source Global

A catalogue record for this work is available from the National Library of Australia

KAT ORGOVANY

Georgie

*For Ben Iser*
*Who left for the big library in the sky,*
*before he had a chance to read this*

**Content Warning**

This book contains mild references to and inclusions
of physical abuse.

# CHAPTER ONE

I snuck through the back door of Purgatory Palace hoping to avoid Mother, but it wasn't to be.

'Where have you been until this godforsaken hour?' she bellowed, champagne glass in hand, drunk as usual and reeking of Chanel No. 5.

Mother loved using words like *godforsaken.* Any word that referred to God was top priority in her vocabulary.

'I've been with Troy, *Mother.*'

Then it began.

'What are you doing with your life, Georgina? Spending all your time with that loser; are you having intercourse with him? You are, aren't you? You are eighteen years old and your only ambition in life is to be a pizza deliverer. What sort of career is that for a daughter of mine? And when are you going to take out that ridiculous nose ring? You look like a punk!'

And on it went.

I was already skipping through Purgatory Palace's kitchen as Mother's wailing continued and was soon joined by the love of my life, my red and tan kelpie, Chocky. My pooch and I had been together for three years, since she was a pup, and were inseparable. I loved her more than anyone else in this world.

I spied my soon-to-be-step-dad watching TV in the living room. The old, bald fool. He peeked up at me through his specs and shook his judgmental head. I hated his guts. We had absolutely nothing in common yet I was forced to live with him because Mother had found 'true love' again. Vomit. I could never forgive her for bringing a creep like that into my life.

I couldn't move out of Purgatory Palace though, as much as I wanted to, because if I left this hellhole before my twenty-first birthday I would lose my inheritance. Mother insisted on it.

Great, huh?

'Hello there, Mr Peters.' I smirked. 'Mr No Personality Peters,' I continued under my breath as I climbed the stairs, tripping over my own feet.

Purgatory Palace's stairs were always a mammoth task to climb, especially when drunk. To my right, the eyes of my dead relatives looking sombre and miserable watched my every move from their faded black and white portraits framed in gold. There was one in particular that gave me the utter creeps. An old man with a bug-shaped head and huge Coke-bottle glasses who was the spitting image of my nun-nemesis, Sister Catherine.

Shudder.

A gaudy 1920s chandelier hung from the ceiling above the stairs. It would slowly move back and forth as my bored dead relatives took turns pushing it. I'd always hurry when directly under the Devil's Light, fearing the decrepit contraption would fall on me. I would usually keep my eyes fixed on the golden candlesticks that sat purposelessly on a table at the end of the stairs, knowing when I reached them I was safe, but tonight Mother was distracting me.

I turned to look at her as she staggered after me, spilling champagne everywhere. Her dyed yellow hair was always worn in a 1960s beehive but was messy, like Patsy from *Ab Fab* after a three-day bender. She wore a white silk dressing gown with her trademark pink feather boa draped around her turkey neck like she was about to do a number from *Priscilla Queen of the Desert.* There was something very drag-queen-like about Mother.

'Remember, you are coming to our engagement party at The Hilton tomorrow night, young lady, no excuses! And don't you dare wear black!'

I locked my bedroom door and put Nirvana's *Bleach* on my record player to drown out her noise. I jumped up and down on my bed for a while, playing air guitar, before catching my reflection in the mirror and winking at it.

I certainly wasn't the sort of daughter Mother had expected. Always clad in poor clothing, black hair askew and totally ambitionless. I loved playing the rebel. After all, it was the only thing that kept me sane in my horribly rich and upper-class family.

I also knew that I could get away with almost anything.

One smile was usually all it took.

Mother needn't have worried.

I was definitely planning on going to the engagement party.

# CHAPTER TWO

I stepped out of the elevator and strolled into The Hilton's pretentious penthouse with my head held high in an attempt to out-snob Mother and Mr No Personality Peters' guests. I wore black as usual, but this time it was a knee-length dress with a white collar I had found in an op shop. I only decided to buy it after the shopkeeper assured me it had been worn at a funeral. The dress went perfectly with my long black socks and scuffed Doc Martins, so lady-like.

I wandered past a gaggle of old biddies only to be tapped on the shoulder.

'Oh, waitress!'

I turned sharply, spying an old crow, complete with tiara. 'Can we please have some champagne? We seem to have been forgotten about!'

I summed up the situation. Should I, shouldn't I? Would it enrage Mother?

'Certainly ma'am,' I said with a bow. As I headed towards a real waitress, I smiled when I noticed how similar my dress and the waitress' uniform were. She smiled back and offered me a glass of champagne. I took the whole tray.

I headed back to the old biddies.

'Why, *thank you.*'

They huddled around me like vultures, grabbing at the glasses, leaving only one on the tray.

'Well, lookie here.' I grinned. 'A glass for me!'

I sculled the champagne, burped and sauntered off, hearing the faithful words, '*Oh really! I never!*' behind me. Mrs Tiara wouldn't leave things there, though. She wanted vengeance. I followed her as she scuttled off to find Mother.

'Alicia! Alicia!' she yelled in her near-heart-attack state.

'What is it? What's happened?' Mother asked.

'One of the waitresses was so rude. *I never!* She drank one of the glasses of champagne right in front of us. You need to reprimand her immediately. I don't know where you got your catering staff from but...'

'Calm down, dear. Point her out to me. I will fix her.'

Mrs Tiara grabbed Mother's arm and led her off to find the *rude waitress.*

'That's her!'

I turned around, pretending not to have heard their entire conversation. 'Hello, Mother!'

'What?' Mrs Tiara was dumbstruck.

'This is my daughter,' Mother said through clenched teeth.

'What? Your daughter is a waitress?'

'No, actually I'm a pizza deliverer but my ambition in life is to become a waitress when I grow up!' I quipped before fleeing.

I headed towards the kitchen, leaving Mother to clean up my mess as usual.

On my way there, I noticed a figure in a heavily starched black nun's habit standing by the window. I began to freak, thinking it was my nun-nemesis Sister Catherine, but it was only the lesser of two evils, her sidekick Sister Virgilius. What the hell was she doing here? I couldn't believe Sister V was still alive, actually. She must've been older than Granddad by now. I remembered the story the girls a year above me had told of her falling into the bushes, legs askew. When the girls asked if she needed help, she had said, 'No, I am fine.' And there she stayed. I guess nuns have weird hobbies.

I looked away before Sister V noticed me and before my breathing was affected, as my fear of nuns had escalated, resulting in nightmares that plagued me relentlessly. I was also worried Sister Catherine was here.

I pushed open the kitchen door and smiled as I spotted Troy sitting on the counter, sipping a green drink with an umbrella while the catering staff gave him evils.

'My platonic boyfriend Troy!' I yelled, throwing my arms around him.

Troy and I had been friends since primary school. We'd never hooked up, never really wanted to. There was an awkward moment in our early teens when we kissed but both of us burst out laughing and never did it again. It was kind of like the whole kissing-your-brother thing; too creepy. We were far too similar and it would never work, so best friends for life it was. He was easy on the eye though. Long dark hair, deep brown eyes, tall, slender and a smartarse. He would be a real catch for some girl one day. I hoped that day was far away though. I didn't want to lose him.

He pushed me away. 'Now, now, dear, do not rumple the suit. I need to get it back to the funeral parlour before midnight.'

I smiled at how similar we were.

He looked amazing as usual in his black suit, shirt and tie but on his feet were his trademark red Converse sneakers.

'Troy, you're so dapper!'

'Indeed. So, Grasshopper, have we caused any mayhem yet?'

I grabbed Troy's drink, taking a sip. 'Well, my new pal Mrs Tiara thought I was a waitress so I played along until *Mother* caught me. I did see Sister V though…'

Troy grabbed my arm in concern. He was well aware of my nun phobia.

'And Sister C?' he asked.

'No, not so far, I don't think she's here. It's okay, I'm fine,' I said, forcing a smile. 'This pompous farce is actually a really good opportunity to cause mayhem, as there's hardly anyone here I know. It's mainly Mother's posh friends who I avoid like the plague, and Mr No Personality Peters' posers. We could have a lot of fun – are you game?'

Troy stood up, outstretching his arm. 'Let us do what we must.'

We snuck out of the kitchen, managing to avoid Mother, and headed towards our prey.

I put on my snootiest voice. 'Good evening. I am Georgina Appleby, daughter of Alicia, whose fine engagement ceremony you are attending. I'd like to introduce my platonic boyfriend Troy, who has been looking after me since I left therapy. I was in therapy because I have issues with my mother. I'd wanted to kill her many times but I feel the episodes have somewhat lapsed recently. Have a grand evening!'

The shocked looks on their faces almost made me lose it, but not quite. I grabbed Troy by the tie and headed back to the kitchen. A cliché-ridden food fight ensued until the catering staff threw us out.

# CHAPTER THREE

I didn't go home for a couple of days after that, fearing the inevitable fallout. Troy let me crash at his flat. He shared it with his mum but she didn't mind. Mrs J loved me; thought I was hilarious. She was just one of those typical late-40s, mid-life-crisis-types, trying to fit in with young folk by acting all cool and funny. She was all right, I suppose. I mean, I liked the attention, but it did get a bit much. Sometimes I thought the only reason she fussed over me was because of my rich, snooty family. I hated thinking that.

Troy's clan weren't well off like mine. Mrs J was a single mother trying to make ends meet after Troy's dad did a runner when he was a baby. I know Troy had issues with not knowing his dad and here I was with two of them. Not that Mr No Personality Peters was my dad. He was my fake dad. My real dad lived in Sydney. I loved my dad heaps but I didn't think he loved me as much as I loved him. It's hard to explain. Like I always had to make that first phone call, make the effort. Would he even call me if I stopped calling him? He was there for me sometimes, though, like he never forgot my birthday. I guess that was better than nothing. It was sure better than what Troy had anyway.

Troy and I went to the same Catholic primary school in Prahran, but after that he was off to a public school in Richmond and I was incarcerated at Saint Patricia's College, more commonly known amongst the girls as Satan's Prison Camp.

The college was in Brighton on a side street property so huge it could be used as a cattle ranch. The surrounding concrete walls were grey, depressing monstrosities of ridiculous height, with broken pieces of coloured glass sticking out the top. I remembered staring up at those ominous walls when I was a kid, terrified of the glass. Obviously, it was to keep out the unsavoury, but to me it always felt like it was to keep the girls from escaping.

Saint Patricia's College was the last remaining convent of its kind, an archaic abomination that hadn't moved with the times. As soon as you walked through the imposing metal gates you felt like you were stuck in a weird time warp. The macabre mansion that housed the nuns reminded me of the house from *Psycho*. I used to fantasise about Norman Bates sitting up at the window dressed in his mother's clothes, clutching a sharp blade against Sister Catherine's throat; that always brought a smile to my face. Most of the buildings were Gothic and quite beautiful. Troy did love them. I always thought they could have filmed an episode of *Buffy* there, but alas there was no mausoleum for Spike.

My school was the only one left that still had nuns. Its sister schools only had teachers these days. I figured the last of the sadistic nuns had been deliberately hand-picked by Sister Catherine to live and teach at Saint Pat's. It was the school Mother and her mother had gone to so I had no escape. A nauseating tradition. Mother always used to say, 'School years are the best years of your life!' But they weren't. My school was like living in a tiny hierarchy five days a week, bar weekends and holidays, with its own rulers (priest, principal and vice-principal) princes and princesses (teachers and nuns) and peasants (students). When you're at school it becomes your whole world and everything is just so important. Then you get out into the real world and realise how unimportant school really was in the scheme of things.

Whenever I played up, Mother would threaten to institutionalise me as a boarder or send me to a Swiss finishing school. I was terrified of both prospects so I would be good for a while and then the whole thing would repeat until I became older and realised Mother was crying wolf. From then on, I just kept playing up. Luckily, I got to go home after school. The creepy boarders could only go home during holidays.

The flashbacks could not be contained.

*** 

*Shelley walked into class confidently. She was smart; she knew she was smart but she was still considered weird because she was a boarder and what's worse, she looked like a sheep.*

*Her white blonde hair was thick like wool and piled high on top of her head. She wasn't very attractive either. She had a weird-shaped face. It was both long and round at the same time and her thick neck had wrinkled lines across it. She spoke in a posh accent and said things like 'nonchalant' and 'debauchery', which didn't help matters.*

*I couldn't stand Shelley The Sheep Girl. She played a prank on me once. My friend Mel put her up to it but still, the fact that Sheep Head was in on it at all made me very uncomfortable.*

*I was sick and had a day off from school. Mel made Shelley ring me at home. Shelley told me I'd won a competition to meet some musician I was really into at the time. Her voice was unrecognisable. She put on this English accent and sounded really old. I got sucked in. The next day at school I rushed over to Mel to tell her. The Sheep Head just happened to be standing next to her, of course. Mel's reaction to me telling her I was going to meet my idol was strange, and when they both burst out laughing, I felt like I had been slapped in the face by the smelliest wet fish ever. I felt deflated, like a balloon that had just popped. I never entirely forgave Mel, and the fact that Sheep Head played a prank on me and got away with it was the most distressing thing ever.*

*I even had to go on holidays with her once, when Mel invited her along. It was the worst two weeks of my life. On the way home, when we were on the bus from Adelaide to Melbourne, I could hardly control myself from throwing her off the bus and into a paddock filled with her own kind. We always used to wonder whether it was her mother or father who had had sex with a sheep.*

***

I was snapped back to reality as Troy walked into my temporary bedroom, his lounge room, clutching a bowl of cocoa pops. His hair was slightly dishevelled, but his black pyjamas were immaculate.

'That phone call was your mother,' he said mid-chew. I rolled my eyes. I'd vaguely heard the phone ring but was too deep in Shelley The Sheep Girl dung to register.

'She wanted to know when you're coming home.'

'Did you tell her never?'

Mrs J walked past the lounge. 'You can stay as long as you want, Georgie!'

'I fear your mother will kill you if you do,' Troy continued, his eyes narrowing.

'Let her.' I sunk deeper into the couch, my huge Snoopy slippers stretched before me. I always kept a spare pair at Troy's. My feet couldn't live without them. In fact, I pretty much kept a spare wardrobe of clothes at Troy's, I stayed there so often.

'But what about Chocky?' Troy asked a little too innocently.

My heart began to race as my thoughts returned to my beloved kelpie. I'd only thought of her a hundred times over the last few days. But I relaxed, knowing Mr No Personality Peters would have looked after her. He loved that dog, but the feeling wasn't mutual as Choc hated him as much as I did. As for Mother, she would have had her eye on Chocky for a fine red and tan fur coat by now.

'I better go. Have to see my Chocky and I'm working tonight, anyway.' I stood, stretching.

'Do you think you should change first?' Troy asked, looking down at my monstrous feet.

'Hmmm, maybe.'

'Goodbye then.' With that, Troy and his cocoa pops were gone.

# CHAPTER FOUR

Chocky did her trademark bum wiggle when I walked through the back door of Purgatory Palace. She was so happy to see me, she even stopped eating her dinner. She let Mr No Personality Peters feed her when I was away but due to Choc's hatred of him, I was certain he fed her at arm's length. I gave Choc cuddles until I noticed NPP in the kitchen. He was bending down getting something out of the oven, draped in a frilly apron, the old fool. His backside was all that was visible. Not a pretty sight.

'Oh, Georgina, you're home,' he said slowly, straightening up and putting a tray of peanut butter cookies on the kitchen table. They smelt great but there was no way in hell I was gonna eat them.

We employed a woman who cooked for us, whose nickname sadly enough was Cook, but he insisted on baking, much to my disgust. I never ate anything he made. Just the thought of those clammy little hands preparing baked goods made me dry retch. He tried to win me over once by baking a pecan pie, my favourite food in the whole world, but I didn't touch it. Cook bakes my pecan pies and nails it.

'Your mother was worried about you,' he continued in his ridiculously high-pitched voice.

'She knew I was at Troy's,' I said, trying to grab a cookie to give to Chocky.

He slapped my hand. 'No, no, no!' he yelled. 'They are for your mother's get-together this evening and she will be mighty cross if there aren't enough for everyone.'

I watched him silently as he bent down and got another tray from the oven, whilst holding my burning hand. I looked at it. It was crimson. That was quite a slap the bastard had given me.

The flashbacks could not be contained... again.

*\*\**

*I hit the wrong key on the piano and shuddered, knowing what would follow.*

*Sister Catherine's HB pencil swooped quickly hitting my knuckle many times until the pain was so intense, I hid my hand.*

*A single tear rolled down my cheek and I started sobbing, which helped drown out the frantic nun's abuse.*

*'You wretched thing, you haven't practised at all, have you?'*

*'Yes, I did,' I lied quietly.*

*'How long did you practise for, five minutes?'*

*'Yes.'*

*I was still too young to grasp any concept of time and thought five minutes was good a time as any to practise.*

*Out came the HB again. She grabbed hold of my arm and hit the same hand's knuckle over and over. The pain zapped through me and I felt the tears welling up, making it hard to see.*

*When she finally let go, I clutched my aching hand and started crying.*

*'Stop that sniffling, you brazen child!'*

*She handed me a box of tissues; clean, white and pure, unlike her.*

*I took one gingerly.*

*'What do you say?' the beast roared.*

*'Thank you.'*

*She sat down next to me, straightening her skirt. 'Continue.'*

*I did. My hands shook uncontrollably as I attempted to proceed, but it wasn't long until another wrong note was audible. I stopped playing and instinctively hid my hands behind my back, watching her through cloudy eyes.*

*Sister Catherine was purple. The same purple as Violet who turned into a blueberry in Willy Wonka and the Chocolate Factory. Blueberry purple.*

*The blood vessel on her forehead throbbed as she clenched her wrinkled mouth tightly, glaring at me.*

*The punch in the back came swiftly, resulting in my head hitting the top of the piano.*

*I started howling.*

*How can someone like that go to Heaven?*

*She is the Devil.*

***

'Georgina, have you been listening to me?'

NPP was standing a foot in front of me. His bald spot was sweaty, eyes squinting through his spectacles. I took a step back as his Old Spice penetrated my nostrils.

'I was asking if you have decided on what university you will go to next year.'

'Oh, give it a rest.' I sighed. 'You're not my father.'

I grabbed a cookie when he wasn't watching and threw it into Chocky's mouth before heading towards the back door. NPP called after me saying I had a letter.

I read it in my car. It was an invitation to my graduation, even though I had dropped out and never graduated, but dropouts were still invited.

Lucky me.

The reason my alumni's graduation was so late was because it was cancelled due to a fire in the Chapel. Was it God's work or did Father Luke just forget to butt out his cigarette after a night of binge drinking? We never knew, but were told our night of nights would be rescheduled at some point so I guess this was it. Took them long enough and it was ages away! Why send it so early? God, Satan's Prison Camp was hopeless. I seriously doubted I would be putting myself through that kind of hell.

Or would I?

# CHAPTER FIVE

Tony's Pizza was on Fitzroy Street in St Kilda, a tiny old-school dive not far from Leo's Spaghetti Bar. It was a cash-only business because Tony detested credit cards, but for some strange reason it worked. Probably because the pizza was incredible. Tony was a great boss and adored Troy and me as we did him.

There is a fine art to delivering pizzas. Knowing the back streets of Melbourne usually helped, as did a love of driving at night, but the best thing was, you didn't need to have a love of people. Let's face it, as Troy says, most people suck, and when you deliver pizzas you only need to have contact with the customer for a minute or so before you're gone. No 'Can I help you with that?' crap and no 'The customer is always right,' because to be honest, the customer *isn't* always right, and who wants to suck up to a stupid customer, anyway?

Delivering pizzas was fun but what I *really* wanted to do was work with animals, especially dogs. But I had absolutely no idea how to do that, so for now, pizzas it was.

The night started off with the usual suspects.

*The Druggie:*

'Hey dude! How much was it again?' asked a teenage boy with eyes so bloodshot there was no white visible.

'$39.50,' I answered as a waft of marijuana entered my nostrils.

The boy handed me two twenty dollar notes.

'Keep the change. Hey, do you wanna come in for a bong?'

'Ah nah, it's okay,' I said with a shy smile as I hurried off.

*The Sleazy Drunk Guy:*

The front door swung open revealing a shirtless man with a hairy chest and a grin on his face that immediately made me shudder. He wore a large gold crucifix around his neck that made me uneasy. A Catholic priest on his night off perhaps?

'Would you like to come in and share the pizza with me sweetie? My beers are cold and you're hot,' he purred after paying me.

'Don't call me sweetie. Call me savoury,' I said before running away.

*The Cheapskate:*

'That's $19.95.' I yawned.

The woman dressed in Dolce and Gabbana handed me a twenty dollar note and didn't move. I fished around through the coins in my bum bag for ages trying to find a five-cent piece while she just stood there patiently holding her hand out. Finally, I found one and put the coin in her stingy palm. That's why she was rich, literally.

*The Disabled Person:*

The guy in the wheelchair took a while to open his front door and even longer to find his money but I didn't care as none of this was easy for him to do. The order came to $39.99. He handed me a fifty dollar note, smiled and said, 'Keep the change.' That's why he was rich, metaphorically.

*The Blind Woman:*

The blind woman's sweet-natured daughter, who looked around ten, would always open the door. She would hand her daughter the money and her daughter would hand the money to me. They always tipped. Their teamwork was incredible.

*The Football Club:*

I arrived at the footy club with forty 'piping lukewarm' pizzas stuffed into my Mazda 121's hatch.

As I took the first bag into the building I stepped back in horror as strippers who had pretty much already stripped danced on the table surrounded by a group of bogan drunk guys yelling filthy things. When one of them saw I was a female driver he yelled, 'Are you gonna strip too?'

I hurriedly got the hell out of there.

*The Girls from The Brothel:*

I always found it interesting when I took food to places that I would never step foot in normally. As I walked on the red velvet carpet to reception, I passed door after door to my left and my right and imagined what kind of sex was going on in each room and how far along they all were and whether there was one room where the guy just wanted to talk.

The woman from reception took me to the break room to get my money. I was shocked when I saw the girls that worked there looked younger than me.

*The Rudest Customer in the World:*

'I've been waiting for an hour!' the woman yelled, all dressed up for a night on the town in her hair curlers and fluffy pink slippers. 'What did you do, get lost?'

'No.' I sighed. 'It's very busy.'

'Well, you shouldn't say half an hour on the phone then!'

'I don't answer the phones,' I said through clenched teeth as I handed her the pizza.

'Where's my small Aussie? I ordered a small Aussie too!'

I started to panic until I looked in the pizza bag and found the small Aussie hiding up the back. She snatched it from me.

'That's $19.80,' I forced out. I wanted to strangle her; right there. It was dark. Who would know?

She threw a crumpled twenty dollar note at me. 'Give me back my change too, I'm not tipping you.'

That was the straw.

'No, I'm keeping this,' I said venomously as I held the twenty-cent coin in front of her ugly head. 'There's a surcharge for having to put up with rude arseholes like you!'

As I walked away, I could hear, 'You have an attitude problem!'

How I loved compliments.

When I got back to the shop she was on the phone to Tony.

'Oh really, she was rude, was she?' Tony said, winking at me. 'The rudest driver you've ever met?! I'll be sure to have a word to her when she gets back.'

Tony put the phone down and laughed before throwing a baby octopus at my head.

God, I loved my job, apart from the poor baby octopus that is.

Things changed soon afterwards though.

One night a customer opened the box to check if the pizza was right.

'I hope this is a Supreme with Seafood,' she said, then promptly screamed, dropping the box. 'There was a silverfish on that pizza!'

'Well, you did order seafood.' I smiled.

The Health Department soon found out about the Silverfish Special, and Tony's Pizza went on holiday for a while.

Troy and I had to find new jobs. He was okay as he went to work at his friend's building site, although heavy lifting was never Troy's strong point. I, on the other hand, needed to think long and hard about another job that would infuriate Mother.

Our last night at the pizza shop needed to be celebrated and there was only one place where we could do that.

# CHAPTER SIX

'Let's sing another 80s song!' I yelled excitedly. The alcohol was beginning to work. Troy was dubious.

'Bingey, don't you think we've sung *enough* 80s songs?' Bingey was Troy's nickname for me when I was hammered. He seemed to call me that a lot.

'No, we haven't!' I grabbed him by the tie and dragged him onto the stage for *Like a Prayer* by Madonna.

Friday night karaoke was the only place to drown your sorrows after a horrible night of work. In fact, I drowned my sorrows there many a night with Troy in tow.

After we were done, I stumbled off stage with the words, 'You suck!' ringing in my ears and headed to the bar. 'One more Jim and Coke!' I yelled. The bar guy rolled his eyes. My drinking must have gotten to extreme idiot stage by then but I didn't care, I was having a ball.

I looked around for Troy and found him nearby, being harassed by some princess. The number of times he got picked up was legendary.

I guess all the girls were into his long dark hair and goth-like looks, but he didn't want a bar of any of them. I hardly ever got picked up. Apparently, I was good-looking, but I needed to show cleavage; Mother's words.

I staggered up to them, spilling my bourbon onto her silicone breasts. I'm sure Mother would be proud if I had *her* cleavage.

'Watch it, bitch!' she yelled. She was every bimbo you've ever seen in your entire life rolled into one. It was astounding.

'Who you calling bitch, bitch?' I said as I moved closer to her, staring into her heavily made-up eyes. 'You trying to steal my man, are ya?'

She started to look worried.

'Oh, honey bunny,' Troy said to me meekly, in his best country hick accent. 'Don't hurt her. She was only talking to me. Remember what the cops said, if you put one more person in hospital, they're gonna lock you up…'

'I don't care!' I screamed. 'This whore's goin' down!'

By the time I rolled up my sleeve, she was gone. Troy and I burst out laughing.

'Good one, honey bunny.' He smiled. 'But what happens when one day I actually like the girl who tries to pick me up? What then?'

'That won't happen,' I said, finishing my drink. 'You hate everyone.'

'Indeed, all except you.'

'Seeing as you love me so much, you can come to my non-graduation with me. It's in February,' I blurted out. 'I'm thinking of maybe going, but not alone.'

'So, they have finally re-scheduled your night of un-nights! I wouldn't miss it!' He kissed my forehead, took my empty glass and went to order me another drink.

I felt a tap on my shoulder and turned sharply, thinking it might be the princess with her come-back, but instead, I was confronted with 'Cute Guy'.

Cute Guy was at karaoke every Friday night by himself. He always sat at the same table and just watched people. He was kind of skinny, seemed a little shy. He had this short messy blond hair that was natural blond, you could tell, like he was Nordic or something and I adored blond hair. His eyes were ice blue. They sliced you in half with one look, like they had lasers in them or something. He was no Kurt Cobain but there was just something about him. Troy was unaware of Cute Guy as he'd never said a word to us before, but *I'd* noticed him.

'Hi, um.' Cute Guy straightened his glasses just like Dad did. Oh my dog, maybe that's why I liked him? 'I was just wondering if you'd like to…'

'Excuse me!' It was Troy. My heart sank lower than a home boy's jeans. 'Are you tryin' to pick up my woman?'

'Oh no, I… sorry.' With that, Cute Guy was gone.

I looked up at Troy as he handed me my drink.

'What a geek,' he laughed.

'Yeah,' I mumbled, looking away as I took a sip.

# CHAPTER SEVEN

I stepped behind the cash register slowly.

'Stop moping. I'm sure you were born to be a check-out chick!' Troy said enthusiastically before running off to work. His quip wasn't enough to lighten my mood.

I'd found myself a job at a small, family-owned supermarket in Brighton; a tad too close to the convent for my liking but beggars, choosers. Although it would make Mother furious, I still wasn't looking forward to it. I finally looked up at my first customers in horror as I came face to face with Leticia 'I am beautiful, deal with it' Caulfield and her dumb sidekick Prudence Miller from Satan's Prison Camp. They hadn't changed a bit since school. It was frightening. Leticia's big blonde bouffant looked like it had been blown by an industrial sized fan then immediately hair-sprayed to within an inch of its life. It was beyond hideous. Prudence, on the other hand, wore her long blonde hair in a ponytail with pieces hanging from the sides so she could conveniently put them in her mouth. Prudence's wardrobe could be best referred to as 'Prostitute Chic', with copious amounts of pink but what was even more alarming was that Leticia was dressed like Mother. She was all pearls, expensive high heels and a tight little Armani jacket. No pink feather boa in sight, though.

The memories came flooding back as I morphed into my green school uniform all over again.

\*\*\*

*'You'll never amount to anything, you loser!' Leticia roared. She had snatched my Maths test from my hand and was running around the playground while the girls around us giggled.*

*'Georgie got three out of ten on her maths test! She's too dumb to even work at McDonalds!'*

\*\*\*

I just couldn't give those two the satisfaction.

I quickly turned around before they got a good look at me and started fumbling through the lost and found box for anything to disguise my appearance. I found a pair of huge Coke-bottle glasses and put them on. I bet they magnified my eyes as much as Sister Catherine's. I shuddered at the thought. The glasses seemed to work though, as the girls didn't appear to recognise me, although I became extra slow, as I couldn't see a thing through them.

'For God's sake,' Leticia snarled. 'They give any imbecile a job here, don't they?'

That was enough for me.

I grabbed Leticia's feminine hygiene product and called for a price check.

'Price check on Libra extra-thick for extremely heavy flow incontinence pads...'

Leticia turned beetroot as the customers around her laughed.

'What are you doing? They don't say that!'

She ran off in embarrassment, leaving Prudence to foot the bill. I found that strange considering Prudence was the dumbest person I'd ever met. (My brother Andy's girlfriend was the second dumbest, but more about her later.) After fumbling around in her bag for ages, Prudence eventually took out a fifty dollar bill and threw it at me, telling me to keep the change. Their shopping came to $49.99.

Sigh.

I thought I'd done a good job embarrassing Leticia until I heard her yell from a distance, 'Did McDonalds sack you, Georgie Porgie?!'

Uh-oh.

My smelly manager took me off register due to that little outburst and I was demoted after only ten minutes on the job. What an achievement, Troy would be proud.

As I stacked the supermarket shelf miserably, I caught a whiff of mothballs before being tapped on the shoulder.

It was Sister Catherine.

I had nowhere to run, nowhere to hide, no huge, ridiculous glasses to conceal my appearance anymore. I was bare, naked, see-through, and there she was, the nun who ruined my life.

She stood there with her huge glasses and bug-like head, holding a can of no-name spaghetti like she was going to complain about the price. Then, in an instant, I saw her expression change as she recognised me.

'Georgina Appleby,' she croaked.

I stood to attention as I was transformed back in time to the principal's office.

'Well, well, well,' she continued, scratching at the hideous hair that grew from the mole on her chin.

What she meant by 'well, well, well' was obvious.

She meant, 'My, haven't you become exactly what I thought you'd become… nothing.'

I couldn't escape. My mind was ablaze with excuses about why I was working at a supermarket, not that I personally thought there was anything wrong with working at a supermarket, but she wouldn't believe any of them. I was a loser, plain and simple, in her eyes at least. Although deep down I knew she was right.

'The spaghetti is on special – ninety-nine cents, I think,' I rambled, trying to avoid the inevitable conversation.

'Ah yes,' she said, her thoughts shifting back to the can in hand. She always was a thrifty old bag.

'Thank you.' She limped away slowly.

That was it.

No put down, no smart-arse comment, no nothing.

I felt deflated, cheated, like I was ready for a comeback but wasn't given anything to come back to. As I watched her walk off, I noticed my smelly manager heading towards me and thought I'd impress him after my demotion.

'Hope you enjoy the spaghetti!' I called after her. 'I've tried it and it's very good!'

Sister Catherine turned around and glared at me.

'It's a treat for my dog's birthday,' she said bitterly. 'I wouldn't eat this abomination if it was the last can of food on Earth!'

I stood there like an idiot. She'd done it to me again.

'You know you're going to Hell, don't you?' I yelled.

'I'm sorry?' my manager said.

'Not you! I didn't mean you. I was singing that new song, you know the one, have you heard it? It goes, "You know you're going to Hell, baby",' I sang in an out of tune voice.

God I was an idiot.

My manager rolled his eyes before walking off.

I faked a smile and shot myself in the head with my pricing gun.

I remembered one of the last times I saw Sister Catherine.

*** 

*'But I passed, you told me I passed!' I yelled.*

*She glared at me through her thick glasses.*

*'Almost passed,' she corrected, shuffling papers.*

*I slammed my hand onto the desk, making her jump. 'No... you told me... I passed,' I said slowly, feeling the tears start to well.*

*'I was wrong. You failed the final examination,' she said bluntly, refusing to look at me.*

*'Where are my results? I want to see them!' I demanded.*

*She finally looked up. 'That is impossible.'*

*The office door suddenly opened, revealing Bird Girl, Sister Catherine's assistant. Sister Catherine needed an assistant because my nun-nemesis was also the school's vice-principal as well as being one of its piano teachers. I always wondered why she bothered to teach piano because she didn't need to; purely to torture the girls, I thought.*

*Bird Girl walked in holding an arm full of manila folders. She looked at me in contempt. I did the same. She wore a beige business suit which blended into her beige hair. I could not stand the colour beige. Even the word made me vomit. To me it isn't even a colour; it is a no-colour, worn by lifeless conservatives wanting to blend into society's shallow shadow.*

*Bird Girl got her nickname due to her nose, which was long and beak-like and hung down way too far, almost touching her pencil-thin mouth. Bird Girl thought she was above us all, working for the vice-principal, being such a hot shot, always giving us foul looks when we were sent to the office. We were all shocked when we found out she was the same age as us yet thought she was so superior. But her superiority complex was due to the fact she was some kind of genius, not dumb like us, and had done Year 12 last year. Apparently, she was on a gap year before she went to study Law at Harvard and her uncle, the principal, had given her this job. We hated her even more after we found that out.*

'Don't you know how to knock, girl?' Sister Catherine yelled at her.

A smile formed on my lips.

'But Sister, I have the piano exams here,' Bird Girl chirped.

Sister C's eyes widened, as did mine.

'I'll look at them later!' she roared.

Bird Girl jumped, dropping the folders.

I quickly bent down, soon finding mine.

'How dare you!' my nun-nemesis screamed.

Ignoring her, I read my results. 'This says I passed the final exam.'

Sister Catherine said nothing, just sat there staring at her mountain of paperwork.

Bird Girl said nothing either, as she looked from me to her.

Finally, Sister Catherine spoke. 'It must be a mistake,' she muttered.

Bird Girl suddenly remembered the authority she had over me, snatching the folder from my hand. 'Sister,' she began meekly, looking at the folder. 'Appleby is right. It does say she passed.'

'Fine!' Sister Catherine roared as she threw a metal paperweight shaped like the ocean's waves to the floor, barely missing us. Then she stood upright, scrunching the papers with her claws, instantly transforming into an evil vulture-like creature who was about to murder her prey. 'My mistake, you passed. Now go, I am busy!'

As I exchanged glares with Bird Girl, I realised she'd actually saved my skin. I knew what Sister Catherine was up to. She was going to change my pass to a fail when no one was looking. That's how she worked. She probably would have got away with it too, being so high up on the examination board. But now that Bird Girl was a witness, her plans had been foiled. It all seemed too much like an episode of Scooby-Doo.

As I walked out of the building, Bird Girl followed. 'Back to class now,' she said smugly.

*I stopped walking and turned around to face her.*

*She took a step back when she witnessed the Georgie Death Stare.*

*'I know where you live.'*

*She swallowed uncomfortably before hurrying off.*

*I didn't know where she lived, how would I? Gullible fool.*

*The next day Sister Catherine called me into her office. I didn't need to be a brain surgeon to know why. She told me if I ever said anything to anyone about what happened yesterday, she would hit me so hard I would end up in hospital.*

***

'Georgina, are you deaf?' I was back at the supermarket and my smelly manager was yelling at me. He was a very unattractive man who smelt like Snappy Tom Tuna and Sardine variety.

'There has been a complaint about you,' he continued.

It didn't take me long to figure out who'd been doing the complaining.

'That nun you were talking to before claimed you had an attitude problem.'

There it was again, my epitaph.

'I don't think it's working out, Georgina. I'm going to have to let you go.'

'No problem.' I took off my red apron and handed it to him. 'And by the way, it's Georgie not Georgina and has anyone ever told you that you smell like Snappy Tom Tuna and Sardine variety?'

I walked off, leaving him smelling his armpits.

I was depressed.

I rang Troy to tell him of my day in Hell. He suggested drowning my sorrows at a party we'd been invited to that would be serving free booze. I was dubious but couldn't pass up the opportunity of free alcohol. Can any amateur alcoholic?

\*\*\*

The sign on the front door said, 'Door is open! Come in!'

'I really don't want to be here,' I muttered.

'Oh, come on,' Troy said as he opened the door and gave me a push. I stumbled inside and looked around, noticing everyone seemed to be dressed in religious attire.

'What the hell is this, some kind of Catholic reunion?'

'Not really,' Leticia Caulfield answered. I was shocked to see her wearing a white habit. 'It's actually a Catholic fancy dress!'

'Where's your outfit?' Prudence asked me. Her habit was pink. Bright pink!

I went into shock and started to fan my face with my hand.

'Are you okay?' a nun asked.

'Do you want a glass of water?' another nun questioned.

I started to hyperventilate as I realised I was surrounded by a flock of cackling nuns.

The last time that happened I was on my way to the principal's office.

\*\*\*

*We entered reception and took a step back in horror. The room was full of squawking penguins. Some in blue habits, some in black; there was even one in white. She must have been the purest, or evilest – nuns were never what they seemed. We had walked into some horrid nun convention about their whacking sticks no doubt. They looked us up and down in distaste before they huddled off into another room. I finally caught my breath just as Bird Girl saw us, rolled her eyes and told us the principal was ready to see us. In other words, her uncle was ready to see us.*

*There I was again with my best friend and partner in crime, Titania, by my side. We stood with our hands behind our backs as we stared at the grey chequered carpet in silence. I thought I saw a splotch of blood and pictured Sister Catherine in boxing gloves, punching some poor girl out.*

*'Look at me when I'm speaking to you!' Sister Catherine yelled. We looked up hesitantly, straight into the magnified eyes of the fuming nun. Her ridiculously large glasses made her eyes so huge and black she looked like an evil, bug-like cartoon character.*

*We were defenceless. I started to chuckle, which made Tits chuckle, and so on and so forth until we were full on laughing. Then Tits got to the point where she was laughing so hard no sound was coming out, which made me hysterical. Principal Valencia turned a shade of red I hadn't seen before. I feared he'd burst a blood vessel. He roared at us as we kept laughing.*

***

'Georgie! Georgie!' Troy yelled in alarm, a glass of water in one hand, my head in the other. I came to, realising I was on the floor, and started to panic until I saw the nuns had dispersed.

'Don't worry, I got rid of them,' he said, helping me up. 'I told them you nearly died in a bizarre nun-related accident.'

Troy didn't know why I had a fear of nuns but hoped I'd tell him one day. After years of friendship, I fear he hoped it would be soon.

'What the hell did you bring me here for anyway? If this was a joke it wasn't funny!'

'I didn't know,' Troy pleaded. 'I thought a party might cheer you up. Leticia and Prudence invited us. I thought you'd have fun.'

'Leticia and Prudence?! Have you forgotten they're not my friends? They know about my phobia. They made you take me to this party on purpose!' I scanned the room frantically, spotting them in the corner, giggling and waving. I headed towards them.

'You okay, Georgina?' Leticia asked patronisingly.

'Look at that!' I yelled, pointing at something non-existent behind them.

As the girls turned around, I grabbed their drinks, pouring them over their heads.

Leticia growled, ready to pounce.

Troy stepped between us. 'Now, now ladies,' he said in his charming way.

'This isn't over,' Leticia threatened before stomping off with Prudence sulking behind her.

'You bet it isn't,' I said.

Troy watched me in concern.

# CHAPTER EIGHT

The next morning Chocky jumped onto my lap and began stealing kisses as I attempted to read *The Age*'s job classified ads. I couldn't find my phone and the computer was too far away, so it was old school or nothing.

I glanced up at Troy as he started to make coffee, the aroma soothing my semidetached senses. He'd stayed the night at Purgatory Palace after the triple whammy of me seeing my nun-nemesis, losing my shit job and the horrendous Catholic Fancy Dress. Seeing as I had been diagnosed with reactive depression, he knew me being alone would not be a positive move at this time.

'You know what I really hate?' I asked him.

'Hmmm, let me see… nuns, posh people?'

'Besides the obvious.'

'I give up.'

'I really hate it when job ads ask for a bubbly personality. I mean who actually has a bubbly personality? Let's see… The Wiggles in a bubble bath?'

'What about a game show host in a bubble bath blowing bubbles?' Troy asked.

'You win.'

I flung the paper across the table.

Troy picked it up and opened it.

'Look, I've found two jobs for you already! One in telemarketing and here's another one in a mail house, both kind of better than pizza delivering and check-out-chicking but still crap enough to get on your mother's goat!'

'Do they require a bubbly personality?'

'No!'

'Great! I'm in!'

***

A few days later I had the misfortune of having a trial at the mail house and telemarketers on the very same day. As I walked into the mail house, my heart sank. I really wished this job was working with animals but as usual it wasn't, so here I was. Before I had a chance to walk out, a skinny bald man wearing a grey overcoat that was three sizes too big for him approached me nervously.

'Hello, I'm Mr Papp. What's your name?'

'Georgie Appleby.' I sighed.

'Um, I have a Georgina Appleby on the list, is that you?'

I gave him the *Georgie Death Stare.* Could this actually be the most stupid person I had ever met?

He cleared his throat. 'Okay then, this way.'

I followed him to a table that had a group of people huddled around it. Most of them looked around my age. Mr Crapp told me what to do and left me to it. I had to stuff pamphlets into envelopes. It was kind of a production line type thing, with each of us handing the envelope to the person next to us so they could put their pamphlet in. It was pretty boring, as you'd imagine. As I joined in, everyone was silent, lost in the monotonous rhythm of it all, until one of the girls screamed.

'Oh my god, a mouse!' she cried, jumping onto a chair. No one else seemed to mind as they watched the little critter scurry off.

'Who cares?' the guy beside her said. 'They're just trying to make a living like the rest of us.'

I smiled as I pictured mice wearing Armani suits and carrying miniature briefcases, jumping into their Lego cars and driving like maniacs so they wouldn't be late to the office.

I worked hard stuffing envelopes for a few hours and soon realised the more repetitive and inane the job, the more I tended to stuff it up. It was almost as if the simplicity of it became too difficult. Go figure. Luckily, I wasn't working in a sweatshop as the afternoon tea bell finally rang. Mr Crapp told us to go upstairs to the tea room. As we got to the top of the stairs, the nasty old biddies who'd worked there for an eternity gave us the cold shoulder so we bunched together at a small table. I was desperate for coffee so I jumped up and made one. I found a teaspoon in the sink, rinsed it off and started to stir my coffee when an extremely tall woman with a head that resembled a maggot invaded my space.

'Can't you see that's my teaspoon?!' she roared as the entire room fell silent. I looked up into her huge snot-filled nose in disgust and then began to inspect the teaspoon closely.

'Well, I can't see your name on it. Is it engraved or something? Oh, hang on, here it is. *Stupid Bitch*, no worries, you can have it back now.'

That's all I remember. When I came to, I found myself lying on the tea room floor with Mr Crapp and my fellow casuals huddled around me. My right eye hurt like hell.

'I'm so sorry, Georgina,' Mr Crapp pleaded, helping me up. 'I just fired Sharon for what she did and if you want to press charges against her, I will fully support you, but please don't sue us!'

What a day. Troy would be so proud.

*** 

When I arrived back at Purgatory Palace, Mother was sitting on the couch watching her soap operas. She stood up and wobbled towards me, taking a step back in shock when she saw my black eye.

'What in God's name has happened to you, Georgina? Are you all right? Do I need to call the doctor?'

I said nothing.

'COOK!'

After Cook defrosted a veggie burger, as I refused to put steak on my face, Mother forced me to lie on the couch with the burger on my eye as she asked me a barrage of questions. Before I could answer any of them, I was saved by the doorbell. It was Mrs Tiara, complete with tiara, turning up for some meaningless meeting about how often they get their maids to polish their gold-plated candlesticks or something or other that Mother and her plastic posh posers held at daily intervals. While Mother greeted Mrs T, I got up off the couch, letting the veggie burger fall to the ground. It wasn't there for long as Chocky promptly grabbed it and made a run for it. I headed towards Mrs Tiara and noticed her expression turn to shock.

'What has happened to your eye, child?' the old biddy asked. There was slight sympathy resonating from her, which I thought strange as I was sure she hated me.

I glanced at Mother in fear. 'I-I-I walked into a-a-a... door,' I stuttered, pretending to burst into tears.

Mrs Tiara glanced at Mother in horror. Mother swallowed uncomfortably as she cursed me under her breath. I left Mother to clean up my mess as usual and ran upstairs to ring Troy and fill him in on my wonderful day so far. He couldn't wait to see my black eye so we organised to meet up at karaoke later that night. I hoped Cute Guy would be there as it felt like ages since I'd seen him. Maybe he would find me even more attractive with a black eye. But before karaoke I had another job tryout from hell waiting for me; telemarketing.

Good God.

***

The room was massive, with dull grey cubicles stretching far and wide. The telemarketers wore head-sets and talked over the top of one another. The constant murmur of voices reminded me of people praying out aloud in church. I suddenly felt faint. I was really going to hate this job. An ancient woman wearing a hideous bright orange dress approached me.

'Are you Georgie Appleby?' she asked.

'That I am.'

'What happened to your eye?'

'My dog punched me.'

The old woman watched me strangely for a minute before speaking again.

'Oh... all right then, my name is Mrs Sweet. I'm your supervisor and you'll need to take that nose ring out as it's against company rules. Follow me.'

Double sigh.

Mrs Sour led me to my desk and filled me in on my duties, which were to ring a list of customers and ask them if they were interested in buying Tupperware.

I hated Tupperware. I didn't know why but it just made me feel ill. It was so Stepford Wives, so plastic, so see-through and clean, and all the various sizes that fitted into each other were well and truly what nightmares were made of. I shuddered.

I sat down and rang my first customer while Mrs Sour watched me. After a few calls, she left me to it, as she thought I was doing well. I had a few hang-ups, which was normal, a bit of abuse, which was also normal, and then I struck gold when I stumbled upon my target market: The Old Biddy. The Old Biddy loved Tupperware. But Tupperware wasn't the only thing The Old Biddy loved. She loved a lot of things and after an hour of telling me all about the things she loved, my patience was wearing thin.

'Yes, dear, I am happy your grandchild got an "A" in English but can I just have a minute of your time to tell you about this wonderful Tupperware I am selling?'

Close but no cigar. My reference to Tupperware made her think of her late husband who worked at a plastics factory and would serenade her every night while they danced under the moonlight conducting their fantasy orchestra with plastic knives and forks... enough!

'Listen, you old biddy, are you gonna buy my stupid Tupperware or not? By the way, do you actually know how much I hate Tupperware? Did you know that Tupperware tried to kill me in my sleep? You don't even know how much I hate this stupid thing I'm selling and add to that having to listen to all your boring drivel as well, seriously just give me a gun and put me out of my misery...'

By now, my surrounding telemarketers, including Mrs Sour, were listening. Let's just say The Old Biddy was the last phone call I made.

***

It was so good to finally get to karaoke after stuffing up three jobs in such a short space of time. Well, my lucky number was three. I started to search for Troy and soon found him leaning on the bar, complete with a girl hassling him. No surprises there.

'Troy Boy!' I yelled as I threw myself onto his neck. The girl, who looked about twelve and was primped to the max, gave me a dirty look.

'Excuse me, we were in the middle of a conversation,' she snarled.

'See this?' I asked, pointing at my eye. 'Do you want me to give you one?'

The girl started to look uncomfortable and left. Troy laughed as he examined my shiner.

'That is sensational.'

'Why thank you.'

'Now please fill me in on your exhilarating day.'

I ordered a drink and had begun to tell Troy of my latest adventures when Cute Guy suddenly walked past with a girl I used to go to school with; Emily Mears. I couldn't believe it. Emily was the quiet girl in my class. I didn't really have much to do with her; most of the time I forgot she was even there. How did Cute Guy know Emily Mears? Did this mean he'd be going to our graduation with her? I never knew what he tried to ask me the last time I was here, thanks to Troy ruining it. I guess I'll never know. But I did have a strange feeling he liked me. But maybe that was just my ego babbling.

Cute Guy didn't notice me all night. My heart sunk. Was Emily Mears his girlfriend now? I couldn't believe I'd missed my chance. A heavy weight settled in the pit of my stomach.

I didn't stay long at karaoke after that. I made an excuse to Troy about not feeling well and dragged my sorry arse home.

# CHAPTER NINE

It was Sunday, the Sabbath. I needed peace not riot. The last few days had really taken it out of me. I needed to visit my brother Ben.

I grabbed my backpack and jumped aboard the bus. My car was out of petrol, I had no money to fill it up and the limo driver had the day off, so it was the bus or nothing. Melbourne was in a good mood that day and let the sun out to play, but the grey buildings depressed me. As angle grinders sawed through my brain whilst passing a building site, all I could think about was putting on Sister Catherine's boxing gloves and pounding all my nemeses until they were dead. Sister Catherine included.

I thought about my other brother, Andy. The one I didn't like. I didn't have much time for him anymore. Not since he moved out of home and became such a hotshot. But come to think of it, I never really liked him anyway. He was such a pretentious arsehole. Always wearing a ridiculously expensive suit and tie. He didn't look a thing like me or Ben. We looked more like Dad. Andy was a male version of Mother; cold eyes and judgmental, not gentle. He fancied himself as a blond Tom Cruise. Tom Cruise made me projectile vomit.

When we were growing up, Andy was always a nasty piece of work. Mean for the sake of it and basically a bully. Being the oldest and Mother's favourite, he could never do any wrong. I hated that. So, when Ben was born, it was my duty to shield him from Andy's wrath.

But that's all I could shield him from.

I put my flowers onto Ben's grave; yellow roses. He always loved yellow. He had a toy yellow car when he was little; slept with it every night.

*Wello Ca,* he used to call it. I smiled and lay down next to him as Nirvana blared through my headphones. I turned up the volume to drown out the violent thoughts I always had of what I would do if I ever found Ben's killer, and instead played imaginary drums along to the music.

# CHAPTER TEN

When I was a kid, I used to think that when a woman was ready to marry, she would be presented with a row of bachelors holding flowers and would slowly walk past each one until she decided on which she liked best. I wondered whether Mother would have chosen NPP if this was the way marriage happened but enough of that, because today was the day. The day I had dreaded for so long; the wedding of Mother and Mr No Personality Peters.

Troy and I were late. We hurried down the aisle of Saint Joseph's Church in Brighton to the sound of deafening organ music.

'Is this a wedding or a funeral?' Troy asked, grinning.

I remembered Ben's funeral and suddenly felt cold. This was the first time I'd been in a church since then. I also felt faint surrounded by religious paraphernalia and started to breathe heavily. Troy gave me a concerned look but I smiled, pretending to be fine.

We hurried to the front pews with the disapproving looks of a hundred pretentious posh people following our every move.

Mr No Personality Peters stood at the altar with his back to me, but turned around in order to give me a glare. I glared back and poked my tongue out, embarrassed when the priest noticed. He shook his head. Yet again I had offended a religious person. Would it ever end?

Troy and I sat in the front row, next to my brother Andy and his girlfriend, Debbie; the second dumbest person I have ever met. She was a lingerie model who I nicknamed Barbie, for obvious reasons. She was a total stereotype; long blonde hair, short, short skirt and the brain capacity of an ant. Actually, no, I think ants are more intelligent. I once saw one carrying a huge chunk of bread that was three times larger than itself. There is no way Debbie could ever do that.

'Hello, little sis.' Andy smirked. 'And Troy.'

Troy waved but I said nothing.

'You remember Debbie?' Andy continued.

I glanced at his princess. Today she was dressed from Barbie's disco selection. I watched in awe as she chewed gum and texted whilst wearing headphones. I couldn't believe she was able to do all these things at the same time.

'How could I forget?' I muttered, pushing my sunglasses back to the ridge of my nose. I'd cleverly worn them to hide my black eye from the judgment of hundreds of pretentious plebs.

I started adjusting my salmon pink, puffy dress in frustration. 'I hate this bloody dress, I feel like a bloated peach,' I whispered to Troy, who tried to suppress a laugh.

As I continued to wrestle with my dress, I felt someone's eyes drilling through the back of my skull and turned around, seeing none other than Mrs Tiara, complete with tiara. I lifted up my sunnies and pointed to my black eye, mouthing the words, 'Mother did it,' to which Mrs Tiara responded with the usual, 'Oh really, I never!'

The ceremony began.

Mother and her messy beehive staggered slowly down the aisle. She was wearing an off-white strapless little number, with Granddad holding her arm. I feared Granddad was only there to hold Mother up due to the case of champagne she'd had before the event. Granddad didn't look so hot. I figured he was around 120 years old by now and looked it. That meant Sister Virgilius must be going on 130.

I remembered how Mother had wanted me to be bridesmaid and how I'd refused. The last thing I wanted was to be traipsing in front of her in my salmon pink puffy dress, throwing rose petals or whatever bridesmaids do, like some kind of demented flower-child. After all, that would show I was happy about this union when in fact I wasn't. The only reason I was there, and in that dress, was because Mother had threatened to get rid of Chocky. She would have done it, too. In the end, Mother decided on no bridesmaids at all, as she didn't want to be upstaged by anyone.

The wedding was long, dull and depressing. Watching those two fools marry was almost too much for me to bear, with Mother in that off-white strapless little number.

'Well,' I remembered her saying before the wedding, 'I *have* been married before. When I married your father, I wore white, so I feel off-white is more fitting for me as a mature woman...'

I remembered dry-retching after that little speech, thinking black a much more fitting colour to ascertain Mother's virtue.

The only way I was able to get through this ridiculous little union was to occasionally pinch Troy's thigh until he shrieked.

The reception wasn't much better. The Brighton Savoy's function room was decked out in hundreds of white balloons alongside pale yellow and violet curtains, transforming the place into what looked like prom night from a really bad 80s movie.

I felt ill.

'Look at this place,' I said to Troy. 'Is this Hell? Have we been sent to Hell?'

'Obviously.' He nodded, pointing at something behind me.

I turned around, shocked to see Sister Catherine talking to Mr No Personality Peters.

'What the hell is she doing here?'

'To torment you, no doubt,' Troy said wryly. 'But seriously, didn't Mr Peters' law firm donate money to the convent? Remember, Sister V was at their engagement party as well.'

'I'll never be rid of them.' I sighed.

A waiter approached, holding a tray of bubbly. I did my usual trick and took the entire tray just as Mrs Tiara rattled past. 'Don't worry!' I yelled after her, 'I'm off duty tonight, ma'am!'

Troy gave me that *sometimes you go too far* look that I knew and loved so well. I put the tray on the floor and picked up two glasses, handing him one.

'It's a shame Mrs J had to work. She woulda dug the free booze.'

'She *always* has to work.' Troy sighed.

Picking up on Troy's sadness about his mum working herself into an early grave, I attempted to snap him out of it.

'Let us celebrate this momentous occasion together!' I said in a puffed-up voice.

We clinked our glasses together, sculled the champagne, burped and begun to scan the room for potential victims.

Uncle-Rock-Star-Has-Been Jack was doing his best bad 80s dancing, complete with arms swinging high up in the air. My uncle (Dad's older brother) was a total pain in the nether regions. He almost made it as a rock star in the 70s but not quite and never failed to remind me of that every time I saw him. He also had the ego of a lion on steroids. Troy and I imitated his dancing for a while until he unfortunately saw me and headed over with Auntie Elm in tow. Troy did a runner as usual. The bugger.

'Georgie, honey!' he roared giving me a suffocating hug as Auntie Elm moped beside him.

His fruity aftershave pierced my nasal cavities, causing me to sneeze.

'Do you hear this song playing? Do you know who it is? It's the band Dragon. The name of the song is *Are You Old Enough?* Did you know Dragon used to support my band Jack and The Meanstalks? Yes, I said *support*! That's how big we were! We nearly made it but we never had a hit! That's the only reason! Blah, blah, blah, blah…'

When I couldn't take anymore, I excused myself from my ulcer-inducing uncle and soon found Troy propping up the bar. After we got drinks, my attention focused on Granddad, who was waltzing with Mother. She'd drunk so much by this stage she was passed out on his shoulder. NPP came to the rescue and pulled her off Granddad, sitting her down on a couch. I laughed and yelled 'timberrrrrrr!' as I watched her body slowly fall into a heap. NPP just stood there awkwardly, hands on hips.

'Do you believe that old fool thinks he's my dad now?' I said bitterly to Troy, turning my back to them.

'He'll never be your dad. You already have a dad.'

'I know, but he thinks he's my *new* dad.'

'May I have the next dance?' a familiar voice said behind me. It was Mr No Personality Peters. His bald spot was shinier than ever and he was holding out his clammy little hand for me to hold. I seriously thought I was going to be ill.

'No, I, can't, I have to… bathroom.' I said quickly, dragging Troy by his tie.

'That was a little obvious,' Troy said after we were safe.

'What was I supposed to do, dance with him? How could I possibly do that and keep a straight face?'

'Look.' Troy pointed at something, smirking.

I looked over, seeing Mr No Personality Peters attempting to dance with Barbie. Barbie was all disco-diva with ten moves a second while NPP was struggling to keep up with her.

Troy and I exchanged meaningful glances before we started imitating them.

We stopped when a scowling Sister Catherine stood in front of us with her bug-shaped head and ridiculously huge glasses.

Back into my green school uniform and principal's office I went.

'Appleby,' she grunted. 'Got the night off from the supermarket, have we?'

Little did she know about the other shit jobs I'd stuffed up since then.

'I always knew you were never going to get anywhere in life,' she continued, eyes narrowing, 'even though you have such a prestigious family. Some eggs are rotten and will always be rotten.'

With that she strolled off with her ugly bug head held high, leaving nothing but a whiff of mothballs.

'Don't listen to her,' Troy said as he hugged the life out of me.

But the sad thing was Sister C was right. I was a loser. I always was and always would be. Troy helped me regain a slightly better mood after Sister Catherine's vitriol, but it wasn't easy, as my nun-nemesis had really got to me.

Luckily, the night wrapped up soon after Mother passed out. NPP was piling her into the limo, legs askew, when he noticed Troy and me grinning nearby.

'Are you coming, Georgina?' he asked as he tried to stuff one of Mother's legs into the car.

'No, I'm staying at Troy's. Look after Chocky for me.'

'Gladly,' he said as he successfully put Mother's legs into the car and closed the door.

'She's pissed again, eh?' I asked with a grin.

'No, your mother is just tired,' he corrected sternly.

The old fool. How stupid did he think I was?

'Remember tomorrow night we are having a special family dinner,' NPP continued. 'Your brother and his girlfriend are coming so we will expect you at 6 pm.'

'May I be invited, sir?' Troy quipped eagerly.

'Very well, I shall tell Cook,' NPP muttered as he got into the limo.

As the car sped off, I gave Troy a strange look.

'What?' he asked.

'You called him *sir.*'

'Anything for a free feed.' Troy smiled.

# CHAPTER ELEVEN

Family dinners; what can I say? Think of the worst movie you've ever seen being played over and over with you being tied to a chair with something to prop your eyes open, and you still wouldn't be close to the pain of family dinners.

Tonight, starring Mother, Mr No Personality Peters and featuring special guest stars Andy and Barbie. I hated eating with Barbie. She always opened her mouth as wide as Luna Park when she ate so she wouldn't smudge her lipstick. It was beyond annoying.

Thank dog Troy invited himself. We sat down at the dining room table next to each other. I felt Mother's ice-cold stare slicing through me as I sat there in my sunglasses and tucked my huge white napkin into my collar. Troy did the same.

'Marlene!' Mother yelled, resulting in our skinny maid tip-toeing in, looking terrified. Troy gave her a wink, making her nearly drop the plates she was carrying.

'For God's sake girl, watch yourself,' Mother said sharply.

Marlene the maid was a meek young girl around my age. She had long brown hair that was always worn in a tight bun, giving her an older appearance. Her face was plain, her skin pale and translucent; she never wore make-up. Her eyes were an eerie light grey that sent a chill up my spine when I bumped into her on the stairs at night; maid by day, axe murderer by night. She wasn't ugly, she was just Marlene. She always wore a classic black and white maid's uniform that looked like it was either from the 1950s or a porn movie. Sadly, Mother insisted on her wearing one. What that said about Mother I do not know. I have never seen Marlene in casual attire. Sunday was her only day off and she was always gone before any of us rose and would sneak home in the middle of the night when we were all asleep. I often wondered what she did on that day off, her only day of freedom from oppression. I imagined her laughing and partying with her friends, staggering home drunk hoping not to wake us as she tripped and giggled on the stairs, but the reality was, she probably sat in a park all day feeding ducks food they didn't even want as they had already gorged themselves to the brim from earlier duck feeders, so she would eat the duck food herself before crying her way home.

Marlene the maid had no money, no education and no prospects whatsoever. I think Mother only had her around to make her feel better about herself. I tried to befriend our maid many times, but she was scared to death of me. No surprises there, I guess.

Marlene put the plates down and left. She came in and out a few more times until mountains of food covered the table, and deliberately avoided Troy's eyes every time.

'Time to say grace,' NPP ordered as Troy and I began to help ourselves. After thanking God for what felt like an hour, he finally let us eat. He took a breast of chicken and passed the plate to me.

'I don't eat animals, Mr Peters.'

'Georgina!' Mother roared.

We ate quietly and uncomfortably to the sound of cutlery clinking together and Mother's diamond ring tinkling against her champagne glass. She was on a liquid diet, as usual. Barbie commented on how good the fish was. Pity it was chicken.

'So, Georgina,' NPP began, wiping his thin, wrinkled mouth with a napkin, 'have you decided on what university you will go to yet?'

I gave NPP the *Georgie Death Stare*, making him shift uncomfortably in his chair, before I glanced at Mother. Her champagne glass was at the ready.

Andy and Barbie were sitting opposite. Andy was grinning at my uneasiness, but Barbie had no idea what was going on. She was delicately eating one pea at a time.

I fantasised about jumping on the table and kicking food in their faces.

'Well, are you going to answer him?' asked Mother.

I handed Chocky a piece of chicken under the table. She snatched it from my hand and gobbled it down quickly.

'I'm not going to university,' I began slowly, taking off my napkin and folding it neatly. 'I have found my calling in life and that is to be a pizza deliverer, which I hope to return to when the Health Department re-open the shop. You see, a silverfish was found on a seafood pizza. Unbelievable! I thought it was one of the ingredients! I *have* tried other careers, like being a check-out chick and telemarketer, but I keep getting fired on my first day! I even tried to work in a mail room and look what happened!'

I took off my sunglasses, shocking everyone except for Mother (who rolled her eyes) and Troy (who laughed).

'It's my attitude problem, you see,' I said with a smile, putting my sunnies back on.

Silence filled the room.

'Marlene!' Mother yelled. 'More champagne!'

Dinner continued silently, becoming increasingly boring when Andy started boasting about his Ridiculous Real Estate Firm's annual turnover. Mother was licking her lips at the thought of all that delicious money.

Barbie tossed her hair.

Then Mr No Personality Peters put in his two cents, gushing about his Lame Law Firm's annual turnover.

Mother started dribbling.

Barbie tossed her hair.

Troy and I looked at each other in anticipation, smiling deviously.

Mother was beginning to get wise. 'If you dare talk about how much money you earned at that ridiculous pizza shop, Georgina, you can leave the table right now!'

Marlene walked nervously into the room, giving me an idea. Mother may have been beginning to get wise, but she wasn't wise enough.

'Actually,' I began, all eyes centred in on me, except for Barbie's (I don't need to tell you what she was doing), 'I was going to talk about the money Marlene earns.'

Marlene glanced at me in horror.

'What is your annual turnover, Marlene, five dollars?'

'That is enough!' Mother roared, standing. 'You leave this table right now and don't come back until you are able to have a civilised conversation!' Her heavily made-up eyes narrowed into slits, making it hard to see how bloodshot they really were.

'Well, I guess I won't be coming back then,' I said calmly, throwing my huge white napkin into the air as I left the room. Shadow dog followed. Troy excused himself in his usual gentlemanly way that made me want to puke, but I figured he needed to act like that in order to get fed again. Cook was amazing. She made the most delicious vegetarian dishes in the entire universe.

As I left the dining room and walked into the kitchen, I could smell something baking, but this time it wasn't my step-fool's clammy little handmade treats. I was pleased to find Cook in her usual position, behind the stove.

Cook was a fifty-odd, big ball of love. She was always happy, no matter what. I had never seen her anything but happy.

'I've got your Pecan Pie in the oven, dear,' she said with a wink. 'I won't tell Hubert our little secret!'

I laughed as I gave her a high five.

'Let's go outside,' I said to Troy. Chocky followed us out the back door as we sat down on the veranda.

'You shouldn't have come. Dinner at Purgatory Palace is always like this, except tonight we had the added pleasure of the Andy and Barbie show.' I stroked Chocky's soft fur. It glistened from the swim she'd had earlier and turned rust-coloured in the moonlight.

Troy said nothing. I looked at him, noticing a sad expression that worried me. I knew something was up. 'What is it?'

'I have to tell you something, Georgie.'

'What?'

'I'm going away.'

# CHAPTER TWELVE

Troy walked into my room, finding me slumped on the bed, staring blankly at my kelpie calendar, Chocky's head in my lap.

'You mad at me?' he asked in a baby voice.

I threw my stuffed Snoopy at his head. He swerved and missed it.

'What about my non-graduation? You said you'd come with me,' I moped.

'When is it again?'

'Ages away, February next year.'

'I'll be back by then! It's not forever,' he continued, sitting beside me. 'If you actually let me explain, you'll realise it's only for around six months.'

I glanced up at his puppy-dog expression, complete with bottom lip protruding. 'Okay, explain, but it better be good.'

He went on to tell me about his uncle in Perth, Mrs J's brother, who had just started a new business and was paying Troy and his mum to help with his new enterprise. I knew money was tight for them, so I started to feel Catholic guilt about giving him a hard time – but I had to, just for a little longer.

'How can you leave me here with Mother and Mr No Personality Peters?' I whined.

'It's only for six months or so, like I said.'

'What about work? I hear Tony's re-opening the pizza shop soon.'

'Work will be here when I get back. I'm sure Tony will put me back on the roster. I'm pretty replaceable – you don't need a degree to be a pizza deliverer!'

'God, but imagine if we did!' I laughed, finally lightening up. 'Maybe we'd actually make some money out of it!'

'Nah.' Troy grinned. 'We wouldn't be doing it 'cause we wouldn't have a degree!'

We rolled about laughing until a knock on the door brought us to.

'Who is it?' I asked, although I already knew it would be Mother or NPP, as Andy and Barbie never came to my room.

'It is your mother and new father!' Mother yelled.

I rolled my eyes at Troy. 'New father,' I said through clenched teeth. My five-second good mood was over. I unlocked the door to see the two fools standing there gawking at me. Mother was wobbling. She was on her third case of champagne by this stage.

'I hope we're not interrupting anything,' she began coyly.

'No, it's fine Mother, Troy and I have finished having sex.'

'Really! I never! You can talk to this ridiculous child of mine, Hubert. I have had enough!' Mother stormed off in a flurry of pink feathers and champagne bubbles, leaving NPP standing before me, clutching a coloured pamphlet in his clammy little hand.

I had a bad feeling about this.

'Georgina... I have taken the liberty of applying to Melbourne University for you, as I am in the Alumni with the Dean of the Faculty of Arts.'

He cleared his throat.

'You have an appointment with him on Tuesday at 9am.'

Chocky's growl combined with the *Georgie Death Stare* made the old fool take a step backward, which was just in time, as I slammed the door in his face.

'I've had enough of this place,' I said to Troy. 'I'm leaving, too.'

# CHAPTER THIRTEEN

Dad opened the door, his face turning to shock when he saw me.

'Georgie… what are you doing here?!'

Dad and Ben were the only ones who called me Georgie in my family. Dad gave me the nickname in the first place and it stuck, much to Mother's distaste.

Before I was able to answer, he grabbed me and hugged me to the point of suffocation. I hated people hugging me unless it was Dad, Troy or Ben. Not that Ben was ever going to hug me again. At least Dad seemed happy to see me; I was worried about that. Even if the hug was out of guilt for being a crap father, it was still nice to be hugged by him.

Dad looked good for his age. He was tall, dark and slim. Like me, except for the tall bit. He worked out and seemed to always care about his appearance, unlike clammy little Mr No Personality Peters and his protruding Buddha belly.

Shudder.

'What happened to your eye?'

'I walked into a doorknob.'

'Hmmm… are you here for a visit? You should have called me…'

'I'm here for good,' I said defiantly, dropping my suitcase to the floor, giving Chocky a start.

Dad glanced at the pooch incredulously.

'What's going on, Georgina?'

Uh-oh, he called me Georgina.

'Well, Dad, I can explain if you let me…'

I suddenly heard an unfamiliar male voice ask who I was. Then the door opened fully, revealing a tall, bleached-blond man with a fine head of hair standing next to Dad. He looked around Dad's age, forty-odd, but had an incredible tan. Dad looked uncomfortable.

'Hello, darl.' The man's smile radiated like a heater. 'Are you Georgie?'

I nodded.

'Oh, I'm so glad to meet you. I've heard so much!'

This strange man was shaking my hand so furiously that my dog stood to attention to sniff him, but I feared Chocky was only interested because he smelt like coconut. It seemed the pooch thought she had encountered a light snack.

'Georgie, this is Josh,' Dad said quietly.

'Hello there, Josh.' I smiled, my hand still possessed by his.

'Josh, you can stop shaking her hand now. I need to have a serious talk with my daughter, do you mind?'

Josh nodded his head and disappeared.

Dad led me to the living room. I'd visited him once before, a year or so ago, but it looked different now, new furniture maybe. There was definitely a different vibe.

I threw myself onto the couch. Chocky curled up beside me and soon started snoring.

Dad sat opposite in the armchair and leaned forward to look at me. He still had a nice head of hair, a little thinning, but not too bad, and his glasses were small, frameless ones you could hardly even see. I wondered if Sister Catherine even knew you could buy glasses like these. He wasn't a bad looking guy, for a dad, I guess. I realised Cute Guy didn't look like him at all – must have been the glasses. Thank dog, incestuous much.

'How did you get here? Did you drive all the way from Melbourne?'

'Yeah! It only takes ten hours to drive to Sydney. We slept in the car when we got tired.'

'Chocky share the driving with you, did she?'

'No, she's still trying to get her Ls.' I laughed.

Uncomfortable silence; then:

'What's going on, Georgina?' he asked again, still with the Georgina.

I took a deep breath. 'Well... I think I should be asking what's going on with *you*.'

Dad moved uncomfortably in his chair.

'Who's Josh?'

He didn't say anything for ages after that. He just sat there staring at the carpet, taking off his specs to clean them. All Giles-like, from *Buffy*.

He finally put his glasses back on and looked me straight in the eye.

'Josh is my partner.'

I laughed. I didn't mean to; it just happened. I wasn't laughing that he was gay or anything, but this was my dad and it was a little weird. I was gay-friendly; in all honesty, I was bi, but Dad didn't know that. No one did. To this day there had only ever been one girl I had a massive crush on.

Dad was looking really uncomfortable.

'Hey it's cool, it's cool, I'm okay with it, I think it's great, really!' I said in between giggles. 'Actually, I'm really not surprised that after being with my mother, you turned gay!'

Dad stood, seemed upset.

'It wasn't just that, you know,' he said, pacing the floor. 'It's a lot more complicated than that...'

'I know, I know.' I stood up, grabbing his arm to settle him. 'I'm sorry, of course it's complicated and if you ever want to tell me about it, I'll listen, but I just want you to know I'm okay with it, Dad, really!'

His face softened and he half-smiled, taking off his glasses to clean them again.

'I never thought I'd experience coming out to my daughter.' He laughed. We hugged for a while, then he let me go abruptly.

'Oh, and anyway, back to my original question, what's going on with you, Georgie?'

Ah, Georgie. That was better.

'My turn, is it?'

'Yes.'

We sat down and I told Dad the whole story of my escaping Purgatory Palace. He listened to me patiently as I rambled on about Mother and Mr No Personality Peters and the sheer horribleness of my existence in that house, and the whole time he just sat there and listened patiently. So patiently, it was incredible. He was nothing like Mother. How he listened to all my crap, I have no idea. *I* wouldn't listen to it.

I finally came up for air just as Josh arrived with tea and biscuits. He set the tray down on the coffee table carefully before leaving us to it. He was well trained.

After Dad cleaned his glasses for the hundredth time, he looked at me. I could feel the words of wisdom looming.

'If you don't stay in that house until you're twenty-one,' he began, all guru-like, 'you'll lose your inheritance to Andy and you'll never forgive yourself for that, Georgie.' He picked up his tea, taking a sip.

'Andy!' I yelled. 'Mother never told me that!'

'Well, *I'm* telling you, so now you know.'

Jesus. Andy. He'd probably waste my money on Debbie so she could buy Barbie's After 5 Collection. I shuddered.

Fuck, I hated my family.

'Of course,' Dad continued. 'If you ever need a break from Purgatory Palace, you're welcome to visit me and Josh whenever you like.'

I jumped up, giving him a kiss on the cheek, nearly making him spill his tea.

'I love you, Dad.'

'I love you too, kiddo.'

# CHAPTER FOURTEEN

After a few weeks of 'quality time' with Dad (which included me hardly even seeing him, as he was always working) and being promised to be taken sight-seeing (which never eventuated), it was time to go home. At least my black eye was almost gone. I was sick to death of being asked about it and running out of lies to explain what happened.

Driving back to Melbourne from Sydney took even longer than the other way around. Maybe it was because I was preoccupied thinking about Dad and Josh. I was actually really happy, though. I thought it was really cool. I did wonder about Mother's reaction and imagined the shit hitting the feather boa big time, or did she already know but hadn't told me? Hmmm…

Chocky started getting restless and I needed to stretch my legs. I thought of Mother's legs being stuffed into the limo and let out a chuckle. The old fool.

I pulled over at a truck stop somewhere between Woop and Woop Woop. I found a stick on a patch of grass, throwing it for Chocky before I gave her dinner. I had to wait for it to come out before I bundled her back into the car.

Then I entered the truck stop, observing the familiar base-ball-capped tourists and starved-for-coffee truck drivers. I stood in line and was soon tapped on the shoulder. I'm always being tapped on the shoulder. I turned around and was shocked to see my old school friend and partner in crime, Titania, behind me.

'Oh my dog!' I said, genuinely surprised. 'What are you doing here?'

'We're on our way back to Melbourne,' Tits said. 'We were visiting John's grandparents in Newcastle.'

She looked tired; very tired. Her miniature brown eyes had deep dark circles beneath them and her long dark hair sat limp and greasy. She looked so different. Her Greek goddess style was gone. I couldn't believe she was wearing a moo moo and thongs of all things.

'John. Are you still with John?'

I think Tits heard my distaste as she immediately flashed an engagement ring at me. 'We're getting married...'

'Congratulations,' I forced out.

John was a sleazebag and an idiot. Tits started dating him halfway through Year 12 and he became everything to her. It was around then our friendship started to dwindle, as her main hobby became smoking weed. She dropped out of school soon after. I did the same. In fact, it wasn't long until I lost contact with Tits and Mel altogether. I became a hermit after Ben's death. The only person I let in was Troy.

Most people don't know what to say when a tragedy like that happens, so they just end up saying they're sorry even though they did nothing wrong or they just disappear. Losing a sibling changes you forever, especially when they're your favourite. There is a constant emptiness, a feeling like you've misplaced something, like you've lost a metaphorical limb. Then you start living your life for both of you because they never got the chance to live longer and that makes you live in the moment because you don't know if you'll be around tomorrow. Putting the finality of death in front of someone at a young age is its own kind of trauma. Troy was the only one there for me; he got me through it and that's something I'll never forget.

'And I'm pregnant,' Tits continued, holding her protruding belly.

'Pregnant?' I repeated in shock.

'Yeah, six months gone.'

John was beside me now with his toothless grin. The guy was such a bogan. He had his front tooth knocked out in Year 11 but didn't care. He just always smiled his toothless smile like he was proud of it or something. His party trick was putting a cigarette in the gap.

Puke.

'G'day, Georgie...' he said, looking down at my boobs, even though I hardly even had any and they were totally covered by a loose black T-shirt. He always creeped me out so bad. He had no idea how much I disliked him. I guess he was too thick to realise. 'Fancy bumping into you down this way,' he continued, winking.

My mind started racing one hundred kilometres an hour. I couldn't believe that Titania, my cool, sarcastic, smart-arse friend, was engaged to this sleazy moron, wearing a moo moo and thongs and carrying his child. She used to be so cool but he'd turned her into a bogan. She also seemed to have aged so much since I'd last seen her, yet I hadn't aged at all.

'We better go, honey.' John grinned. His missing front tooth was like a magnet and I couldn't look away. It was very disturbing.

'Are you going to our graduation? Did you hear they rescheduled it?' Tits asked as she started to walk away. 'You can still go even if you dropped out, like us. Hope to see you there!'

My best friend Titania.

\*\*\*

*Tits and I escaped from school during lunchtime for a wander down Church Street. It was against the rules but we didn't care, we needed some nun-free air. After our little adventure we passed a pub. Tits stopped me and grabbed my arm.*

*'That bag looks like it's full of beer,' she whispered, eyes wide.*

*We checked it out and sure enough, the brown paper bag that sat on the pub's doorstep contained an unopened six pack of VB. Tits and I looked around but couldn't see anyone, so we went in for the kill. We weren't allowed to eat while wearing our school uniform out of grounds but no one said anything about not being able to drink.*

*The park seemed the right place for a drink or three, so we sat on the swings and guzzled the cans down quickly, then went back to our next class, which was Sacred Singing, better known as, you guessed it, Sacred Screeching. We sang a lot louder than usual that day. Luckily the nuns, high on God's songs, didn't notice.*

*After school, Tits invited me back to her place to watch TV; anything to avoid me going back to Purgatory Palace. As we entered her house, we were confronted with the horrific sight of Titania's mother vacuuming topless. I wondered if that was why she gave her daughter the name she did. It was an image that has unfortunately haunted me to this day.*

***

I hopped back in the car, put on Chocky's dog seat belt and continued on my journey. Thoughts of Titania plagued my mind. My thoughts then turned to my non-graduation. Surely Leticia and Prudence, Shelley The Sheep Girl and Mel would be there, and of course Sister Catherine and Sister V. Bird Girl might even fly in for the occasion. I could give them all heaps. I think I'll be going to my non-graduation after all.

Chocky and I got home around 3am. Luckily, no one was awake. I went up to my room and threw myself onto my unmade bed in exhaustion. Marlene was forbidden to clean my room. The last thing I wanted was her creeping around, sniffing things and touching all my stuff.

But I missed Troy. Being at Dad's had wasted a few weeks, but now I was back I had no Troy and no job. I felt the tears start to well as I stroked the fur under Chocky's chin. She yawned as her golden eyes met mine.

I wasn't looking forward to the scene that awaited me due to my sudden disappearance and no-show at the Melbourne University appointment that NPP had set up for me weeks ago. Why couldn't he just leave me alone? What did it have to do with him whether I went to Uni or not? It was just Mother's influence. He was trying to do the right thing by her, the old fool.

The last thing I thought of before falling asleep was Chocky's vet appointment, which I'd organised for tomorrow morning while still in Sydney, so I set my alarm and soon drifted off.

# CHAPTER FIFTEEN

The next morning, I dragged myself out of bed just in time for Chocky to get her booster and check-up, the vet telling me she was in tip-top shape for a three-year-old kelpie dog. I was so proud I bought her a new red studded collar to celebrate. As we were leaving the vet, a cat was brought into the waiting room. It reminded me of a cat I used to know.

*** 

*'She's over there!' Tits yelled. We ran after the feline, finally catching up to her as she rubbed her back on one of the teacher's car's wheels. She was black with white spots, which included a white chin and four white socks; two pulled up and two pulled down.*

*Titania and I bent down and stretched out our arms so she would come over. She did, then promptly flopped to the ground, rolling continuously as Tits and I took turns in patting her. The feline's purr sounded like she was making popcorn.*

*A group of girls walked past, turning their heads as they watched us pat the cat.*

*'Do you know what her name is?' I asked the girls.*

*'I dunno.' One of the girls shrugged.*

*We thought 'I Dunno' was a strange name for a cat but who were we to argue?*

\*\*\*

After the vet, I took Chocky to visit Ben. I bought some yellow roses and made my usual way to his grave, only to be stopped short when it was in sight as I noticed someone was there. As I moved closer, I saw a figure in black kneeling at his grave but when I got closer still, the figure had vanished. All that remained were three long-stemmed yellow roses and a note that said, *'I'm sorry.'*

I freaked, frantically looking around, but saw no one. Who the hell was that? It must have been the piece of shit who ran over Ben. I bet it was! Who else would leave a card saying *'I'm sorry'*? But there were yellow roses... how would the hit and run driver who killed my brother know that yellow was Ben's favourite colour? Who the hell *was* that?!

After an hour of trying to calm myself down, Chocky and I headed back to Purgatory Palace but I couldn't stop thinking about the stranger at Ben's grave and the mysterious note. My thoughts distracted me from the inevitable backlash that awaited me at home. Luckily, I had avoided it in the morning.

I found Mother alone in the living room, crying. She was sitting on the couch, bawling into a white handkerchief. She looked older than usual and there seemed to be a strange vulnerability surrounding her that alarmed me. Ben's death was the likely cause of her tears. She had totally shut down after that tragedy. She never talked about him anymore and it was only after he died that she really started to hit the bottle big time. I couldn't even imagine how hard it was for Mother and Dad to lose their child.

Dad kept Ben's memory alive – I'd seen photos of him when I was at his house recently – but Mother did the opposite. All photos of Ben had disappeared from the living room. Whenever any of us spoke about him, she would seize up and either leave the room or change the subject. She behaved similarly when ads for funerals were on TV – you never notice how many ads there are until you lose someone. Mother obviously needed to see a shrink or grief counsellor but of course didn't; she preferred to pretend Ben never existed and the booze definitely helped with that. Sometimes I actually worried about her, especially when I saw her cry, which wasn't very often. She was so skinny now, frail. I imagined what it would be like if she wasn't around anymore, how that would affect me. Sometimes I wished we got along but usually we just carried on despising each other. It was the way things worked best between us. But I did believe that somewhere underneath all that plastic surgery, Mother did love me, just a little. Or so I hoped.

'So, you're back, are you?' she spat, wiping her eyes self-consciously and smudging her mascara in the process. 'You do realise you missed your appointment with the Dean at Melbourne University?'

'Yes.'

My thoughts turned to Mr No Personality Peters just as he walked downstairs. He called out Chocky's name but, as usual, she growled at him. Clever girl. NPP watched me silently with his arms crossed. His bald spot glistened like a lone disco ball at a two dollar a pot RSL. I dreaded hearing his ridiculously high-pitched voice. Luckily, he remained silent.

'Have you found yourself a job yet, Georgina?'

'No, I haven't found myself a job yet, Mother,' I said, throwing myself into the armchair. Chocky jumped onto my lap and kissed my face gently.

'Thought as much,' Mother said, reaching for her champagne glass. She took a few sips as I watched her ominously. Her sudden sedateness was alarming.

'It has been decided that Hubert will be giving you a position at his law firm in one week's time.'

'That is correct,' NPP croaked, hands on hips.

'You're joking,' I said in shock. 'There is no way I'm working in that hellhole!'

'Hubert and I have been talking,' she went on, ignoring my outburst. 'You have had more than enough time to find a job. You have had three opportunities recently and you ruined all of them…'

'The mailroom job wasn't my fault! I got punched in the eye!' I pleaded but, ignoring me, she continued.

'You refuse to go to university, yet continue to live here, working dead-end jobs. You're just wasting time until you receive your inheritance, which you will fritter away on reckless abandonment, after which you will come crawling back as you won't have a cent left.'

She glanced at me. A volcano of venom erupted from her that sent a shiver through my soul.

'This is your future, Georgina.'

'Since when did you become a fortune teller?!' I roared, startling Chocky, who jumped off my lap.

'I can see it as clear as the nose on my face,' she continued. 'There are a few years before that happens, so the least you can do is work a decent job like any other human being. And finally,' Mother said as she stood shakily, tossing her pink feather boa around her turkey neck, 'if you decide not to work at Hubert's law firm, you can kiss your inheritance goodbye.'

With that she left the room, with NPP scuttling behind her.

I was speechless.

***

Sometime later, Marlene tiptoed into the living room to retrieve Mother's empty champagne glass and noticed me sitting with my head in my hands.

'Are you all right, Miss?' she squeaked.

Marlene didn't usually say a peep to me unless she was talking in maid-speak. This was a breakthrough. I looked up at her through cloudy eyes. She picked up the tissue box from the coffee table and held it towards me. I took one and blew my nose.

'I hope you feel better soon, Miss,' she whispered, placing the tissue box carefully back in its rightful position.

'Thanks, Marlene,' I said quietly, totally in awe of this moment between us. As she scurried off, I called after her.

'Marlene!'

'Yes, Miss?'

'My name is Georgie, not Miss.'

'Okay, Georgina.'

'No, it's Georgie.'

Marlene blushed and looked to the floor as she held the edge of her apron in one hand and Mother's empty champagne glass in the other. She was like a child; vulnerable, innocent and totally clueless.

'Okay, Georgie.'

Then she smiled, revealing beautiful teeth and dimples. I'd never seen her smile. I was shocked at how attractive she actually was. As she tiptoed out of the room, my mind was ablaze with thoughts of how I had always wanted to be her friend and gossip about Mother. It seemed now I finally had the chance. I was happy for a moment until I remembered what Mother had said. There was no way in hell I could possibly get out of working for Mr No Personality Peters' Lame Law Firm, as I didn't want to lose my inheritance.

Triple sigh with a twist of lemon.

***

I was so depressed I locked myself in my room for an entire week, awaiting the inevitable; thank dog I had an ensuite bathroom.

I had resigned myself to my fate.

Troy was still away and, apart from my canine companion, I felt all alone. Luckily, Marlene brought food and sweet Jim Beam and Coke up to my room as often as I wanted. She really looked after me. She even looked after Chocky by feeding and walking her for me. I refused to see Mother and NPP.

When Marlene dropped off supplies, she would always say hello and hope I was feeling better, but not much else, as she could no doubt sense my mood. But today, she said a lot more.

There was a knock on my door.

'Georgie, it's Marlene,' a little voice said.

I jumped out of bed and unlocked the door, then jumped back into bed.

'Enter.'

Marlene opened the door slowly, spying me on my bed, totally under the doona. Chocky was beside me, being the good electric blanket she was.

'I brought you a drink,' she said softly.

I threw the doona off me instantly. Chocky got annoyed and chicken-scratched until she was under again.

Marlene handed me my special Snoopy glass I'd had since I was ten. I sculled the entire contents in two seconds, burped and wiped my mouth on my sleeve.

'Why can't you just bring me a barrel of Jim Beam?' I sighed, throwing myself back onto the bed.

'I don't think drinking yourself to death is a good idea, Georgie,' she squeaked.

I sat up and looked at her.

'Why? You do know that tomorrow morning I'm starting my job at Hubert's Lame Law Firm as a filing clerk, don't you? What is the purpose of living?'

'I do know that, Georgie, but I'm sure it won't be as bad as you think!'

'Do you like your job?' I asked her seriously.

Marlene didn't answer; she just stood there, awkwardly staring at the silver tray she was holding that held my empty glass.

'I mean, seriously, I don't know how you put up with my mother!' I continued. 'She treats you like shit!'

'Your mother took me in when I had nowhere else to go,' she finally piped up. 'My parents threw me out, I had no money. I saw her advertisement for a live-in maid and she gave me the job.'

'Why did your parents throw you out?'

I was shocked; I had no idea that had happened to her. She put down the tray, sat on the end of my bed and finally spoke.

'Well, Georgie, my biological parents died in a car accident when I was ten; my adoptive parents never loved me, they just used me to cook and clean and look after their baby. I was just their maid. My room was as small as Harry Potter's. Then when I turned seventeen, they said it was time for me to start my life on my own and they threw me out. The only thing I knew how to do was to be a maid, so that's what I became.'

I had no words. I just watched her sitting there sadly on the edge of my bed. I wanted to hug her so bad but resisted because a) I didn't like hugging and b) I was worried she would think I was a weirdo, or worse, in love with her, so I just sat there staring at her with no words.

# CHAPTER SIXTEEN

The next morning, I was forced out of self-imposed exile and, what's worse, I had the utmost pleasure of NPP chauffeuring me to my new prison camp.

Quadruple sigh.

For my first day in hell, I wore my black op shop dress with the white collar I had worn to Mother and NPP's engagement party. It was the only dress I owned, apart from the salmon pink puffy monstrosity I'd worn at their wedding and there was no way I was wearing that. Mother was not happy about my lack of boring office attire, so had instructed Marlene to go shopping for me. I didn't have a chance to talk to Marlene before this was organised. Now that we were friends, I hoped she would buy me things I could actually wear but let's face it, would I ever be seen dead in office clothes? And what if she bought everything in the colour beige? I would be Bird Girl; Beige Bird Girl. Shudder. I think if I wore beige, I could safely commit suicide by jumping out a window and never be noticed by anyone as beige just blends into everything.

When we arrived at NPP's Lame Law Firm he led me to a woman called Ms Wright, who I would be working for. Ms Wright was a human matchstick. She was in her forties with a shock of bright red hair that was worn in a messy bun. Marlene's bun was way neater.

'I'll check up on you later, Georgina. Have a good day,' NPP said, attempting a pathetic smile.

I shot him the *Georgie Death Stare,* making him jump, then clear his throat and scurry away like the rat that he was.

Ms Wrong led me to my desk.

'This is where you'll be doing your filing, Georgina.'

'It's Georgie,' I corrected.

'Oh, is that the name you prefer?' she asked.

'Yes.'

'Okay then, I'll make a note of that, so basically throughout the day your inbox will be full of documents that need to be filed by number, so you have to file them by number. For instance, here you have 1004, 1005, 1006, etcetera, and above you are the folders they need to go into. They are marked by month, so you can see that you will be using the one from this month.'

I never knew I was able to sleep standing up but the nap I just had was awesome.

'Well, good luck, *Georgie.* I'm around the corner if you need me – oh, and your lunch break is an hour. Just take it at twelve. The tea room is just over there. You can have coffee whenever you like and the toilets are down the hall on your left. That's pretty much it, have a great day!'

As Ms Wrong walked away, I sank deeper into my uncomfortable plastic chair, staring at the monstrous pile of filing that awaited me. I could not believe this was the job NPP had given me. The lowest of the low. The shittest of the shit. And why was filing even a job at his Lame Law Firm anyway? Couldn't this crap just be stored on a computer? I bet he created the position especially for me to drive me insane. I felt like screaming banshee-like, throwing the filing all over the office, tearing my hair out and drowning myself in the toilet bowl.

Instead, I started filing.

It wasn't long before I was greeted by the natives.

'Hi there!' an excited girl's voice said. I looked up and saw born-again-Christian Barbie, bible sold separately. I wondered if Deb owned this outfit.

'I'm Cherie,' the girl continued. 'This is Pierre…'

I glanced at the guy next to her.

He looked like a male model.

'And Patrice.' Patrice was the spitting image of Sylvester Stallone. It was uncanny, and scary.

'We're interns! How are you enjoying your first day?' Cherie asked, beaming. She was literally beaming. I had to squint my eyes, her rays were so bright.

'Well, I only just got here…'

'You'll have to have lunch with us,' Pierre insisted, touching my arm.

'We always sit at the same table in the cafeteria,' Patrice piped up. I imagined her dressed as Rambo; it wasn't pretty.

As they walked away, I realised they were going to be my new work BFFs. They were the people I would talk to every day; they were the people I would have lunch with; the people I would have after-work drinks with. As I stared at my mountain of filing, I realised how trapped I was. I seriously felt like a caged animal. Mother and NPP had sucked the life right out of me and all that remained was a filing zombie. I found it harder and harder to breathe until it got so bad my filing grew a mouth and started to laugh at me. So, I had no choice but to run to the tea room, as it was closer than the toilet, fill the sink with water and stick my head in it.

'Are you okay?'

I looked up, as water poured off my face and hair, into the eyes of none other than Cute Guy! What the hell was he doing here?! As soon as he recognised me, he started to look uncomfortable.

I just stood there like an idiot, my face and hair soaking wet and dripping onto my op shop dress, while my major crush stood there gawking. He grabbed a handful of paper towels and handed them to me. I attempted to wipe my head.

'You're the girl f-from karaoke. D-do you work here now?' Cute Guy stuttered. His hair was gelled down, just like Bart Simpson's when he had to go to church, no doubt due to his conservative office job and/or Emily Mears, and his glasses were nowhere in sight.

'Yep, I just started. I'm the Executive Filing Jerk.'

Cute Guy smiled and seemed to blush.

I melted.

'Oh, okay,' he continued. His eyes were as blue as an unpolluted ocean. Oh shit, I was starting to think in clichés.

'Well, I don't know if you remember me, but my name's Justin.'

I remembered.

'I'm Georgie.'

'Hi, I work in accounts so if you need any help, just ask; oh, and b-be careful of Mr Peters, he can be a bit of a, um… arsehole.'

I didn't know if it was humanly possible, but I think I fell for him a little more just then.

'He's my stepdad,' I deadpanned just for a reaction, which I immediately got.

'Oh sorry, I…'

'But I hate him and you're right, he is an arsehole.'

With that, I handed Cute Guy the wet paper towels and walked off, leaving him standing in total confusion as he attempted to catch up with what I just said.

My first day was long, dull and so excruciatingly boring. Filing was such an inane job. The mail room was way more fun than this, minus the punch in the eye, and at least there were executive mice to look at. As soon as I was beginning to catch up, another pile of crisp white monotony was thrown onto my desk. I was dying for coffee but didn't move. I just sat there like a malfunctioning robot stuck on the continuous filing switch. It was Bible Barbie, Model Pierre and Mrs Stallone who snapped me out of Production Line Purgatory. Sister Catherine always did say I would end up in purgatory before I moved onto Hell. I already lived in Purgatory Palace anyway.

'It's lunchtime, Georgie, come on!' BB beamed.

As I stood slowly, grabbing my backpack, I realised my bum had fallen asleep. I gave it a rub as I miserably followed them to the lunchroom. I could hear them gossiping about Ms Wrong ahead of me and how they were certain she was anorexic. Sigh. When we got to the lunchroom, I bought myself a cheese and salad sandwich and a can of Coke and sat down at their table. As I took a bite of my stale sandwich, Cute Guy appeared in my peripheral vision, giving me an idea.

'Hey Justin, is it okay if I sit with you?'

'You can't sit with accounts!' Mrs Stallone yelled as Bible Barbie and Model Pierre nodded in agreement. 'We have to sit in our own sections.'

'There is no rule like that, Patrice,' Cute Guy said in annoyance. 'Yeah, sure, Georgie.'

As I stood, grabbing my food and backpack, the Thorny Threesome watched me with narrow eyes.

'Gee, they're weirdos,' I said as we sat down at Cute Guy's table. I noticed we were the only ones there. 'Are you the only accounts person?' I asked.

'No, there's Annie as well, but she takes lunch later, so I usually get peace and quiet and get to read my book.' He held up a copy of one of the five million *Harry Potter* books. Such a geek. God, I loved geeks; God, I loved him.

'Sorry to disturb your peace and quiet,' I said innocently.

'No, it's fine, don't worry, don't worry. It's nice to have company sometimes.'

'So, what's with the high school mentality of where you sit at lunch?' I pushed my sandwich away and took a sip of my Coke. If only it had bourbon in it. Maybe I could ring Marlene to bring me some?

'It's only them,' he answered. 'The interns. No one else is like that.'

I suddenly remembered that time at karaoke, before Cute Guy was with Emily Mears, when he had attempted to ask me something. I was feeling courageous enough to mention it.

'Do you remember at karaoke ages ago you came up to me and tried to ask something but my friend Troy cut you off?'

'You mean your boyfriend,' he corrected, or so he thought. 'I think he referred to you as his woman.'

'No, that was a joke!' I laughed. 'He was joking, we've only ever been friends.'

'Oh.' CG started looking uncomfortable.

'So, what were you gonna ask?'

He stared at *Harry Potter* for a long time, trying to find magical words that just weren't coming, until finally he had enough of trying to find them.

'Actually, I don't remember,' he said, standing abruptly. He gripped his book so tight I feared Harry's glasses would break. Maybe Cute

Guy's glasses broke, that's why he never wore them anymore. 'I have to go back to work now, see ya.'

With that, Cute Guy, his uneaten lunch and *Harry Potter* were gone. What the hell just happened? As I sat there wondering what I had said to scare off the geek of my dreams, a revolting sight appeared before me. It was Mr No Personality Peters attempting that God-awful smile again. He sat down in Cute Guy's chair. Beauty had become the Beast.

'Hello, Georgina, how is your day going? I see you were having lunch with Justin. He is a very nice chap indeed.'

I said nothing. I just sat there, counting NPP's protruding nostril hairs. I was soon into double digits.

'All right then, thank you for the chat. Can you tell your mother I will be working late tonight so Cook needn't worry about my dinner? Oh, and by the way, I just had a meeting with the Christmas party committee, which included your vice-principal Sister Catherine. She has some wonderful ideas. We are having a beach theme! I expect you to attend. It's at the Hyatt.'

Sr Catherine was in the Christmas party committee!

Kill.

Me.

Now.

Satan.

When my vision had returned after resting my head on my arms for a minute or so, I noticed a tall, voluptuous blonde woman in her thirties standing at the table. She had the cleavage Mother wished I had and wore a – wait for it – leopard print dress. I felt like I had time travelled back to the 1980s. I looked for the glitter in her hair but sadly there was none.

'Mr Peters. Sorry to disturb you, Sir, but that important phone call you were waiting for has come through.'

'Oh yes, Sharon, of course, of course.'

NPP stood up with a groan and tip-toed after her. He didn't even say goodbye; the prick. I figured Sharon was his secretary. Well, she looked like how a secretary looked in the 1980s. I hadn't had the pleasure of meeting her yet and by the looks of it still hadn't.

The Thorny Threesome took their place.

'Why was Mr Peters talking to you?' Bible Barbie questioned anxiously. 'Did you do something wrong?'

I thought long and hard about my answer. I could play along and say I did do something wrong which would give me endless fun or I could be honest and tell them he was my Pretend Father, but would it result in them giving me special treatment? That would suck. I was already so sick of getting special treatment for being an Appleby. I don't think I have mentioned this before, but Appleby is my dad's surname, not Mr No Personality Peters' surname obviously. Dad's family, the Applebys, made their fortune in textiles and the fashion industry, insert Toorak here.

I don't know if my parents were ever really in love. Their marriage wasn't arranged but I figured they had been deliberately pushed together by their wealthy and prestigious families but weren't compatible, and now Dad lived as a gay man, so it did make you wonder.

A year after Ben was born my parents separated and Dad took over the Sydney branch of the company. I knew it was to escape Mother, although leaving her alone with such a young family was not ideal. Her coping mechanism became alcohol, so our nanny started to pretty much do everything for us. Mother still doted on her favourite, Andy, so it really was Ben and me who suffered the most. Nanny was let go when we were all old enough to fend for ourselves and we were devastated. We weren't allowed to see her again.

Mother loved being an Appleby as she felt it made her important. She didn't want to change her name to Peters when she married NPP which, considering how much she disliked Dad, made no sense, but of course it was the prestige, darling. It was the Toorak Applebys, with or without Dad living there. Mother had come from money as well, as I'd mentioned. Her family, the Greedy Gosfords, were boringly wealthy, old money sweetie; old money.

I opted for neither answer to Bible Barbie's question about why NPP was talking to me. I wasn't in a smart-arse mood and I didn't want her attention either.

'Mr Peters told me about the Christmas party, that's all.' I sighed as I stood up and walked away.

*** 

One good thing about Mr No Personality Peters' Lame Law Firm's employees though, was they were basically a bunch of alcoholics. After-work drinks were a nightly event. As suspected, these boring buffoons became the people I spent the most amount of time with over the coming months, which included seeing them socially.

Weekdays my life became this:

1. Work 9 to 5 Monday to Friday.
2. After work, go home to spend time with Chocky, including plenty of cuddles, a big walk and giving her dinner.
3. Head back out for after-work drinks at the RSL near the Lame Law Firm.
4. Stumble home and pass out.
5. Rinse and repeat.

I always enjoyed having to sign in at the RSL. My latest name was Tess Tosterone. (Previously I had been Kat A. Tonic and Dee Pression.)

There would always be someone from work getting plastered and making a fool out of themselves at the RSL; it was great. I would join in the revelry, hoping Cute Guy would be there but he never was. I figured Emily Mears had him under lock and key, although I still didn't know for sure if they were an actual couple.

After copious amounts of drinks, I would stumble home, fall into bed with my Chocky electric blanket, wake up hung over the next day and do it all again.

The weekends were spent in my room with my faithful pooch. Watching movies, crying and drinking alone. Troy and I would Skype every Saturday night. I missed him like crazy, as he did me. My reactive depression was in overdrive. There were many weekends I would fantasise about the least painful way I could kill myself.

So, this was my life.

All I did was file and drink and file and drink and file and drink – I became the sort of person I detested. As suspected, Marlene had bought me office clothes in my most loathed colour, beige, and I wore them. I even started to take my lunch to work in Tupperware and I hadn't worn my nose ring for so long the hole was closing up. My hair wasn't dyed blue/black anymore either. It had reverted to Boring Brown. I lost myself in corporate hell and was sinking deeper and deeper into the murky depths of enjoying gossiping about Ms Wrong around the water cooler.

Then one day, this happened...

# CHAPTER SEVENTEEN

It was the night of the Lame Law Firm's Christmas party. I had been working there for six months already and Christmas seemed to come early that year. I was so depressed I wore my – wait for it – salmon pink puffy dress. Why? Why not, I was still lost. I'd become a passionless princess, a corporate chimp, a soulless sage. I was Georgina Appleby. I was nobody.

I also had the misfortune of sharing Mother and NPP's limo. Although it was summer, this particular Melbourne evening was unusually cold and wet, which didn't help my mood. Don't get me wrong, I way prefer winter to summer but there was something not quite right about this night. There was an Armageddon-type feeling in the air. I feared my recurring dreams of Christianity's version of the end of the world were finally becoming non-fiction.

I was miserable. I sat slumped in the limo's cold leather seat with my dress puffing around my ears. Mother and NPP were dressed in their best elitist posh beach-themed garb. I looked like a bloated peach. Well, it does rhyme with beach.

'I must admit, Georgina, lately you have been looking so pretty, like the daughter I had always wanted, and that dress looks so beautiful on you. I remember you wore it at our wedding, didn't she, Hubert?' Mother gushed.

Mr No Personality Peters wasn't listening. He was staring at his iPad, looking like he had the weight of his Lame Law Firm on his shoulders.

'Stop the car!' I yelled suddenly.

The limo came to a screeching halt in the middle of the road. Luckily, there wasn't a car behind us.

'What is it, what's happened?' Mother yelled in anger, her Louis Vuitton dress awash with champagne.

'I think a dog just ran across the road!' I said in shock. Sure enough, I saw the tiniest Jack Russell standing in the middle of the road, soaking wet and shaking in fear, through my foggy window. A lightning bolt zapped through me and without a second thought I jumped out of the limo, ignoring Mother's objections, and was headed towards the terrified little creature. Cars swerved and honked around a bloated peach and a pooch, barely missing us both.

Finally, I scooped him up and found I had made it to the safety of the footpath across the road. The little guy looked up at me with big brown eyes and nibbled my nose gently in thanks. As I caught my breath, I realised I was surrounded by a family with a young boy of about seven who was hysterically crying, 'Muppet, Muppet!' and holding up his arms for me to put the dog into them. I did. Muppet promptly kissed the little boy with such gusto his tears soon turned to laughter.

'Oh my god, thank you, thank you so much,' said the boy's mother as she hugged me. This hug I didn't mind that much.

'Yes, thank you,' the dad continued. 'Muppet saw a cat across the road and pulled so hard Billy dropped the lead. I don't know what would have happened if you hadn't done what you did! Can I give you a reward?'

'No,' I said sternly. 'I just did what had to be done.'

I felt like a superhero, like my soul had re-entered my body, like I was re-energised. I had saved this little dog's life and it felt amazing. How had I forgotten that this was what I had wanted to do with my life? How could I just work as a filing clerk and do a job that was so unimportant, when what I wanted to do was so important? How had I got so lost? I had an epiphany, an awakening; this little dog was the sign from the universe that I needed.

By now I noticed the limo driver had parked next to the commotion. Before anyone had time to get out of the car, I bid farewell to Muppet and his family and jumped back in.

'You may continue on to the Hyatt now,' I said in my best posh voice.

The driver did as I asked. I glanced at Mother and NPP, who were sitting opposite. Mother was scowling at me whilst wiping her expensive dress with a tissue. She would have preferred that little dog die than have her dress ruined. NPP was still staring at his iPad. I doubt he'd even noticed that anything had happened.

I wished Troy was here. He would have squeezed my hand and said, *'Good on you, Grasshopper.'*

\*\*\*

As we entered the Hyatt ballroom, I was in awe of the grandness. This would have cost NPP's Lame Law Firm a mint. The drinks were free. *Every* drink was free. Not just beer and wine like at weddings, but everything, including bourbon; sweet bourbon. I soon ditched my limo buddies and headed towards you-know-where. I intended to get totally shit-faced and bourbon by the glass just wasn't going to do.

'You obviously have a bottle back there; hand it over,' I said to the shocked waiter. I guess he was surprised a bloated peach could be such an aggressive alcoholic, but I was on a mission and no one was going to stop me from completing it. He slowly handed me a bottle of Jim Beam. I grabbed it from him and went to hide in a dark corner. I drank about a quarter of it straight from the bottle. I was immune to bourbon these days; it took a lot for me to start to feel it but when I did, it was heavenly. If only Satan's Prison Camp had taught me about this type of heaven.

Eventually, I stumbled to my dinner table, bottle in hand. Needless to say, I was seated with Mother and NPP, along with Ms Wrong and her Humourless Husband. I couldn't believe how much a skinny chick like Ms Wrong could eat. She must have stored food in her feet. I did think she had unusually large feet. The table also had a handful of other bland people I worked with and their partners. I was glad none of them talked to me as I was so drunk, I couldn't make out their faces.

Finally, the food arrived. They kept putting meat in front of me. I told them I didn't eat meat but then they would take it away and put another plate of meat in front of me. This just kept happening and happening until I lost the plot.

'I'm a fucking vegetarian!' I yelled. I think I might have actually stood up and clenched my fists as well.

Uh-oh.

As expected, all eyes were on me. Other tables' eyes as well, including the Thorny Threesome, who were seated nearby. They had already been eyeing me off due to the fact I was sitting at the boss' table. By now some old fool would have told them he was my Pretend Father.

My hissy fit worked though, as my next meal did not contain dead animal. I ate just enough to stop me from passing out but not enough to vomit. I was so proud of myself.

'So, Georgie,' Ms Wrong began, 'do you enjoy filing?'

'Hmmm, let me think, on a scale of one to ten, I would have to say zero,' I said seriously.

Ms Wrong was awash with champagne by now and found this hilarious, but her Humourless Husband did not. He just sat there giving me endless evils as he lifted his glass to his mouth in a robotic fashion and sculled the remainder of his champagne. I figured his sexual fantasies probably involved filing; that was no doubt the reason I had offended him. I needed to un-attach myself from his serial killer glare, so I glanced over at Mother and NPP, finding her angrily whispering into his ear while he rolled his eyes; trouble in paradise?

NPP stood, wiping his mouth carefully with his napkin. 'Please excuse me, I need to attend to something,' he muttered before scurrying off.

I glanced back at Mother. She was drinking champagne straight out of the bottle.

Good God.

After dinner, I took a walk to clear my head. I kept scouring the room for Cute Guy, finally seeing him with, you guessed it, Emily Mears.

Sigh.

CG smiled as he glided past with the girl that should have been me. He always had his hair gelled down now. I had to resist a very strong urge to mess it up. He never wore glasses anymore either. My sweet geek was gone; sad face. Luckily, Emily didn't notice me, as I really wasn't in the mood for a school reunion.

Then predictably, the night got worse when I stumbled upon my number one nemesis.

Sister Catherine was standing next to the chocolate fountain wearing a Hawaiian lei around her neck and chatting to my other most-loved person, NPP.

My conspiracy theory all made sense now. Sister C and NPP were working together to make my life a misery.

I needed to know what they were saying, stat.

I casually made my way over to them, eventually positioning myself on the opposite side of the chocolate fountain. The stupid thing was so high they couldn't see me. Now that I was finally in listening range, this is what I heard:

'Oh, yes, Hubert,' my nun-nemesis gushed. 'I do enjoy giving the girls piano lessons! It is so beautiful to hear the Lord's music and I love my students so much, in fact, I shower them with love! They make me so very happy!'

Angry.

Angrier.

Angriest.

Furious.

I felt myself morph into one of those cartoon characters that have steam coming out of their ears.

My face was hot, then burning.

I could feel and hear the steam.

I began to lunge into the chocolate fountain but stopped when I was tapped on the shoulder. Yeah, that again.

It was Mother.

'Georgie, I have been looking for you. Your dessert is on the table. Are you coming?' Mother hiccupped.

'Yes… but first I have to pee.'

As I stumbled off to find the restroom, I walked straight into the path of Sister Virgilius and her stark, black habit, carrying a beach ball. Damn, all the penguins were out tonight.

'Madelaine! It's so nice to see you. Have you made up with Catherine?' she croaked joyously.

'No… I'm… Georgie Appleby,' I said in confusion.

Sister V leaned closer to look at me, squinting her eyes.

'Oh, so you are! So sorry child, I have had a lot of Christ's blood, but I did always think you were the spitting image of Sister Catherine's younger sister.'

'Sister Catherine has a younger sister?' I asked in surprise.

'Yes, oh yes. It is a shame about what happened between them,' Sister V mumbled.

'What happened?' I asked, incredulous to be getting Sister C gossip from her sidekick who, lucky for me, was full of Christ's blood.

'All that jealously Catherine had. Madelaine was so beautiful, she had all the suitors, she married a diplomat. Nobody wanted to marry Catherine because she was so plain, and those wretched glasses didn't help. So, her parents made her enter the nunnery. Catherine told me she hadn't spoken to her sister for many years... oh, I'm sorry. Christ's blood has made me giddy. I must sit down. Nice to see you, dear.'

As the old penguin waddled off, I wondered if what she had said was part senility or part Christ's blood, but maybe it was the truth. I mean, she would know!

It seems I had inadvertently found out the reason why Sister Catherine hated me.

Wow.

Just wow.

I continued on to find the restroom, which was miles away. I had to go through all these corridors and hallways until naturally I got lost. My sense of direction was never that great and being quite drunk didn't help matters. After asking yet another waiter for directions I got to a hallway with three doors. Without bothering to look at the sign, I opened the first door I came to. As soon as I did, what I saw could never be unseen.

# CHAPTER EIGHTEEN

Mr No Personality Peters was kissing Sharon, his secretary. I would recognise that leopard print dress anywhere; yes, she was wearing it again. So, this was what he'd had to attend to.

They both glanced at me in shock. NPP quickly started to wipe the lipstick off his mouth with a handkerchief while Sharon rushed past me and ran out of the tiny room.

'Georgina, this isn't what it looks like,' NPP pleaded, his clammy little hand outstretched towards me.

'Oh, so it wasn't you kissing your secretary? What was it then? Were you playing chess? God, you're such a cliché!'

He kept walking towards me, waving his stupid arms around. I had never seen him look so worried.

'We were just talking, dear, that's all.'

'Don't come any closer,' I snarled as the *Georgie Death Stare* throttled him at warp speed.

He froze and stiffened like a martini glass that had just been filled with ice.

I had an idea. It was the best idea I ever did have.

'I presume you don't want me to tell my mother about this.'

'Oh, Georgina, it would be so wonderful if you didn't tell Alicia.'

'Okay, I won't tell her – on one condition.'

'That's fine, dear. Anything. What is it?'

'You retrench me from this stupid filing job pronto and you explain to Mother that there was no more work for me, that's why I was let go, not because I did anything wrong and you also tell Mother that I'll be getting a job working with animals. And while I'm at it, I want my inheritance now!'

NPP just stood there gawking at me. His bald spot was so shiny now I could almost see my reflection in it. I could tell he was trying to think of how to worm his way out of my blackmail, but he didn't have a hope in hell.

'Very well,' he whispered.

'What was that?'

'Very well, Georgina, I shall do everything you ask, except for your inheritance as I cannot change the age you receive it. This has been set up by your mother. You still need to wait two years.'

'All right. As long as I don't lose it.'

The old fool made a quick exit after that, no doubt after his Leopard Print Mistress.

After I'd found the actual women's loo instead of the supply closet, I rang Troy to tell him my amazing news.

'Hello, Bingey, how's the party going?'

'Troy! I caught NPP kissing his secretary!'

'You're kidding.'

'For reals! He didn't want me to tell Mother so I blackmailed him into retrenching me from the law firm and guess what?'

'What?'

'I won't lose my inheritance!'

'That is sensational. Well done!'

'I know! Hey, did you know Sister C had a younger sister?'

'No.'

'I bumped into Sister V and she thought I was Sister C's younger sister.'

'What?!'

'Sister V said I'm the spitting image of Madelaine, Sister C's beautiful sister she was jealous of. She married a diplomat but no one wanted to marry Sister C so she was forced into the nunnery by her parents.'

'Jesus… so that's why she hates you.'

'Yep, I mean, Sister V was high on Christ's blood but yeah, it all makes sense now.'

'Wow.'

'She's here, too, of course. Sister C, I mean. She was on the Christmas party committee; she made it beach-themed. I just can't get away from her!'

'She sure seems to be everywhere you are.'

'Should I be worried? When are you coming home?! It's been six months already!'

'I know, I know. Mum and I are nearly done. It won't be long, I promise. At least now you won't have to work that shit job anymore and you can finally get a job working with animals.'

'I know, but I still don't know how to do that!'

'Ask Siri.'

I burst out laughing.

God, I loved him.

Troy and I wrapped up our chat, which included me telling him Marlene and I had become friends in his absence, which I don't think he quite believed.

I started heading back to my table when I came face to face with Sister Catherine. I thought of what Sister V had told me and imagined my nun-nemesis looking straight into the eyes of her sister.

Trippy.

'Appleby,' she muttered, looking me up and down. 'Get out of my way.'

She pushed past me and stomped off, her colourful Hawaiian lei swinging from side to side, at odds with her deathly black habit.

'Happy Christmas!' I yelled after her. 'You old goat,' I finished with a whisper.

I finally reached my table, finding NPP sitting there alone, head in his hands. The slimy bastard. Having the upper hand was such a great feeling. I was so happy I didn't have to work at his Lame Law Firm anymore. I guess that also meant not seeing Cute Guy but honestly, what was the point in having a crush on someone who wasn't available or interested? It's a lose-lose situation.

I looked around for Mother and saw her dancing with the rest of our table, having a great time. She had no clue about his affair with Leopard Print Sharon. I felt a little sorry for her then, seeing as they were only recently married and all. Did she pick a dud or what?

I couldn't stand being at that farce anymore. There wasn't one person at that party that I could even tolerate. I always seemed to be around people I didn't like and who didn't like me, and I was starting to get sick of it. The only new friend I had made recently was Marlene, and as if she would have been invited to this shit show, being a maid and all.

I finally had enough. I jumped in a taxi and went back to Purgatory Palace to be with my Chocky.

\*\*\*

A few days before Christmas I was woken by the most horrible noise ever in existence – opera. I hated opera. It made me nervous. I didn't know why, it just did. The bombastic loud shrieking and languages I didn't understand: you guessed it, what nightmares were made of. A Tupperware party playing opera would result in me becoming a lifer at a mental institution. I rushed downstairs to find Mother singing along, champagne glass in hand. It was nauseating. I ran over to the record player and lifted the arm off violently, making sure the needle scratched the witch's wax.

'Leave it alone, Georgina! I have to listen to your heavy metal every day!' Mother shrieked.

'Nirvana isn't heavy metal.' I sighed.

'Of course it isn't. Nirvana is a state of enlightenment.'

Mother's vacant stare told me to quit while I was behind.

'Where's Hubert?' I asked, eager to change the subject. 'I haven't seen him for days.'

Of course, I was happy about that, but just curious what the slime bucket was up to.

'Your new father is working all week so Christmas is cancelled. Your present is under the tree,' she spat before throwing her pink feather boa around her turkey neck and gliding out of the room. Later, she would be staggering.

New father. Ugh. I bet he wasn't at work. I bet he was spending Christmas in the arms of Leopard Print Sharon. Shudder. Mother was totally clueless and had no idea whatsoever. Was she going to get the surprise of a lifetime!

I was glad Christmas was cancelled, though. I hated Mother's Christmas celebrations. I didn't even bother looking at my present. I knew it was a Victoria's Secret gift card so I could buy something for my cleavage. That's what she gave me every year and every year

I would throw it in the goodwill bin so a homeless person could stay warm in lingerie.

But seriously, I hoped the less fortunate would exchange it with someone for food or something, I dunno. I sure as hell didn't want it.

# CHAPTER NINETEEN

The following month of waiting for Troy to come home was uneventful. I desperately looked for jobs with animals, but with no experience in things like animal husbandry (I had no idea you needed to be a husband of an animal to work with them) I began to drown in a sea of bourbon. At least I always had Marlene to top up my glass.

Mother, in her wisdom, had organised a party for my nineteenth birthday which I dreaded more and more with every passing day. She had taken it upon herself to invite every single person that annoyed the hell out of me. I'm sure Leticia and Prudence were top of the list.

I started drinking early that day. Marlene wished me happy birthday as she handed me my bourbon and Coke in my special Snoopy glass. Marlene wore her usual non-judgmental expression; sweet, sweet Marlene. My new friend.

Luckily, I got to spend the daylight hours of my birthday doing exactly what I wanted; lying on the couch in my PJs having a Netflix *Buffy* marathon as Marlene, Cook, Mother and NPP fussed around me, preparing for my birthday festivities. Whenever my bourbon and

Coke ran out, Marlene was at the ready with a refill. Needless to say, when it was time for me to get ready for my guests, I was giving *Mother* a run for her money.

People started arriving early. I woke to Mother yelling at me as I was fast asleep on the couch and still in my PJs. It took both Mother and NPP to yank me off the couch and drag me upstairs to get ready but NPP did most of the work. Mother was useless. All she did was sway uncontrollably, so much so she kept hitting the wall. Upon reaching my bed I promptly passed out.

'Bingey!'

The voice was familiar and warm, just like Linus' blanket. I opened my eyes and found myself staring at Troy. I threw my arms around his neck, knocking him off my bed, and came crashing onto the floor with him, Chocky included. We lay there giggling until I noticed a pair of poo-coloured loafers, which could very well have been made from gophers, in front of me. I looked up to the horrific sight of Mr No Personality Peters attempting a smile. I felt like I was going to vomit.

'Georgina, are you well enough now to get ready and come down to greet your guests?'

Troy and I stood up shakily.

'Well, I'm not as drunk as I was before so I guess I can manage it.' I smiled sarcastically, brushing off my pyjamas. NPP nodded uncomfortably before slipping away.

My attention returned to Troy.

'What are you doing here? You didn't tell me you were coming! I'm so glad you're here!' I yelled in excitement.

'Of course, how can I not be with my Bingey for her birthday?' He smiled. 'Now, you have many guests awaiting you downstairs, my dear. Do you think it appropriate to greet them in such attire?' he said, inspecting my Peanuts PJs with alarm.

'Are Leticia and Prudence here?' I asked, ignoring his question.

'Yes, I believe I saw them.'

'What about an old biddy wearing a tiara?'

Troy eyed me strangely. 'Since when did you become a nanaphile?'

Nanaphile was a word we invented for people who had the hots for nanas. There were more of them out there than you think.

'Mrs Tiara!' I laughed, grabbing his sleeve. 'You know Mrs Tiara, she's at practically every single function I go to. Why wouldn't she be here to celebrate the birthday of someone she can't stand?'

'I believe I did spy a lady with a tiara downstairs,' Troy said quietly.

I threw myself onto my bed in horror.

'That's it. I'm not going down there. Why the hell are the three people I hate the most here, anyway? I'm gonna *kill* Mother. I really mean it this time!'

'But there is someone else downstairs you might like to see,' Troy began coyly.

'Who, the woman who punched me in the face at the mailroom?'

'No, I believe it is your *real* father.'

'Are you serious?' I jumped off the bed, shocked Dad had made such an effort.

'Yes.'

I pushed Troy out of my bedroom, telling him to wait right there as I had a quick shower and frantically got ready.

As I hurried downstairs in my best attire – barefoot with worn-out Levi's and a black hoodie – I was surprised at the number of people gawking up at me. I immediately grabbed Troy's arm and started gliding down the stairs, waving like the queen. The fools below me actually started to applaud. I felt like it was Oscars night and I'd just won 'Most Condescending Performance'.

Mother was swaying as she waited for me to reach her. She looked me up and down with distaste. 'Couldn't you wear something a little more fitting for your birthday celebration?' she muttered through clenched teeth.

Ignoring her, I shimmied over to Marlene, who was holding a tray with my Snoopy glass on it, no doubt full of sweet, sweet bourbon and Coke. She held the tray up to me, smiling. I grabbed the glass and begun to pour the brown liquid into my mouth. When I finished, I put the glass back onto Marlene's tray, wiped my mouth on my sleeve and burped. Marlene hurried off but Mrs Tiara was at the ready. 'Oh really, I *never*!' she announced, tip-toeing off in disgust.

'I'm not interested in your opinion. I don't remember inviting you, you old biddy!' I yelled after her as Troy whispered 'nanaphile' into my ear. We started giggling just as Leticia and Prudence approached us. My smile instantly evaporated.

Leticia was wearing a necklace with a large gold crucifix, complete with a tiny Jesus. It was quite disturbing but at least she had left her white habit at home. Prudence was decked out in pink and, as usual, had her hair in a ponytail with pieces hanging from the sides so she could conveniently put them in her mouth.

'Hello, Georgina,' Leticia said, all snakelike.

I said nothing, looking from her to Prudence and back again, waiting for a drink to be poured over my head, but nothing happened.

'Many happy returns.' Prudence smiled as they both slid off.

I looked up at Troy in shock. He shrugged.

'Georgie!' a male voice yelled in excitement. I knew it was Dad. I turned sharply, seeing him beaming before me.

'Dad!'

Dad and I bear-hugged before letting each other go.

'Happy birthday, kiddo!' He handed me a small parcel wrapped in shiny gold paper. I opened it hastily. It revealed a cheque made out to my name for one thousand dollars.

'I know you run out of money for petrol from time to time. This might help,' he said with a smile, taking off his glasses to clean them. I threw my arms around him. When I let him go, I noticed Josh for the first time.

'Happy birthday, Georgie,' he said in his male flight attendant voice. I hugged him too, even though, as I said earlier, hugging people outside the secret circle was never my strong point; but I liked Josh and his coconut smell.

'Your birthday party was perfect timing as we were in Melbourne for a convention anyway,' Dad announced.

My heart sank. Ugh. How convenient for him. But what did I expect? I always got my hopes up and I always got disappointed when it came to Dad. I should have been used to it by now.

NPP scuttled past us, waving his clammy little hand.

'Do you believe Mother calls that creep my new father?'

'Does she? Oh... don't worry about it,' Dad said. 'Just ignore it. You know what she's like.'

After the singing of *Happy Birthday* and the cutting of a doily-infested, three-tiered wedding-like cake from hell, my party became extremely tedious. Besides my 'best buds' Leticia and Prudence, the only other people I knew were Andy and Barbie, who I was avoiding, Uncle-Rock-Star-Has-Been Jack, who I was also avoiding, Auntie Elm and Granddad, Nana and Gran. The rest of the guests consisted of Mother and NPP's Pathetic Posh Posers decked out in their diamonds and furs that *weren't* fake. I was extremely tempted to pour red paint on them. Alas, we had no red paint.

Leticia and Prudence were on their best behaviour all night. It was scary. I figured they were going to get me back when I least expected it. I spent most of the night huddled next to my posse, ignoring the occasional glares of Mrs Tiara, whose tiara seemed to sparkle more than usual that evening. I imagined the old biddy keeping her maid up all night, demanding she polish the stupid thing until it glistened like the queen's.

Mother and Mr No Personality Peters hadn't given me my present yet. I dreaded thinking about what it was. But unfortunately, the time had come.

'May I have your attention, please!' a woman slurred.

Yes, it was Mother.

She was tinkling a silver spoon against her diamond-encrusted champagne glass. When everyone gave her their attention, she cleared her throat.

I began to feel seriously ill.

'Thank you for attending my daughter Georgina's birthday celebration this evening,' she spluttered. NPP was beside her, at the ready in case she collapsed.

'Georgina.' She waved me over.

I gave my posse a final terrified look before I made my way over to her.

'Would you like to say anything to your guests?' Mother asked. Her eyes were the colour of a Bloody Mary minus the celery.

I cleared my throat and glanced over at Troy, who began to smirk in anticipation of my speech.

'Well, what can I say?' I began slowly, my face being drilled by the eyes of a hundred pompous fools.

But Mother was getting a little too wise these days.

'Thank you, Georgina!' she said, cutting me off.

The bitch!

'We just cannot wait to give you your gift. Actually, your friends Leticia and Prudence were the ones who gave us the idea, so here it is!'

Leticia and Prudence!

I couldn't breathe.

Mother gestured towards the front door.

Everyone looked over in anticipation.

My heart was racing faster than an extreme sportsman on speed.

Marlene opened the door slowly.

I collapsed in horror.

# CHAPTER TWENTY

The nuns walked into Purgatory Palace single file. They just kept coming. There must have been thirty of them. The last one to walk in was Sister Catherine. I shuddered. They positioned themselves choir-like with Sister Catherine in front of them holding her whacking stick. Then they began to sing.

Their Sacred Screeching went on for well over an hour. By this time, I was in my bedroom huddled next to Troy with a drink in each hand, swaying back and forth like a mental patient.

'I can't believe it... I just can't believe it.'

My meltdown was interrupted by a knock on the door, which made Chocky bark.

'Who is it?!' Troy yelled impatiently.

'Troy, it's Georgie's dad!'

'Let him in, let him in.'

Troy unlocked the door. Dad walked slowly into the room. There was no Josh in sight. He was probably in the kitchen preparing tea and biscuits.

Dad sat down on my bed, taking off his glasses to clean them. 'I've just come to tell you the nuns have stopped singing.'

A sudden feeling of relief came over me.

'This fear of nuns, Georgie, it seems to be getting worse. Maybe you should talk to someone about it,' Dad began, putting his glasses on again. 'I know you had problems with Sister Catherine at school, but that was years ago now.'

'She is evil.' I sniffed, trying to hold back the tears.

'Isn't a nun being evil an oxymoron?' Dad said light-heartedly.

'She *is* evil! She wanted to change my piano exam to a fail when I'd passed! If I hadn't seen the exam myself, she would have gotten away with it, too. Oh, and she used to bash the hell out of me during piano lessons as well.'

Dad and Troy's expressions turned to shock.

'Why in God's name did you never tell anyone this, Georgie? We could have done something!' Dad cried.

'I never said anything 'cause she said she'd hit me so hard I'd end up in hospital.'

By this time, the water from my eyes was flowing as rapidly as the melting polar ice caps in Antarctica. Dad was pacing around my room while I hugged Chocky and sobbed into Troy's long, dark hair.

'She was also the reason Ben died!' I continued, stopping Dad in his tracks.

\*\*\*

*'Where do you girls think you're going?' Sister Catherine sneered.*

*As Tits and I turned around to face the Loch Ness monster's ugly cousin, it was difficult to hide our smiles.*

*'Home,' I said finally.*

*'No, you are not! You two have detention due to your constant giggling at the back of the classroom, so I suggest you sit down and start studying!'*

*'But I have to pick up my brother from school!' I protested.*

*'Did you not hear me, girl?!' Sister Catherine's face once again started to contort into her alias, the evil vulture-like cartoon character we all knew and hated so well.*

*'Well, can I at least text him and let him know?' I asked.*

*'No, and while we're at it, you can give me your phones.'*

*Tits and I sighed, handing over our mobiles and sitting back down at our desks in despair.*

*Our usual English teacher was ill, so our nun-nemesis had stepped in for the day – and had had it in for us the entire lesson.*

*'You will be kept back for two hours,' she announced, sitting down at her desk, smoothing her skirt with her hideous hands. 'I suggest you begin your English homework as you are both failing this subject, so I am actually doing you a favour.'*

*Tits and I looked at each other in horror, shaking our heads.*

*It was while I was in detention that Ben was run over.*

*By the time I got to the hospital, he was dead.*

*He died in the ambulance.*

*I wasn't allowed to see him.*

*I never saw him again.*

***

'Georgie,' Dad said softly, kneeling beside me. 'It was the hit and run driver's fault Ben died, not Sister Catherine's.'

'No, you're wrong, it *was* Sister Catherine's fault! If she hadn't given me detention, I would have picked up Ben on time and he'd still be alive. She didn't even let me text him!'

Dad left things there. I'm sure he could see he wasn't going to be able to change my mind any time soon.

'All right, calm down. Are you going to be okay?' he asked. His expression was as soft as kitten fur.

'Yeah, yeah,' I muttered.

'Are you sure?' Dad asked, standing.

'Yes.'

'Okay then, just stay here with Troy for a while. I'll be downstairs. I better see what the hell Josh is up to anyway, and I might just have a word with Sister Catherine as well.'

'No, don't, Dad!' I pleaded. 'Don't. Just leave her to me. Please leave her to me.'

Dad nodded, closing the door behind him.

I moved away from Troy, grabbing a tissue to wipe my eyes. 'Before you ask if I'm okay, I'm okay, okay?'

'Okay.' Troy got up and left the room. I found this strange and wondered what he was up to. He soon returned carrying a large box wrapped in black shiny paper. My mood suddenly lightened.

'Happy birthday, Bingey.'

I ripped the wrapping paper and opened the box. I could not believe my eyes.

# CHAPTER TWENTY-ONE

Inside the box was an extremely cool black bikie jacket. I was speechless. I slipped it on. It was a perfect fit and instantly transformed me into a rock star. Finally, I had something to wear while playing air guitar in front of the mirror.

'Please don't tell me this fell off the back of a truck.'

'The back of a van, actually.'

I eyed Troy suspiciously until he folded.

'Well, dear, you know my uncle from Perth I've been working for? Remember I told you on the phone he opened a motorcycle store? I got that thing really cheap!'

'Oh, thank dog.' I sighed. 'I was worried the cops were on their way; although if they were, maybe we could blame the theft of the jacket on Sister Catherine!'

'Indeed! Could you imagine her sitting on a motorbike wearing it?' Troy giggled.

I fell onto the bed in laughter. 'Yeah, it'd really suit her glasses!'

After we stopped laughing, Troy suddenly looked serious and I knew what was coming.

'Speaking of Sister Catherine,' he began. 'All that stuff you said, Georgie, it's pretty full on.'

'I know.'

'I mean, I get that you blame her for Ben's death but the fact she was bashing you and the reason you didn't tell anyone, I mean Jesus!'

'Mary and Joseph, I know.'

'She is the Devil,' he said.

'Yep, and here's a question for you. If she's not the Devil, then who actually is the Devil?'

We pondered this for quite some time with no conclusion. Troy then told me he and his mum had finished helping his uncle in Perth and they were back for good, which made me all sorts of happy. I then promptly filled him in on my adventures since he'd been away.

'So, you still don't have an animal job since you left the law firm?' he asked.

'Nope. Apparently, I have to become their husband or something.'

Troy's bushy eyebrows shot up and he gave me a strange look.

'Well, for a start, you're the wrong sex.'

'I know.'

We burst out laughing.

'By the way, Tony's Pizza is open again. I got my shifts back straight away. You could go back there for a while, if you're desperate.'

'No, I've made my mind up. I'm gonna work with animals and that's that.'

'Good for you!'

After an hour or so of catch-up, we finally ventured back downstairs. By now the alcohol was flowing freely amongst Mother and NPP's pretentious posers; Marlene could barely keep up with their demands.

Andy and Barbie were drunkenly waltzing, Uncle-Rock-Star-Has-Been Jack (who had been bragging about taking LSD before the party) was being whisked away by Auntie Elm. My grandparents were either dead or asleep on the couch. Mrs Tiara stood scowling at everyone, Leticia and Prudence had vanished and, thankfully, the nuns seemed to have dispersed as well; all except Sister Catherine of course. Troy and I spotted her talking to Dad and Josh and moseyed on over at just the right time.

'Homosexuality is a sin and you shall go straight to Hell!' she roared, her eyes bulging with ferocity from behind her ridiculously huge glasses.

Dad and Josh were speechless.

I wasn't.

'No, they won't go to Hell as being gay isn't a sin. Bashing kids and lying to the examination board about someone failing their exams when they passed is a sin, which means *you* will go straight to Hell!'

Silence surrounded us as Sister Catherine's magnified eyes narrowed into large slits. I automatically flinched as I seriously thought she was going to hit me but we were in public; that was the only reason her boxing gloves remained off.

She glared at me a minute longer before turning around and walking out of the house silently, whacking stick in hand.

Dad and Josh stared at me open-mouthed.

'I told you to leave her to me.' I smiled before leading Troy away by his tie.

Andy and Barbie stepped in front of us. I sighed. I could only avoid them for so long. Barbie had bleached her hair even blonder for the occasion. It looked like white straw. She was wearing a strapless little number which revealed more cleavage than I ever imagined possible; Mother's dream come true.

'What was up with Sister Catherine?' Andy asked.

'Nothing,' I deadpanned.

'Okay, well, here's your present, li'l sis. We think you'll like it. Debbie picked it out.'

Andy handed me a girly-looking gift bag. I felt ill at the thought of Barbie choosing my present. I opened the bag and slowly lifted out a pink bra. Troy covered his mouth so they wouldn't see him laughing. I gave him a small kick.

'It's padded!' Barbie began excitedly as she chewed gum with her mouth open. 'I thought you could do with one. Your mother told me you needed more cleavage.'

I said nothing, just stood there holding the stupid padded bra whilst staring into Barbie's heavily made-up face.

'My cleavage thanks you,' I eventually forced out.

We walked away from them backwards. When we were safe, I handed the bra to Troy who promptly put it on over his jacket.

Mrs Tiara shook her head in disgust.

'Nice bra, Troy, really suits you.' Dad smiled as he walked past with Josh.

Then suddenly Troy and I heard shouting coming from the kitchen and headed towards the racket. It sounded like Mother and Mr No Personality Peters. I opened the kitchen door. They immediately stopped yelling when they saw me and instead gave me a fake smile. Had NPP told Mother about Sharon? That'd mean I wouldn't be able to blackmail him anymore! God no!

'What's going on?' I asked.

NPP ignored me, leaving the kitchen.

'It was nice not talking to you!' I called after him.

Mother wobbled towards me.

'Did you like your present, Georgina?'

I gave her the *Georgie Death Stare* in high volume definition.

'No.'

'Why not?'

'Well, hmmm, let me think, maybe because it was nuns singing!'
I yelled.

Mother stepped back in surprise. 'And what is wrong with nuns
singing? Your friends Leticia and Prudence told me how it was your
*dream* to have them sing at your birthday!'

I was too emotionally distressed and exhausted to say another word
to her. I left the kitchen with Troy and went back upstairs. We locked
ourselves in my room and drank shots until we passed out.

*** 

After saying goodbye to Dad over the phone early the next morning
– as he and Josh had to fly back to Sydney, no surprises there – all I
was left with was a hangover and a head full of memories of my worst
birthday party ever.

'Do you want me to make you breakfast, Georgie? It's Cook's day
off,' Marlene squeaked as Troy and I sat at the kitchen table nursing
our heads. Saturday was Cook's day of freedom. Sunday would be
Marlene's. I bet she was counting the seconds.

'No. I need the hair of the dog,' I whimpered.

Marlene left the room then re-entered holding Chocky in her arms.
Troy and I burst out laughing. Our heads hurt like hell but what choice
did we have? Marlene started to look distressed as she put Chocky
on the floor. I must admit I did feel a little sorry for her. She had
absolutely no clue.

'Don't worry about breakfast, Marlene,' I said quietly. 'I really
don't think we could keep it down.'

'All right then.' She smiled, leaving the room.

'So, you weren't lying about becoming friends with Marlene,' Troy
said in surprise.

'Why would I lie about that? I haven't even had a chance to tell you about the shit life she had before working here.'

Marlene was back. I wondered whether she'd heard what I said as she placed dirty glasses onto the kitchen bench.

'Hi, Marlene,' Troy said with a little wave.

Marlene glanced at him in absolute horror before running out of the room.

Troy and I exchanged WTF looks before he spoke.

'I guess she's only friends with you.' He shrugged.

# CHAPTER TWENTY-TWO

As I walked into Satan's Prison Camp with Troy, I wondered why the hell I was going to my non-graduation. Sister Catherine probably only invited drop-outs so they would feel bad about themselves, knowing it was inevitable they would end up being unemployed and lined up in endless Centrelink queues.

I thought of Leticia and Prudence and remembered it was my turn to get them back. I hadn't seen them since that horrific screeching-nuns-from-hell birthday present they gave me and I knew they would be here tonight. I had no idea what I was going to do to them, but I guess time would tell.

Before we got to the school hall I stopped and faced Troy nervously.

'Are you okay?' he asked. He looked so fine in his just-dry-cleaned shiny black funeral suit and red Converse sneakers. I remembered when he used to wait for me after school, on the frequent days that I had detention. All the girls would be checking him out. I was so sure he would be picked up tonight, like every night.

'I'm okay, I think,' I said meekly. Troy grabbed the collar of the bikie jacket he had given me for my birthday and looked sternly into my eyes.

'Don't let any of them get to you, Georgie. You know you are better than all of them.'

'I know,' I said, starting to get my mojo back. 'But what I really wanna know is which one of us is Romy and which one of us is Michelle, 'cause I'd really like to be the one that invented post-its.'

Troy threw his head back in laughter. *Romy and Michelle's High School Reunion* was our favourite movie of all time and we were looking forward to imitating their dance tonight. It's all we had talked about for weeks. Although this wasn't my school reunion, it was close enough.

Troy and I walked into the hall and started to scan the room. The decorations were pretty cheesy, but what else would you expect at a girls' school graduation except soft pastels and girly pink? I often wondered why black was never used in decorations. Surely Troy and I weren't the only two vampires in town.

We were pretty late so there were already a lot of people standing around talking, but the lights were so dim it was hard to make anybody out from a distance. At least we were all over eighteen now, so there was booze. My thoughts turned to Titania, presuming she wouldn't be able to drink as she was pregnant. Then I realised it had been months since I'd seen her, which meant she had probably popped. I really hoped she wasn't bringing Sleazy Toothless John with her tonight.

Troy and I wandered over to the bar and ordered some drinks. When we turned around Leticia and Prudence were at the ready.

'Well, hello Georgina.' Leticia smirked. Her hair was so blown out she looked like she'd been stuck in a wind tunnel. 'I love that jacket. Five dollars in the op shop bargain bin, was it?'

I went in for the kill but Troy held me back, whispering, 'Not yet, she'll keep,' in my ear. I did as he said and took a step back, my heart pounding through my expensive jacket. Leticia then turned her attention to Troy.

'My, don't you look handsome tonight,' she purred as Prudence looked on sheepishly. 'Tell me, sweetie, are you still single?'

That was enough for me. I dragged Troy away by his tie to a corner where we were able to hide and assess the situation.

'I swear tonight will end up in so many tears, a new ocean will be formed.'

'I love the way you speak, honey bunny.' Troy laughed.

Apparently, I was always funny when I wasn't trying to be. I found this extremely annoying.

'We have to come up with a plan 'cause I really need to fix those bitches tonight.'

'Relax, Georgie, it will happen when it's meant to happen,' Troy said in his guru voice.

I took a deep breath and tried to steady myself, but that didn't last long, as I noticed Sister Catherine limping by with Sister Virgilius in tow. Sister C glared at me, resonating pure evil. I hadn't seen her since I told her off about her homophobic comments towards my dad and Josh. I was sure she had put me on her hit list. I was positive she had a .45mm under her habit with the safety off, ready for a kill at a moment's notice. All she needed was her own TV show, *The Assassin with a Nasty Habit,* and Sister V could be her bumbling sidekick.

'What's so funny?' Troy asked.

I must have been smiling but didn't realise it.

'I'll tell you later. Let's get drunk.'

We walked back to the bar, but were stopped an inch away by none other than Mel and Shelley The Sheep Girl. I couldn't believe Mel was still hanging out with that Sheep Head. I don't know what she saw in her besides a potential woollen jumper.

Mel hadn't changed. She still had long scraggly red hair and was standing there eating a Mars Bar through her braces. Her pantry used to be full of Mars Bars. She even stashed them under her bed for late-night munchies. She was always the easiest person to buy a birthday present for. A Mars Bar was sufficient. A box of the things and you were her friend for life. Mel's sister Hayley was my one and only girl crush that no one knew about. She was stunning, funny and smart, a perfect combination. I was pretty obsessed with her. I used to love going to Mel's house just so I could see Hayley. She had such a sarcastic sense of humour, much like mine. We were both Aquarians after all and I always felt we had a special symmetry. I used to get jealous when her boyfriends were there, as she didn't give me any attention. Hayley was two years older than Mel and me and had also attended Satan's Prison Camp. I remembered seeing her at school before she graduated. All the lesbian boarders were in love with her. You would see them carrying her books, Hayley lapping up the attention, even though she was straight. She was such a flirt. There was something about Hayley. I'm not surprised I had a crush on her; I think everyone did. I often wondered whether Mel was jealous of her older sister, but she never let on.

'Hey, Georgie!' Mel came in for a hug and I let her, although as I said earlier, hugging was never my strong point.

'Hey, Mel. Been a while,' I said, attempting a smile after she let me go.

'Hi, Troy Boy,' Mel said as they exchanged a quick hug.

'Hello, how *are* you this grand evening?' Shelley gushed pretentiously, holding out her hand to me and Troy. I swear she wanted me to bow and kiss it. I shook her hand limply. It felt clammier than Mr No Personality Peters' hand, if that was even possible. Troy shook her hand properly and bowed, always the cavalier idiot.

'I will be making a speech in a few hours, no doubt you heard I was Dux of the school for our year. I'm sure you will all enjoy it, so please pass it around. And now I must dash.'

Shelley rushed off with her signature walk, leaning forward with her butt sticking out so far it could be used as a coffee table. I followed her, imitating her walk for a few seconds, evoking giggles from Troy and even Mel. When I finished, I glanced at Mel incredulously.

'Oh, Georgie,' she pleaded. 'Shelley actually has some really good qualities.'

'The only good quality I can think of is a lack of a wool shortage in the future,' I quipped.

Mel burst out laughing, although I could tell she felt bad about it.

'I'm off to the bar. Back soon with drinks for you lovely ladies,' Troy announced.

'Thanks, Troy.' I smiled.

'Hayley dropped me off,' Mel continued. 'She says hi.'

'How is she? I haven't seen her for ages.' A sudden excitement zapped through me.

'She's good. She's gay now,' Mel said with raised eyebrows.

'What?!'

'Yep, got a girlfriend and all.'

'Cool.'

But it wasn't cool. I felt jealous! My god, what was happening? I thought I was over her.

'She volunteers at an animal rescue, too, in between Uni. Thought you'd like that. You two always drove me nuts with your animal addictions!'

Hayley volunteered at an animal rescue! My dog! That was it! That's what I wanted to do! Finally! Now I didn't have to ask Siri...

although volunteers didn't get paid. How could I work at an animal rescue and get paid?

'You should come around for dinner and catch up with the family. They always ask about you.'

'Yeah, for sure, I'd love to.'

If I saw Hayley again, I'd be screwed. I think the not seeing her at all for years thing dulled my feelings, but did I really want to put myself through that again? And then there was Cute Guy, who I dug so much; but what was going on with Emily Mears? Sigh.

I was snapped out of my thoughts by a flash of spectacularly un-coordinated clothing as one of our teachers, Mrs Faulkenstein, rushed past. 'Hello girls, all good, yes, yes, very good, all well, must dash.'

Mrs Faulkenstein, better known as Mrs Frankenstein, was a dowdy woman in her mid-fifties who wore the daggiest dresses in history. She also had one mighty temper on her. I recognised Mrs Frankenstein's dress as she scuttled away. There was a green stain on her bottom.

The flashbacks could definitely not be contained.

***

*Before class, Tits and I carefully put a dollop of green slime onto Mrs Frankenstein's chair. The class cheered us on. Everyone hated her. She was mean and her neck always moved like a pigeon's when she said the word 'An-tarc-tica'.*

*Sure enough, Mrs F pulled her chair out and sat straight into the slime. The entire class was in hysterics. She was totally oblivious.*

*As class went on, Mrs Frankenstein's temper came to the fore as she got sick of girls talking while she was trying to. Her punishment was making us stand on our desks. This particular lesson, half the class were standing on their desks, all holding their skirts close to their thighs in embarrassment as the girls sitting next to them could see everything. If you were sitting next to a lesbian boarder you held your skirt extra tight.*

*Teachers always threw me out of class, usually for talking or laughing or deliberately making myself fall off my stool in Science every single lesson. Being thrown out of class was a daily occurrence and I had stood on desks in Mrs Frankenstein's classes many a time, but today I had crossed an imaginary line that was unknown to me.*

*'Appleby, get in the corner!' the old goat screamed as the girls giggled. She pushed me towards the piano but there was no way I could stand there, as the corner was full of sports bags and tennis racquets.*

*'I can't get in there,' I muttered.*

*'Yes, you can!' she spat, grabbing one of the racquets and using it like an oar to push everything out of the corner. The class were dumbfounded. Mrs Frankenstein had never lost it like that before. I always did wonder whether she had failed the nunnery. Eventually, the old goat succeeded in squashing me between the piano and the wall.*

*'All right, settle girls,' she said as she sat back down into the green slime, attempting to calm herself after her mental breakdown. 'We have time for one more oral presentation before the end of class. Shelley, are you ready?'*

*Mrs Frankenstein taught Australian History and our oral presentations were on an Australian industry of our choice and how it had evolved. I did mine on Vegemite. So did half the class.*

*'Yes, I am ready Mrs Faulkenstein,' Shelley said confidently. I couldn't see due to my prison corner, but I heard her walk to the front of the room and clear her throat. The girls started to chuckle.*

*'Good morning, class,' she began in her posh accent.*

*'Today I would like to talk to you about the Australian wool industry.'*

*All hell broke loose. There was no way on Earth Mrs Frankenstein could contain the girls, so she ended class early. She instructed me to stay in the corner for an extra half hour though. As the girls started to leave, some of them looked at me sadly, asking if I was okay.*

\*\*\*

'God, Mrs Frankenstein gives me the shits,' Mel sneered, bringing me to.

'She's wearing the green slime dress,' I deadpanned before bursting out laughing.

'Oh my god!'

Mel and I shot a look at each other.

'Friends forever, aren't we clever, don't worry about the old bag, she's just a hag. We shall pass, and she can stick it up her arse!' we sang, before cracking up.

After sharing a giggle, Mel got serious.

'So, have you been insulted by Leticia and Prudence yet?'

'Yes, I have had the pleasure.' I sighed.

'So have I.' Mel continued. 'Leticia said people with red hair should be drowned at birth.'

I growled.

'Georgie! Mel!'

We turned to see Titania approaching. As predicted, she had obviously had the baby. She looked way better than she did the last time I saw her, which was at that truck stop between Sydney and Melbourne. Her long dark hair was shimmering and she was wearing an attractive gown with a plunging neckline. The type of gown girls who aren't tomboys wear; the type of gown I would never wear. It was bloated peach or funeral dresses for me and I accepted nothing less. She looked more like the Titania I used to know. Luckily, Sleazy Toothless John was nowhere in sight. Tits came in for a hug as well. If I'd known this was hug night, I'd have worn protective clothing.

'Hey gals! Guess what? I had a son!' she cried. 'John Junior. John Senior is at home looking after him.'

Thank dog.

'Great,' I forced out.

'Congratulations!' Mel beamed.

'Was that Mrs F I saw walk past before?' Tits asked.

'Yes,' I piped up. 'And she's wearing the green slime dress.'

We laughed hysterically for a few seconds and then a few more seconds when Tits' laughter turned silent, as it always did.

'Do you know what Leticia just said to me?' Tits asked after our giggles had subsided.

'I can only imagine.'

'She said people like me should be sterilised so they can't breed!'

'That's it, she's really gonna get it tonight,' I said as I scoured the room for her.

'What are you gonna do?' Mel asked excitedly.

'Yeah, and can we help? Tits added.

Before I could answer, Troy arrived with drinks – just as none other than Emily Mears and, you guessed it, Cute Guy, approached us.

Nooooooooooooooooooooooo!!!

'Hi everyone,' Emily said shyly.

Cute Guy seemed surprised to see me and smiled. His hair was gelled down again, just like Bart Simpson's church hair. No doubt Emily's influence. I preferred his hair the other way. His glasses were AWOL too.

'This is my partner, Justin.'

Partner?! Damn! It finally was confirmed!

Or did she mean business partner? No, I don't think she meant business partner.

'Justin, this is everyone.'

'Hi everyone,' Cute Guy said with an awkward wave.

Everyone said hello.

I said nothing.

'Look out, Bird Girl is swooping this way!' Tits yelled suddenly.

That was all I needed.

Bird Girl approached us, smiling like we were all best friends. Her beak seemed to have grown; no doubt due to the lies she'd been telling.

'Hello all,' she beamed.

None of us said anything.

For some strange reason, she turned her attention to me.

'How have you been, Georgie? You're looking well. What have you been up to since school finished?'

'Oh, just the usual, shop-lifting, burglary, street fights, etcetera,' I said before leading Troy away by his tie.

Bird Girl seemed to think we were best friends. This made me extremely uncomfortable and I just had to get the hell away from her.

Troy and I ended up back at our safe place, the bar.

'What the hell am I doing here, Troy? Sometimes I think I only do things to make myself miserable.'

'Poor Bingey,' he said in a baby voice, complete with bottom lip protruding.

I sighed and scanned the room, catching the eye of The Coolest Girl in School, Mary-Louise. She was still slim, blonde and sun-kissed. She nodded her acknowledgment of me before slipping away. There was a flashback there but I'll leave it for another time.

After the graduates got their pieces of paper which prevented them from ever standing in Centrelink queues, my alumni got more and more lubricated until predictably, there was dancing, waking Troy and me from our bored stupor. It wasn't long until Shelley The Sheep Girl was pumping and grinding, with her butt sticking out so far I was tempted to put my drink on it.

We couldn't believe it when Cyndi Lauper's *Time After Time* came on. After copious drinks, Troy and I were ready to do our dance from *Romy and Michelle*. We took a deep breath, held hands and headed onto the dance floor. Just as I was about to start a ballet move, the music stopped and a loud croaky voice followed.

'And now it's time for a request from Sister Catherine, *The Lord's Prayer*!'

Kill.

Me.

Now.

It was the rocked-up version of *The Lord's Prayer*, done by an actual nun, Sister Janet Mead, in the 1970s. I unfortunately knew the song, due to it being played by Sister Catherine before every Sacred Screeching class. I used to envision Sister C dancing to it every evening in her nightgown, singing into a hairbrush whilst winking in the mirror through her bottle top glasses.

Shudder.

My nun-nemesis was beaming as she rushed onto the dance floor and started to boogie with her homey Sister Virgilius in tow. Sister C's dancing could best be described as a female version of *Mr Bean* while Sister V just stood there, frozen, occasionally thrusting her arm high up in the air in a way that had Troy and me mesmerised.

'What the actual fuck?' I asked.

Troy nodded seriously before we started imitating them.

I was suddenly grabbed from behind. It was Titania. Mel was beside her, looking nervous.

'The Portables!' Tits yelled, running off. 'We're going to The Portables!'

The Portables were two small portable classrooms tucked away near the playground. They were hardly ever used and usually kept open. Back in the day, we used to have séances in one of them every lunch time.

When Troy and I arrived, we noticed the door was slightly ajar and saw candlelight flickering. A shiver went through me as I remembered David.

***

*As soon as the school lunch bell rang, Tits and I rushed to The Portables. Mel would never rush as she was terrified but addicted, nevertheless. Girls were already sitting around the table with a homemade Ouija board, putting letters and numbers in a circle. As usual, we had onlookers who would only watch and whisper.*

*We had been doing séances every day with not a lot happening, apart from some girls pushing the glass for fun. We soon kicked them out and as our group got smaller, only the real believers remained.*

*Lately, we'd picked up a spirit called David, who visited now and again, mostly when Jane Queen of Pain was there. Jane's nickname came from having an incredible threshold to withstand pain, which was pretty lucky considering she was seven months pregnant. This was quite the scandal in a Catholic girls' school of course.*

*Jane was tough but attractive and that made her seem softer. She had shoulder-length strawberry blonde hair, baby blue eyes and a mole on her face where Marilyn Monroe's was. Most of us felt sorry for her, as predictably the nuns treated her like the Devil's Spawn. To them, it was fine to get pregnant before marriage via The Immaculate Conception but not by having actual intercourse. Strangely, Mr Valencia hadn't expelled her. We heard it was due to her parents having money and donating it to the Prison Camp. I wondered if Mother would have done the same had it been me, but I seriously doubted it. I would have been shipped away to Siberia for a messy abortion then left to freeze to death in the worst winter for fifty years.*

*As we sat down, Jane told the group she was only going to spectate today. When everyone was ready, the glass was turned upside down and we all put our fingers on it. Tits asked if anyone was there. Nothing for a while and then the glass slowly began to move and YES was spelt out. I asked if it was David.*

*YES.*

*'I've got a question for him,' Jane piped up from the corner. We all glanced at her in anticipation.*

*'I wanna ask him something none of you know the answer to.'*

*We all nodded.*

*'David, I just found out what number I am in the talent quest and I haven't told anyone. Can you tell me the number?'*

*The glass slowly navigated itself towards the numbers and joined a one and a five together before returning to the middle of the table.*

*'Well, is it fifteen?' Tits asked.*

*Jane's face turned deathly white. We all knew the answer.*

*But what followed stopped us from ever doing séances again.*

*David's spirit crush on Jane had been escalating and every time she was there, it was guaranteed he was, too. Jane would always sit in the corner and had stopped touching the glass altogether, for fear it would be like touching his spirit, and she didn't want to get that close. In a previous séance, David said he was going to visit Jane that night. The next day when we got together, we asked her if he did. She said she didn't know as she'd slept in her parents' bed that night; clever girl.*

*On this particular day, we asked David where he wanted to take Jane.*

*'Come.' The glass started to move quickly as it went from letter to letter.*

*'With.' We felt a strong force behind it.*

*'Me.' The glass was moving by itself!*

*'To.' It felt so light, our fingertips barely touched it.*

*'H...E...L...'*

*David didn't get the chance to spell out the second L as we all let go of the glass. It was mayhem. Girls who were onlookers started to cry, Mel was screaming, then Tits yelled, 'Let the spirit out, let the spirit out!' turning the glass right side up. Everyone knew a trapped spirit could do us a lot of harm. We all looked at Jane. She had turned whiter than a snow drift.*

*David probably got really bored after that because we never had another séance again.*

***

'Come on, Georgie!' Tits said, bringing me to. I was back at my non-graduation and back at The Portables.

As we all entered the dimly lit room, we saw Jane Queen of Pain sitting in her usual corner. We knew she'd had to give away her baby and had heard how depressed she was. Jane half-smiled at me. I smiled back awkwardly, not quite sure what to say, as I was never close friends with her.

'We're gonna see if David's around,' she whispered.

'Great,' I said, although to be honest I was scared to death. We'd only done séances during the day. Doing them at night was something else altogether.

I looked around the room. The candlelight created eerie shadows on the walls, making the girls around the table seem otherworldly, while the complete and utter blackness outside felt like the vortex to Hell David would soon be taking us into.

'Why don't you turn the light on?' Mel asked in a shaky voice. It was then I realised she was holding my arm.

'The Portables never had power. But you wouldn't have known that during the day,' Jane said matter-of-factly. She always knew everything.

Troy positioned himself next to Jane. She smiled sweetly at him. Tits, Mel and I sat down next to each other nervously and started chatting.

'Shhh,' Jane said in annoyance. 'We need total quiet or David won't come!'

'Since when is she such an expert?' I whispered to Tits.

She shrugged.

Everyone became silent as they stared ominously at the Ouija board. The glass was turned upside down; we put our fingertips on it and one of the girls asked if David was there. Nothing. She asked again. Still nothing. This continued for quite some time.

'Why isn't he here? Where is he?!' Jane yelled. It was all right for *her* to speak.

We sat with our fingertips on this stupid glass for ages, too scared to move or do anything in case Jane yelled at us. I felt like I was back in class and that Jane had morphed into Sister Catherine, complete with personalised Ouija whacking stick. Boxing gloves sold separately. I was getting so bored and what's worse, was starting to sober up, so I needed to get the hell out of there pronto.

Then something happened.

Jane pointed at the window, her face pale as vodka. We turned to look and saw a figure outside. It was white; pure white. It had no head, neck or body, just a white blob with no beginning or ending.

That's all we needed.

Everyone ran out of The Portables screaming until we heard Troy yelling something behind us.

As our screams subsided Troy's words became audible.

'Guys!' he yelled. 'It's Shelley! The ghost is Shelley!'

As we slowly headed back towards The Portables, we could see Troy holding a white sheet and beside him stood Shelley grinning sheepishly (pun intended).

'I am going to kill that rotten piece of mutton!' I fumed, pushing up my jacket sleeves as I headed towards Shelley, but I was stopped in my tracks by a sudden gust of cold wind that seemed to freeze me from within. It was coupled with an ethereal whistling that made every hair on my body stand up. All of us saw the white puff of smoke that darted around for a few seconds before disappearing as quickly as it appeared. We knew it was David. He had deliberately been saving his strength by not communicating with us so he could scare the shit out of us visually.

As I ran in terror, I remembered the rumours about an 1800s graveyard beneath The Portables. I never knew whether those rumours were true or not, but after witnessing what I just did, I think I became a believer.

After an hour of composing ourselves, we went back inside. Predictably, my night of non-nights became an utter bore. All these people I didn't give a toss about kept coming up to me and bragging about what they had been up to. The only thing that helped to get me through the night was my posse and copious amounts of alcohol.

But just when I thought things couldn't get any worse, the speeches began. The principal, Mr Valencia, started them off with some boring drivel I wasn't even listening to, then it was Shelley's turn to tell us what being Dux of the school meant to her.

'You know,' I whispered into Troy's ear. 'I was offered ducks of the school but I refused 'cause I told them I wanted geese instead, but they didn't have that.'

We started giggling, making the idiots around us glare.

Shelley's speech went on and on, so Troy and I snuck outside for a breather. We soon spotted Tits and Mel nearby. As we got closer, we saw they were patting a cat.

'I Dunno!' I said excitedly as I ran over to them and scooped the feline up into my arms. She rubbed her face onto mine and did the familiar purr that sounded like she was making popcorn.

'We had to get out of there.' Tits sighed. 'I don't think Shelley is ever going to shut up.'

'Poor Shelley,' Mel continued. 'Practically everyone has already walked out. I think she's only talking to a handful of teachers now. I feel so sorry for her.'

'Maybe they would have stayed to listen if she was wearing her white sheet!' I piped up. 'At least you wouldn't be able to see her face.'

Everyone laughed, even Mel, although as usual she looked guilty about it.

'And speaking of white sheets, were you in on it, Mel?' I asked, remembering the prank her and The Sheep Head had played on me at school.

'No!' she yelled, open-eyed. I could tell by the look on her face she wasn't lying.

'So, Sheep Head did it alone! I'll have to add her to the list of idiots I have to get back at now.' I sighed.

'But it gets worse!' Tits said suddenly. 'You'll never guess who's performing next.'

'Who?' Mel and I asked in unison.

'Leticia and Prudence.'

'What the hell are they doing?' I questioned.

'They're doing a piano recital together 'cause they were Sister Catherine's best students.'

'Oh, give me a break!' It was then I wondered if Sister C ever used to bash them too, but seriously doubted it.

'Maybe we should all just leave now and go to the pub,' Tits said.

'No.'

A light bulb had suddenly gone off in my head and in that instant, I knew how I was going to get Leticia and Prudence back.

# CHAPTER TWENTY-THREE

'Where's Helen?'

Helen was the school's drug dealer. She had everything from weed to pills, uppers, downers, inbetweeners, you name it. Helen never let on who her supplier was, but drugs were always rampant at Satan's Prison Camp. If only the Lord knew, he would be mighty cross on his cross.

'We should probably check the back toilets. That's where Helen always used to be,' Mel said.

I kissed I Dunno goodbye and we headed towards the toilets, leaving Troy to stand guard outside. Sure enough, when we walked inside, a thick layer of smoke hung in the air and there stood Helen, leaning on the sink having a cigarette.

You guessed it...

\*\*\*

*Helen wasn't very well liked. Most of the girls would cringe when they saw her having a 'chewy' in the toilets. Chewy was the code word for smoke, something the girls could say in front of the teachers without getting caught. As Helen and I exchanged glances I rolled my eyes, but was shocked when she did the same. That felt wrong. It was normal for me to not like her but it wasn't supposed to work the other way around. Why didn't she like me? I was almost in the cool girl gang; she was in the trailer park trash gang. I was uncomfortable and angry.*

*'Give us a drag,' I said, trying to sound tough.*

*'You don't smoke!' she teased.*

*'Yes, I do!'*

*Helen gave me her cigarette and watched me intently. There were a few girls around and I knew this was my moment to show them how cool I really was. I took a drag, immediately blowing the smoke out of my mouth. Helen wasn't impressed.*

*'You didn't draw back!' she yelled, embarrassing me no end. Luckily the girls had dispersed and I only had her to deal with. Ignoring her comment, I walked out hoping she wouldn't tell anyone. I had been stealing Mother's cigarettes for a while now and thought I knew how to smoke perfectly well. What the hell did draw back mean?! God, I really needed to work on my cool factor, pronto.*

***

'Well, hello girls, can I interest you in anything?'

Helen smiled deviously, revealing rotting yellow teeth. Her hair was greasy and she was covered in spots. I guess that's what being a drug addict will do to you.

I stepped forward. Tits and Mel were always scared of Helen but I wasn't and Helen knew it.

'Learnt how to smoke yet, Georgie?' she teased, holding out her cigarette to me. I grabbed it, took a puff, drew back then blew the smoke right into her face before throwing the ciggie to the floor and stepping on it with my Docs. She coughed, moving backwards.

'Do you have any ecstasy?'

Helen threw her head back in laughter.

'Well, do you or don't you?' I asked seriously, taking a step closer. I wasn't in the mood for her shit.

She stopped laughing when she noticed my expression.

'Yes, I do. How many pills would you like?'

'Two.'

We made the exchange, I paid her and as we left, I heard her call out, 'I'll be here all night if you need any more!'

'Loser,' I muttered under my breath as we rushed back to the hall. When we got there, I explained my plan of attack to my posse.

'But how are you gonna slip Leticia and Prudence the eccys?' Mel asked.

'I'll find a way.'

The four of us went backstage and soon found my nemeses limbering up in the corner.

'Tits, go get me two shots of vodka, stat!' I ordered. She did as I asked.

'They're not gonna accept vodka from you, Georgie!' Troy laughed.

'No, but they will accept it from you, *sweetie*.'

'Ah!'

Tits was back and holding two shot glasses of vodka. I crushed the pills with Troy's tie clip and slipped them in the glasses.

'Will the pills dissolve?' Mel asked nervously.

'Yes, Mel,' I said, handing the glasses to Troy. 'Work your charm, Sir.'

Troy took the shot glasses and walked towards Leticia and Prudence as we watched from a safe distance. His back was to us so we couldn't see him work his magic, but what we did see was the girls' faces light up when they saw him. It didn't take long for them to take the shot glasses, clink them together and scull the vodka.

Troy returned with a Cheshire Cat grin.

'Oh my god, they took the bait, they took the bait!' Mel cried in excitement. I told her to shut up and made everyone leave backstage before we asked Troy what happened. When we were safe, we huddled together like American footballers ready for a showdown.

'Well?' I asked eagerly.

'Well,' Troy began, clearing his throat, 'I said I got them the shots of vodka for good luck, not that they needed it, as they were the most talented pianists in the whole school.'

'You're such a suck!' I laughed.

'How long will it take to kick in?' Mel asked.

'Oh, half an hour maybe, about the time they come on,' I said with an evil grin. 'So now we wait.'

We found some chairs together in a good viewing position and waited in anticipation. Half an hour later, Sister Catherine took centre stage to introduce Leticia and Prudence. The old biddy was gushing about how wonderful they were and that she had never had such talented students in all her days, blah, blah, blah, pass me the sick bucket. When my nun-nemesis finally shut up, Leticia and Prudence entered stage left, bowing to rapturous applause from everyone except, you guessed it, us. Instead, we sat silently, grinning like Devils in Heaven.

The girls started their piano concerto and as much as I hate to admit it, they were actually quite good, playing a duet from some famous old composer, I don't know who. I suddenly had a flashback of Sister Catherine whacking me with her whacking stick for not knowing that.

Then about ten minutes in, something happened. Prudence started to sway; a little at first, then more and more. The E had obviously affected her first, as Leticia still seemed fine. Soon Prudence's swaying became almost uncontrollable and then she started playing wrong notes left, right and in between. Leticia shot her an evil look but Prudence was oblivious, she just kept swaying whilst hitting wrong notes and then stopped playing altogether and just burst out laughing. Leticia glared at her for a moment before suddenly laughing as well. Then they started to bash the piano like two kids who had never had a lesson whilst laughing like lunatics, the highlight being when Prudence started to bash the keys with her head.

By this stage the audience was in hysterics, apart from Mr Valencia, Sister Catherine and the teachers, who had watched the whole thing with horror from the side of the stage. It was Sister C who pulled the curtain to end the performance, which resulted in rapturous applause from the crowd with many yelling, 'Encore! Encore!'

'Well,' I said in a satisfied voice, 'that was well and truly the best piano recital I have ever heard.'

After we'd wandered back to the bar to toast our victory with a drink or ten, we heard an ambulance siren growing closer and closer, until it sounded like it was right out front.

Troy and I glanced at each other.

'Who called 911?' he asked.

Calling 911 was one of our running jokes due to all the American film and TV we watched.

Everyone went outside to see what all the fuss was about. We were shocked at what we saw. Prudence was lying lifeless on a stretcher as it was being lifted into the ambulance. Leticia was standing next to her crying whilst being comforted by Sister Catherine.

'Oh my dog,' I said in shock. 'I've killed her.'

# CHAPTER TWENTY-FOUR

We waited at the hospital for hours along with Prudence's family, friends and half the school until we got the all-clear that she was going to be okay. I'd heard of ecstasy killing kids before but I couldn't believe this whole thing had happened, a stupid joke almost ending in someone's life. Had Prudence died, I'd never have forgiven myself.

At that moment, I think I grew up a little more and vowed to end our constant torment of each other, which would mean I'd have to confess about the eccys; God help me if Prudence's parents ever found out.

Only family were allowed to see Pru, so everyone else went home except for me and Troy, who loyally stayed with me all night.

Finally, early the next morning, a nurse wandered past, having noticed us crumpled in two uncomfortable plastic chairs.

'Who were you waiting to see?'

'Prudence,' I said, suddenly waking. 'Prudence Miller.'

'Are you relatives?'

'No, but he's her boyfriend and I'm her best friend, that's why we've been here all night. *Please*, Nurse, you just have to let us see her, even just for a minute!' I pleaded.

It worked.

The nurse said she wasn't supposed to let us see Prudence, but seeing as we were so close to her, we could go in for five minutes. She led us to Prudence's room. I made Troy walk in first and I snuck in behind him. The nurse left us to it.

As I appeared from behind Troy, Prudence's expression turned from excitement to shock. I noticed Leticia was slumped in a chair next to the bed. She must have snuck in when no one was looking. Leticia looked like she had slept there all night. She woke when we came in.

'What the hell do you want, Appleby?' Leticia growled, standing. Troy quickly positioned himself between us.

'I'm here to see if Prudence is okay.'

'What do you care?!' she yelled. 'I didn't know you were her friend! Did you know someone spiked our drinks with ecstasy last night? Prudence nearly died!'

'It's okay, Leticia,' Prudence said softly, shutting Leticia up. 'I'm sure Georgie's here to apologise for spiking our drinks.'

My god, Prudence knew! When had she grown a brain?

'What?!' Leticia roared. 'Is this true? Did you do this to us?'

Troy was separating us like a referee at a boxing match. I thought of Sister Catherine's boxing gloves and wished I'd had them with me.

'Yes,' I admitted.

'You bitch!' Leticia tried to jump me but she didn't have a hope in hell with Troy between us.

'I'm sorry!' I gushed. 'I don't think I've ever regretted anything as much as I regret this! It was a stupid thing to do. I was just... so angry and I knew Helen would be around like always. I didn't think!'

I took a breath.

'And don't blame Troy,' I continued. 'I made him give you those shots.'

The girls remained quiet, Leticia backing off from wanting to bash my brains in.

'Can you forgive me?' I asked Prudence.

She glanced at Leticia for a moment before turning her attention back to me and nodding.

'Prudence!' Leticia yelled, unimpressed.

'Leticia,' Prudence said seriously. 'It's over. Georgie has apologised. This getting each other back all the time, it was bound to end in something like this one day. Luckily, I'm okay and maybe, just maybe, we can learn something from all this.'

Prudence took the words right out of my mouth. It was a real Meat Loaf moment. In that instant, after what she said, I realised I could maybe be friends with this girl, especially since she had suddenly seemed to grow a brain. A sudden calmness filled the room and, seeing as Troy felt his security wasn't needed anymore, he left us to it and went to hunt for coffee.

I sat down and started to chat to Prudence, feeling like we were really starting to warm up. Leticia was still wary though and chose to stand in the corner as she eyed us both cautiously. Soon enough, the conversation shifted to Sister Catherine.

'By the way, I never thanked you two for the nun choir birthday present and I still won't!'

'Sorry,' Prudence said quietly. 'In all honesty, it was your mother who organised the whole thing. She asked us what you wanted for your birthday and we said a nun choir for a joke and then she went and organised it.'

'It was pretty funny though!' Leticia said with a giggle, starting to warm up.

'Maybe for you!' I laughed. 'Sister C really loves you guys, though. Asking you to play that piano recital; I was just her punching bag. All she ever did was hit me.'

Leticia and Prudence exchanged serious glances. Eventually Prudence spoke. 'She hits us too.'

'Prudence!' Leticia roared.

'Leticia! Nothing will happen to us now! It happened to Georgie, too! We have to talk about it!'

Leticia quieted down, nodding her head.

'I can't believe it,' I said in shock. 'You too?'

'She hit everyone, Georgie, not just you,' Prudence said.

A memory I forgot I had come flooding back.

\*\*\*

*The Bridge to Hell was the small overpass you had to walk across to get to Sister Catherine's piano room. The bridge was so narrow it was hard for two people to pass each other without having to walk on the side or rub shoulders. Every time I had to walk across The Bridge to Hell, I wondered whether this was one of the rare days when I only got hit a little, as it did happen from time to time, but more often than not, Sister Catherine's boxing gloves were on.*

*On this particular day as I crossed the bridge, I noticed a girl walking opposite. When she saw me, she immediately became self-conscious and started to wipe her eyes with her hand. As we passed each other I noticed the tear stains down her cheeks and in that instant, I knew I wasn't the only one.*

\*\*\*

'She made us do that stupid recital,' Prudence continued. 'We had to go to school every day to practice and God help us if we hit a wrong note.'

'She was *still* hitting you? *Now?!*'

'Yes,' Leticia piped up from the corner, hanging her head sadly.

'I had no idea... did she threaten you if you didn't do the recital?' I asked, certain of the answer.

'Yes,' Prudence replied. 'She said she'd go to both our parents and tell them we cheated on our final piano exams, which would result in us failing.'

'We didn't cheat!' Leticia pleaded.

'I believe you,' I said compassionately. I would never have thought in a million years I would be talking to Leticia with compassion.

'So we had to go through with it,' Prudence continued. 'You don't know our parents, especially our mothers, there is so much pressure, failing anything is just not done in our families and we feared the consequences so much we just had to suck it up and go and get bashed one last time.'

Everyone was silent for a while, lost in their own thoughts until I finally spoke.

'The truth about her has to come out. We *have* to rally together, guys. Are you with me?'

Leticia and Prudence glanced at each other seriously then both nodded.

The door suddenly opened but it wasn't Troy or the nurse, it was Mrs Miller, Prudence's mother. Thank dog the ecstasy part of the conversation was over.

'Oh, you have another visitor, Prudence. And you are?' Mrs Miller asked as she looked me up and down in distaste. I could tell she didn't approve of my appearance but no plastic posh poser ever did.

'This is Georgie, Mummy. Georgie *Appleby*.'

That did the trick.

'Appleby?! Of the Toorak Appleby's?! Why didn't you say so! So nice to meet you, Georgina!' the pretentious fool gushed. I had heard Mother talking about her once, something about a diamond-tiled bathroom.

Vomit.

I started to feel sick and needed to get out of there, pronto.

'Do you believe some deranged person spiked the girls' drinks with ecstasy?!' Mrs M continued. 'My princess nearly died! If I ever find out who did this…!'

I shot a terrified look at Prudence but she reassured me with a calm smile.

'We'll never find out, Mummy. It could have been anyone.'

I glanced at Leticia, making sure she was on the same page, and saw her nodding in agreement. My heart started beating again, but I still had to get out of there before Mrs M started to gush over me again.

'I better go, I have to go home and count my money.'

Mrs Miller's eyes lit up while Leticia and Prudence grinned. The girls seemed to have clued in to me. This impressed me no end.

'I'll see you girls soon, okay?'

They both nodded and gave me a smile.

I walked out of the room just as Troy was returning with coffee. As we left the hospital, I filled him in on what had gone down with my former nemeses.

***

A few days later Prudence was out of hospital, so the Scooby Gang's new recruits convened at a café near the convent. Troy and I sat down at a table outside and waited for the girls to arrive. It felt so weird to suddenly be friends with them, but I needed to give it a chance. The more the hairier, when it came to bringing Sister Catherine down. Soon enough I saw them heading towards us. Leticia was walking ahead, decked out in her usual pearls and designer garb while Prudence followed behind. She was dressed from top to toe in fluorescent pink. I immediately had to put my sunglasses back on to prevent a migraine.

'Hi, hi!' Leticia said with a little wave as she sat down. Prudence sat beside her. The waitress came over and asked them what they wanted.

'Can I have a black decaf with a hint of turmeric and just a drop of soy milk on the side, make sure it's on the side please, otherwise I can't drink it!' Leticia gushed as Troy and I gave each other a look.

'That's fine, and for you?' the bored waitress asked Prudence.

'Do you have water?' she asked.

'Um… yes.'

'I'll have that; in a glass.'

I kicked Troy under the table as we shared a WTF look. I thought it strange that Prudence had become dumb again.

'So!' Leticia said in excitement clapping her hands together. 'What's the plan?'

'Yeah, what's the plan?' Prudence repeated, also clapping. This was going to be more painful than I had originally thought. I began to regret the whole thing.

Troy sensed my uneasiness and piped up for the first time since they'd got there.

'Well, ladies,' he said, all James-Bond-like as he rubbed the palms of his hands together. 'Here goes. We have to break into the convent, then break into the nuns' quarters, then break into Sister Catherine's room so we can find more dirt on her.'

'That seems like an awful lot of hard work.' Leticia sighed as she began to file her nails.

'Or,' I said, my mood suddenly lightening, 'we could just follow her now!'

The gang looked in the direction I was pointing, seeing Sister Catherine walking out of a shop, two doors away. She bent down to untie her mop dog before starting to walk away from us.

We quickly paid the bill and started to follow her. Luckily, there were a lot of people on the street, so even if she had turned around, she wouldn't have seen us. After limping down the street for what seemed like an eternity, she finally went into an op shop, leaving her dog tied up out the front.

'We could steal her dog! Wanna do that?!' Prudence yelled in excitement, making the people around her turn and look at us suspiciously.

'Shhh,' I said, grabbing her fluorescent pink arm. 'There's no way in hell we're doing that! I would never steal anyone's dog, even someone I hated. That'd be the worst feeling in the world. I can only imagine how hysterical I'd be if Chocky was stolen!'

'Yeah, Georgie's right, that's the worst idea you've ever had, Pru!' Leticia scolded. Prudence looked like she was going to cry.

'Come on!' Troy said as he slipped through the op shop's door. We all followed, soon spotting Sister C near the back of the store looking at a Hawaiian shirt. We hid behind a row of men's coats and watched her.

Prudence started to giggle. 'This is so exciting!'

'Shhh,' the rest of us said.

We spied on my nun-nemesis whilst she examined the shirt for a little longer before looking around to see if anyone was watching, then she quickly stuffed the shirt into her bag and hurriedly left the store. We all looked at each other in disbelief. Leticia put her hand over Prudence's mouth just in case. When we got outside, we were in shock.

'She's a shoplifter,' Leticia said in bewilderment. 'I can't believe it.'

'So not only does she bash students and fail them when they've passed, she shoplifts as well? What else does she do, I wonder?' I asked.

'The only way we'll ever know is if we break into the convent,' Troy Bond stated with a charming smile.

'Troy's right. We have to. You guys are in, yeah?' I asked my former nemeses.

'For sure, right Pru?'

Prudence looked at Leticia innocently for a moment before smiling and nodding.

# CHAPTER TWENTY-FIVE

While I waited for the perfect time for us to break into the convent, I kept researching animal rescues that would pay me, but I'd get overwhelmed and start drinking instead so I didn't really get anywhere, which left me frustrated. NPP hadn't told Mother about Leopard Print Sharon, so their farce of a marriage continued, as did my blackmail. Mother hadn't been hassling me about getting a job at all, so they were currently both off my back, which was a nice change but I knew it wouldn't last.

Finally, the day to break into the convent came as we knew Sister C and some of her nun-posse were away on the annual retreat.

Here we go again…

***

*Fifteen was the perfect age for us to spend a weekend with Jesus at the retreat. So we decided the best thing we could do to honour him was to get drunk for the first time. After an exhausting day of hearing all about the amazing things Jesus had done for us, word spread amongst the virgin drinkers that the party was in the room shared by me, Tits,*

*Mel and, even though we weren't really close friends with her, Emily Mears. We needed a fourth in our room as there were two bunk beds, so before Mel could discuss a certain piece of mutton, I grabbed Emily and made sure she was our fourth. I knew due to her shyness and withdrawal no one would want to share with her, and I was right. Mel seemed upset but Shelley ended up sharing with The Mathletics Club, her geeky study group, so the universe definitely aligned.*

*After dinner, while the teachers sat huddled around the campfire and the nuns had gone to bed far from our cabin, the party was getting started in our room. Most of us had alcohol in our bags that weekend, stolen from our parents' liquor cabinets or bought for us by older siblings/friends. Girls were piling onto my top bunk bed with bottles of Stoli, Jim Beam and Baileys that, thrown together, would create the hangover of the universe, but we were losing our drunk-virginity so anything went. Soon the other bunks were crowded too, as excited chatter reached fever pitch and alcohol flowed into plastic cups that were filled and guzzled down ceremoniously. The coolest girl in school, Mary-Louise, made herself the mixologist and even Emily Mears seemed off her face as she started handing everyone a square of toilet paper, even though she didn't appear to drink a drop. Placebo effect?*

*All of a sudden there was a thump on the door.*

*It wasn't the secret door knock.*

*Everyone froze.*

*Of course, I was elected to see who our unwanted guest was, but before I even had a chance to ask, our visitor had made themselves known.*

*'This is Sister Catherine! Open this door immediately!'*

*I glanced at the girls in horror as I slowly opened the door. To my surprise, instead of seeing Sister C and her ridiculous glasses, all I saw was an ugly Sheep Head.*

*'Ha ha! Hello, hello!' Shelley laughed as she pushed past me into the room. The girls looked horrified, except for Mel, who predictably jumped up to hug her. I gave Mel a look but she shook her head innocently.*

*Shelley, as usual, had ruined everything. How did she even find out about our party if it wasn't Mel that told her? I had deliberately made sure she was in the dark, along with her fellow Mathletics Club and assorted other geeks and dorks. I bet Sister Catherine was on her way to our room right now with year-long detentions for all of us.*

*Sigh.*

*'Ladies, I believe you are having a celebration for Jesus...' Shelley piped up in her usual pompous way. 'So, I have brought you something.'*

*She pulled out three bottles of wine from her backpack and placed them carefully on the table. They were covered in dust.*

*'This is my parents' wine; Penfolds Grange 1955, a very famous vintage I believe, and seeing as Jesus turned water into wine, He would approve!'*

*'My god, Shelley, won't your parents miss them?'*

*'Oh no, Mel, they won't. They have an entire cellar full of this type.'*

*I couldn't believe it. This was definitely the coolest thing Shelley had ever done and I must admit she slightly redeemed herself in my eyes. But I guess she was from the country and wasn't every kid from the country an alcoholic? It finally seemed we had something in common, anyway.*

*It was after Shelley and her wine's arrival that the party really kicked into gear. Her parents' wine was a totally LETHAL acquired taste. We got smashed. Later, the few of us left standing went to sit around the campfire with the teachers and fell off our stools sideways, landing on top of each other. We just lay there laughing hysterically as we couldn't get up. The teachers thought we were just being silly and the snoring nuns were none the wiser.*

*None of us got caught.*

*Best.*

*Retreat.*

*Ever.*

*This was the first time I had alcohol, well, REALLY had alcohol. Dad gave me a sip of his Jim Beam and Coke when I was ten, thinking I would scrunch my face up and run to spew in the toilet. Instead, he had to pry my hands open to get the glass back. I had never tasted anything so amazing in my entire decade of existence.*

***

I'd spoken to Tits and Mel recently and had told them of my newly formed friendship with Leticia and Prudence and our plan to take down Sister Catherine. They begged me to be involved. I caved in, although I did worry six people looked a little more conspicuous compared to four. I was fine for Tits to come (without John, of course; he could stay home and look after John Junior) but I was worried about Mel's vomit-inducing friendship with Shelley The Sheep Girl and feared Mel would let it slip. That shady Sheep Head was not to be trusted, especially after her recent white sheet incident. The retreat was a one-off. She had never been that cool again and there was no way in hell she was going to wreck this adventure.

We met at midnight in the park next to school and sat down on the wet grass. It was the same park that Tits and I had drunk our stolen VBs. Why midnight? Well obviously, it was because we watched way too many horror movies. Troy, Mel, Tits and I were there early, clad head-to-toe in black, including black beanies. I had warned the newbies of the Scooby Gang that they needed to wear black, not florescent pink, white pearls and Armani jackets, although I did worry about my former nemeses, especially Prudence and her stupidity. Or, as it seemed lately, selective stupidity.

'God, they're so late.' I sighed as I checked the time on my mobile. 12.35am.

'Oh well, we may as well have some fun before they get here,' Tits said, lighting up what looked like a joint.

'What are you doing?!' Mel roared. Mel was so straight and scared, sometimes it was annoying. I bet she'd tell The Sheep Head who would immediately find Father Luke and get him to perform an exorcism on Tits to remove the Pot Devil from her. I wasn't surprised Tits still partook, although I was a bit worried that she would get a little too stoned, and end up ruining everything.

'Okay, Tits, but not too much,' I said sternly.

'Yes ma'am,' Tits mocked. 'I haven't had any for ages, you know,' she added. 'Not since I've become a mum.'

Hmmm, if you say so.

I must admit that I found it a little unsettling that I was the unelected leader of the Scooby Gang; I was basically Buffy, which was cool and all, but I wasn't always comfortable with being a leader. Being a typical Aquarian, I was comfortable both as a leader and a follower, depending on the situation, though apparently I was a natural leader, my horoscope had told me recently.

'They're here!' Troy piped up.

Two black shadows headed towards us. My breathing relaxed as I saw they were both dressed in black, well, designer black, but still black. It was as they got closer that I found myself rolling my eyes in disbelief when I looked down at Prudence's feet, spying hot pink stilettos that were so tall I don't think any of the Kardashians would be able to walk an inch in them.

'Jesus, Prudence!' I yelled, pointing at her feet. Everyone bar Leticia looked down and laughed.

'What?' she asked innocently. 'You didn't say anything about footwear! I can't wear all black *ever!* If I don't have some pink on, I like, freak out!'

'How are you gonna climb over the gate in them? Hmmm?' I felt like I was about to lose it and began to regret palling up with this total moron and her spoilt side-kick.

'Don't worry about it, Georgie,' Leticia said in her usual blasé way. 'Hi everyone!'

I think judging by everyone's faces, they were sure our former nemeses should have stayed former.

And then it got worse.

'Oooh, a joint. Can I have some?' Prudence gushed, pouncing at Tits.

'Do you really think you should be having that?!' I roared into her deaf ears.

'No, leave her,' Leticia said calmly. 'It will do her good.'

I shook my head incredulously as I grabbed the joint out of Prudence's mouth, after she had already had a long drag, and stomped it out on the grass.

'That was A-grade stuff ya know!' Tits protested.

'I don't give a fuck! Has everyone forgotten why we're here? This isn't a stiletto pot party! I need people to focus! What we're doing could land us in jail, for Christ's sake!'

I think the girls finally got it as they stared with wide-eyed guilt.

Troy unravelled the convent's blueprints, which he had managed to somehow get off the internet, and spread them out on the grass. We shone our torches onto them.

'Okay, ladies. The gate at the back of the convent is smaller than the others. I think I should be the one who climbs over the top and tries to open it,' he said authoritatively.

'Lucky for you,' I said to Prudence, whose sudden stone-cold expression started to worry me.

We started heading toward the gate, with me leading.

Troy caught up to me.

'Are you okay?' he asked.

'I swear this whole thing has turned into *Dumb and Dumber*. We aren't even prepared! How are we gonna break into the convent? None of us are criminals or thieves, none of us can pick locks!'

'I can,' a small voice said behind me.

I turned around, seeing Prudence watching me sternly. She pulled out a black pencil case from her backpack and unzipped it. It was full of devices that looked like what cops and criminals on TV and movies use to break into houses.

'What the...?' I trailed off as I watched Prudence swing her backpack over her shoulder and take the lead.

'I told you the joint would do her good!' Leticia smirked, following her. The rest of us watched each other sceptically.

'Are you thinking what I'm thinking?' I asked Troy. He didn't have time to answer as Prudence yelled, 'Sometime today, ladies; that includes you too, Troy!' ahead of us.

As soon as we got to the back gate, Prudence had the lock opened in 3.5 seconds. I glanced at Leticia in bewilderment. She just smiled and shrugged like what Prudence was doing was as normal as Sunday mass.

'This way,' Troy whispered. We followed him through the grounds cautiously. There were a couple of old-fashioned lantern-looking lights here and there, but apart from that it was pretty dark. All we could make out was the path and surrounding bushes. Troy led us with his torch but none of the rest of us had ours on, to avoid being too conspicuous.

'What's that?' Mel asked suddenly, pointing to a small shadow nearby. Troy shone his torch in the shadow's direction.

'It's I Dunno!' I cried, running over to the feline as she did her usual flop on the ground while turning continuously as she asked for pats. The familiar popcorn purr began as Tits, Mel and I stroked her soft fur.

'For God's sake, it's just a cat, what's the big deal?' Leticia moaned, hands on hips.

'It's not just a cat, it's I Dunno!' I said in defence of my fur baby.

'Whatever, can we just go?' Leticia kept on. She was really annoying me. There was always time to pat I Dunno as far as I was concerned.

We finally got to the ominous Gothic building that housed the nuns and looked up at the majestic mansion in awe. Gargoyles moonlighting as security guards stared down at us. Mel grabbed my arm nervously.

'I want to go home,' she whispered.

'It's a bit too late for that now!' I said in annoyance as I pushed her hand off me.

Prudence stepped up to the imposing front door and began to work her magic as the rest of us stood behind her nervously.

'Be careful,' Leticia whispered. Prudence shot her a look as if to say, *don't question me, I was born picking locks!* Her behaviour was so strange after having smoked that joint, I was beginning to put two and two together and for once it didn't equal three.

The front door creaked open.

We were in.

'How do we know which room is Sister Catherine's?' Tits asked.

'It's the first on the left at the top of the stairs,' Mel answered. 'Shelley has been there once, she told me.'

'She'd better not be here today!' I warned as I shot a look at Mel.

Mel shook her head.

'What about her mop dog? It'll bite us!' Leticia whined.

'She takes it to the retreat.' I sighed.

'Come on,' Troy whispered.

We followed him up the grand staircase slowly. The stairs were fully carpeted and the bannisters were incredibly wide, perfect to slide down. For a minute I wanted to, but there was no way. Today I was a leader and being a leader usually meant being boring. My horoscope never told me that. As soon as we reached the top, the door directly in front of us began to creak open. Panic-stricken, we scattered and hid as best we could. An old nun dressed in an 1800s long white nightie hovered out of her room and went downstairs.

'Oh my god, was that a ghost?' Mel whispered in horror.

'It's a nun,' I whispered back in annoyance, pushing her hand off me yet again.

'Quick, before the ghost nun comes back,' Troy grinned as he tried to turn Sister Catherine's door knob, but predictably, it was locked. He shot a look at Prudence, who instantaneously worked her magic again and soon we were all inside. I locked the door as Troy shone his torch shakily towards Sister C's bed.

'Empty.' He sighed.

Whew!

I turned on the light and we gathered in a circle.

'Okay,' I began. 'There are six of us so it shouldn't take too long. Everyone needs to go through all her stuff and if you find anything strange, tell me. Oh, and if anything is locked, tell Prudence.'

We searched for over half an hour, cautious when we heard the old nun go back to her room, but remained safe. After Sister Catherine's quarters had been combed from top to bottom, including Prudence picking a few locks, our secret circle reconvened.

'Nothing!' Leticia cried. 'There's nothing here! What a waste of time.'

I sighed as I scanned the room, soon spotting something I hadn't noticed before.

'Hang on, look at those drawers,' I said.

'What about them?' Tits asked. 'Mel and I looked inside but there was nothing in them at all.'

'I'm not surprised nothing's in them; it's so they're lighter to move.'

I pointed to the track lines in the carpet from the drawers being moved back and forth many times.

Troy and I walked over to the chest of drawers, moving a couple of beach souvenirs that sat on top, before standing either side and pushing the drawers forward. A small *Alice in Wonderland*-size secret door was soon revealed with a padlock attached to it. After Prudence picked the lock, Troy cautiously opened the door.

'I bet there's skeletons in there!' Mel whimpered. She was holding my arm yet again. Troy shone his torch inside. It revealed a dark, narrow staircase that looked like it led to the attic.

'Look at those stairs!' Leticia yelped, hands covering her mouth. 'What the hell do you think she keeps up there?'

'Definitely skeletons!' Mel cried.

I knew what had to be done.

'You lot stay here and keep quiet. Troy, Prudence and I are gonna go investigate,' I commanded. I really only wanted Troy and I to go but we needed Prudence's new-found lock-picking skills, so I had no choice.

Troy got on all fours and crawled through the little door. Prudence and I followed him. When we got through the door, we immediately were able to stand up. Troy pointed his torch towards the steep, narrow staircase in front of us and shot me a look.

'Are you sure you wanna go up there, Georgie?' he asked, looking a little scared.

'We have to! Don't worry, she won't be there. She's at the retreat.'

'Yeah, I know, I'm just worried who *else* is gonna be there.'

Ignoring his Mel-like behaviour I shook my head and gave him a push to start climbing the stairs. I went next and Prudence was last. I had watched enough horror movies to know you are always safer when you're the veggie burger in the sandwich.

Each wooden stair creaked under our feet as we took a step up. Some of the stairs had rotted away and had gaping black holes leading to Lucifer's Lounge Room. The staircase was lengthy and took forever to get to the top. When we did, we were confronted with a wooden door of normal size. It was then Prudence started to become a little hesitant with the lock. I feared the drugs may have been leaving her system. Finally, she got the door unlocked.

Troy pushed it open slowly and shone his torch into the room. We jumped out of our skin as a hundred faces peered back at us.

# CHAPTER TWENTY-SIX

'Turn on the light! Turn on the light!' I screamed. We frantically fumbled our hands across the walls until one of us found the light switch and hit it.

'Oh my god, they're only dolls.' Prudence sighed in relief.

The damp, musty room was covered in shelves choc-a-bloc full of antique-looking porcelain dolls with the kind of eyes that open and close. There was a weird vibe in that room that made me feel extremely uneasy, as though one hundred faces were staring into my soul. I found myself holding Troy and Prudence's arms, then realised they were doing the same with me.

'Maybe she's a doll collector?' Prudence asked.

'So why aren't they displayed in her room? Why are they hidden up here in this creepy attic? There must be something going on with them,' I said.

'And how did she fit the shelves through that tiny door?' Troy asked in bewilderment.

Prudence and I had no answer.

'My god, look at this.' Troy stepped towards one of the dolls and picked it up. 'Who do you think this looks like?'

He turned around to show us. I couldn't believe what I saw.

I saw me.

Black hair, blue eyes, nose ring, green uniform but there was more to the doll's resemblance of me than just that. Its face actually looked like mine. I grabbed the doll from Troy and studied it closely; I was creeped out big time.

'It's not as cute as you are, though.' Troy grinned, attempting to lighten the mood.

'You're right,' I said, giving him a smile. 'For a start, it doesn't even have dimples.'

'Guys, do you think it's voodoo?' Prudence asked nervously.

'I can't see any pins,' Troy answered.

'This isn't good,' I muttered, starting to freak out again. 'She is totally gonna put some kind of curse on me!'

There was a sudden crash. We all jumped and saw one of the dolls had slipped off the shelf and broken into pieces.

'What the hell is that?' I asked, seeing something lying amongst the broken pieces. I bent down and picked up a bag full of something green.

'Jesus, is this weed?' I laughed, inspecting the bag.

'Oh my god it is! Sister C's a pot dealer!' Prudence yelled, snatching the bag from me.

I grabbed the bag back off her and opened it, taking a sniff before putting a little bit in my pocket, then I placed it back on the floor next to the broken doll.

'So that explains it.' Troy smiled.

'It doesn't explain this, though,' I said anxiously holding my voodoo doll up to him.

'Shake it, is there anything in there?' he asked.

I did. There was no sound. 'Maybe she's yet to put something in it,' I mumbled.

Troy was starting to look nervous. 'Come on you two, we better get outta here,' he said abruptly.

Prudence started to kick the broken pieces of the doll under one of the shelves until Troy stopped her.

'No, that'll look conspicuous! Leave the smashed pieces where they are. She'll think the doll just fell by itself; the shelf's pretty crowded.' He took mini-me carefully from my grasp. 'We better put you back too, I'm sure she'd miss *this* doll,' Troy said as he carefully placed me back onto my spot on the shelf.

'Hang on, I need proof of this,' I said as I quickly took a photo of myself in doll form with my phone.

We hurried back downstairs and when all the doors were closed, locks were locked and drawers and ornaments put back to their rightful place, I told the girls everything.

'I can't believe it. What are we gonna do now?' Tits asked.

'I guess we'll have to get the cops to catch her selling the pot dolls, that's if she's even the one that sells them. It won't be easy – she is a nun and vice-principal,' I said slowly.

I felt like I was in a dream. This was big, really big. My nun-nemesis would totally go down for this. Add to that, failing exams when girls had passed, and shoplifting as well. But was there more to her evil superhero persona or was that it? As I stared out her window, which faced the back of the convent grounds, I noticed a massive area of grass, dimly lit from the odd light.

'What's that?' I asked. The Scoobies looked out the window and shook their heads.

'Looks like some kind of paddock. I didn't even know it was there,' Mel said.

'I bet it has a barbed wire fence and a lock or ten,' I said, glancing over at Prudence who had started to hum the theme song from *Play School*. 'We have to come back another day.'

'Why can't we just look at it now?' Leticia protested.

'Because our locksmith is out to lunch and I don't think we have time for a lunch break,' I said as I took the small amount of marijuana out of my pocket to inspect.

'Awesome, Georgie, we can have another smoke in the park!' Tits said in excitement.

'This is for Prudence for next time, not for us!'

'Why does she get it all?'

Luckily, Leticia spoke before I had a chance to throttle Tits.

'Drugs make Prudence smart, really smart,' Leticia deadpanned as we all glanced at Pru who stayed silent, looking oblivious to the whole thing. 'Even after she came down off that E that luckily didn't kill her,' she said, shooting me a look, 'she was reciting Shakespeare to me. I almost puked it was so horrible! But it doesn't last long, it can wear off pretty quickly, depending on what drug it is. E's last the longest.'

After we had all digested what Leticia said, we left Sister Catherine's room, managing to escape the nun's building without incident. We made our way to the back gate, Troy leading us with his torch as he'd done before. We were almost there when we heard a loud voice that scared the hell out of us.

'Hey! Who's there? Stop!'

We turned and saw what looked like a security guard with a torch walking towards us. We bolted out of the gate and ran in all different directions. Luckily the security guard didn't run, so we all got away.

As Troy and I ran, I tripped over something on the footpath in the darkness and toppled over. Troy helped me up and we kept running until we felt safe then leaned against a wall to catch our breath.

'Are you okay? Did you hurt yourself?' he asked.

I looked at my hands and noticed a small cut in the middle of my left palm.

'Stigmata!' I yelled, stretching my arm out toward Jesus above.

'I always knew you were the chosen one.' Troy grinned.

As we stood there laughing in between catching our breath, I recalled the last time I ran from school.

***

*The public school next to Satan's Prison Camp was rough-as-guts. Stabbings weren't uncommon. Public schools weren't all like that though. Troy's school was fine. Most were but Brighton Bay High was terrifying.*

*Green Gorbies was our name as far as they were concerned. They would yell it out from across the street; they'd even spit at us sometimes. They considered us to be rich, snobby girls with trust funds. Well, okay, they had the trust fund bit right with me but I was barely even given enough money to buy lunch and I sure wasn't a snob, but there were poor girls at the Prison Camp too that had come from divorce with dads that didn't give a shit and mothers who worked two jobs, like Titania's, so we weren't all rich, but stereotypes remain.*

*One afternoon I decided to walk home from school instead of taking the tram, and soon regretted it. A bunch of girls from BB High caught up and jumped in front of me, blocking my path.*

*'Look, it's a Green Gorbie!' the ringleader spat. She looked like a typical Shazza (a bogan with badly dyed blonde hair) so that's what I'll call her. 'You think you're really special goin' to that stupid posh school, don't ya?'*

*'No, I don't, my mum forces me to go,' I protested. As tough as I was, I was worried. There were four of them and only one of me, not really a fair fight, so my usual trademark sarcasm was kept under wraps.*

*'Yeah, sure,' Shazza continued. She was right up in my face, holding the collar of my blazer. Her teeth were crooked and her breath stank of alcohol. 'You're just a rich posh shit.'*

*'Not her,' one of Shazza's scrags suddenly piped up. The girl looked scared to death. 'Let's get another one.'*

*Why this chick was sticking up for me, I had absolutely no idea. Maybe she could sense that underneath all the layers of bottle-green fabric I was basically a punk, a rebel, a person who couldn't stand tradition and my stupid school, but had no choice but to go. I was rich, which I hated, but I wasn't posh and unlike Leticia and Prudence, I didn't look like a typical Barbie. Green uniform or not, I couldn't hide my dyed blue/black dishevelled hair and nose ring that I would always put back in as soon as school was over. My friend that was a stranger couldn't manage to convince Shazza though, she was dead set on me.*

*'No, this one will do,' Shazza said with an ugly grin. Her hand that wasn't holding the collar of my blazer formed a fist. I didn't wait to see what was going to happen next.*

*I ran.*

*I broke away from her and ran as fast as my terrified legs would carry me, and then I heard laughter. The bitches were laughing! Was it all a joke? Were they just trying to scare me? I never knew. I'd always wanted to get them back but never saw Shazza and her scrags again. That was also the last time I ever walked home from school alone.*

\*\*\*

'Georgie,' Troy said, bringing me to. 'We better get outta here.'

We started walking quickly towards my car. 'I think we've lost everyone,' I puffed, still catching my breath.

'Don't worry, they can find their own way home. Lucky that security guy didn't run!' He laughed.

'I know! Sister C hired "We Don't Run" security to save money 'cause she's such a tight arse!'

We jumped inside my car, locking the doors and sitting in silence for a minute, remembering what we had just uncovered.

'My god,' Troy began. 'Those pot dolls... what are we gonna do, Georgie?'

I sat silently for a minute staring through the windscreen into the black abyss of the night. 'Well, Sir, the next thing we're gonna do is go back and check out that dodgy paddock.'

'Agreed, Miss,' Troy said with a nod.

I started the engine and drove us home.

*** 

A few days later I messaged the Scoobies and organised part two of 'Take down Sister Catherine' for the following night. Everyone was ecstatic that we were going back there so soon.

After I talked to Mel, she insisted I go around to her place for dinner that night as her parents had been asking about me. I must admit I had been thinking about Hayley since Mel had talked about her at graduation and now that Cute Guy was basically unavailable, the fact that Hayley was now with a girl kind of intrigued me.

I knocked on Mel's front door. A few seconds later it was flung open by none other than Hayley. My jaw dropped. Hayley was even more stunning than she used to be, if that was even possible. Her hair was still short but instead of being mousy brown she'd bleached it white blonde. As I said before, I loved blonde hair and suddenly, she'd become more adorable. There was something about blondes that killed me; probably because I was the exact opposite. The lighter hair really suited her. It seemed to bring out her blue eyes even more.

She was barefoot and wore ripped jeans and a bright red T-shirt that said 'South Melbourne Animal Rescue', which must have been the shelter she volunteered at. She was still skinny; clothes just hung off her. It was so good to see her again. Her face broke out into a wide smile when she recognised me. Fuck, she was gorgeous.

'Appleby,' she began seriously, looking me up and down. 'Have you been to a funeral again?'

I was all clad in black; black Converse, black jeans, black shirt, black rosary beads, (worn ironically), black hair, black eyeliner, black disposition. If only I still had my black eye.

Before I had a chance to respond, Mel appeared, grabbing me and pushing me inside. She led me to the dining room, where her dad and a girl I didn't know were already seated at the table.

'It's so nice to see you again, Georgie!' Mel's dad said happily as he got up and hugged me; yeah, that again. He was a big, burly man with a quick smile and larger than life laugh. I always thought he was a pretty cool dude.

'Georgie, this is Kylie, Hayley's girlfriend,' he said, gesturing toward the girl.

I didn't like her one bit. Not only for the obvious reason, but because of the way she treated me. She basically looked me up and down with a bored expression then looked away. She was an arsehole, but an attractive arsehole. I stood there taking in her long black hair, hipster black-framed glasses, dark smoky eyes, lip rings, nose stud, eyebrow ring and tattoo sleeve. I thought of my one piercing and little Aquarian symbol tattoo on my left shoulder and felt pathetic. I couldn't believe a nasty piece of work like her was with my Hayley, speak of the Devil.

'Cool, you guys met, yeah?' Hayley asked as she entered the room and threw herself onto the chair next to The Bitch from Hades.

Mel's dad suddenly stood. 'Come on, girls, let's go help Mum. Leave the guests to talk,' he said as he pushed Mel and Hayley out of the room.

Nooooooooooooooooooooooooooooooooooooooo!!!!!!!!!!!!!!!!!!!!

I sat down awkwardly, trying to look anywhere but at Kylie's face. She did the opposite. She just stared at me with a pissed off expression. Finally, I couldn't stand it any longer. I met her gaze.

'Who are you?' she asked.

'Err, I'm Georgie.'

'No, I mean who *are you*? How do you know these people?'

This girl must have been high. She was a complete and utter nutter.

'I went to school with Mel... and Hayley.'

'Are you into chicks?'

'Well, I like baby chickens but I wouldn't have a relationship with them.'

'Are you into WOMEN?!' she was yelling now.

'Not really.'

This conversation was getting weirder by the minute. I could barely breathe as I prayed for the others to come back in.

'What does "not really" mean? You either are or you aren't!'

'I prefer guys more,' I blurted out. I sounded like a moron. I hated how this girl was making me feel. I almost started to sink under the table with discomfort.

'Are you into Hayley?'

Ah, okay so this was where she was headed.

'No,' I lied.

'Well, you better not be.'

The others suddenly walked in, carrying all the food. Mel's mum was with them. She looked the same; big, blonde and jovial.

'Hi, Mrs Summers.' I smiled.

'So nice to see you, Georgie! Now dig in. I made a vegetarian lasagne especially for all you vegos!'

Who else was vegetarian besides me? Was Hayley? I didn't think she used to be, but then neither was I back when we were at school.

The lasagne was delicious. So much so I complimented Mel's mum and told her I'd like to grab the recipe to pass onto Cook, but soon regretted it.

'Do you have a cook?' No need to tell you who asked this. 'Are you rich? Are you the one per cent?'

Hayley burst out laughing. I could tell she was enjoying watching my panicked expression.

'Now, let's not talk about that at the table, Kylie,' Mrs Summers said sternly. 'So, Georgie, Mel tells me you saw a ghost at your graduation!'

After dinner I offered to stack the dishwasher, anything to get me away from Kylie. After a little more chatter and merriment, Mel's mum and dad went to bed. I was in the kitchen with Mel as she raided the pantry looking for her precious Mars Bars when I caught Hayley checking me out. She was in the lounge room wrestling with Kylie, who announced she was going to bed as she was staying the night. After Kylie left the room, Hayley just stood there, staring at me. I could feel her unflinching gaze. Eventually I gave in and tentatively looked over at her. As soon as our eyes met, she gave me a cheeky smile and winked.

I melted; Cute Guy? Who was that again?

'Damn! Where are my Mars Bars?!' Mel yelled, making me jump. She was getting annoying.

'Don't you have a stash under your bed?'

'Not anymore, Mum found them and threw them out. She's put me on this strict no Mars Bars diet but I hid a few back here, or so I thought,' Mel whined.

'I ate them,' Hayley piped up from the lounge. 'To save you becoming as big as the planet they're named after!'

I started laughing but hid my smile with my hand so Mel wouldn't see.

'Yeah, well at least I don't replace meals with water and pass out 'cause I have no energy!' Mel yelled back at her sister. Hayley poked her tongue out.

I was starting to get tired. Tomorrow night's 'Take down Sister Catherine' part two was going to be huge and I needed sleep. After I had said goodbye to Mel and Hayley, which included my personal highlight, a hug and kiss on the cheek from the only girl of my dreams, I jumped in my Mazda and turned the ignition, but there was nothing. I tried again and again; still nothing. My car was dead.

I eventually gave up and went back into the house to tell the girls.

'Are you in the RACV?' Mel asked.

'No,' I said solemnly.

'I'll drive you home!' Hayley suddenly piped up, grabbing her keys. 'You can leave your car here. Dad will get it going in the morning – he's a genius.'

'I can drive her, Hayley,' Mel chimed in.

Nooooooooooooooooooooooooooooooooooo!!!!!!!!!!!!!!!!!!!!!!!!!!!!!!!

'You've had too much wine, Mel. I haven't had any. You may have had too much yourself, young Georgie.'

'Ha, yeah, maybe,' I said shyly. I felt like I was twelve years old.

Hayley drove a vintage car, of all things. She told me it was a Valiant S. To me it was white and had wings on either side with red leather seats. It was the coolest thing I had ever seen.

It took around twenty minutes to get to my place, so we had time to chat. It was so great to have some alone time with her.

'So, ah, Kylie seems nice,' I lied. I just needed to say something to get the conversation started as she had so far said nothing and we were well into our journey.

'Nice? You mean rude, don't you?' Hayley said.

I remained silent as I wasn't sure what to say to that.

'I mean, she wasn't very nice to you tonight, was she? She's like that, gets jealous of everyone, as if anything would happen between *us!*'

'Ha, yeah,' I said with raised eyebrows as I stared out the window.

'It's just some fun, you know. She's my first-ever girlfriend. I've only ever dated guys but girls were always after me. I was curious.'

'Like the lesbian boarders.'

'Ha ha, yeah, they did like to carry my stuff around. I wish I'd had one of those things from the Roman days, you know, those couch things where you get carried around. I reckon they would have done that.'

'Yeah, for sure!' I laughed. 'Did you ever like any of them?'

'No way! You saw what they looked like, like Mel's friend, what's her name...'

'Shelley.'

'Yeah, my god, who'd wanna tap that?'

'A sheep?'

We both burst out laughing.

'Mel said you're at Uni and volunteer at an animal rescue?' I said after our laughter subsided. I didn't get a chance to ask her about the rescue at dinner as the conversation had been monopolised by Kylie.

'Yep, at Latrobe Uni, studying Arts part-time like every other loser and...'

'Hang on, weren't you gonna study Law?'

'That was the plan until it all got too much, the study, the pressure, the expectations. I just couldn't handle it anymore so I decided to switch to Arts instead.'

'Oh okay, I didn't know that. I just remember at school you kept saying you wanted to become a lawyer.'

'No biggie,' she said casually. 'And I also volunteer at SMAR, that keeps me sane.'

'SMAR?'

'South Melbourne Animal Rescue,' she said, pointing at her T-shirt.

'Oh yeah! I'd love to work with animals. Can anyone volunteer?'

'Yeah of course, I can let them know you're interested, if you like.'

'That'd be great! Do they have paying jobs?'

'What do you mean?'

'I mean paying jobs as well as volunteer jobs.'

'No, just volunteer. If you wanna make money, you don't work at an animal shelter!' She laughed, making me feel stupid. 'Anyway, aren't you a millionaire? You don't have to work! You *should* volunteer!'

I felt a little hurt after that. Sitting around counting money and living off the interest wasn't my ideal life at all. Not that I even did that. She didn't understand that even though I was a *cough* millionaire, I never had any money. I was basically broke until I turned twenty-one. I needed a job that paid so I wouldn't have to keep begging Mother for petrol money. I also wanted that job to be with animals. I did have Dad's cheque for a thousand dollars, but I wanted to hang onto that and use it for something special.

'Anyway,' she continued, oblivious to the fact my feelings had been hurt, 'I've been helping SMAR out for a few years, I've loved animals since I was a kid but I had to stop eating them after watching *Fast Food Nation,* that made me a vegetarian instantly.'

'Me too…' I said slowly, watching her in awe, shocked at our similarity.

'Cool. Mel told me you were vego,' she said with a smile and a nod.

Hayley and I really were two peas in an iPod. She had also helped me realise volunteering at an animal rescue was the way to get my dream job.

'Did your mum and dad crack it when they found out you had a girlfriend?' I asked after we shared a moment of silence.

'No, they don't care. Dad's brother is gay. No one cares about that stuff anymore, unless you're a right-wing bible basher from the Liberal Party.'

'My dad recently came out to me. He lives with his boyfriend now.'

'That's awesome! What about you, Appleby? Do you think you'll ever turn to the dark side?' she asked in a Darth Vader voice.

'Maybe,' I answered. 'There's only ever been one girl I've been interested in.'

'Shelley? Ha ha but seriously, who? Do I know them?'

I was so ready to say, '*Yes, it's you.*' I could feel the words forming on my lips and the red wine had made me giddy but I just couldn't say it, so I didn't.

'No, you don't know them.'

'There *was* a girl I had a crush on at school but it wasn't a boarder,' Hayley began.

Here we go. I bet it was the most popular girl in her year, or worse, a teacher.

'She was two years younger than me so it was cradle-snatching, I guess.'

God! My year! She must have liked Leticia, or Prudence maybe? Or Tits? Or none of the above?

'She was close friends with my sister.'

It's gotta be Tits! Surely it wouldn't be me.

'And she usually dressed like she was going to a funeral.'

I shot a look at her. No way.

She glanced at me while driving and smiled that stunning smile.

'It was cool when she came around on weekends 'cause I got to hang out with her,' she continued.

Now that I knew it was me, I felt sick, but in a good way.

'There was just a connection between us, mental and physical, and I knew it was mutual.'

'Why didn't you ever tell this girl you liked her?' I finally squeaked then regretted asking.

'I was never in a position to. I didn't see her often enough and when I did, my stupid sister never left her side.'

I felt even sicker. My whole body was tense, I had butterflies and moths in my stomach at the same time and they were fighting.

'Pull over!'

I jumped out of the car and promptly vomited, barely missing the red leather seats. After the great purge was over, I dragged my sorry arse back into her car. I was totally mortified. Trust me to ruin a magical moment. The most magical moment I'd ever had in fact. I was such a loser. I didn't deserve Hayley, or Cute Guy, or anyone. I should just resign myself to my fate and get the Crazy Cat Lady Starter Pack and be done with it.

Hayley just sat there laughing at me. 'Something I said?'

She gave me a box of tissues to clean myself up. Lucky my projectile had missed my shoes, clothes and hair. She also found half a bottle of vodka in the back seat and handed it to me; I gargled it for ages and sculled the entire thing during the rest of the drive home. We didn't talk at all during this time but the cogs in both our brains were working overtime. By the time we got to my place, I was more than a little drunk.

'Jesus! You *are* the one per cent!' she yelled as she pulled up outside Purgatory Palace.

I felt like I was going to cry but instead I just burst out laughing. We sat there giggling together for ages. Everything was just hilarious.

Hayley was so different to Cute Guy; pretty much his exact opposite. She was outgoing, confident, funny, easy to talk to and not awkward in the slightest. She definitely had that spark. It was effortless to be around her. Cute Guy was so geeky and shy; it could be a lot of hard work to be around someone like that, even though I still thought he was adorable.

'Well, thanks for the lift, I'll ring Mel tomorrow to see what her, your… dad says is up with my car,' I said slowly, slightly slurring my words.

I glanced at her. Our eyes locked and we just sat there staring at each other. It was one of those *'Is something gonna happen? Or not happen?'* moments before someone gets out of a car. It was fully intense. And then all of a sudden it went from us staring at each other to her kissing me. It was magical. I felt like I was flying but I'm sure the wine and vodka had something to do with it. It seemed to last forever. I felt like I was dreaming, like I thought it couldn't possibly be her doing that to me. And then it was over.

'I'll see you tomorrow when you pick up your car, then,' she said matter-of-factly.

I nodded as I glided out of the car. I felt the car's wings lift me out of my seat and then I fell flat on my face onto the wet grass and promptly passed out.

When I woke up in the middle of the night, I was tucked in my bed fully clothed with Chocky curled up and snoring beside me. There was a note from Hayley on my pillow saying not to forget to pick up my car tomorrow at 11am. I thought it was weird she had specified a time but I didn't dwell on it for long as I soon fell back to sleep.

\*\*\*

The next morning, I got the limo driver to drop me off at Hayley's. My car was where I'd left it last night. I saw Hayley's Valiant in the driveway but didn't see any other cars.

I knocked on the door. Hayley soon answered it. She was wearing a black silk dressing gown that was done up kind of loose. I could tell she didn't have anything on underneath. She had this seductive look on her face. The butterflies killed the moths in my stomach. Before I could say a word, she grabbed me by my Birthday Party T-shirt, slammed the front door and led me to her bedroom.

\*\*\*

'Where is everyone?'

'Church.' Hayley sighed, lighting up a cigarette which I thought was pretty funny, all things considered. We were still lying in her bed with the doona over us. There were no cuddles afterwards. Once the deed was done, we seemed to become friends again which bugged me a little.

'I don't go to church but they all do, so I'll be the only one going to hell.' She took a long drag then passed the cigarette to me, which I declined. 'That's why I wanted you here at 11 'cause I knew they wouldn't be. Smart huh?' She glanced over at me with that cheeky grin of hers.

'Where's Kylie?' I asked tentatively.

'Under the bed.' She attempted to say this seriously but it wasn't long before we both burst out laughing. I did have a look under the bed just to be sure, though.

After our laughter died down, I had a strong urge to kiss her and started to move closer but suddenly she had jumped out of bed. I didn't know where to look. When she had finally put her black silk dressing gown on again, I remembered my car issues.

'Did your dad know what was wrong with my car?'

'Yeah, flat battery,' she said as she started to throw clothes out of a drawer. 'He replaced it before he went to church.'

'Oh, okay, how much do I owe him?'

'Nothing, he loves you.' She was throwing clothes out of another drawer now. I wanted to ask her a question; I was nervous but decided to ask it anyway.

'So, are you gonna break up with Kylie now?'

'I want to,' she said, finally finding a Ramones T-shirt that was worthy of wearing. 'But she's gonna go postal so I probably won't. Anyway, I know she cheats on me, so I cheat on her too. It all balances out in the end.'

This disturbed me no end.

So, I was just someone to cheat with? A one morning stand; a calculated conquest; she had admitted to having a crush on me for years. It seemed like I was something that had to be attended to, confront that annoying sexual attraction and move on.

Yet again I had fallen and fallen hard. I couldn't do the sleep around thing without feeling emotion; I hated that about myself but it was just the way I was wired. I lost my virginity to a boy when I was in high school and had fallen for him; of course, he dumped me. Hayley was the second person I had ever slept with, my first girl and I kind of liked it – no, I kind of loved it, I kind of loved her. I was screwed, tighter than a light bulb, tighter than a bottle top, absolutely, positively, screwed.

'I'm just gonna jump in the shower, won't be long, unless you wanna join me?' Hayley asked. The seduction had started again but this time I was immune. I shook my head without looking at her. As soon as she closed the bathroom door I got up, got dressed, got in my car and drove to my brother's grave.

As I lay down next to Ben, a yellow honeyeater flew past, hovering for a moment before continuing on its journey. The bird gave me comfort as I felt it had been sent by Ben. I told my brother I had officially given up on love and that he would be proud of me, especially as he had always said love was 'gross'. How I wished with all my essence he was still alive; Ben and I used to have the best conversations, even though he was only fourteen. I closed my eyes and found myself drifting off to sleep, dreaming of Hayley and Cute Guy sword fighting *Game of Thrones* style to the death.

When I woke, I noticed someone had been to visit Ben while I was asleep. Again, there were three long stemmed yellow roses and a card. This time the card said 'Please forgive me'. It must have been the hit and run driver who killed him! It must have been!

# CHAPTER TWENTY-SEVEN

It was midnight and as I waited for the Scooby Gang in the park with Troy, I told him everything. Cute Guy, Hayley, how I felt about them and especially how I currently felt about her, Ben and the strange notes. After I had blurted it all out, I felt such relief; the Ben thing wasn't a biggie but why I chose to not tell him about these crushes that turn to love that turn to loss, I don't know. I was three-dimensional, I wasn't a cardboard cut-out, and my best friend needed to know that.

After we finished talking it all out, he hugged me. We just sat there on the grass in the darkness with our arms around each other, being serenaded by cicadas. When he finally let me go, I noticed a glimmer in his eye.

'Well, I must come clean about something too, Grasshopper.'

For a moment I felt terrified, hoping he wasn't going to tell me he had realised he was in love with me, but I kept that to myself as I sat there holding my breath waiting for him to fess up.

'I seem to have developed feelings for someone too.'

'Who?' I asked, shaking in fear.

'Your maid.'

Whew!

'Marlene! Really? She's a bit plain for you, isn't she?' I asked.

'I don't know, I just think if she did herself up a bit and wore something other than that maid's outfit, she would be a real stunner.'

The cogs in my brain went into overdrive.

'Why don't you come over for dinner tomorrow night? I'm cooking; Marlene will be there. You know we're friends now.'

'I do know that, but she just seems to ignore me.'

'Maybe it's because she likes you too?'

'You think?'

'How's 7pm?'

'Doable,' he said with a Cheshire Cat grin.

The Scoobies' torches were upon us.

'Hi, everyone.' Leticia waved. She was dressed in her designer black again, as was Prudence, whose footwear had changed from pink stilettos to pink Converse.

'Hi, hi,' Prudence said in giggle-speak. 'I'm wearing sneakers just for you, Georgie, but my stilettos are in my backpack just in case!'

That was all I could take. I quickly took a joint out of my pocket, lit it and handed it to Prudence, who started to puff away as Tits looked on sadly. I'd made the joint from the pot I'd stolen out of my voodoo doll the last time we were here. That reminded me: I needed to steal that evil abomination tonight.

'I'm just glad we're together again.' Tits smiled before snatching the joint from Prudence and finishing it; typical Tits.

I shot a look at Mel, who was standing there shaking her head in disgust as she watched Tits smoke the joint. She would die if she knew I'd slept with her sister this morning. I still couldn't believe it had even happened. I'd tried to put the whole thing out of my head, although it wasn't easy, as what we'd done would flash back in my mind and erupt into a swarm of butterflies that felt like my stomach had taken a roller coaster ride without me.

'Hayley wants you to call her,' Mel suddenly piped up.

I became tense. 'I don't have her number.'

'I can give it to you. What does she want to talk to you about, anyway?'

'It must be about my car, she probably wants to know if it's working now,' I lied, consumed by Catholic guilt.

'Oh yeah, she told me you came by this morning to get it while we were at church. Lucky Kylie left early. I don't think she likes you!'

'The feeling's mutual,' I said bluntly.

'Give us your phone then.'

I handed Mel my mobile. Great; I didn't even want Hayley's number. What's the bet she'd get mine off Mel and kept ringing me until I had no choice but to answer. I really didn't feel like talking to her at all after the way she'd treated me. And if she just wanted to hook up another cheating session behind her girlfriend's back, especially since during the heat of the moment she'd said I turned her on more than Kylie did, I just wasn't interested.

'Ladies, ladies, please, we have a mission to complete,' Troy said as Mel handed my phone back to me. As everyone followed Troy and me across the road towards the first convent gate for Prudence to unlock, I thought it the right time to tell him of my *other* plan.

'Troy.'

'Yes.'

'I wanna steal my voodoo doll tonight.'

'What?' he asked in surprise. 'You can't do that! Sister Catherine will be in her room. She's not at the retreat anymore.'

'I know that, but we have to find a way!'

'All right, but it won't be easy.' Troy sighed as he watched Prudence unlock the gate. We followed Troy and his torch silently, aware of the security guard who'd nearly caught us last time, but he was nowhere in sight. I searched the shadows for I Dunno but didn't see her either. Troy had worked out where the pot paddock was and that was where we were headed. We passed the nuns' building and a small forest of trees. A high fence with barbed wire surrounded the paddock. The gate had the largest padlock I'd ever seen chained around it. They sure didn't want anyone entering this dodgy place.

Prudence had the padlock open in seconds. As we were now far away from the convent buildings, we switched on our torches and scattered around the paddock looking for the marijuana, but there was nothing. It was just a paddock of grass, nothing more. After we had searched every nook and granny, our secret circle reconvened.

'There's no pot here,' I said quietly.

'I know!' Leticia huffed. 'This has just been a massive waste of time!'

As we headed miserably toward the gate to begin our journey home, I stopped everyone as we passed the nuns' building.

'I need Troy and Prudence, the rest of you can go home,' I said in my leader voice, ignoring their objections.

After the pack had dispersed, I turned toward The Mini Scoobies – or should that be The Scrappy-Doo's.

'Prudence, I have to get my voodoo doll. I realise Sister Catherine is in her room so there's only one solution.'

'Kill her?' Prudence asked with an insane glimmer in her eye. I began to worry and hoped weed didn't make her smart and a serial killer at the same time.

'No,' I said through clenched teeth as Troy cackled beside me. 'I need you to break the glass and push the fire bell button and then hide until you see us wave you to come out.'

The fire bell was situated on the left wall of the nuns' building. I had noticed it when we were on our way to the pot paddock.

'What do I break it with?'

I looked at the ground and picked up a nearby rock, handing it to her. She did as I asked and ran off. Troy and I hid in the bushes, laughing as we watched dozens of wrinkled penguins in 1800s nighties run and scream out of the building.

When the penguins had dispersed, the three of us ran up the stairs. Sister Catherine's door was wide open, as was everyone else's. We pushed aside the chest of drawers. Prudence opened the lock on the *Alice in Wonderland* door. We creaked up the steep narrow staircase towards the attic, making sure we didn't fall through the rotted wood, and when we got to the top, Prudence unlocked the door. We stepped inside and I switched on the light.

We could not believe what we saw.

# CHAPTER TWENTY-EIGHT

The room was empty; totally empty. Even the shelves that held the dolls were gone. Everything was gone, including my voodoo doll.

'Noooooooo!' I yelled, falling to my knees, hands covering my face. Troy bent down to comfort me.

'It's as though the dolls never even existed,' Prudence said in bewilderment.

'I don't care about those stupid dolls; I only care about *my* doll. Where is it? What has she done with it? I know she's gonna do something nasty to me with it!'

'You don't know that for sure, Georgie,' Troy said.

'Yes, I do!' I objected, standing up in anger. 'Why else would she make a doll that looks exactly like me?'

I walked across the room, noticing a fireplace I'd never seen before as previously there'd been shelves in front of it. I rested my arms on the mantelpiece deep in thought when I noticed something strange.

There appeared to be a small doorknob behind the fireplace's grate.

'Guys, look at this,' I said as I moved the grate aside. Sure enough, there was another *Alice in Wonderland* sized door behind it with a padlock.

'Oh God, what do you think she keeps in *that* room?' Prudence asked in fright.

It was then that we heard a faint fire truck siren that was getting closer.

'Well, if we're going to have a look, we better hurry before the fire-fighters get here,' Troy said, shooting a look at Pru. She worked her magic and pushed the door open slowly.

'I'm not going first,' she squeaked.

'Guess I have to be the man again,' Troy said in a husky voice as he switched on his torch and crawled through the door. I went next and Prudence went last; always safer when you're the veggie burger in the sandwich.

When we'd made it through, Troy found the light switch and turned it on. The tiny dank room was completely empty apart from a large black strongbox sitting in the middle of the floor. After Prudence picked the lock which she had a lot of trouble with, uh-oh, she insisted Troy open the lid.

The strongbox was full of money. Piles and piles of fifty-dollar bills were neatly tied together by rubber bands. There would have been thousands of dollars in there.

We all glanced at each other in shock.

'We're going to have to discuss this later, ladies,' Troy eventually said. 'The fire-fighters sound like they're here.'

The three of us managed to escape Sister Catherine's secret rooms, bedroom, nuns' building and convent grounds without being seen. How we managed to do that seeing as there were ghost nuns and fire-fighters everywhere, I have no idea.

We talked about the money in the strongbox as I drove Troy and Prudence home, although by now Pru had put her pink stilettos back on so she really couldn't contribute much. Troy and I figured it was the money Sister Catherine had made from selling the pot dolls, but how could we prove it and take her down? And more importantly, where was my voodoo doll? That was my main concern.

By the time I dropped them off, my eyes were barely staying open. When I got back to Purgatory Palace it was almost 4am. I dragged myself up the stairs to my room and was greeted by an exuberant Chocky, who insisted on kissing my entire face, including my eyelids, before curling into a ball and falling back to sleep. I threw myself on the bed and checked my phone, noticing I had quite a few text messages. There were five in total but as I'd had my phone on silent all night, I'd never heard any of them.

They were all from Hayley. She must have got my number from Mel. Damn.

'It's Hayley, can you ring me I need to talk to you.' 'Please ring me, Georgie.' 'Still waiting for you to ring me.' 'Me again, can you ring me?' 'If you don't ring me, I'm gonna ring you.' The last text had been sent ten minutes ago.

My phone suddenly started ringing; uh-oh. I didn't want to pick it up but I did. Why? I don't know. I was exhausted, miserable, angry and depressed but amongst all these conflicting emotions I just wanted to hear Hayley's voice.

'Hello, Hayley.'

'Jesus Appleby! It's about time!'

'Why are you ringing me at four in the morning?'

'Sorry, I just need to talk to you; in person.'

'Why?'

'I just do. Can I come 'round later today?'

'No, I won't be home,' I lied.

'What about the day after?'

'I still won't be home. Can't you just talk to me now? I don't have time to see you.'

This of course was an outright lie, as all I had was time now that Mr No Personality Peters had retrenched me from his Lame Law Firm. Lately I'd been living in luxury in my PJs and due to NPP suddenly being on my side, he'd started sticking up for me whenever Mother complained about me not having a job again. Life was good.

Hayley fell silent.

'Hello?' I said sarcastically. I appeared to have the upper hand and it felt great.

'I told SMAR you wanna volunteer for them, they're waiting for your call,' she said a little too quickly.

'Thanks,' I said, slightly bewildered. 'I don't know why you needed to talk to me in person to tell me that, though.'

'Okay,' she said after a long sigh. 'I can't stop thinking about you.'

I was quite certain my heart skipped more than one beat when I heard her say that.

'Oh,' was all I could muster.

'I *need* to see you again.'

There was an urgency in her voice that took me by surprise. Here I was thinking I was a dud root, especially since it was my first time with the same sex, but it seemed quite the opposite applied. My confidence shot through the roof.

'And what does Kylie have to say about this?' I asked. 'Are you still with her?'

There was silence for a few seconds before she said, 'Yes.'

'Yeah, well I'm not into seeing people who're already taken. Why don't you give me a call when you've broken up?'

With that I hung up on her, turned off my phone, threw it across the room and attempted to go to sleep.

# CHAPTER TWENTY-NINE

The next morning, I sat down on the couch with Chocky and checked my phone. Nothing; Hayley had obviously given up. She didn't know what she wanted, but I did. I just wanted to be with someone I liked who was single and unfortunately, neither Hayley nor Cute Guy was. My thoughts were interrupted as Marlene entered the room.

'Hi, Georgie,' she squeaked.

I remembered what Troy had said in the park and started to smile deviously.

'Hi, Marlene, come and sit next to me for a tick,' I said, patting the couch.

She did as I asked and sat down.

'Can I ask you a personal question?'

'Um… okay.'

'Do you have a boyfriend?'

I presumed she was straight.

'No, Miss – I mean, no, Georgie.'

'Have you ever had one?'

'Once,' she eventually mumbled. 'Long ago, but it didn't last long.'

'What happened?'

'I was still living with my adoptive parents. They made me end it; said I didn't have time for a boyfriend with all the work I had to do.'

I watched her as she sat there miserably staring at her hands, wearing that ridiculous maid's uniform with her hair in that unflattering tight bun, and I had an idea.

'Marlene,' I began.

'Yes?' she asked, glancing at me nervously.

'I'm gonna give you a makeover.'

Her eyes widened in shock. 'What do you mean?!' she shrieked.

'Haven't you ever heard of a makeover? You will look amazing when I'm finished with you!'

'I will?' she whispered.

'Yes! We'll do it tonight, I just have to get a couple of things first, okay?'

'All right, but I don't have any money to buy anything,' she said, uncomfortably straightening her skirt as she stood.

'My treat.' It was actually Mother's treat, not that she knew that yet.

'Okay, thank you. Well, if you're sure. See you later then,' she said, leaving the room.

I smiled, knowing my plan would come off without a hitch. Troy was coming over for dinner tonight which I was going to make as it was Cook's night off. Mother was going to be out for the evening as well, which was even better. When Troy saw the new Marlene, he would be even more smitten. Maybe they could even have dinner together if I made up some emergency I had to attend to; not Hayley.

I was happy for a moment until I remembered my missing voodoo doll. What the hell had Sister Catherine done with it? Maybe I'll never know. Sigh.

That afternoon I rang SMAR about volunteering. I also asked what days Hayley Summers volunteered. She did Mondays, Tuesdays, Fridays and Saturdays, making me wonder what time she even had to go to Uni. I told them I could do Wednesdays and Thursdays. They said I could come in this Wednesday. I couldn't wait.

Then I went off to the shops with Marlene's measurements and Mother's credit card, which I had stolen earlier. I was pretty excited about Marlene's transformation. I hoped she would look as awesome as she looked in my head.

Later that day I got to work. The first thing I did was dye Marlene's hair black. Her brown hair was boring. Besides black making her look more gothic, I thought it would also bring out her grey eyes and I was right. Her hotness level had already accelerated.

Next on the list was make-up; black eyeliner and dark eye shadow to make her eyes really pop and a smatter of red lipstick. I didn't think she needed powder as her skin was already so pale and flawless. I wasn't really an expert at applying makeup on anyone, all I ever wore was black eyeliner, but I think I did a pretty good job on my protégé.

Then it was time to address her clothes. I could tell she was more of a dress wearer than I was, so I'd bought her a long black dress with lace on the sleeves and a neckline that showed just enough cleavage. You guessed it, Mother would be proud. I'd also bought her a necklace with a large black crucifix that matched her dress perfectly.

Finally, I put a pair of black patent leather Doc Martins on her feet and stood back to take it all in.

She looked amazing; no, stunning; no, stunningly amazing. She didn't even look like Marlene. She looked like a gothic supermodel who was about to do a fashion show in Milan.

No kidding. It was breathtaking.

'How do I look?' she asked in a worried whisper. I smiled and led her to a mirror. She stared at herself for a long time before collapsing to the floor in a heap.

'What's wrong?!' I asked in despair.

She looked up at me. Her tears had made her eyeliner smudge, damn it.

'I look beautiful. You made me look beautiful.'

She threw herself onto my neck and bawled her eyes out. Let's just say it took a while for me to get her face up to scratch again, but I was glad I'd made her this happy, it gave me a good feeling. No one had ever really paid much attention to her before or even noticed how attractive she actually was, apart from Troy. Everyone deserved to be noticed, especially when they were a good person like Marlene.

After I fixed her face, we went downstairs, noticing Mother putting on her coat ready to leave. I quickly put her credit card back in her purse without her noticing.

'I am off to dinner at the German Club now, Georgina,' Mother said, turning to look at me and seeing Marlene for the first time.

'Oh, you have a friend over, that's nice. Have a good time. I shall be home late so don't wait up.'

With that she was gone. Marlene and I glanced at each other incredulously before bursting out laughing.

'Marlene,' I begun cautiously, after our laughter had subsided.

'Yes?' Marlene asked, worried.

'I've invited Troy over for dinner.'

'What?!' Marlene said in horror.

'He likes you! It'll be fun!'

'He likes me?' she asked, suddenly calm.

'Yes, and I have a feeling you might like him too.'

She stared down at her hands for ages before looking up at me and saying, 'I do like him.'

Bingo!

At 7pm sharp the doorbell rang. I made Marlene open the door. She didn't want to but I forced her, literally pushing her toward it and then I hid behind the curtain to watch. She opened the door slowly and smiled a radiant smile. I noticed a shocked expression on Troy's face which soon turned to confusion.

'Marlene?' he asked quietly.

'Yes, it's me,' she said with an innocent giggle.

Suddenly Troy was on bended knee. 'Will you marry me?' he asked in his charming way.

Marlene burst out laughing just as I came out from behind the curtain.

'Dear guests, please walk this way,' I said in a posh accent before limping to the dining room.

Troy took Marlene's arm and limped after me.

After they were seated opposite each other, I made them my one and only specialty, something that was so deliciously mouth-watering and sought after I had been approached to create a cook book around it; cheese and tomato toasted sandwiches.

'Eat it and weep.' I bowed.

'Mmmm, this looks delicious!' Troy tucked his napkin into his collar.

'Aren't you joining us, Georgie?' Marlene asked, turning to look at me. I noticed Troy shaking his head while Marlene's attention was focused on me.

'No, sorry, I was going to but I have to visit a sick friend, in fact I have to leave now.' It was a pretty crap lie but the only thing I could think of.

As soon as I closed the front door it started pouring. I was certain the rain gods had been playing poker, biding their time waiting for me to leave the house. By the time I ran to my car I was drenched, yet another typical 'four seasons in one day' Melbourne summer.

Summer; Summers; Hayley Summers; no! Stop!

I started my car, drove to the nearest McDonalds drive-thru and got my usual, a cheese burger without the meat, fries and a Coke. I sat in the car soaking wet and began to eat my junk food miserably. After only one bite I felt the tears start to well and soon enough I found myself crying uncontrollably.

# CHAPTER THIRTY

Wednesday was my first day of volunteering at SMAR. I was happy there was a reason for me to get out of bed. Recent events had all become too much. My unrequited love for Cute Guy, my requited love for Hayley, the strange notes at Ben's grave, my missing voodoo doll and the strongbox full of cash and, although I was happy for them, I couldn't help feeling that setting up my best friend with my maid was the beginning of the end of Troy and my friendship.

Quadruple sigh.

I walked into the shelter, which was busy and chaotic and told Mary, the owner, my name and why I was there. She greeted me with a wide smile and thanked me for wanting to volunteer. My day basically consisted of washing dog and cat bowls, changing kitty litters, loading the washing machine with towels and blankets, cleaning out pens and, my favourite thing of all, walkies, when I got to walk a selection of dogs around the block. Everyone who worked there was really friendly and obviously animal lovers so I had loads in common with them. They spoke very highly of Hayley. She did the pick-ups and drop-offs. Dogs and cats were picked up from death row pounds with only a few days, sometimes only a few hours, until their time was up, then she'd drop them off at the shelter and help get them ready to be re-homed. The amount I had in common with her was actually quite daunting, but is it really a good idea to go out with yourself?

Volunteering at the shelter was hard work but thoroughly enjoyable and I knew it was something I could do every day without getting sick of it, as I was actually helping the animals and doing a job that was worthwhile, unlike filing.

During my lunchbreak I found out Mary was the only person paid to do this job. Everyone else volunteered, otherwise there would be no money going towards caring for the animals. The shelter basically existed through fundraising and donations and sometimes when times were tough, Mary didn't even pay herself to make sure the animals could eat. Things were pretty dire; they'd almost closed recently as they were so desperate for money. I thought of all that ridiculous wealth my family had and it made me feel sick. Mother and her stupid diamond-encrusted champagne glass and designer garb, NPP's ridiculously expensive cars that were barely used and pathetic golf course on the grounds of Purgatory Palace so he could entertain his rich clients. The animals needed money for basic survival, they didn't. I thought of the thousand-dollar cheque Dad had given me for my nineteenth birthday that was just sitting there. I decided to cash it and give it to them anonymously, but it wasn't enough. I still had years before I could claim my inheritance.

My inheritance. I needed to know how much money I actually had. Stat.

*** 

Troy and I organised a catch-up on Friday so I could get the face-to-face goss on his dinner with Marlene, as he wouldn't give away anything on the phone, while he accompanied me to the bank to check on my inheritance.

'So... spill,' I said, starting to drive.

'Has Marlene told you anything?' he asked sheepishly as he put his seatbelt on.

'No, I haven't seen her. I've been flat out at the shelter.'

'Well, we did enjoy your exquisite cuisine,' he began with a wry smile.

'Enough with the exquisite cuisine, did you guys click or what?' I asked in annoyance. He was always like that, taking forever to get to the point just to annoy me.

'Well… if you must know, we did.'

I smiled.

'In fact, we clicked so much we are going on a date this weekend.'

'That's great!' I said happily, although inside I felt that slight pang of loss.

'Yes, it is.' He grinned. 'And before you ask if we did the sex…'

'I wasn't going to ask that!' I objected.

'We didn't. We are going to wait. Marlene has had a pretty tough life, so she finds it hard to trust people. I would like her to trust me before we even thought of such intimacy.'

'Fair enough,' I said with a nod, not that I wanted to know any of that.

'What about you? Have you heard from Hayley?'

'No, why would I? She's not breaking up with Kylie, she's made that pretty clear, she only wants to use me for sex.'

'Is that such a bad thing?' Troy asked with a cheeky smile.

'Yes!' I yelled. 'You know I can't do that, Troy! I can't just sleep with people, especially when they're with someone else. You know I develop feelings.'

'Poor little sensitive Georgie,' Troy said in a baby voice, complete with bottom lip protruding as usual.

'Shut up!'

'Also, dear, in case you are worried I won't have time for you anymore if Marlene and I start going out, you really don't have to worry about that.'

I said nothing, even though that was exactly what I had been thinking.

'Marlene respects our bond so we can continue doing immature things together at frequent intervals.'

I burst out laughing. He was such an idiot.

'She does love you,' he continued.

I shot him a terrified look.

'In a platonic way.'

I sighed, shaking my head. He was at it again.

'She said the makeover you gave her was the nicest thing anyone has ever done for her.'

I smiled. It gave me a fuzzy feeling knowing that.

When we arrived at the bank, to my surprise I found a car park right out the front, which I considered a good omen. I had a meeting scheduled with the bank manager and as usual had dressed appropriately, including sleeveless black T-shirt with a giant white skull on it; classy.

Not long after we got there, I was called into the bank manager's office with Troy tiptoeing after me. Let's just say this dude looked like a bank manager. Without going into boring detail, just picture the dad from *Beverly Hills 90210*.

We sat down opposite 90210 Dad. He shot a look at Troy. I could tell he was wondering who the hell he was and why he was at my meeting.

I was on it.

'This is my financial adviser, Mr Head. You can call him Dick,' I said casually before kicking Troy's leg as I heard him start to chuckle.

90210 Dad nodded then unfortunately said:

'Nice to meet you, Dick.'

That was it. Troy burst out laughing then turned it into a fake cough before excusing himself and running out of the room.

I turned back to face 90210 Dad after Troy's embarrassing outburst, knowing I had damage control to do.

'So sorry, Dick is stressed, lots of finances to advise, I'm sure you can relate.'

90210 Dad was looking sceptical but instead cleared his throat and asked why I had wanted to see him.

I told him my inheritance was with the bank and that I knew the roundabout figure but wanted to check exactly how much. He nodded and promptly keyed a few things into his computer before staring at the screen for so long I became concerned.

'How much did you say you thought was in there, Ms Appleby?' he asked slowly.

'Well, it should be around five million I think.'

'I'm sorry but there isn't anything close to that amount.'

'What do you mean, how much is there?'

'Seven dollars.'

He turned the computer screen toward me so I could see.

'That can't be right!' I yelled. My good omen feeling was a fake. 'Who's been authorised to take it out?'

'The only person authorised is your mother, Alicia Appleby.'

I raced out of the bank and ran toward Troy who was leaning on my car in wait. I filled him in as I sped home to confront Mother.

I found her in the kitchen, stirring a pot of rat stew. Well, that's what it looked like. Troy went to hide in my room to give Chocky cuddles.

'Hello, Mother.'

'Oh, hello Georgina. Cook has asked for the night off, something about a wedding anniversary and being the kind soul that I am, I gave it to her so tonight I am making my famous veal stew!'

Champagne glass, check; the fact she still hasn't processed the fact I am a vegetarian, anger; but let it go, Georgie, let it go, just like Elsa.

'I just went to check on my inheritance, *Mother*, and there's only seven dollars in there. You told me ages ago that there was around five million!' I yelled.

Mother stopped stirring her pot of muck and shot a distressed look at me.

'Of course, there should be around five million. There must be a mistake!'

'There is no mistake; you spent it, didn't you!'

'I did no such thing! I haven't touched it!'

NPP suddenly scurried in, no doubt listening from the other room.

'Did you hear that?! Do you know anything about this, Hubert?!' Mother roared.

'No, I don't. It must be a mistake. I will go into the bank myself on Monday and sort it out.'

***

The next day NPP disappeared and so did Leopard Print Sharon. All that remained was the lingering smell of Old Spice. I braced myself and told Mother about his affair and how I'd seen them in the supply closet the night of the Christmas party. She was pretty upset and cried and then cried some more. I felt so bad for her I uncharacteristically gave her a hug.

She eventually pulled away, wiping her eyes with her hand-embroidered handkerchief that had the letters 'AA' stitched in pink cotton. I chuckled at the other meaning of AA. Not the Alicia Appleby one.

'Why didn't you tell me about this when you first found out, Georgina?!'

Why didn't I tell her? Oh, that would be because I was blackmailing NPP that I'd tell her unless he retrenched me from the Lame Law Firm. I felt a bit guilty about that now.

'I was going to,' I lied. 'I just didn't get around to it.'

'I'm such a fool.' She sniffed. 'I should have known.'

'How could you have known? He hid his dirty little secret so well.'

'I don't know… he just seemed so wonderful, so loyal, and he loved me… or so I thought… and your inheritance, Georgina! Oh, my Lord! A rotten thief as well! How could I have been so stupid!'

Mother burst out crying again and buried her face in her hands. My heart ached for her at that moment. It was a surreal feeling. She must have really loved that old fool. I hated him so much. I'd always hated him. Even more so now. I wished I could Coward Punch him to death with Sister Catherine's boxing gloves.

After a few minutes Mother wiped away her tears, had a sip of champagne and glanced at me, her eyes cloudy and forlorn.

'I know you miss Ben.'

I was shocked she had even mentioned my dear departed brother's name.

'I do, too. He was a little ray of sunshine, that boy; my pride and joy and so different to Andrew, so happy all the time. If I had one wish, it would be that I would die so he could live.'

I started crying.

Mother hugged me, like when I was a little girl, before our relationship capsized. I don't know how long we remained like that; time stopped. I was warm and loved and wished the moment would never end.

***

So that was that.

No huge inheritance, no future of being able to do what I wanted to do, which was to give a million dollars to SMAR so they could move to a larger and better-equipped shelter and eventually start my own shelter; there was nothing, nada, zilch, zero, zip.

Sigh like there is no tomorrow.

The Scoobies were talking about part three of 'Take down Sister Catherine' when we heard she had disappeared too. Troy, Prudence and I snuck back into the second *Alice in Wonderland* room she had the strongbox full of cash in to see if she had taken it with her. The answer was obvious.

Was Sister C having an affair with NPP as well? Gross, I know, but still weird they disappeared around the same time. Something was up and I had my conspiracy theory about the both of them as well. Maybe he was in on her pot dolls? Maybe she was in on him stealing my inheritance? Who knows? They were gone and that was that. No more Mr No Personality Peters to drive me insane or drive me home when the limo guy had the night off.

NPP's partner took over the Lame Law Firm in his absence while the cops searched for him so they could charge him with embezzlement as, apparently, I wasn't the only one. Many of his Lame Law Firm clients were missing money too. As far as my inheritance was concerned, the cops soon worked out he had been forging Mother's signature and bit by bit, sucking my money dry.

And now that Sister Catherine, her trusty mop dog and the strongbox full of cash were gone, there were no more Scooby Gang adventures and no more breaking into the convent. I hardly even saw the Scoobies anymore. I felt cheated that I hadn't been given the satisfaction of bringing down my nun-nemesis or finding my voodoo doll, but after racking my brain I realised there was only one thing I could do to help SMAR financially, even though I only had seven dollars to my name.

# CHAPTER THIRTY-ONE

Leticia had gone to dance school with vomit-inducing popstar Candy Dee before Candy moved to America and had five consecutive number-one hits, and they were still close apparently. So after hassling Leticia to the point of her wanting to kill me, I got her to ask Candy to perform at a fundraiser I wanted to organise for SMAR. I'd done my research and knew Candy was an animal lover, so presto, she said yes. She flew out to Australia for the benefit and all.

The gig was massive and raised over a million dollars for SMAR, which kept them going and then some. Mary moved the shelter to a bigger space, which meant she could rescue and re-home even more animals. SMAR also opened another rescue in Sydney and were able to ramp up the Adelaide shelter, too. Candy got all the kudos, even though it was my idea, but I didn't care. I just wanted to help Mary and I did. I guess it felt good to get off my butt and do something myself, now that I wasn't waiting in limbo for my stupid inheritance, which, let's face it, I didn't work for at all.

Maybe I was finally growing up a little?

Nine months had passed since Mr No Personality Peters had done a runner. The cops were still looking for him, but the case was growing cold. Sister Catherine was still on the missing persons list as well, but I hadn't heard anything about her dodgy doings, so basically, they had both gotten away with it. I was still sure of the connection between them, especially how Sister C had been at the Lame Law Firm's Christmas party chatting away to NPP and all the 'donations' the law firm had given to the convent; dodgy.

Eventually I went to the cops to tell them about the Sister C pot stuff and the strongbox but there was no evidence, so they couldn't do anything and I almost got done for breaking and entering at the same time. Luckily, I had a young male cop who seemed to like me and had decided to let the matter go.

Home life had been hard since NPP had gone AWOL. Without him there to at least try to curb Mother's alcohol consumption, she naturally became worse. That tender moment between us had unfortunately become a distant memory. She rarely got out of bed these days. She just lay there watching soap operas and demanding more champagne. She had pretty much stopped eating. She was a sorry sight. Her spark had gone and no matter what any of us tried to do, she wouldn't snap out of it. Even her golden boy, Andy, had attempted to help her but she was beyond help. We had no choice but to put her into rehab for a few months and now that she was gone, the house was like a morgue.

The only inhabitants of Purgatory Palace were me, Chocky and Marlene. Troy was over a lot but didn't live there. Cook came and went. I let the limo driver go. He had another job lined up so I didn't feel bad. I was totally capable of driving the limo myself and enjoyed wearing the uniform. It made me feel like Watts from *Some Kind of Wonderful*. Troy and Marlene's relationship was going great, though; so great I'd given them a Hollywood name, Troylene. They were basically joined at the rib. Troy hadn't said anything about them 'doing the sex' yet, so I figured they hadn't or maybe he decided not to tell me, which was fine as I didn't want to know anyway.

Troy kept his word as we still did immature things together at frequent intervals, like getting the limo stuck in a McDonalds drive-thru. Sundays were the hardest, when Marlene had her day off. These days she would spend it with Troy and stay over at his place, leaving me and Chocky totally alone. I would never sleep properly on those nights. I'd just sit on the couch and watch all my favourite TV shows until I passed out from sweet Jim Beam and exhaustion and hope the ghosts of my dead relatives would leave me be.

Money wasn't a problem as there was still Mother's fortune to get us by, being the ridiculously rich cow she was. I was allowed access to her cash while she was in rehab so I kept the household going, paying Marlene, Cook and the bills. I had to grow up even more and it sucked big time, but until Mother came back, I felt a huge responsibility to keep things going, especially after NPP did what he did. I still volunteered at SMAR's new HQ and that kept me sane. I was part of the furniture now. Hayley did her shifts too but as we were there on different days, we never saw each other, which was fine by me. Apart from the occasional silly limo ride, I had become a sad, serious adult.

Troy noticed this, so one Friday night he forced me to go to karaoke with him and Marlene…

'Come on, Georgie, you love this song!' Troy yelled as he ran to the microphone with Marlene to sing my old standard, *Right Here, Right Now* by Jesus Jones. I declined. I really wasn't in the mood to be there. I had so much on my mind it was exhausting. I decided to walk outside to the beer garden to get some fresh air when I heard a voice behind me say my name. I turned around and looked straight into Cute Guy's, sorry for the cliché, ocean blue eyes.

Our eyes locked, I melted.

'Georgie, it *is* you. How are you?'

It was good to see him. He was rocking a black, short-sleeved shirt, grey tie with tiny Darth Vader heads on it, black trousers and shoes;

no doubt what he had worn to work that day. I'd always loved the fact that he was my height. He was basically a short-arse for a guy. I really found it hard to be attracted to tall guys. I liked guys that were at my eye level for some strange reason. He looked different though. I realised it was because his hair looked like he had just got out of bed, like it used to. No more Bart Simpson church hair and his glasses were back. He was smiling that shy smile I loved. He was still adorable.

'Hey Justin,' I said absentmindedly, mesmerised by his hair.

'I saw you at Emily's graduation...'

'Yeah, we went to school together. Same year.'

'Oh, and what happened to you at work? You just disappeared,' he said.

'Yeah,' I muttered, thinking of what to say. 'I needed to move on.'

'Was it because of your step-dad? Pretty full on the way he stole his clients' money.'

'Yep,' I said, looking away. I didn't feel comfortable discussing this with him. He noticed.

'Sorry, it must be difficult,' he said softly.

'Yeah, well, he also stole my inheritance so, yeah, it's pretty difficult!'

'Oh shit, that's terrible! D-do you want a drink? We can sit down and catch up if you like.'

I nodded and sat down at a table in the beer garden, waiting for him to return. When he did, he placed a bottle of Jim Beam Black in front of me and took a swig from his Crown Lager.

'Who are you here with?' he asked.

'Troylene.'

'Who?'

'Troy and his girlfriend Marlene.'

'Oh, Troy has a girlfriend now, wow. I heard you do, too. A girl called Hayley.'

'Who told you that?!'

'Oh, Emily heard it from someone you guys went to school with.'

'Well, I don't anymore and she was never my girlfriend anyway,' I said in a huff. I was worried that seeing as girls from school had inexplicably found out about me and Hayley that Mel would too, and somehow I don't think she would be cool with the fact it was her sister.

'I didn't know you were gay,' he said.

'I'm not! I'm bi!'

I may have yelled that.

The trouble with being bi is people don't get it, they just end up thinking you're gay or straight. They don't understand how you could possibly be attracted to both sexes.

'What girl from school did Emily hear that from?' I asked in annoyance.

Cute Guy cleared his throat and moved uncomfortably in his chair.

'Um... Mary-Louise?'

How the hell did The Coolest Girl in School, Mary-Louise, find out about Hayley and me? God only knows. So, Mary-Louise thought I was a lesbian and I wasn't even a boarder. Not that there's anything wrong with being a lesbian. I think there's way more wrong with being a boarder. I wonder if ML thought I had the hots for her because I sure as hell didn't, even though she was attractive. I wasn't attracted to many girls. Hayley was one of the exceptions.

Good old Mary-Louise, here's that flashback you knew was coming...

***

*As I entered the waiting room to see the principal, I was surprised to find it full of our year's misfits, freaks and rebels all chattering amongst themselves, including Tits, who had beaten me there, and bang smack in the middle was the ultimate queen of cool, Mary-Louise.*

*Mary-Louise, as mentioned before, was skinny, blonde, sun-kissed and beautiful. The typical stereotype of the Aussie beach girl, but she was also tough, intimidating and the leader of the Cool Girl Gang. It was such a privilege to be in her presence. No one could touch her gang and they weren't looking for new members, but I was close, I was there, I was in her stratosphere. As I walked in, she shot a look at me. There was no smile, only a slight nod of acknowledgment. My heart skipped the jump rope it usually tripped on.*

*It was the beginning of Year 12 and all the girls in our year who were likely to cause trouble were cattle-called in to see Mr Valencia, who warned them off bad behaviour before they had actually done anything wrong. Being there meant you weren't a geek or goody two shoes, it meant you were cool and a rebel. It was such an honour to be told off. I'd never felt so at home in my life.*

***

'So, where's Emily?' I asked Cute Guy after coming to.

'Emily and I broke up months ago,' he said, staring at his bottle of beer.

This came as a surprise but I didn't really know how I felt about it.

'What happened?'

'She got a job teaching English in Europe.'

'How'd she manage that? She's *my* age!'

'Her dad's connections. She doesn't need to be qualified.'

'So why didn't you go with her?'

'I didn't have a job there. Anyway, I just got promoted at work. You probably think my job is boring but I'm saving to buy a house. It's something that's always been important to me.'

As he sat there miserably inspecting his hands in such an innocent manner, I felt like I wanted to jump over the table and kiss him. These feelings took me by surprise. The fact I had any feelings left at all took me by surprise.

He looked up at me shyly. I could tell he wanted to ask something but was working up to it.

Then this happened.

'Do you want to go to dinner with me sometime?'

It must have taken a lot for him to get that out.

I was amazed he was asking me out, but then I always did have a sneaking suspicion he kind of liked me, but Emily got to him first. There was also that question he never got to ask me at karaoke ages ago that Troy ruined.

I took so long to answer he started to sweat and shake, so I thought it best to put him out of his misery.

'Yes,' I said finally.

Cute Guy broke into the widest smile, revealing a set of perfect white teeth that blinded me in a good way.

'Great, can you put your number in my phone and I'll call you.'

I did as he asked and gave his phone back to him.

'I better go find my mate, I think he might be a little drunk by now. I'll call you soon, okay?'

'Okay.'

And then he was gone and I was smiling.

***

Cute Guy called me the next day and asked if I was free that night. I was, so we met at this swish Chinese restaurant complete with white tablecloths and candlelight. It was a little too sickly romantic for my liking, but whatever. He wanted to pick me up but I didn't want him to see the embarrassment that was Purgatory Palace so I said I'd meet him out front of the restaurant. He turned up in a blue suit with that damn Bart Simpson church hair again and although I noticed a weird look on his face when he saw what I was wearing – ripped Levi's, green Converse and a Nirvana T-shirt – wisely, he said nothing.

I ordered the only vegetarian option on the menu, mixed veggies and tofu, while he decided on the chicken. It was fine. Hayley was the only other vegetarian I knew but that didn't mean she was more perfect for me. We ordered and sat there making small talk as we waited for our drinks. I was pretty bored. CG seemed more nervous than usual and was shaking and stuttering a lot. I just wished he would chill the fuck out.

Finally, I noticed the waiter coming towards us carrying our drinks on a tray. He was balancing the tray with one hand and seemed to be holding it a little too high. This feeling of dread engulfed me whole. Sure enough, the waiter tripped when he was right in front of me and the entire contents of the tray, which, besides our drinks, included a jug of iced water, ended up on my lap. I sat there in shock with the whole restaurant's eyes on me, drenched, covered in ice and surrounded by broken glass. CG jumped up and started abusing the waiter who was apologising profusely. As the owner came over to see what all the fuss was about, I stood up slowly. Dozens of ice cubes navigated their way down my clothes and on to the floor. Remembering my Scottish heritage on my Gran's side, I realised I had literally become a scotch on the rocks. The owner was now in my face begging forgiveness but ignoring him, I strolled over to the front door, calmly opened it and walked out. CG ran after me.

'Georgie! Are you okay? Oh my god, I can't believe that waiter!'

I turned to look at him, noticing the absolutely adorable look of horror on his face. Something clicked in my brain. Like a demon possessed, I grabbed him around the neck and started to kiss him.

We ended up at his flat. It was tiny and immaculate and bursting with *Star Wars* toys that looked like they were dusted every day. Hayley's room was the opposite. I remembered I couldn't even see what colour the carpet was due to it being covered in clothes. Cute

Guy lived alone, which was convenient. After we had sex (mind blowing) I noticed yet again he was the opposite of Hayley. Instead of getting the hell out of there, he wanted to cuddle and then cuddle some more. I honestly didn't know which behaviour I preferred, as both were poles apart; indifference versus suffocation. Why couldn't I sleep with someone who was in the middle of these two extremes? After a while I just had to get the hell out of there and made some lame excuse about needing to desperately walk my dog, even though it was after midnight.

'Are you sure you can't stay a little longer?' he pleaded as I headed toward the front door. 'I'll make you hot chocolate.'

I turned to look at him. He was so cute standing there shirtless, displaying his skinny hairless chest and wearing his Spiderman boxer shorts, but he was just too much, so I said I'd call him and left.

When I got home, Troylene were watching TV in the lounge room with Chocky curled up asleep on her blanket until she saw me and went mad.

'How was it? Did you get lucky?' Troy asked cheekily as Marlene looked on in anticipation.

'Well, I had sex but I don't think I got lucky,' I deadpanned as I threw myself into the armchair. Chocky jumped on my lap, kissing me furiously. Cute Guy was not the last being I had been kissed by now.

'You don't consider sex getting lucky?' Troy laughed.

After I filled them in on my dinnerless dinner and how I now knew what it felt like to be an actual full glass with ice, Marlene handed me a letter.

'This came for you today, Georgie.'

I took the envelope from her and turned it over.

'It's from Tits... and John,' the last word I said with disdain. 'I know what it is.'

Sure enough, when I opened the letter, I saw an invitation to their wedding. Oh, how I was dreading this moment, Tits marrying that sleazy bogan piece of crap. How the hell could I get out of this?

'What is it?' Marlene asked anxiously.

I threw the invitation at her.

'Oh, how exciting! I love weddings!'

'Well, why don't you go then?' I mumbled as I stroked Chocky's fur under her chin.

'Georgie doesn't like her friend's future hubby very much, Marlene,' Troy explained with raised eyebrows.

'And it says plus one. I don't have anyone to go with.' I sighed.

'What about the person you didn't get lucky with?' Troy asked, eyes gleaming.

'Oh, my dog, if I ask him to a wedding, he'll plan our own!'

'Well then I would be honoured to accompany you, my dear,' Troy said gallantly.

'Of course!' Marlene piped up, being the sweetheart she was. 'You should go with Georgie.'

'When is it?' Troy asked.

'Next month.' I sighed.

'Perfect!' He grinned. 'That will give me plenty of time to raid the funeral parlour for a new suit!'

Marlene and I both laughed at the silly boy we loved so much.

'Now it's time for the next item on the agenda,' he continued, rubbing his palms together. 'It's almost January 24, young Georgie; you turn the big two-zero; no longer a teenager, now an actual bona fide woman.'

I threw my cushion at his face but he caught it just in time.

'What about *your* birthday?' I asked him. 'It's just before mine but we never do anything for yours, do we?'

'You know my birthday is not something to be celebrated *ever*,' he said with furrowed brow.

'Until now!' Marlene piped up.

Troy glanced at her in dread.

'I'm taking you out to dinner, Troy. I will not take no for an answer.'

'Well, I do like to eat.' Troy grinned.

As I sat there watching them, Troylene held a staring competition to see who would laugh first (Marlene lost) and then they bear-hugged each other. They were such an awesome couple. Marlene still looked as amazing as she did when I gave her the initial makeover. She had maintained her black hair, wore a little make-up now, but even without it she looked great and she'd given the maid's uniform the flick, just as I had instructed. Before Mother had gone to rehab and was still in her champagne-induced coma, she had no idea that the woman who was serving her was Marlene. This would make us chuckle at regular intervals.

'But back to your birthday my dear,' Troy continued after they stopped hugging.

'What are we doing?' I said with a sigh. I had given in. There was no point fighting him.

'Well, you know your mother's holiday house in Lorne that is sitting there idly...'

'Yes,' I said sceptically.

'That's where we're going; it's beach holiday time! And all your friends are invited!'

Great. I hated the Ludicrous Lorne Lodge.

I hated the beach. I hated it during the day in summer. I liked it at night in winter when the moon was full and the sea swayed back and forth in the darkness like a hypnotic seesaw. Nice image, huh?

There was no use protesting, though, Troy's mind was made up.

'Okay,' I said miserably.

# CHAPTER THIRTY-TWO

My twentieth birthday party was organised in one week thanks to Troylene. Mother was still in rehab so we didn't have to worry about her objections to us having it at the Ludicrous Lorne Lodge. After much inner turmoil I decided it was best for Chocky to stay with Mary from SMAR for a few days rather than come with me. Although I had taken Choc to Sydney with me to visit Dad, knowing she would be safe, the Lorne house had no proper fencing and basically just sat on the foot of a strictly 'no dogs allowed' rich, snooty beach. I knew Chocky would be fine with Mary and her pampered home zoo.

Troy had invited the Scoobies: Tits, Mel, Leticia and Prudence, the usual suspects. He had asked whether I wanted Justin or Hayley there. I'd said no to both. Hayley, I hadn't had anything to do with for months, and Cute Guy, I was avoiding after he'd started ringing me every day, desperate to see me. He was freaking me out and I was seriously worried that if I saw him again, he would go down on bended knee. So, avoidance was a must.

It was a surreal feeling being back at that house. We used to go there all the time for Fun Family Holidays before Ben passed away.

Now it was just a sad reminder of happier times. Troylene noticed my expression when I had walked back into that dusty, sheet-covered morgue. They instructed me to go for a walk on the beach while they got things in order. January 24 wasn't a horribly hot day this year and feeling the crisp sea breeze on my face was refreshing. As the sun set and the sky turned a spectacular orange, I almost felt at peace, but I knew the feeling wouldn't last.

An hour or so later I returned to the lodge and found it cheery and inviting. Troylene had even put food and drinks out, covered the lounge room in decorations and put on Nirvana's *Bleach* album. As I thanked them with an uncharacteristic group hug, I felt incredible gratitude that they were both in my life and cared for me as much as they did.

Whilst Troy poured my first glass of sweet Jim Beam and Coke in my Snoopy glass, which had been shipped from home in industrial-strength bubble wrap, there was a knock on the door. Marlene opened it, revealing Leticia and Prudence's beaming, made-up faces. As usual, Pru was dressed from top to toe in fluorescent pink, immediately giving me a migraine, and Leticia was dressed like Mother minus feather boa.

Sigh.

'Happy birthday, Georgie. The party can start now we're here!' Leticia yelled, snapping her fingers. Prudence pushed past her but their smiles soon evaporated when they walked inside.

'Where is everyone?' Leticia asked.

'There's only a few people coming,' I said as I took a swig of my drink and promptly burped.

'Well, a few people aren't enough! We saw some cute surfer boys earlier; they said they'd be here later.' Leticia winked as I cringed. 'And what is this horrible music? Pru! Put Beyoncé on!'

I gave Troy a pained look, remembering why my ex-nemeses were actually nemeses in the first place.

As Beyoncé's commercialised pop bled through my ears and drowned out the room, I noticed other people walking through the door. It was Tits and Mel. My smile turned upside down though when to my horror I also saw Shelley The Sheep Girl, Hayley and – wait for it – Kylie, walk in after them. They all gathered around me as I began to choke on my Jim Beam. Marlene started to frantically pat my back.

'Happy birthday, Georgie!' Mel and Tits yelled in unison as they both gave me a bear hug.

To me, bear hugs were the equivalent of Superman being given kryptonite.

When they were finally done, they handed me a gift bag that looked like it could have a bottle of Jimmy in it. It did. Unbeknown to them, they had just been given slight redemption.

'I hope you don't mind all the plus ones,' Mel continued.

I minded.

'You see, Hayley drove us. Kylie was at our house anyway and poor Shelley, her parents left her all alone in the country. She was so sad, I thought she needed cheering up, so here we all are!'

In-fucking-deed.

I finally got the nerve up and glanced at Hayley. I hadn't seen her since the morning we hooked up last year. Annoyingly, I think she might have gotten hotter. Her hair was cut a little shorter and suited her even more. She was wearing a tight black T-shirt, purple jeans and black Converse. I found her staring at my T-shirt, soon realising it was the same Birthday Party shirt I wore the morning she seduced me. I guess I was trying to be ironic by wearing it for my birthday – I didn't wear it for her. It wasn't like I knew I would be seeing her tonight or anything. She smiled at my tee then our eyes met. As usual, our gaze lingered a little too long as everyone else in the room seemed to disappear.

'Happy birthday, Appleby; nice T-shirt.' She grinned.

Kylie was beside her, holding her hand. She looked hot too, but she was a bitch. I'd felt her stupid stare burning me from within. When I finally looked at her, she smiled sarcastically.

'Thanks for the invite, *not*,' she said whilst swaying.

Weirdo; it took all my strength not to lunge at her and bash her head in. Sister Catherine's boxing gloves would definitely have come in handy. Why was she here? Why were any of them here? I only wanted the Scoobies here, even the new recruits I could only handle in small doses. Why does this always happen to me? Why are there always people I hate at my birthdays even when Mother isn't here to invite them?

But it was about to get worse.

'Many happy returns, Georgina, so good to see you,' Shelley pontificated as she stepped forward with her trademark butt sticking out and put a large box covered in pink wrapping paper in my hands. She looked different. I soon realised it was because she had been shorn. Her sheep head looked smaller than it usually did. I wondered how many woollen jumpers her hair had made.

'I took it upon myself to buy you Twister,' she went on. 'My favourite game in the world; perhaps we will play it later!'

I was seriously about to throw up in my mouth when I remembered something.

'Shelley, did you happen to bring any of your parents' Penfolds Grange 1955 by any chance?' I asked her, recalling the lethal vintage she had brought to the school retreat long ago.

Shelley suddenly broke out into a wide smile, revealing uneven teeth and vampire fangs that worried me.

'Yes! How did you know?' she finally yelled, much to my relief. 'There is a box in the car!'

Troy offered to get them. He opened a bottle and put it straight in my hand, no glass required, before being called away by Marlene.

As everyone settled in and mingled, I just stood at the open door miserably taking it all in. A birthday text from Dad brightened my mood momentarily. He apologised for not calling as he was stuck at some conference, but I was just happy for the text and glad he remembered.

I took a swig out of the bottle of wine just as I noticed someone else entering the house through my peripheral vision.

Good God... it was Cute Guy.

I began to choke again. Marlene was on it.

I glanced at Troy, who was at the stereo attempting to put *Bleach* back on. He shrugged and shook his head.

'I'm okay now, Marlene,' I said bluntly. Sensing my mood, she soon disappeared.

Cute Guy was decked out in his usual garb: a dark blue suit, matching shirt and tie; but his hair was scruffy and the glasses were back again. So, it must have been Emily Mears who favoured the Bart church look and contacts; interesting. He was carrying a huge bouquet of flowers and had a big grin on his face. Damn he was gorgeous; if only he understood sarcasm and wasn't the male version of Glenn Close in *Fatal Attraction*.

'Hi, Georgie. Happy birthday,' he said shyly, handing me the flowers.

'Thanks... Justin, so... great to see you. Who told you about my party?'

'Mary-Louise.'

Damn that Mary-Louise! She knows everything!

'How did Mary-Louise find out about it?' I asked calmly, although inside I felt anything but calm.

'Well, your friend Leticia told Mary-Louise who told Emily, who is back for a visit, by the way, but we're not back together...'

Obviously.

'And Emily told *me*. I hope you don't mind me crashing it. It's just I've been trying to see you for a while now, but it's like you work 24/7 at that animal rescue place.'

'No, she doesn't.'

It was Hayley. I gave her the *Georgie Death Stare* in High Volume Definition.

'She only works there a few days a week...' she went on.

I wanted to kill her and kiss her at the same time. I was very conflicted.

'So, Georgie must be lying to you. Will you introduce us, Appleby? Is this your *boyfriend*?'

'Yes.'

Cute Guy beat my 'no'.

'Hi, I'm Justin.' He held out his hand and Hayley shook it limply. I could tell she was jealous, even though it was fine for her to be with Kylie.

'Hi Justin, I'm Hayley.' She looked around to see if the coast was clear of presumably Kylie and her sister before she said, 'I'm the first girl Georgie ever slept with and that wasn't long before you came along.'

'Yes, I have heard of you,' Cute Guy muttered uncomfortably.

I couldn't take it anymore. I ran out the front door as fast as my tipsy legs would carry me and plonked myself on the sand at the ocean's edge.

The salt water smelt inviting as I sat there staring at the sea. An unusually icy summer wind froze my soul as the waves washed over my orange Converse, relentlessly beckoning me to be wrapped in its cold, dark blanket, but the moon was full; watching me, protecting me. Maybe it was Ben up there, but I was scared and not drunk enough, so instead I kept swigging that bottle of wine.

It wasn't long until Troy was sitting beside me.

'You okay?' he asked sweetly.

I said nothing for a while, instead handing him the bottle. He took a swig then promptly started coughing.

'What the hell is this?'

'It's old wine.'

'Really, you sure Shelley's sheep didn't pee in it?'

I began to laugh uncontrollably. God, I loved him.

'So... is it nice to have all your lovers here? And before you ask, no, I had nothing to do with it.'

I shot him a pained look.

'Why are they here? I don't want them here, and bloody Kylie as well! Not to mention a certain Sheep Head. Stupid Mel, I'm so sick of her bringing Shelley everywhere.'

'At least she brought vintage sheep pee with her.' Troy smiled.

I shook my head, staring at the sand.

'Are you coming back in?'

'Maybe later.'

'I don't want to leave you here by yourself,' he said in concern.

'I'll be okay. I'm not gonna kill myself. I just wanna be alone for a while.'

'Okay, but I'm coming back to check on you. You're going to need more sheep pee soon anyway.'

'Get outta here!' I laughed, giving him a push.

I was barely alone for five minutes before I had my next visitor.

It was Hayley.

I gave her the *G.D.S* as she sat down beside me.

'Hey, Georgie, I'm sorry about being a bit of a dick before,' she said innocently.

'Why are you here?' I asked after a long pause.

'Because I'm the designated driver and I… wanted to see you. It's been so long. I'm sorry about Kylie, she was just over at my place like usual and had to come.'

'I'm not in the mood for her shit.'

'Oh, you don't have to worry about her, she just passed out. She drank a bottle of vodka on the way up.'

So that's why she was swaying.

'Tell me about Justin,' Hayley continued.

'What about him?'

'How long have you guys been going out?'

'We're not, he just thinks we are 'cause he's delusional. We had sex once and he became too obsessive so now I'm avoiding him.'

'You had sex?'

'Yes Hayley, we had sex! You're not the only person I've ever been with, so get over yourself!'

I stood up and tried to get the hell away from her as quickly as possible but the combination of bourbon, lethal sheep pee and sand soon had me falling flat on my face.

Hayley came to my rescue, turning me over and laughing as I spat a mouthful of sand at her. I just lay there on my back, comatose, as she leaned over me, gently brushing the sand off my face and hair. I had seen that look in her eye before. I knew what was going to happen next and I was drunkenly ready to give in to it when I heard an angry voice yelling and getting closer. Hayley and I stood just in time seeing a psychotic Kylie frothing at the mouth in front of us.

'I knew it! I knew it! That's why you wanted to come here!' she yelled at Hayley.

'No, I didn't!' Hayley protested.

'Nothing happened,' I deadpanned. Well, it was true, nothing had happened; yet.

'Bullshit! God, it's all so obvious now, how could I have been so stupid?!' Kylie screamed, pacing up and down in the sand. Then her eyes locked on me.

'And you, *you,*' she said venomously, taking a step closer as I began to back away. Hayley jumped between us but one push from Kylie and she went flying. Hayley and I were both skinny short-arses, but Kylie was tall and built like a brick shithouse. I knew I was in big trouble. She kept walking towards me and I kept walking backwards, soon finding my Converse in the ocean. It wasn't long until she had her hands around my neck, had pushed me into the sea and was holding my head under the water. Whenever I was able to pull my head up and catch a breath, I would hear Hayley screaming frantically and trying to pull Kylie off me.

I soon started to fade. I'd swallowed salt water and the alcohol had left me lethargic. The last time I managed to draw a breath I saw blurry people running toward us and then I saw Ben.

# CHAPTER THIRTY-THREE

I suddenly woke in agony as salt water shot from my lungs and out my mouth. The taste of the ocean engulfing me. When my eyes began to focus, I saw Cute Guy leaning over me.

'She's gonna be okay, she's gonna be okay,' I heard him say.

'We should call an ambulance,' said someone else.

'No,' I objected, slowly sitting up.

'We really should, Georgie, just to be on the safe side,' CG said softly.

'No, I'm okay,' I whispered looking up through foggy eyes at Troylene and Hayley, but my potential killer was nowhere in sight.

'Where's Kylie?' I asked, a sudden pang of fear zapping through me.

'It's okay, she ran away after the boys got her off you... shit, I'm so sorry, Georgie,' Hayley whimpered, beginning to sob. Troy put his arm around her.

That was the first time I had ever seen Hayley cry, but I was way too out of it to react.

Cute Guy helped me up.

'Did you give me CPR?' I asked him, suddenly aware of his closeness to me when I woke from the dead.

'Yes, sorry, but I had to. I was the only one that knew CPR. We thought you were a goner.'

I threw myself around his neck. He had, like, saved my life. This was huge.

'We better get you inside, Georgie, you're soaking wet,' Marlene said.

I felt a sudden shiver as Kylie ran over my grave in an alternate universe.

'Don't tell any of the others what happened,' I ordered. 'Especially Mel, and someone needs to get Kylie the fuck out of here.'

'I volunteer to drive her off a cliff and jump out of the car just in time,' Hayley said with a salute.

I smiled at her irresistible quick wit whilst wondering what the ramifications of tonight would really be.

When we got back to the lodge, Shelley, Mel and Tits were playing Twister while Leticia and Prudence looked on in boredom.

'Decide on a swim, did we?' Leticia asked me, making the Twister players all turn around and look, resulting in them falling on top of each other.

'Yep,' I said with a fake smile.

'What were you guys doing out there?' Mel asked suspiciously as she untangled herself from Tits and Shelley. 'And where's Kylie?'

'She went for a walk,' Hayley answered in annoyance as she started to head upstairs with us.

'Why are you all going upstairs?' Mel wouldn't let up.

'Georgie's had a bit to drink, sis, we're taking her for a lie down.'

'Since when did *you* become her best friend?' Mel went on.

'Since now!' Hayley snapped.

Just as we reached my bedroom door, I heard the words I was dreading from Shelley:

'We are ready for a game of Twister when you are, Georgina!'

'Guys, you can leave me to it now,' I said to my Scooby rescuers. 'I'm just gonna get changed and come back down. I'm fine, really.'

'I'll go find Kylie and drive her home and then I'll run over her before she reaches her front door,' Hayley said seriously as everyone laughed. She didn't though. I was a little worried she wasn't joking. 'But I'll have to come back to give the girls a lift home,' she continued. 'If that's okay.'

'Of course it is. I want you to come back,' I said. As we smiled at each other, I noticed Cute Guy cough and look uncomfortable.

After I got changed into my pink penguin PJs (as I didn't bring any other clothes with me) I had a quick crying fit before a few shots of Jim Beam set me straight; bloody Kylie, the bad vibes I got from her were genuine. I don't know what would have happened if Troy and Cute Guy hadn't got her off me. I remembered seeing Ben's face before I passed out, but then nothing. I knew he was around. I usually felt his presence around my birthdays and I'd dream about him more often. I guess it wasn't my time for us to be together again.

A little while later I ventured downstairs. I heard Nirvana's *Bleach* was back on and noticed a group of surfer boys moshing in the lounge room. Troy greeted me at the bottom of the stairs.

'How are you feeling?'

'Fine. I don't need an ambulance, okay?'

'Okay, but I still want you to be checked by a doctor.'

'Yes, Dad.'

'Nice PJs by the way.' He grinned.

'I thought it best to be wearing them when I pass out from alcohol poisoning. I see the guys Leticia invited are here.'

'Yep,' Troy said. 'They seem okay, pretty harmless. One of them seems to have the hots for Shelley!'

'Hmmm, must be into knitwear.'

'Also, we found Kylie,' Troy went on, turning serious. 'She was like a zombie, like someone had turned the lights out in her head. We think she needs serious help. Hayley's driving her home to her parents and Justin went with them in case Kylie had another turn. They're both coming back.'

'Okay,' I said slowly, processing what he said.

'They're pretty cool, those two,' Troy continued. 'They seem to care about you a lot.'

I nodded absentmindedly.

'Anyway, now onto more important business,' he said with a smile, putting his arm around me. 'How would the birthday girl like another drink?'

'Intravenously.'

After the singing of *Happy Birthday* and the devouring of a Snoopy birthday cake I was totally in awe of, I was intercepted by the surfer boys who wanted to meet me. As Troy introduced me to them, I noticed the three of them seemed to be pretty out of it.

'Hey pyjama girl, it's your birthday huh?' the blonde one with a goatee who went by the name of Stu asked. 'How about we have something special to celebrate?'

He grabbed his backpack from the couch and pulled out something that made my knees turn to jelly, promptly followed by my mouth letting out a blood-curdling scream.

# CHAPTER THIRTY-FOUR

He was holding one of Sister Catherine's pot dolls.

I took the doll from him and shook it. I heard something was inside so I threw it to the floor and watched it break into a million pieces. I soon spied a bag of weed amongst the rubble, quickly picking it up whilst holding Tits at bay.

'Ah, you know the dolls, huh? Pretty cool, don't ya reckon?' Stu grinned.

'Where did you get this?' I asked in a voice that sounded so possessed Stu backed away a little.

'From the shop in town, Lorne Clippings, the souvenir shop.'

'Do you know the woman who supplies them with these dolls?'

'Woman? No dude, I don't know the supplier, all I know is it costs fifty dollars a doll, the stuff is A Grade and they aren't on the shelf, you have to ask the guy behind the counter for a "special doll" and he'll sell it to you.'

I glanced at the Scoobies who had congregated around me and had heard everything.

'Guys, Sister Catherine must live nearby! Troy and I are going to that souvenir shop tomorrow. We're gonna catch that satanic witch after all!'

As the Scoobies started to cheer, I felt so proud standing there in my pink penguin PJs.

***

The next morning my hangover accompanied me downstairs. I also had a sore throat and red marks on my neck from being choked by Kylie; yet another nightmare memory to add to the collection. Apart from that I felt okay. I guess I probably should have been checked out by paramedics, seeing as I could have drowned, but I wasn't out for long, so whatever. Troy would be dragging me to a GP soon anyway. There was no way I'd be able to get out of that.

As I walked into the lounge, I noticed Leticia and Prudence had gone but I knew they wanted an update on the souvenir shop as soon as I had one. The surfer boys had gone too, but I was surprised to see Tits, Mel and Shelley asleep on the couch and armchairs. Didn't Hayley come back for them after I had gone to bed? And what about Cute Guy, where was he? I looked out the window, spotting his Toyota in the driveway, and began to worry something had happened to them. Had Kylie come to and veered Hayley's car off a cliff, killing all three of them? I started to panic and shook Mel to wake her up.

'Georgie, what are you doing? I was asleep,' Mel said with a yawn.

'Didn't Hayley come back with Justin? His car is still here! Did something happen to them?!' I said in a frenzy.

'It's okay, Georgie,' Mel said softly. 'Hayley rang me after you went to bed saying they were too tired to drive back here last night and were gonna come this morning instead… it was weird they had to drive Kylie home, though, and she looked so out of it. What happened on the beach? You were there.'

'Oh, nothing, I think Hayley and Kylie had a fight,' I lied. 'I don't think they're together anymore.'

'Shit, really?!' Mel cried, wide-eyed.

'Did Hayley drive Justin home after dropping off Kylie at her parents?' I asked, ignoring Mel's reaction to her sister's break-up.

'I think so,' Mel said slowly, giving me a weird look.

'So, she has to pick him up before she comes here.'

'No, that's right, she said she was gonna crash at his place 'cause she was too tired to drive herself home.'

I felt weird about that; those two alone, together and both absolutely gorgeous specimens of their species. He was straight and single and she was bi and now single as well... *oh God no, no way, you're just over-thinking this, Georgie...* but what if they started to drink red wine and discussed the insane events of the evening and found a connection, besides me; an Aquarius/Libra connection, the same connection I had with Cute Guy, the air sign connection I had with both of them, and then they kissed and kissed again and ended up in bed...

'Earth to Georgie,' Mel said, searching my face.

I came to and shot her a fake smile.

'Hey, wouldn't it be funny if those two got together?' Mel grinned.

Had she just read my mind?

'I mean, Justin's single and Hayley's single now too. I think they'd make a cute couple. I was secretly hoping Hayley would go back to guys anyway.'

'Why? I didn't know you were a homophobe.'

'I'm not!' Mel said defensively. 'But Hayley's my sister, it's just weird she suddenly became gay.'

Weird indeed; I wondered how Mel would feel knowing I was weird too, and that her sister and I had been weird together.

There was a knock on the door. I jumped up and flung it open. There stood Cute Guy wearing a freshly ironed, crisp white shirt and Hayley wearing what she had worn last night.

'Speak of the Devil!' Mel yelled from her armchair.

I stood there looking them both up and down, giving them the once over, looking for a clue in their faces that would give away any sexy time between them, but they both looked normal and just smiled at me as I stood there in my dishevelled pink penguin PJs and messy bed hair.

'Kylie's at her parents,' Hayley whispered, not wanting the others to hear. By now Tits and Shelley had been woken up too. 'We told her folks what happened. They said this isn't the first time she's tried to hurt someone.'

'You mean kill someone!' I interjected.

'Kill someone,' Hayley corrected, her blue eyes narrowing. 'Let's just say she's being put out to pasture for a long, long time so you won't have to worry about her doing anything to you ever again.'

I sighed in relief.

'How are you anyway, Georgie?' Cute Guy asked. 'Are you okay?'

I nodded just as Mel strolled over to us.

'Hello, you two.' She smirked.

Oh dog.

'So, what happened with Kylie last night? Why did you guys have to take her home? She looked so weird; spill.'

'She didn't feel well, Mel, that's all,' Hayley said shortly.

'Georgie said you guys had a fight and broke up,' Mel went on.

I suddenly realised Hayley and I hadn't got our stories straight so I shot her a panicked look.

She was on it.

'That's right. That's why Kylie didn't feel well, 'cause we had a fight and broke up and Justin just came along for the ride,' Hayley quipped, slapping Justin on the back, making him cough.

'I see. So, tell me, is love in the air?' Mel asked in a stupid baby voice as she glanced at both of them.

She was beyond annoying.

'Between us?' Cute Guy asked in surprise, pointing at Hayley then himself. 'No, I don't think so. I think there's more love in the air between us and Georgie.'

SHIT!!!

The next hour or more was spent calming Mel down due to the fact she literally, yes, literally vomited when she found out there had/ has been something going on between her sister and myself. I swear the way she was acting was almost as if she thought it was incest. I guess I kind of knew this day was coming, not that I was ready for it, not that anyone would ever have been ready for it, as obviously Mel wasn't. After all the vomit and tears there was a quick exit from Hayley (who said she would call me later, not sure I wanted that, well, maybe a little sure; I wasn't sure) and her sister who now hated me and Tits who had to get back to John Junior; and Shelley, not that she mattered, and Justin, sweet innocent Justin, who jumped into his Toyota and took off back to Melbourne like a banshee without a cause. As I stood there frozen, in my dishevelled pink penguin PJs and messy bed hair, Troylene yawned their way downstairs and asked what was for breakfast.

***

As I drove Troylene to the souvenir shop, I filled them in on the morning's unsightly events.

'That's pretty full on,' Troy said as he watched me seriously from the passenger seat. 'Do you think Mel will ever speak to you again?'

'I dunno,' I muttered. 'She was pretty sickened. The way she was acting you'd think I had the hots for *her* or something, which I sure don't, yuck.'

'I guess it must be hard for her though,' Marlene piped up from the back seat. 'I mean, it's her best friend and her sister.'

'It's only hard for her 'cause she's a homophobe. I'm sure she wouldn't care if I was a guy. I don't give a toss what sex someone is, it's the person I'm interested in.'

'Not everyone is that open-minded, Georgie,' Marlene mused.

'Yeah, well, she can fuck off then. All I know is everything has gone to shit and the Scoobies are slowly splintering.'

'Hey, there it is!' Troy yelled, ending the sombre mood. I looked out the window as we passed a decrepit looking souvenir shop that was desperate for a paint job.

Marlene decided three people asking for pot dolls was one too many and opted to stay in the car. As Troy and I walked into the souvenir shop, we observed the usual sad, touristy trinkets any seaside store would carry, but they weren't very appealing. They were covered in dust and the store itself looked as though it was rarely cleaned. It also had a strange smell. I wouldn't say it was pot, although it could have been pot mixed with incense.

I gave Troy a look and whispered, 'Obviously a drug front,' before heading toward the counter. A tall guy with a scraggly beard who resembled Shaggy from *Scooby-Doo* looked up at us through thin spectacles. The type Sister Catherine didn't know had even been invented.

'Can I help you?' he asked.

I looked around suspiciously before leaning forward.

'I'm after a *special doll*.'

He looked at me like I was an idiot.

'A what?'

'A *special doll*,' I repeated, starting to get nervous that Stu the surfer boy had got the instructions wrong.

There was a long pause while Shaggy looked both Troy and me up and down.

'Um… we don't sell blow up dolls in this shop, you might want to try the internet,' he said as he rolled his eyes and went to the backroom.

Before I was able to utter another word, Troy had whisked me out of the shop.

'Troy! What are you doing? I'm sure that stupid surfer boy just stuffed up what I had to say!'

'Marlene just texted me, this is the wrong shop.'

'What do you mean?'

As Marlene got out of the car, she pointed across the road to a store with a sign out front saying *Lorne Clippings. Souvenirs and bric-a-brac.*

We filled Marlene in on what had happened in the wrong store and promptly all burst out laughing after Troy said, 'Would you like a blow-up doll with your pot doll?'

When we had come to, we ran across the road, this time taking Marlene with us, and entered the right souvenir shop. This store was clean; it was actually sparkling clean. Everything was dusted and immaculate. After waiting until a few customers had left, we approached the counter, seeing a well-groomed man in his fifties who looked like he could be a bank teller – stereotypes; oh, sweet stereotypes.

'Yes, love,' he said.

I took a deep breath, not looking forward to going through this again.

'Hi, I'm after a *special doll*,' I said in a half whisper.

His eyes narrowed as he looked the three of us over.

'You're not cops, are you? You don't look like cops,' he said suspiciously.

'Of course we're not cops, look at us!' I said in annoyance.

'Okay.'

He went to the front door and locked it, turning the open sign to closed, then led us to the back of the shop, to a door which he unlocked with a key. When we were all inside the tiny room, he shut the door after us and took a large box from a shelf, opening it. I found it hard to breathe and suddenly had a pang of '*my god, what if he is a serial killer and is going to take an axe out of that box*' fear zap through me, but it rapidly diminished when I saw the inside of the box contained Sister Catherine's pot dolls all right; assorted shapes and sizes, all with those creepy eyes that opened and closed. I searched through them all, disappointed to not find mine.

'You don't happen to have a doll that looks exactly like me, do you?' I asked as I showed him the picture I'd taken on my mobile.

'Um… no, love.'

I sighed in disappointment.

'Georgie, isn't there another question you want to ask?' Troy said, trying to move things along.

'Yeah… look, I need to get in touch with the woman who supplies you with these dolls,' I said matter-of-factly.

The guy gave me a panicked look and quickly put the box back on the shelf. 'I thought you said you weren't cops!'

'We're not, I promise,' I said, trying to calm him down. 'We just need this woman's contact details, she's an old friend of my mother's. You see, my mother died recently and we need to tell her.'

My lie was successful.

'Oh,' he said softly. 'I'm sorry for your loss… look, I don't have her details, she's very secretive, but she delivers here on the first Monday of every month. You'll have to come back in three weeks.'

'Damn!' I yelled.

'Or if you prefer, leave me your number and I'll get her to call you when she comes in.'

'No! I have to see her in person, so, three Mondays away, what date is that?'

'The fifth.'

'Okay, does she come in at a particular time?'

'Midday, always midday.'

'Great, we'll be back then, but don't say anything to her!'

'All right, love.'

We quickly left the shop and stood out the front in a Scooby circle.

'So, what's the plan now, Georgie?' Marlene asked in excitement.

'Well, we're coming back with the cops in three weeks and we're gonna take down Sister Catherine once and for all!'

# CHAPTER THIRTY-FIVE

By the time we got back to Melbourne it was already late afternoon and raining as usual. After dropping off Troy, Marlene and I picked up an absolutely mental Chocky from Mary's then finally got back to Purgatory Palace, throwing our overnight bags on the floor in exhaustion.

'Can you hear that?' Marlene asked in a whisper.

I concentrated and, sure enough, heard talking coming from the kitchen. I quickly grabbed Chocky to shush her from barking and shot Marlene a panicked look.

'Burglars?'

But it was the lesser of two evils, just, as a waft of Chanel No. 5 floated out of the kitchen, soon followed by Mother, who was accompanied by an expensively suited old man with a ridiculously tall quiff of grey hair.

Mother looked different. Her face seemed fuller, like she had put on weight, and her eyes, which would usually remind me of a Bloody

Mary minus the celery, had morphed into a Bloody Mary minus the tomato juice and vodka. Well, she did have green eyes.

'Hello, Georgina, many happy returns! Oh, your friend is with you again, how nice.'

Mother sounded weird. I soon realised it was because she wasn't drunk. She also still had no clue Marlene was Marlene. Even sober, Mother thought she was someone else. Bizarre.

'This is my gentlemen friend, Mr Deveraux. He is a doctor at the clinic.'

'Very nice to make your acquaintance, ladies,' the Quack said with a bow. Chocky had none of that, though, and lunged, nearly knocking him over. My pooch not only managed to mess up his Quack Quiff, she left muddy paw prints on his suit; so proud. One thing about Choc is she could always pick an arsehole.

'That damn dog!'

The bitch was back.

'Are you all right, Sebastian?' Mother wailed.

Kill.

Me.

Now.

'Yes, Alicia dear, dogs will be dogs after all,' he said, brushing off his suit whilst giving me evils at the same time.

Great; another prick I would no doubt be forced to live with.

'So, where did you go for your birthday, Georgina?' Mother asked.

Of course, she would never consider calling my mobile. As far as she was concerned, it was still the swinging 60s and they hadn't been invented yet.

'I left the clinic early to celebrate with you,' she continued, leaving me no room for response. 'The house was empty and Marlene has disappeared as well! Where is that wretched maid?'

Marlene and I glanced at each other and remained silent. I began to think Mother shouldn't even know that the stunning creature beside me was Marlene and Marlene no longer needed to put up with Mother's shit. I suspected Marlene agreed.

Suspected that is.

'Marlene died, Mother,' I suddenly blurted out. I don't know where that came from, but it must have been from somewhere. Marlene shot me a horror movie look.

'What?! Nobody told me!' Mother yelled.

'You'll have to find a new maid now. Samantha and I are going up to my room,' I said abruptly, pushing Marlene up the stairs with Chocky in hot pursuit.

'What happened?! When is the funeral? Where can I pay my respects?' Mother called after us.

Ignoring her, I slammed my bedroom door.

Marlene switched to panic mode.

'Georgie! What did you do? I live here! This is my job! What am I supposed to do now, pretend I'm someone called Samantha?'

'Don't stress, Marlene, it'll be sorted. You can never go backwards in life, you know. You've gone forwards; you can't go backwards now.'

Marlene just stood there silently, deep in thought, watching me as I lay on my bed while Chocky nibbled my nose.

'You're right,' she finally said. 'I think I need to move out. I have to see Troy.'

With that she was gone.

Oh shit. I didn't expect that to happen. What have I done? So now it was just me, Chocky, Mother and *Sebastian?*

Fuck.

I didn't have time to mull over the problem I had just created as I was late for my afternoon shift at SMAR. When I got there, I froze in the doorway when I saw Hayley standing behind the counter with Mary.

Great, she wasn't even supposed to work today.

'Georgie, Georgie, thank God you're here!' Mary cried in desperation. 'Hayley has to pick up four dogs on death row and the girl that helps her has broken her leg. Can you go with her please, darl?'

'O-of course,' I stuttered.

'Let's go,' Hayley said bluntly, walking out of the shop.

I followed her to a white van and jumped in the passenger seat. She turned the ignition and we were off. As usual she said nothing as we drove. I wanted to say so much, but instead sat there like a stunned mullet for over half an hour until my mouth forced itself open.

'You don't usually work today,' I finally blurted out, then immediately felt ridiculous that that was all I could come up with.

She said nothing.

Either she was pissed off at me or was having a shit day. I was pretty convinced it was the former. I'm sure Mel kept crapping on about how disgusted she was about us in the car all the way home from Lorne and then Hayley had to unexpectedly see me. She probably regretted letting anything happen between us. I'm sure she thought it wasn't worth the hassle it had created.

'Are you all right, after what happened?' she finally said.

'I'm fine.'

'Good. Look, you know my sister is an idiot,' she said, still fixated on the road ahead.

I said nothing. I didn't know what to say to that and thought it best I let her continue to talk; if she wanted to, that was.

'She is, like, disowning us now, that's what she said on the way home.'

'What does that mean?'

'It's pretty obvious what that means! I don't know what the fuck is wrong with her. She's not in love with you, is she?' Hayley asked as she shot me an angry look.

'No!' I protested.

'Is that the reason?' Hayley continued, much to my displeasure. 'Did something ever happen with you guys?'

'No, it didn't! Mel's straight and I've never been attracted to her!' I yelled, sick of where this conversation was heading.

'But we're sisters! We look a little alike!'

'Maybe you do, but the difference is you're hot and she's not!'

Oops. Did that actually come out of my mouth? My face turned the colour of Mother's Bloody Mary – you guessed it – without the celery.

Hayley glanced at me and burst out laughing. I did the same.

'Well, I'm glad that's been established.' She smirked, eyes back on the road.

'Ah, yep,' I said moronically.

'So, tell me,' she continued, sounding ominous. 'What's going on with Justin? He's obviously still into you.'

I thought about how Hayley had just spent the night at Cute Guy's house and how I'd imagined them drinking too much red wine then realising how hot they both were… in my head. Ignoring her question, I asked my own.

'Did you guys have a good laugh about me when you crashed at his place?'

Hayley said nothing, just kept staring at the road ahead.

'Did you drink wine?' I found myself blurting out.

Idiot!

'Yes. How did you know, were you spying through the window?'

It was all getting too weird now. Hayley was a shit-stirrer no doubt, as was I, but my discomfort was beginning to hit the red zone and I had nowhere to go but jump out of a car doing 100, which would result in me ending up in hospital or worse. She wasn't gonna come clean so I had to.

'Okay, look, I'm gonna tell you the truth,' I said, taking a deep breath. 'I have feelings for Justin... and I have feelings for you.'

'Who do you like more?' she asked.

'I don't know!' I yelled in confusion.

Silence followed, which I needed to break.

'So, did you and Justin have a good laugh about me when you crashed at his place or what?'

'We didn't talk about you at all, Georgie,' she finally said, admitting defeat. 'We talked about Kylie and what happened with her mental breakdown, that's all, and by the way, this whole thing has really taken its toll on me. I had feelings for her, you know, and now she is basically in the nuthouse indefinitely because she tried to kill you. Think about it. It's pretty full-on shit.'

I remained silent, embarrassed of my childishness, although the fact I was the person Kylie had tried to kill had obviously had an effect on me too, but now wasn't the time to mention it.

'Anyway,' she continued. 'As far as you, me and Justin are concerned, you'll be glad to hear I'm opting out of this love triangle. Mary needs someone to run her shelter in Adelaide, so I'm outta here.'

I suddenly felt sick.

'What about Uni?' I asked in desperation.

'Who cares?! It's a part-time Arts course! I'm gonna be running this shelter, I'll be getting paid a full-time wage. This is what I wanna do. I'm gone.'

I wish I was gone.

After we picked up the dogs and dropped them back at the shelter, Hayley made a swift getaway without so much as a goodbye. By the time I finished my shift it was late and I went home feeling like crap. As soon as I got out of my car, the heavens opened and I got absolutely drenched. Yet again, the Melbourne rain gods were just biding their time with their buckets. I unlocked the front door and threw myself into the house, pathetically trying to slam the door behind me but I don't think it even closed. I didn't care.

Chocky greeted me with her usual exuberance but lucky for me, Mother and the Quack were nowhere to be found. I remembered some posh dinner was mentioned earlier which meant I probably wouldn't see them at all tonight, thank dog. I dragged myself up the stairs, noticing a note pinned to my door. It was written by Marlene. Oh, shit I had forgotten about the problem I'd caused by telling Mother she was dead.

The note said:

> *Dear Georgie, sorry to do this to you but after telling Mrs Appleby I had died, I didn't feel comfortable living at the house anymore. I could have pretended to be your friend Samantha for a while but it wouldn't have worked. I'm staying with Troy and his mum for the moment but no hard feelings, okay? It was probably all meant to be and time I moved out anyway. Like you said, you can never go backwards in life. You've gone forwards, you can't go backwards. You know Troy and I love you and hope to see you soon.*

I flung open my bedroom door and fell onto the bed, soon realising I was totally alone in that macabre mansion. No more Marlene, sweet, sweet Marlene the meek maid who had become my second-best friend, who I had given a makeover to, whom my best friend had fallen in love with. She was gone, and in a way, Troy was gone too and Justin had gone and Hayley was going and Ben... Ben left a long time ago.

I wanted to see my dad so much but he was in Sydney. He had gone, too. I felt completely and utterly alone.

I hugged Chocky as hard as I could and started to cry uncontrollably. She felt my pain as she always did and started to do back flips on the bed until I laughed but my laughter didn't last long. I went downstairs and opened the door of the liquor cabinet. Jim Beam stared back at me. I started to do the one thing I knew I was good at.

# CHAPTER THIRTY-SIX

I woke up in shock, taking a massive breath of sterilised air whilst staring at a white ceiling with tiny cracks that looked unfamiliar to me. Then I realised I was in bed, a hospital bed. Before I had time to scream, I felt a hand take mine. The hand was warm and gentle. My eyes followed the hand to its owner and I sighed in relief when I saw Troy.

'What the hell,' I muttered with barely any voice.

'Shhh, don't freak out. You're okay, Georgie, everything's okay.'

'What happened?'

'You, ah, had a bit too much to drink last night. They had to pump your stomach.'

'What?! I don't remember anything…'

'Of course you don't, you were passed out. You had pretty bad alcoholic poisoning, Bingey.'

I lay there for a minute trying to take it all in. I remembered getting the bottles of Jim Beam from the liquor cabinet and starting to drink in bed but after that it all became a blur.

'Who found me? I was alone in the house.'

'Me.'

'You?'

'Marlene told me about the note she left you and how bad she felt about it, so I went round to see how you were. The front door was open and when I got to your room, well, it wasn't pretty, so I had no choice but to ring 911.'

I felt like death, the most death feeling I have ever felt apart from when Kylie nearly killed me and here he was, still making me laugh.

And well, yeah, he saved my life… again.

'Well thank dog for 911,' I said with a chuckle but Troy's expression remained serious.

'There's something else, Georgie.'

'What?'

'Chocky got hurt.'

'What?! No!' I screamed at the top of my lungs whilst trying to get out of bed.

'It's okay, she's all right, she's at the vet,' he continued, holding my arm to steady me.

'What happened?' I asked, tears streaming down my cheeks.

'After the ambulance took you away, I found her in the kitchen. There was glass on the floor and her paws were bleeding pretty badly. I took her to the twenty-four-hour vet. They stitched her up and kept her overnight for observation. I have to pick her up soon. Do you remember what happened?'

'I don't remember,' I sobbed.

I didn't. I remembered nothing. I must have broken a glass and left it on the floor because I was so drunk. I hurt Chocky. My baby. My rock. My best friend in the entire world. I hurt her because I was drunk, because I'm an alcoholic, just like Mother. I picked on

Mother's drinking but I did exactly the same thing, minus the pink feather boa.

Rehab helped her. Maybe it would help me? No, I couldn't stand it. I had to go cold turkey. It was the only way. Fuck. What if Chocky had died? I would die too because I would never forgive myself. I couldn't do this anymore. Enough. Enough. Enough.

'Well, luckily Choc is okay, but why did you want to drink yourself to death?' Troy asked sternly.

I remained silent, a hundred thoughts entering, leaving and re-entering my mind.

'Was it because Marlene moved out of the house?'

'No! She was the icing... just the icing on a cake of abandonment,' I said quietly.

'Nice to hear you're still poetic after being on the brink of death.' He grinned just as Marlene came into the room holding a huge Snoopy soft toy with a balloon attached that said *Get Well Soon*. I smiled at how sweet she always was to me.

'Georgie, are you okay? Did Troy tell you about Chocky?'

I nodded.

'Good. Chocky's fine. She'll be okay. Here, I got this for you, I hope you like it.'

She handed me the Snoopy and I gave it a big hug. Hugging Snoopy was never a problem for me.

'Thanks. I love it.'

A middle-aged nurse, whose hair was cut into a conservative bob with a fringe so straight you could use it as a ruler, entered and smiled when she saw I was awake.

'How are you feeling, Georgina?' she asked in a matronly tone.

'Okay.' I could not be bothered to correct her about what name I preferred.

'You were lucky your friend found you when he did. I dread to think what would have happened, silly girl.'

The nurse turned her attention to Troy.

'I just mentioned Georgina's near-drowning incident to the doctor as well, so he will be giving her a thorough examination. Thank you for providing us with this information.'

Told you Troy would make sure I was checked over after that horror. Lucky for me I was already in hospital.

'Now, are there any next of kin you want notified?' she asked me.

'These people are my next of kin. Water can be thicker than blood when it's an ice cube.'

Troylene smiled.

The nurse looked confused, no doubt thinking I was high on some medication and not realising I was actually just weird.

'All right then… the doctor will be here soon and the psychologist will be talking to you as well.'

'Why do I have to talk to a shrink?' I asked in annoyance.

'Well, after drinking the amount of alcohol you did, young lady, she needs to know whether you had actually wanted to wake up.'

With that, the nurse was gone.

'Did you want to wake up?' Troy asked seriously.

'Yes… no. I dunno!' I yelled, starting to get upset.

'We should let Georgie rest now,' Marlene whispered to Troy.

He nodded and gave me a kiss on the forehead before they left the room.

*** 

After I was examined by the doctor and talked to by the shrink, they decided to let me go home. The encounter with the shrink was underwhelming. She couldn't get a lot out of me. As if I was gonna give a stranger my life story. I was basically ordered to rest up minus the alcohol; which was fine by me. When I got back to Purgatory Palace, Marlene was quick to remove all the booze from the house and even started tidying up.

It was already late afternoon and Mother and the Quack were still nowhere to be seen. They had no idea what had happened to me; that I was grateful for.

Troy finally got back from the vet with Chocky, who had a lampshade around her head so she wouldn't rip the bandages and stitches out of her paws. I lay on the floor of the hallway with her for ages, bawling my eyes out while she attempted to kiss my tears away, which was hard seeing as she had a lampshade around her head.

After being reunited, Choc and I eventually made it to the lounge room. While Marlene was in the kitchen making hot chocolate and Chocky fell asleep on my lap, I glanced over at Troy, who was sitting on the couch immersed in the boxing match on TV.

'Hayley's leaving,' I blurted out.

He turned the TV off and gave me his undivided attention; a true friend.

'What do you mean? Where's she going?'

'Adelaide. She got a job running an animal shelter over there. She's quitting Uni. I told her I had feelings for her but she doesn't even care about me.'

'I'm sure she does, Georgie, but she's been through a lot lately – all that stuff with Kylie, she probably just wants a clean break.'

'What about me?!' I cried. The melody of that damn song was in my head, of course. There was no way anyone could utter those words without them being sung in your head. 'Everyone seems to forget I nearly died!'

'And you nearly died again,' Troy said sternly.

'Maybe it'll be third time lucky,' I said, glaring at him, waiting for a rise.

But I didn't get one.

Silence and then…

'Marlene and I are going to stay at Purgatory Palace for a while, Georgie,' he announced, ignoring what I'd just said. 'She will even pretend to be Samantha, seeing as you decided to kill Marlene. We just don't think you should be alone right now.'

I was in such a shit mood, but hearing those words ignited a fire within me that made me feel so warm. I couldn't show it though.

'Okay,' was all I could muster.

Troy smiled as he made himself more comfortable on the couch.

'So, what's the go with Justin then? Is he still interested?'

'That's doubtful. After stupid Mel's blow-up when she found out about me and Hayley, he did a runner. I'm sure he's sick to death of me. Oh, shit, that reminds me, Tits and John's wedding is in a few weeks, which means Mel will be there. Great. Are you still coming? I can't go alone.'

'I'm going,' Troy said quickly, before turning serious. 'Georgie,' he said, leaning forward. The guru words were coming. 'You need to ask yourself which one of them you love: is it Justin or is it Hayley?'

I stared at the carpet in silence for a long time after that; love? What was love? Had I felt love? I didn't know. I'm sure what Troylene were experiencing was love but had I ever experienced it? All I had ever done was sleep with a person once and then it all went to shit. Was I in love with one of them? I didn't even know. Maybe I wasn't capable of being in love.

He never got my answer as Marlene walked into the lounge, distracting us. I took a deep breath and smiled. The smell of hot chocolate would always take me back to when I was a kid and Ben and I would wait in anticipation while Dad made it for us. Without fail, the aroma would always take me back there.

As I took my first sip of delicious frothy chocolate, my tastebuds immediately went on hiatus as I heard the front door open and saw Mother and the Quack standing before us. Chocky woke and gave him a growl. The Quack gave Choc a strange look due to her new accessory, but thankfully said nothing. Mother didn't even notice. No surprises there.

'Oh, hello everyone,' Mother said with a fake smile before turning her attention to me. 'Georgina, you simply *must* tell me how Marlene died and where I can pay my respects! We weren't very close but she was the best maid I ever did have!'

Marlene and I glanced at each other. I knew what needed to be done.

'Mother, Marlene isn't dead. I was just joking. *This* is Marlene,' I said, gesturing toward her.

'What? Samantha is Marlene? I'm confused!' Mother wailed.

'Marlene just had a makeover, this is her!'

I was well and truly over this conversation by now.

'Oh!' Mother said, leaning forward glaring at Marlene. 'I see it now. Well, thank God for that, and Georgina, saying someone has died when they haven't died is not a very nice thing to do!'

'No, it isn't,' the Quack chimed in.

I gave him the *Georgie Death Stare*. He unlocked his judgemental gaze from mine and instead looked uncomfortable as he fiddled with his purple cravat.

'So, Marlene, now things are back to normal,' Mother begun. 'I need you to get rid of all the alcohol in the house. I am in recovery, you know. Sebastian said that needs to be done.'

'I have already done that, Mrs Appleby,' Marlene squeaked, curtseying. I suddenly saw her transform back into Marlene the meek maid before my very eyes. That's what Mother did to her. It was heartbreaking.

'Good, good, oh and Georgina,' Mother went on. 'Before I forget… the police called me. They have had a tip on the whereabouts of your stepfather and his mistress.'

'Oh really?' I said hopefully.

'Yes, they aren't giving too much away but it seems the slimy leech will hopefully be caught soon and maybe some of your money will be recovered. I will let you know if I hear anything. Sebastian and I will be upstairs in the parlour. Marlene, can you bring us some of that hot chocolate you made? Good evening to you all.'

With that, the two pompous fools sashayed upstairs.

'Well, I guess I'm moving back in as myself now that I'm not dead!' Marlene laughed.

'Yeah, sorry about all that… also… I just need to say something.'

'What is it, Georgie?' Marlene asked quietly.

'Well, it's just, it was sad seeing you regress back into a maid with Mother just now,' I said seriously. 'You've come so far from being that person.'

'Oh, don't worry about that, it's just how I am with her. I'm still a different person now, thanks to you.'

I smiled then glanced at Troy.

'Do you mind if Marlene moves back in permanently? You guys weren't thinking of moving in together after she stayed with you and Mrs J?' I asked him.

'No, no, Marlene was just going to live with me and Mum; very romantic, and I'm still staying here for a while to make sure my Grasshopper is all right.'

'Okay,' I said with a big grin, happy to not be alone in that hellhole anymore. Mother and the Quack didn't count.

'Good news about your stepdad though,' Marlene continued as she sat down next to Troy.

'Yeah, I hope they get him, the little prick. He's been on the run for nearly a year with his secretary. I bet he's spent all my money buying her leopard print dresses.'

'Well, we're going to take down Sister Catherine soon, at least that's something,' Troy said brightly.

'Yeah, I can't wait for that. I just wish I knew where my voodoo doll was.'

'She'll probably have it on her. It'll all work out, Georgie, just wait and see,' Marlene said.

I prayed she was right.

# CHAPTER THIRTY-SEVEN

So here I was, at yet another wedding I didn't want to be at. First, it was Mother and NPP – wow, didn't that last – now Tits and stupid Sleazy Toothless John. Whose wedding would I have to suffer through next? Mother and the Quack?

I shuddered in my salmon pink puffy dress. Yes, the bloated peach was back. I was all ready to wear black jeans and a purple shirt until I found out the wedding attire had been changed to ridiculously formal by Tits' mum at the last minute or you weren't let in.

Sigh.

Tits and John didn't have a lot of money, unlike my Frivolous Family, so at least the wedding wasn't a pompous farce. The ceremony itself was held in a tiny nondescript church near Tits' house in Bentleigh.

As Troy, his dapper suit and I sat down at one of the pews, I spotted Mel and her pet sheep sitting a few rows in front of us, but luckily Mel hadn't seen me, which I was thankful for. I wondered whether Hayley had left for Adelaide yet and whether I would ever see her again.

The wedding was boring, as all weddings are. John Junior stole the show. He was dressed in a tiny grey suit with a bright red bow tie and a smile you could die for. Luckily, he looked more like Tits than John, apart from having teeth issues, that is.

To save money, the reception was held at Tits' house. When Troy and I eventually got there, I'd hoped Tits' mum had already done the vacuuming.

So far, I had managed to avoid talking to John, so my boobs got a break. They were a little more obvious in my salmon pink puffy dress. But there was plenty of other cleavage on display for him to ogle. I guess that's why he married a girl whose nickname was Tits. I took a deep breath, knowing it would be hard to keep hiding from Mel, and I was right. I spotted her walking toward Troy and me with Shelley in tow but she actually stopped to talk and didn't look like she was going to axe murder me.

'Hey,' she said uncomfortably.

'Hey,' I said back.

'Shelley!' Troy gestured theatrically, outstretching his arm. 'Would you like to escort me to get some drinks?'

My guru as usual sensed the need for me and my current nemesis to be alone.

'Of course, I would, a gentleman like you!' Shelley gushed, twirling in her frilly yellow gown that made her look like a sheep dressed as a lemon.

Mel looked me up and down with raised eyebrows before saying, 'Nice frock.'

'You can talk!' I laughed taking in her white ball gown. 'Isn't that your deb dress, or are you getting married today too?'

'Shut up, it's all I had.'

\*\*\*

*Memories came flooding back of the horrific Debutante Ball that Mother had forced me to do with Ugly Guy, who she partnered me to dance with, resulting in the framed photo Mother still had of us in the lounge room. Me wearing that hideous white ball gown with Ugly Guy next to me in his tux; there for everyone to see like we were passionately in love and it was our wedding photo or something. I had lost count how many people said they didn't know I was married. I hated that picture to high heaven but the old crow never let me get rid of it.*

*Don't worry I'll spare you the rest of the flashback as I just don't want to think about it anymore.*

***

'Hayley's gone to Adelaide, you probably heard,' Mel continued.

'Yeah, she told me she was leaving.'

'We had a big talk before she left. She said I needed to get over myself... so... I have.'

I watched Mel, silently waiting for her next fateful words.

'I'm sorry!' she cried. 'I dunno why I freaked out, it was just weird, but I was a jerk and it's none of my business if you guys get together or not. I just wanna be friends again, like we used to be, is that cool?'

I watched her genuine expression, complete with sorrowful red eyebrows and folded. I wished I'd had a Mars Bar to give her as a peace offering.

'Of course it's cool, you idiot, but don't hug me!' I said, in case she felt the need.

She burst out laughing and gave my salmon pink puffy shoulder a friendly punch instead.

Then I saw Tits' mum heading toward us, decked out in all her gaudy gold finery, complete with blown-out hair that would make Leticia proud. That reminded me that I hadn't seen Leticia and Prudence yet and wondered if they had been invited.

Tits' mum's face always reminded me of a horse, I wasn't sure why. Then the vacuuming topless memory was back.

Shudder – or should that be udder?

'Come on, girls, Titania is going to throw her bouquet! Let's see which one of you will be married next!' she squealed in ridiculous excitement before galloping away.

Mel and I gave each other a serious look before starting to laugh.

'Your memory of Tits' mum's tits is back again, isn't it?' Mel asked with a grin.

I nodded just as Troy reappeared with our drinks, mine of the soft variety, and no Sheep Head.

'Where's Shelley?' Mel asked.

'She ran to catch the bouquet,' Troy said.

Tits' mum was back.

'Girls, come on!'

She started pushing us over to where a group of girly girls and Shelley stood waiting to catch a stupid bunch of flowers that meant they would be the first to marry Prince Charming out of all these other sad spinsters. As I stood amongst the gaggle of cackling hens, I recognised the back of the girls in front of me and tapped them on the shoulder.

'Georgie!' Leticia and Prudence yelled simultaneously.

I could describe their dresses but am worried doing so would give me an aneurysm.

'We were looking for you!' Leticia continued. 'What happened at the souvenir shop in Lorne? You never gave us an update!'

Oh shit, I had forgotten about that.

'A lot happened. I'll tell you later.'

It was then that I spotted Emily Mears, in bright red from top to toe, walking toward the hen house holding... wait for it... Cute Guy's hand and yes, his hair was back to the way she liked it and his glasses were contacts. They kissed passionately before Emily left him on his lonesome so she could stand in front of the desperate chooks. Cute Guy's eyes and mine met briefly but he unlocked his gaze and instead looked so damn uncomfortable I felt sorry for him.

So, Emily Mears was back from overseas for good and they were back together? Shit just got real. All my love interests had dumped me... again. If only I wrote country songs, I would be dog paddling in millions.

Tits appeared in her flowing white monstrosity of a dress, beaming from ear to ear.

'Are you ready, ladies?'

She turned her back to us and threw the stupid thing. I didn't hold my hands up to catch it but the Mexican wave I was entrenched in did. The next thing I saw was Shelley jumping up and down like a lunatic yelling, 'I caught it! I caught it! Now all I need is a boyfriend!'

Good luck with that.

It took all the strength I had not to start drinking after seeing Cute Guy and Emily Mears back together, but I stayed strong; all I had to do was think about Chocky and her lampshade. Instead I asked Troy to get me another Coke while I filled Leticia and Prudence in on what happened in Lorne after they'd left.

'That's so awesome!' Leticia gushed. 'Can we come with you when you go back there?'

'I think it's better if there's less of us,' I said in my *leader* voice.

'Cheese,' said Prudence suddenly. 'I need cheese.'

With that she was gone.

'No drugs tonight, I presume?' I asked Leticia as Mel giggled beside me.

'Regrettably not, although I'm sure Tits will have some.'

'Speak of the pot Devil,' I said as I saw Tits gliding toward us.

'I was hoping one of you would have caught the bouquet,' she said with a smile.

'Why? None of us wanna get married.' I yawned.

'Speak for yourself!' Leticia chimed in.

'It's perfect that Shelley caught it though,' said Mel. 'She's wanted to get married since she was five. It's her lifelong dream.'

I think I vomited in my mouth a little when Mel said that.

'Ladies, it's time to sit down for dinner,' Tits gushed whilst waving to her mum, who was calling her. 'Choose the chicken *POT* pie,' she said to us with a wink. 'And the iced tea is the best, it's from Long Island.'

After dinner, whilst Prudence was explaining the Theory of Relativity and John had finally accosted me with a hug that was a little too tight and lasted a little too long, I started to sink into a deep depression. I realised I would never have what Tits had. Regardless of how I felt about John, I would never have a love that lasted. No one would ever want to be with me for any extended period of time. And then, to add to my misery, I spotted Emily Mears and Cute Guy pashing in the corner and told Troy he needed to get me home to Chocky, stat.

# CHAPTER THIRTY-EIGHT

The day had finally come; the first Monday of the month. 'Take Down Sister Catherine Day.' I was nervous, but ready. It was decided only Troy and I would go; too many cooks cliché. Marlene needed to stay home to take care of Chocky anyway, which she'd offered to do.

I had already alerted the local cops to what would be going down that day. After much prodding they had agreed to send two plainclothes police in an unmarked car to meet us at the shop. I'd left the make and model of our car with the deskbound cop so the undercover cops would recognise us.

It was right on midday and raining as usual. The sky's tears followed me everywhere. We parked at least five shops away from our target in order to be cautious. Troy and I stayed in the car. As the rain dispersed, we noticed two casually dressed guys with army haircuts stroll toward our car. Troy wound down his window.

'Georgina Appleby and Troy Johnson?' Red-haired Cop said as he leaned into the car, his mirrored aviator sunnies reflecting our nervous expressions.

We both nodded and I squeaked out a 'yep'.

'Stay here,' he instructed as he and Dark-haired Cop headed toward Lorne Clippings.

Troy and I watched them as they stopped at the store, looked in the window, then stared at something on the ground which wasn't visible to us. Then they waved us over.

We jumped out of the car like *Starsky and Hutch*.

I could not believe what I saw.

Lorne Clippings had shut down. The store was empty, completely empty. All that remained was a 'For Lease' sign stuck to the window.

The shop guy must have snitched.

The rat!

But the worst was yet to come.

On the ground in front of the door sat my one and only voodoo doll.

Noooooooooooooooooooooooooooooooooooooooooooo!!!!!!!!!!!!!!!!!!

Sister Catherine had done it again.

Red-haired Cop picked up the doll and studied it closely before turning his attention to me.

'Do you have any idea why this doll looks exactly like you?' he asked suspiciously.

'Well, I wouldn't say it looks exactly like me, I mean, I'm not wearing a green school uniform!'

Red-haired Cop was not amused.

'Okay, look, Sister Catherine made a doll that looks exactly like me and she's been hanging onto it for ages waiting for the right moment so she can do something bad to me with it. This is obviously that moment!' I blurted out, sounding like a complete fool.

'Are you sure this isn't *your* doll?' Dark-haired Cop asked me.

'It's not her doll, Officer,' Troy piped up.

Ignoring Troy, Red-haired Cop turned the doll upside down, inspecting the soles of its shoes.

*'This doll is the property of Georgina Appleby. If found please return to owner and do not break as the contents are valuable,'* he read aloud before giving me evils.

'What!?' I roared. 'I didn't write that! Sister Catherine did! Can't you see she's setting me up!?'

I started to freak out. I had no idea my nun-nemesis had written that on the doll as I hadn't turned it upside down when I'd first found it. I wished I had. I would have got rid of it pronto and none of this would be happening.

Then of course Red-haired Cop started to shake the bloody thing. There was something in there all right. He threw mini-me to the ground and I smashed, revealing a bag of something white, not green.

Kill!

Me!

Now!

Dark-haired Cop picked up the bag and gave it to Red-haired Cop, who promptly produced an evidence bag and before you could say 'Georgie is a drug fiend' I was in handcuffs, being read my rights and driven to Lorne police station.

***

I had been sitting in a cell that stank of pee and perfume with a scary, massive bald woman who had been constantly blowing me kisses for well over five hours when I heard Mother had finally paid my bail. It was quite substantial but the old crow could afford it.

My thoughts turned to Troy, hoping he was okay, but it seemed like all the cops wanted to do was question him, not lock him away. I mean, it was *my* doll after all, wasn't it? Sigh. I figured the cops had sent the white powder to the lab for testing. I hoped it was flour but strongly doubted it. When the cop came to let me out, my prison girlfriend looked like she was going to cry; yet another relationship that had gone nowhere. As the cop led me to the reception area, I saw

Mother and Troy waiting to greet me. Troy rushed over and hugged the life out of me. Mother didn't. She just stood there scowling in her stupid pink feather boa, which was, as usual, wrapped around her turkey neck. I wished I could string her up with it.

Mother instructed Troy to drive my car back to Melbourne and to stay away from me. I wished I was driving my car to Adelaide or over Emily Mears. The ride home was unbearable. Mother sat opposite me in the limo and yelled and yelled. I didn't say a word. As if she would believe anything that came out of my mouth, anyway.

When we got back to Purgatory Palace, the Quack opened the front door with a frown as Chocky limped around him trying to jump on me. Then I noticed Marlene standing by the kitchen door looking sombre, her hair back in a tight bun, no makeup and wearing her ridiculous maid's uniform again. It was all too much, so I made a run for it. I picked up Chocky and ran up the stairs, locking myself in my bedroom. Self-imposed exile, we meet again. At least I had my fur kid, mobile, an ensuite bathroom and Marlene to bring Chocky and me sustenance, unless Mother didn't let her… uh oh.

I immediately rang Dad.

'Kiddo!'

'Dad you have to come here right now and save me! I had to lock myself in my room, I'm out on bail, Mother paid it but I'm in big trouble and it looks like the Quack lives here now! Mother won't let Troy see me anymore and Marlene looks like a maid again!'

It was no surprise that after hearing that, Dad caught the next plane to Melbourne.

Later that night I heard a knock on my bedroom door.

'Georgie, it's Dad.'

I leapt off the bed and swung the door open, frightening Chocky, who started to bark, but her tail soon turned into a helicopter's propeller when she recognised Dad.

He walked into my room and closed the door quietly. Dad looked tired and his grey suit was crumpled. I felt bad for making him come all the way here.

Catholic guilt strikes again.

'Hi, Dad,' I said meekly. 'Who let you in?'

'Marlene did and yes, she looks like a maid, like she always has. What's going on, Georgina?'

Uh oh – there was my birth name again.

And so, it began; yet again there I was crapping on and on, filling him in on everything that had recently happened. Mainly the taking down Sister C and the voodoo doll stuff Mother had tried to get out of me but couldn't. I also touched on Marlene, her makeover and our friendship, which he didn't know about, and her recent regression back into a meek maid, Mother forbidding Troy to see me and the Quack living here. The glasses came off a couple of times for cleaning by the time I had finished.

'I see,' he said a little too sedately.

'Daaad! Help me! I'm gonna go to prison and as cool as *Orange is the New Black* is, I'd rather watch it on TV than live it!'

'Calm down, Georgie, don't worry, you won't go to jail, I'm good friends with a lawyer in Sydney who can help you. But did you try to explain all this to the police, that the doll wasn't yours, and what Sister Catherine was up to?'

'Of course I did! They don't believe me! There's no trace of Lorne Clippings anymore and although they know it used to exist, none of this stuff can be proved. All the evidence has disappeared apart from my stupid voodoo doll, which they now have in pieces along with the hard drugs that were in it, not to mention they're still on the lookout for Mr No Personality Peters, who they're chasing for embezzlement. As far as the cops are concerned, it runs in the family, you know!'

'When are you going to court?'

'After Easter.'

'Okay, look, leave it with me. I'll get onto that lawyer; I'm sure she can help. As for the other stuff, I can talk to your mother about letting Troy see you, but I don't know what I can do about Marlene. Alicia does have a hold on that girl, and as far as your mother having a new boyfriend, well, I can't butt in there!'

'But the Quack has moved in!'

'Your mother can't be alone, Georgie, you know that. She seems to have gone straight to the Quack after Hubert. What can I do about it? Look, I'm going to be here for a couple of days. How about I come by and take you out to dinner tomorrow night to try to cheer you up?'

'Okay.'

Dad stood up and kissed my forehead gently.

'Talk soon, kiddo.'

After Dad left it really hit me that he had become an absent father of late. Although he did come to my rescue, it was probably due to feeling obligated. He wasn't there in any real sense. Months could go by without a phone call. It was hard to maintain any kind of relationship with someone when it was so one-sided. Eventually you just gave up.

Dad did hang around for a couple of days trying to do what he could to alleviate my suffering, although he totally forgot about taking me out to dinner, no surprises there. What he did do was talk to his lawyer friend, who was happy to represent me, and he reversed the ban on Troy visiting.

But the Quack still lived in my house and had started to boss me around, and Marlene still looked like a maid. I'd discussed this with Troy as he was concerned about her regression. Although they were still together, they didn't spend as much time with each other anymore, as Mother had Marlene doing ridiculous chores like washing Mrs Tiara's limo, for real. Mother also had no idea Marlene and Troy were an item, which didn't help. I wished Marlene hadn't come back from the dead. But it was too late now. It was all too late.

# CHAPTER THIRTY-NINE

Easter had arrived and that meant going to church. Shudder. I had managed to get out of it at Christmas, seeing as Mother was in rehab, but not this time and, what's worse, I was accompanying Mother and the Quack. He had turned into a right old prick. He even put a curfew on what time I got home. Like a discarded old pumpkin from 1950, I had to be home by midnight. Do you believe that? Twenty years old with a midnight curfew.

I know, I should have just moved out; I mean, it's not like I was waiting until I was twenty-one to claim my inheritance and run, as I no longer had one to claim, thanks to NPP and Leopard Print Sharon. But in all honesty, I was scared. I had zero money and worked voluntarily. I was also worried about Mother starting to hassle me about getting a job again. I was sure there was an opening as the Quack's personal slave.

Where would I go, anyway? Sure, I could crash at Troy and Mrs J's for a while, or Dad and Josh's, but I couldn't live with either of them permanently. I'd end up in a Centrelink queue just as Sister Catherine had predicted, followed by a dead-end job's depression. I was stuck like a pound dog, waiting in vain for my eventual fate, which was either a new life or death. But unlike a pound dog that had no comprehension of this, I did, and that made it so much worse.

'I think you should go to confession, Georgina, to absolve all your sins. God knows you have enough of them,' Mother ordered.

Unfortunately, we were early for Easter mass so there was no escaping that hell. I dragged myself to confession and stood in line with all the other dirty sinners. When my turn finally came after waiting a good fifteen minutes (there were a lot of guilty Catholics that day) I stepped into the confessional, closed the sliding door and sat down. I felt so claustrophobic in that tiny box. The grate between the priest and I was supposed to stop us recognising each other but a cough and the odour of stale cigarette smoke soon gave it away. It was Father Luke all right. He must have been moonlighting from the Prison Camp.

It's been a while…

***

*R.E. (Religious Education) or more commonly known amongst the girls as Revolting Excrement, was compulsory. There was no escaping it in a Catholic school. Father Luke took the class and would bore us all to tears with his waffling on. He was the Prison Camp's priest. He looked like a priest. Bald on top with white puffs of hair on either side of his huge head, small framed spectacles and a big Rudolf the Red-nosed Reindeer nose. We all knew he liked a drink or twenty.*

*Today one of the girls asked him if animals went to heaven. He said no as they didn't have souls. I had heard this stated before and it always made me feel uneasy. So, they just die and that's it? I doubted that. Everything is energy and energy has to go somewhere. I remembered talking to my old cat after he passed away when I was fifteen and asking him to give me a sign that he was still somewhere. Instantly a zap of pure ecstasy travelled from my feet to my head. The feeling couldn't even be compared to an orgasm and it wasn't sexual either. It felt like for a moment I was in heaven. My cat gave me a sign. Okay, so I did have a joint but that's not why it happened. If anything, the effects helped the cat's message to get through and I have never felt a feeling like that since. So yeah, me and the Catholic religion are very conflicted and don't even get me started on their anti-gay/anti-same sex marriage/anti-contraception and anti-abortion bullshit.*

*But anyway... while my eyes were glued to the clock, counting the seconds until the end of class, Father Luke handed out photocopies with the dates of the Easter holidays. Like synchronised Catholics bathing in a pool of fresh ink we all held the paper up to our noses and took a deep breath, exhaling in a happy stupor. Then I looked down at my sheet, immediately covering my mouth with my hand when I read the fateful words 'PUBIC Holidays'.*

*I guess everything was entitled to holidays, even pubes.*

*I pointed the rather embarrassing spelling mistake out to Tits whose hand soon covered her mouth as well. After we had calmed down, which took a while, Father Luke started randomly asking a few of the girls' different questions about Easter and then came my turn.*

*'What is the meaning of Good Friday, Georgina?'*

*I sat up straight and smiled, putting my palms together in prayer.*

*'Good Friday is very important, Father Luke, as it is the day the Easter Bunny died for our sins.'*

*Mayhem ensued.*

\*\*\*

After I had told Father Luke about my bad behaviour, which included watching too much reality TV, I was given my Hail Mary's as penance and asked to move along like the rest of the Catholic cattle. I was hurt. Didn't he remember me? Or maybe he did and just chose to forget.

During mass I sat squashed between Mother and the Quack like some sort of unsavoury sandwich filling. The poncy fool sang all the hymns so loud and so out of tune I had no choice but to cringe as I pretended to sing along. Mother always sang the hymns in a loud operatic voice. You guessed it; what nightmares are made of. Holy Communion was a highlight. Father Luke put an ash cross on my forehead. I'm sure he probably just used the ash from his cigarettes. He'd have plenty of that stuff lying around. Then to top it all off we went outside to do Stations of the Cross. I get it. Jesus died for our sins. How many more times do I have to be told this? Maybe if I tattooed it on my forehead next to my ash cross, I wouldn't forget.

After church was finally over, I did a runner and jumped aboard the bus to go visit Ben. As I reached his grave, I wasn't surprised to find the usual fresh yellow roses and note. This was becoming a common annoying occurrence by now. If only I could catch the culprit in the act. This time the note said, '*I will see you soon.*'

The plot solidifies…

***

Easter came and went like it always did, with nothing to show for it except a sick tummy that had consumed way too much chocolate. Troy had bought me a ridiculously large Easter egg that we would slowly devour in my room each night while we watched our favourite movies: *Ghost World, The Breakfast Club, Pretty in Pink, Ferris Bueller's Day Off* and *Romy and Michelle's High School Reunion* of course. The Quack still ruled the roost, which meant the majority of my time was spent in my room when I wasn't volunteering at Mary's rescue. Mother still had Marlene under lock and key and riddled her with a million tedious tasks. The only time the star-crossed lovers saw each other was after Mother and the Quack had gone to bed. Marlene would bring Troy and me nightly sustenance during our movie marathons and then they would disappear into Marlene's room for a few hours doing things that lovers did. Chocky and I would usually finish the movie together whilst I kept the chocolate at bay. It was bad for dogs and she was obsessed with the damn stuff, but her name *was* Chocky after all. Her paws had healed by now so she was lampshade-less and I was still sober. I spent a lot of time processing the stuff that happened at school. It was different while straight. I guess I was less angry in general but my hatred of Sister Catherine didn't wane.

In my sober state, I became more and more desperate to move out of Purgatory Palace and actually would have done it too, but being on bail, I couldn't. Always something holding me back.

My court case loomed. I had spoken and met with Dad's lawyer friend from Sydney who was going to represent me and she had done everything in her power to try to convince me that I wouldn't be going to jail, yet I wasn't convinced. My thoughts would return to the five-hour relationship I had with my prison girlfriend and all those blown kisses I ignored. I knew that was only the tip of the iceberg of incarceration.

Prudence's twenty-first was a welcome distraction from my problems. She was a year older than the rest of us, due to her being kept back, no surprises there. If only she had got into drugs earlier, she would have probably become Dux of the Prison Camp.

Oh well.

Prudence's family were rich pigs; *really* rich pigs. Her twenty-first was being held at the nightclub her parents owned called *The Chateau,* but it wasn't a normal nightclub. *The Chateau* was actually a cream-coloured heritage-listed mansion in Toorak built in the 1800s. It had a nightclub downstairs while Prudence and her family lived upstairs in a soundproofed area that was totally blocked off from random drunks entering. Prudence and I obviously weren't friends as kids; her best and only friend was always Leticia, but that didn't matter as every year the Prison Camp's entire primary school class would be invited to *The Chateau* to celebrate her birthday. Even the unpopular ones no one would invite to their parties, like Shelley when she was only a lamb, who one year classically gave Prudence a pair of bottle green undies – the same colour as our uniform – that had the entire class rolling on the floor. Mel wasn't around back then to befriend and defend Shelley The Sheep Girl as Mel only became incarcerated from Year 7 onwards.

To celebrate Prudence's birthday, *The Chateau* would have a ridiculously long table placed in the middle of the floor filled to capacity with party food, drinks and gifts for us all to take home. There were pony rides in the backyard. There were scary clowns who made balloon animals on demand followed by a magic show, then to top it all off, the sugared-up little girls would dance insanely onstage to the current hits of the day at our very own nightclub for kids.

It was high-jinks heaven.

I wondered what Prudence's twenty-first would be like, as I hadn't been to *The Chateau* since her parties had stopped when we finished Grade 6. After that, she had them at Luna Park and Maccas with a few select friends, like the rest of us. We never knew why her *Chateau* parties stopped, although there were rumours her parents had accumulated a lot of debt and couldn't afford the ridiculously expensive invite-the-entire-class birthday parties for their only child anymore.

I had to admit I was more than a little curious about what it would be like being back at *The Chateau*.

Troy and I rocked up dressed for the occasion. He wore his staple – black funeral suit, red Converse – and I wore mine – black hoody, ripped Levi's and green Converse; a stunningly mismatched couple. We arrived slightly later than the allocated time and stood on the front lawn staring up in awe at the stunning historic estate.

'I wish Marlene was here,' Troy said sadly.

I nodded and gave him a gentle pat on the back. Mother had Marlene doing some inane task again, which prevented her from coming. Things were getting tense at Purgatory Palace lately and I feared Marlene would soon crack. I cracked long ago. At least Marlene still had Troy's nightly visits, thanks to Dad stopping Mother's ban.

I pushed the golden doorbell on the mammoth wooden door which ding-donged so loudly it made me jump out of my skin. I half expected Willy Wonka to answer but instead an old grey-haired man with a stoop who was dressed as a butler opened the door slowly.

'Good evening. Please follow me.'

Troy and I gave each other a WTF look as we walked behind him down the hall towards the nightclub. As I looked around, I noticed the place was different to how I remembered it as a kid. Definitely smaller, but everything always seems bigger when you are little. I figured *The Chateau* probably just had a paint job and a bit of renovating that needed to be done on a building this old.

We stopped at the nightclub's entrance.

'Have a grand evening,' the old bloke said with a creepy smile as he opened the door.

Troy and I stepped into the room and I nearly fell over in shock.

# CHAPTER FORTY

It was primary school all over again.

There was a ridiculously long table placed in the middle of the floor, filled to capacity with party food, drinks and gifts for us all to take home. There was a large sign on the back door that said 'Pony rides outside'. There were scary clowns holding balloons ready to make balloon animals on demand. There was a magician setting up his magic show and later, instead of sugared-up little girls dancing insanely onstage to the current hits of the day, there would be drunk women doing the same thing.

It was the craziest déjà vu I'd ever had in my life.

Prudence ran over in excitement, giving us both a hug. She was wearing a hot pink gown complete with hot pink ribbons in her blonde pigtails. I was nauseated just looking at her.

'Oh my god, thanks for coming! Isn't this just amazing, like when we were kids! I asked Mummy and Daddy to recreate it and they got it incredibly right; there's even ponies outside. Well, they aren't ponies, they're horses, as I didn't want adults sitting on ponies 'cause I thought the ponies would get a backache! Sooo excited! Talk later!'

And she was gone.

I noticed Leticia had been standing behind her. She was dressed like Mother, as usual, in designer garb and pearls. It made me wonder whether Leticia actually snuck into Purgatory Palace to steal Mother's wardrobe when we weren't home.

'Leticia, what the hell is Prudence on?' I asked, worried.

'You don't wanna know,' Leticia mumbled.

'Tell me!'

'All right… Helen gave her ecstasy for her birthday. It happened before I got here. I've been following her around with my phone ready to call triple zero; bloody Helen.'

'An E?! She nearly died from an E!'

'I know, the E *you* gave her,' Leticia growled, her brown eyes narrowing.

'Now, now, ladies, the past is the past so let's not go back there,' Troy said in his mediator voice.

'Is Helen still here? I wanna bash her head in.' I rolled up my sleeves, ready to rumble.

'No, she did a runner. I don't know what to do!'

'Maybe this E isn't as strong and she won't react as bad this time,' Troy offered.

'Here's hoping, but we need to watch her like a hawk,' Leticia said before running off after Prudence.

'Why is there always drama? Why?!' I yelled, hiding my face in my hands.

'I don't know, it does seem to follow you around,' Troy said softly, patting my back.

'I can't believe Helen did that though,' I continued. 'She knew what happened to Prudence last time.'

Mel and her pet sheep approached us. Mel appeared to give even less of a crap than I did, not bothering to brush her long tangled red hair and she was dressed like she was going to the milk bar to buy a Mars Bar. Shelley, on the other hand, was wearing a bright pink taffeta dress that made her look like a sheep dressed as fairy floss.

'Did you hear about the ecstasy?!' Mel cried.

'Yep, we just found out,' I sighed, over this conversation already.

'What are you all so ecstatic about?' Shelley asked in confusion.

I eyeballed Troy, resulting in him whisking Shelley away to fairyland, and I literally mean fairyland. There was a sign saying 'This Way to Fairyland'.

'Is Tits here?' I asked Mel.

'She's not coming. John Junior has a fever.'

'Damn. We need her.'

'Prudence seems okay, though, a bit hyper but that's all,' Mel said reassuringly. 'Leticia is watching her every move. Maybe this E isn't as lethal?'

'Yeah, that's what we were saying,' I said, beginning to calm down.

'Shelley's been a bit of a worry, though,' Mel said, changing the subject. 'She's adamant she's gonna get a boyfriend and be married since she caught Tits' bouquet. She even changed her Facebook to "in a relationship".'

'You're kidding,' I said, rolling my eyes. 'Who does she think she's in a relationship with?'

Mel gave me a look, making me soon twig.

'Oh, shit. It's Troy, isn't it?'

Mel nodded.

'Oh, God. Well, Troy's extremely taken and besides, I'm sure he doesn't want lambs as children.'

Mel and I laughed, although as usual Mel looked guilty about it. Starting to momentarily relax, I looked around the room, seeing pretty much all the girls I went to the Prison Camp with, most of whom I hated, and some of their other halves. Mary-Louise, the coolest girl from school, sashayed past, giving me a nod of acknowledgement which I returned. I wondered what the latest thing she knew about me was that soon would be gossiped about to anyone and everyone. She looked the same. She always looked the same; blonde, sun-kissed and skinny. I also spotted Jane Queen of Pain nearby, having an in-depth conversation with someone I didn't know and wondered whether she had had any more séances with her spirit lover David. I sure didn't want to be involved in any more of them after what happened at graduation, that's for sure. My thoughts then turned to Emily Mears, who I hadn't seen yet, and Cute Guy.

'Have you seen Emily tonight?'

'No, not yet,' said Mel.

I wondered how Emily and Cute Guy were going. Last time I saw them at Tits' wedding, they looked like they were about to plan their own. My thoughts then turned to Hayley and there I was standing in front of the perfect person to probe.

'Have you heard from Hayley?' I asked Mel tentatively.

'Yep.'

'How's she going?'

'She's busy and exhausted running the shelter and...' Mel trailed off, giving me a funny look. Something was up.

'And what? Come on, Mel, I'm a big girl, I can take it.'

'She's met some guy, the love of her life apparently. Sorry, Georgie.'

My chest tightened but I said nothing, just nodded, walked over to the bar, grabbed a bottle of Jim Beam when the bartender wasn't looking, and went and sat in a corner by myself.

It wasn't long until Mel had told Troy of my whereabouts. He sat down next to me, noticing me holding the unopened bottle.

'Did Shelley the fairy-floss-flavoured sheep enjoy fairyland then? You do know she has the hots for you, right?' I asked in annoyance.

Troy tried to suppress a laugh.

'She thought fairyland adequate and yes, I did suspect that,' he answered before moving onto more pressing matters.

'You're not going to drink that are you?' he asked. 'Have you forgotten what happened to Chocky?'

'Oh, just take it!' I yelled, handing him the bottle.

'Mel told me about the Hayley thing, Georgie,' he continued.

'What, that she's found the love of her life? Good for her and good for Justin too, being back with Emily Mears. Good on both of them. I'm just the idiot people are with before they find the person that they've been looking for all along,' I sobbed.

'I wish I could make this all okay, I really do,' Troy said, putting his arm around me.

A scary clown with a stupid grin on its face approached us and handed me a poodle balloon animal. After giving it the *Georgie Death Stare,* it had no choice but to back away slowly and run for its life.

'You really need to patent that look,' Troy said with a smile.

'Patent pending.' I grinned, stroking the poodle's rubbery skin.

Then it happened.

'Oh my god!' someone yelled. 'Prudence is on the roof! She's gonna jump!'

# CHAPTER FORTY-ONE

We pushed through the crowd, spotting Prudence standing near the edge of *The Chateau's* roof with Leticia behind her. I slowly moved towards Prudence's best friend.

'I thought you were watching her like a hawk. What happened?' I whispered.

'I went to the loo! I thought she was okay but when I came out, she was up here!'

'Jesus. Have you said anything to her?'

'I've tried to talk to her but she won't budge. She's just been standing there. She hasn't said a word!'

'Are her parents around?'

'No, Prudence didn't want them here. They've gone out to dinner.'

'What about the cops? Has anyone called them?'

'No, not yet, we're worried 'cause she's taken drugs.'

'Do you want me to try saying something to her?'

'It's worth a shot but be careful, Georgie. She could freak out at any second.'

I nodded and moved a little closer.

'Prudence, this is Georgie. Can you hear me?'

Nothing.

'How about we go ride one of those ponies, huh?'

Nothing.

'There's a huge surprise waiting for you downstairs. Don't you wanna know what it is?'

She finally looked at me. I could see she had been crying.

'What's wrong? What happened?'

'I'm a pink butterfly,' she finally squeaked, flapping her arms slowly. 'A pink butterfly without wings.'

I went with it.

'Where are your wings?'

'I don't know but I can't fly without them.'

'I'm pretty sure I saw your wings downstairs.'

She shot me a look.

'Liar!' she yelled, making me jump. 'I see them now. They're down there.'

She pointed below, into the darkness.

'Okay, well, why don't we go inside, go down the stairs and get them?'

'No! They're halfway between me and the ground. I can only get them if I jump.'

Prudence moved further toward the edge of the building, making everyone gasp. I shifted closer to her. Sweat started to bead on my forehead and I was trembling. I had never done anything like this before and had no idea if I was doing the right thing or not, which was terrifying. I tried to remember all the movies and TV shows I had watched that had this happen in them, but how did I even know if this was what you were meant to do? I hadn't been trained in this. I hoped the actors had been. I needed to stay calm and consider ways of getting her away from the edge of the roof.

'Prudence,' I said finally, after having an idea I decided to try. 'You can have my wings.'

I stretched out my arms like Jesus on the cross. At last being brought up Catholic had some use.

Prudence glanced over and watched me through narrowed eyes for what seemed like an eternity before giving me a wide smile.

'They're beautiful.'

'They're all yours, but you have to come over here and get them.'

Prudence hesitated before taking a step back. Troy quickly grabbed her, moving her away from the roof's edge. Leticia and I ran over and hugged Prudence like crazy whilst sobbing. I vaguely heard the sound of applause and figured I'd done a good scene but then realised I wasn't acting.

'Your wings really are beautiful,' Prudence said to me as she started to cry.

As the four of us held each other in an emotional bubble, I remembered what being on a roof had previously meant to me.

*\*\**

*'Hurry up!' Andy yelled from the attic.*

*Ben and I rushed up the narrow stairs just as Andy was climbing out the window. I helped Ben onto the roof and followed him. We made our way to our favourite spot where we would sit and watch the stars. We were fearless. There had been a few close calls in the past but none of us had ever fallen off.*

*Ben was only eight and would bum shuffle down the drain that connected the two halves of the roof. I always kept an eye on my little brother, no matter what. Being eleven, that was what big sisters did.*

*Andy didn't care about Ben or me, he'd just do his own thing. He was almost sixteen by then and couldn't be bothered with his childish siblings. He was always sucking up to Mother, acting like a little angel toward Ben and me, but when we were alone with him on the rare occasions he was forced to babysit, he would ignore us all night and just make us bring him food, like a couple of slaves. I guess it could have been worse – I mean, he never physically abused us, but he was a right little prick and I never forgave him for it, but Ben loved him unconditionally, just like a little puppy dog.*

*When we would finally get to our favourite spot on the roof, we'd lie down and watch the stars. Andy was good at astronomy and would point out every single star and tell us off when we got them wrong, which was often.*

*We used to go up to the roof after Mother passed out and Nanny went to bed. We did it nightly around this time. I loved our roof adventures and usually in that moment, when Andy was pointing out stars that he was so obviously passionate about, I would like him. Just for that moment. My smart big brother; until he decided he'd had enough and yelled at Ben and me all the way back up to the window.*

***

Prudence was *sent away* after her roof incident. Her parents were worried about the erratic behaviour of their only daughter due to excessive drug use. They didn't tell us where Prudence was so we weren't able to visit her. We figured it was some kind of expensive rehab retreat; who knows, maybe it was even the one Mother had gone to. I guess it was fair enough. I mean, this was the second time their only daughter nearly died due to ecstasy. Tits was upset as she hadn't been able to make Prudence's twenty-first but I reassured her that rehab didn't last forever.

I often wondered whether Prudence's folks knew how smart she became when taking drugs, but I doubted it. I figured only the Scoobies knew her amazing lock-picking skills when under the influence, but

I guess we didn't need them anymore now that breaking into the convent was a thing of the past.

Life went back to normal. Boring, mundane normal until one day, everything changed.

# CHAPTER FORTY-TWO

The cops caught Mr No Personality Peters.

They had a tip-off from someone who had seen him spending my money at some posh resort in Bali with Leopard Print Sharon, who no doubt was wearing a leopard print bikini. Shudder. They were whisked back to Australia quick smart and during questioning, the most incredible thing happened.

NPP admitted he was working with Sister Catherine.

My conspiracy theory was right; the pot dolls, the embezzlement, everything. I knew it! He told the cops where my nun-nemesis resided and they found her living not too far from Lorne. Sister C was excommunicated from The Church. I'm sure Jesus wept that day. We also found out she was supplying Helen drugs to sell at the Prison Camp. All the puzzle pieces began to fit together.

Court cases ensued; Sharon, being an accessory, was let off but NPP and Sister C got a few years. They tried to appeal but were denied. At least there was some justice, but knowing they would be walking the streets even sooner with good behaviour really gave me the shits and in fact scared me a little. Spineless, clammy little-handed NPP would leave me alone but Sister Catherine? My recurring dream was of her coming at me with her boxing gloves, wearing a white satin habit with tiny Jesus heads all over it, with her stupid Coke bottle glasses magnifying her eyes, yelling, 'You are going down, Appleby!' while Sister Janet Mead's version of *The Lord's Prayer* played on repeat.

Ridiculously huge shudder.

But the most important thing that happened after they caught Hubert, his mistress and the nun, was that the case against me was dropped.

This meant I could finally move out of Purgatory Palace.

Hallelujah.

Fun and frivolity did not remain, however, as I soon found out my inheritance had been frittered away. It was gone, all gone and Sister Catherine's strongbox full of cash had disappeared too. The cops found some pot dolls at her house but there was no money. I suspected if there was any cash it was well hidden from everyone until their Get Out of Jail Free card.

Chocky did gain a friend though, as Sister C's mop dog, Saint Teresa, was being bundled off to the pound and I wasn't going to have that. I bonded with Saint Teresa as soon as I stopped thinking of her as Sister C's dog but just a dog in her own right. She was cool, apart from her name, but I was stuck with it as she wouldn't answer to anything else. She was a few years older than Chocky, which was good because Choc respected her as pack leader. They soon became best friends, so I guess it's what Jesus wanted.

Then finally, drum roll, I moved out of Purgatory Palace.

After hearing me endlessly moan about the house from hell, Mary asked if the dogs and I would like to move into her spare room, rent-free, as she knew I had no money. I jumped at the opportunity. I guess the fact I organised that fundraiser which helped save SMAR might have had something to do with her wanting to help me, although I didn't do it expecting something in return. That's the way karma works though, when you don't expect anything is when you receive it.

Marlene was a little sad but I told her I'd make time for us to catch up. She was kind enough to relay the news to Mother and the Quack, as I didn't want to spend another minute listening to their bullshit.

So off I went.

Mary's house was in South Melbourne, surprise, surprise. Her home was cottage-like and clean and smelt like potpourri. My bedroom was sunny and huge and even had an open fireplace. I admit it was strange at first, seeing as I'd had an ensuite bathroom at Purgatory Palace and now I was suddenly sharing a bathroom, but I soon got over myself. That was the way most people lived, after all, and I had always been aware of my privilege.

The dogs seemed happy there. Chocky had already stayed with Mary and loved her two Labradors, Sonny and Cher. Saint T liked them too. The cats were another thing, but they just did their own thing so we all got along fine.

Mary was great to live with. When she wasn't at the shelter, she had her feet up in the lounge room surrounded by her zoo where they would watch David Attenborough docos together. She was vegan and cooked amazing meals.

I would say at that moment in time, if I dare to admit it, I was happy, apart from my love life. Considering I had no money, what Mary had done for me made her a saint in my eyes, which made me surrounded by them, seeing as I already had Saint Teresa.

A month after I'd moved in, Troylene were keen to come over for a catch–up, so I decided to cook my specialty for dinner: cheese and tomato toasted sandwiches. Mary was sweet and acted really impressed by my crap cuisine, God love her.

After dinner, Mary went to read in her room with Sonny and Cher and left us the lounge room to catch up.

'Thanks for making your specialty,' Marlene said with a smile.

'Yes, your award-winning toasties that helped get us together on our first date.' Troy grinned.

I laughed, rapt he remembered.

'So, you must be happy the cops finally found those three fools?' Troy said as he sat down, sandwiched between Chocky and Saint Teresa, who had started snoring in unison.

'Happy isn't the word; try ecstatic.'

'Except for losing your inheritance, though,' Marlene said sadly.

'I know, but what can I do about it? At least Mary is letting me stay here for free. I'm so glad I finally got out of Purgatory Palace. Speaking of the house from hell, what's been going on there? I had a few missed calls from Mother but couldn't be bothered ringing back. Nice to see she realises I actually have a mobile phone these days, though.'

'She was quite upset when I told her you moved out,' Marlene began cautiously. 'She wants to put money in your account.'

'Stuff her money!' I spat.

'Also, your mother and her doctor boyfriend have started fighting every day,' she continued.

My mood suddenly lightened.

'So, Mother's having Quack Quarrels, is she?! Are they similar to the ones she had with NPP?'

'I think so,' Marlene said.

I wondered whether another Leopard Print Sharon had surfaced. I mean, let's face it, surely there would be a use-by date for putting up with Mother's shit.

'There's more, Georgie,' Marlene said solemnly.

I had a bad feeling about this.

'Your mother has started drinking again. It's pretty bad. The household has fallen apart and she won't listen to me. I really hate having to say this but... WE NEED YOU!'

Marlene burst out crying. Troy and I rushed to her aid, putting our arms around her.

'It's true,' Troy whispered. 'Purgatory Palace needs you.'

So that was that. One month of freedom and the Hell Mouth had re-opened and sucked me back in.

So many sighs I can't possibly fit them all in here.

When I arrived back at Purgatory Palace, I saw Mother's diamond-encrusted champagne glass had been taken out of mothballs and given a good polish by Marlene, who I noticed had stopped wearing her ridiculous maid's outfit as Mother no longer noticed. Mother was back on a case a day and her nauseating, hateful state returned. The only good to come out of all this was one morning, the Quack moved out, resulting in me spending the rest of the day dancing like Snoopy. I was relieved there would be no woeful wedding I would be forced to attend in the future but it was hard watching Mother's deterioration all over again. As predicted, I had to take over household duties and bill paying, but by now I was an expert at it. I begged Mother to go into rehab again but she wouldn't budge and locked herself in her room to stop us from forcing her to go.

I missed living at Mary's. I couldn't believe how happy I was there and how quickly it had been taken away from me. Mary understood why the dogs and I moved out and told me the room was there if I ever needed it again, which I appreciated.

I got busier at SMAR, picking up a few more days as one of the other volunteers had left. Mary even started to pay me a little, which was great as I could afford luxuries like petrol and mini pecan pies from the bakery next door with money I actually earned myself. Mary would bring up Hayley every now and then and say how wonderfully she was running the Adelaide shelter. She even got on the cover of the local paper for the fundraiser she'd organised. That didn't surprise me, seeing how photogenic she was.

I heard nothing about Cute Guy. I presumed he was still exchanging bodily fluids with Emily Mears. I had pretty much given up on love, anyway. Love just didn't agree with me, the same way some people are lactose intolerant.

Sometimes I'd see someone cute come into the shelter and check me out but I couldn't even do eye contact. I just saw the whole relationship develop in my head up until the break up and I didn't want to go down that path again. I just wanted to work hard and eventually go on the payroll fulltime, now I had no money of my own to start my own animal rescue.

I hadn't seen the Scoobies for a while, either. With Prudence still in rehab, we had all drifted a little. Leticia was in Europe, travelling, Tits was busy being a wife and mother, Mel was eating Mars Bars and Shelley was no doubt pining over Troy, who avoided Shelley like he did Aussie rules football.

The Scoobies were aware the cops had caught my nemeses and were happy the saga was over but I was left feeling empty with nothing exciting in my life. Breaking and entering was sure an adrenaline rush.

Then June arrived and a bitter winter engulfed Melbourne. The days became depressing, dark and dank. One morning Mother was cold. But she wasn't cold because it was winter.

She was cold because she was dead.

# CHAPTER FORTY-THREE

'Mother,' I whispered, trying to push her to wake.

She was lying in bed on her back, draped in her white silk dressing gown and clutching her pink feather boa in her age-spotted left hand. Her right hand was holding her diamond-encrusted champagne glass, which was empty. Beside her on the bed was a bottle of vodka that was empty too. Mother's heavily made-up eyes were closed but her mouth was slightly open, revealing a sliver of saliva protruding from her smudged red-lipsticked mouth. I touched her forehead tentatively then pulled my hand away when I felt she was icy to the touch. Her cold clamminess reminded me of NPP's hands. Then I glanced at her bedside table and witnessed the rest of the evidence. A half-full bottle of vodka, two empty bottles of sleeping pills and an envelope propped against the lamp that said *Georgina*. Before I had time to digest any of this, Marlene walked into the room.

'Is Mrs Appleby all right?'

'No, she's dead.'

Marlene promptly screamed and fell to the ground.

Troy appeared and focused on his beloved until he saw Mother.

'Oh shit, Georgie.' He gasped, hand over mouth.

'She's dead. She killed herself. She's dead,' I said robotically.

As I stood staring at the envelope addressed to me, I vaguely heard Troy talking on his mobile asking for an ambulance, although I wasn't sure why as I thought a hearse was more what the situation called for. I thought I should probably leave the envelope for the coroner or something, as that's what always happened on TV, but I just had this all-consuming feeling to grab Mother's final letter to me, so that's exactly what I did.

The rest of the day was a blur. The ambulance, the police, the doctor, the priest, the coroner, they all came and went and eventually Mother was taken to the morgue. Family and close friends were notified. Andy was the first to arrive and sat downstairs crying. This surprised me as I had yet to shed a tear. Dad was on his way from Sydney. Gran, Nan, Uncle-Rock-Star-Has-Been Jack and Auntie Elm were there too and Mrs Tiara was bossing Cook around. NPP *wasn't* notified. Troylene kept asking me if I was okay but I was fine; just fine.

When Dad arrived, he took care of everything. Mother had a will and her lawyer was soon informed of the goings-on. The funeral was being planned, the classified was organised to be put in *The Age,* and of course the cause of death was kept secret. Everything was taken care of in record time. I didn't have to do anything. When I couldn't bear to be asked how I was feeling one more time and physically wasn't able to stand up anymore, I announced I was going to bed. No one argued with that. I locked myself in my room, threw myself on the bed with Chocky and Saint Teresa and tentatively opened Mother's letter.

> *Dear Georgina,*
>
> *I'm sorry, but if you are reading this I am gone.*
>
> *I want you to know that all my affairs are in order so it will be easy for your father to take care of everything. He is*

*a good man, even though I haven't said that in a long time. You and Andrew will be taken care of and I'm sure you will be happy to know you will finally have your inheritance after that sub-human I regrettably married stole what I had originally put aside for you.*

*Now to come to what I want to tell you. You might have been wondering who has been leaving yellow roses and notes at Ben's grave.*

*Well... it was me.*

*Why was I doing that? The reason was... guilt.*

*I have not told any living soul what I am about to tell you, Georgina. Not your father, your brother, nor anyone. I'm sorry I am about to burden you with this information, but before I die, I need to tell someone and I decided that someone needs to be you. It is up to you whether you tell the rest of the family, I leave that in your hands, for nothing will happen to me now. You can't jail ashes.*

You can't jail ashes? I found Mother's letter from the afterlife a little hard to take at this point so I hugged Chocky and Saint Teresa for a while instead. A single tear streamed down my cheek. I hastily wiped it away, controlling my emotions, as I did so well. I had no idea what Mother was about to tell me. Did I even want to know? Why was she only telling me? As I was about to read Mother's darkest secret, a knock on my door made me hide the letter deep inside a corner of my pillow case instead.

'Come in.'

Dad entered the room.

'Georgie, you're still awake, good. Look, I just realised you haven't eaten a thing all day.'

'I'm not hungry.'

'I know, I know, but you need to keep up your strength. Cook has made a pot of her special vegetable soup just for you. It would mean the world to me if you just came downstairs and had a little bit of it, please?'

How could I say no to that?

I went downstairs and ate a small bowl of soup, which as usual was mouth-watering. The dogs had a little too. Then for dessert I devoured a mini pecan pie which was so delicious it momentarily made me forget about the day's events; momentarily. Then I said goodnight again and strolled back to my room with the pups, closed the door and nearly fell over in shock.

My bedsheets had been changed!

Marlene must have changed them when I was downstairs! I threw my doona and pillow off the bed but couldn't find the letter; the letter! Mother's deepest, darkest secret swirling around in soap and hot water, lost forever; no! I couldn't bear the thought. I rushed into the laundry seeing Marlene emptying the washing machine.

'My sheets!' I yelled at her psychotically. 'Is that them? Did you wash them?!'

'Not yet, they're in there,' Marlene said pointing to a washing basket nearby whilst giving me a strange look.

I grabbed the basket and ran to my room, slamming the door. Chocky and Saint Teresa were sprawled across the fresh sheets, oblivious to my frantic state.

I threw the dirty washing everywhere, finally finding my Snoopy pillowcase and inside it, Mother's letter. I sighed deeply, sat down on the bed and burst out crying. Chocky as usual sensed my pain, whining as she kissed my tears away while Saint Teresa watched on with curiosity.

After my tear ducts were emptied, I hugged both dogs, steadied my nerves and read the rest of the letter.

*So here it is, Georgina.*

Gulp.

*As you know, Ben was killed by a hit and run driver but what you don't know is the hit and run driver was me.*

WHAT THE ACTUAL FUCK?!

I suddenly felt sick and promptly threw up vegetable soup all over my fresh sheets. Before Chocky and Saint Teresa's interest went from sniffing to scoffing down my vomit I took the sheets off the bed and threw them into my bathroom. After quickly cleaning myself up, I sat on the floor and continued to read.

*No one knows this, but that day I thought I would surprise Ben by picking him up from school. But I had been drinking and shouldn't have even gotten into a car. I was so excited seeing him sitting there on the footpath in the gutter and he smiled when he saw my car but instead of pushing the brakes, I pushed the accelerator by accident and ran over him and then I drove away because I was drunk and didn't want to be caught. No one saw. All the other boys had already been picked up. There were no cars around. He was all alone. I wasn't caught. Nobody knew it was me and when I was told of his death my shock was real as I'd hoped to God he survived, but he didn't and by then I couldn't say anything. I fixed the car. I went on that retreat to help get over what I had done, but when I came home my drinking just worsened. Alcohol was the only thing that made me forget, but it's too much now, it's all too much. I don't want to forget anymore.*

*I killed my son.*

*If there is an afterlife, I'm sure Ben will despise me. But he can never hate me as much as I hate myself.*

*I am deeply sorry, Georgina. I truly am.*

*I wish to be cremated and my ashes put where you see fit.*
*I leave that up to you.*

*Goodbye,*

*Mother.*

Jesus fucking Christ, Mother; what did you do?! You killed my brother; my favourite brother; the sensitive one, the sweet one, the one who would have made this shithouse world a much better place. You should have killed Andy, as horrible as that sounds, but he was an arsehole, an evil egotistical piece of shit. Ben was pure, maybe too pure for this horrible world. Maybe you did him a favour.

No, you didn't. He should have lived! He should be seventeen now, doing VCE. He'd have a girlfriend, or boyfriend, I dunno, but someone. He was so fucking cute. For years I'd cursed that despicable piece of shit who killed my brother and got away with it, and it was you. You took his life. YOU took his life!

I was surprised you lasted three years until you topped yourself. No wonder you were always such a drunken fool. And in your rare sober moments, you would visit him at his grave, the grave you put him in, to leave flowers and notes of regret. But that wasn't enough. You re-lived what you did every moment of every single day until the champagne did its job and muddied your guilty mind. You poor fucking thing; you fucking arsehole; you killed my brother; my favourite brother.

There was absolutely no way in hell I was going to be the only person on Earth who knew this. No way in hell. I calmly folded up the letter and put it back in the envelope, stood up, went downstairs and gave it to Dad.

'Oh... my... god...' he said in shock. 'I can't believe it.'

Dad was extremely shaken by Mother's confession, no surprises there. Ben was his son after all. Dad and Mother hadn't been on great terms since the divorce but I think this latest revelation poisoned him in a different way. He said he needed to process what he had just read and went back to his hotel. I would have preferred to talk about it with him but, oh well, in time.

When we showed the letter to Andy the next day, he remained stoic. I'm sure he felt something but I don't know what. He cried when Mother died but now, nothing. He always was a hard one to work out. The three of us agreed it was probably best to keep this horrible revelation to ourselves and those closest to us. I wanted to tell Troy but was so traumatised, I felt I needed to move on. Block it out for a while and bottle it up to the point of needing to see a shrink. Yeah, that'd work. I would probably tell Troy eventually, when the time was right; whenever that was.

# CHAPTER FORTY-FOUR

Mother's funeral was a gallant affair and held at the same church as Ben's funeral; how sickening. Every pompous, posh poser for miles filled Saint Patrick's in Toorak. They held handkerchiefs that resembled doilies to their plastic-surgery noses, pontificating stories and anecdotes I'm sure were made up.

The weather was abysmal that day. Gale force winds and side-ways rain. Mother was no doubt having a laugh up there as our umbrellas broke and our clothes got soaked.

Mrs Tiara arrived in a white horse-drawn carriage, which I'm certain had been conjured from a pumpkin and mice by her fairy godmother who she had sold her soul to because the Devil was busy that day.

Mother had an open casket. I was told she was all dolled up in her pink feather boa, pearls and other such gaudy garb. I said no to the viewing. It wasn't because she was dead. I'd already seen her dead. It's just that since seeing *Six Feet Under* and knowing what they did to dead bodies (draining the blood and replacing it with embalming fluid) I found something unsettling about it. I get that it's so people can see their loved ones one last time, especially if it was a sudden death where the body was able to be publicly viewed but to me it felt wrong. For myself, I would prefer to be cremated immediately, followed by a memorial service, and I didn't particularly care what they did with my ashes. Dying followed closely by cremation is an ancient tradition and much purer than draining blood and replacing life with deadly chemicals. To me, this turned a person into a strange kind of zombie where they still looked alive and you were just waiting for them to sit up in that damn coffin. I don't know, maybe I'm just weird but it's definitely not for me.

My old arsonist friend Father Luke held the service. He stank so bad of cigarettes and whiskey I'm sure anyone at church who had given up either recently would soon fall off the wagon. After he spoke a few slurred words, endless amounts of pretentious plebs took their turn to speak about Mother as if she was some kind of godly saint. Excruciating was the only word that came to mind. I glanced over at Dad and noticed he was becoming increasingly uneasy beside me. He looked upset and started to shuffle uncomfortably in his seat.

'Dad, are you okay?' I asked.

Josh and I sat either side of him in the front pew. Josh noticed his behaviour as well and touched him gently on the arm.

Dad suddenly stood and stormed out. Josh followed him. So did the eyes of hundreds of gawking gossipers.

Troy, who was sitting on my other side, leaned toward me. 'What's up with your dad?' he asked.

'Come with me.'

We went outside and I came clean, telling Troy the difficult truth about the fact Mother had killed Ben. He was shocked and didn't quite know what to say but then, who would? He just wanted to know if I was all right. I told him I probably never would be.

After the funeral I couldn't find Dad anywhere, then noticed I had a text from Josh who said they had gone back to the hotel and that Dad had told him Mother's secret.

Andy and Barbie had also done a runner. I still didn't fathom how my older brother felt about our mother killing our younger brother. I'd probably never know, whereas with Dad I knew he just needed time and would talk to me eventually. I was certain Andy would have told Barbie by now. I was worried that airhead would tell everyone and it would be front-page news in the gutter press the following day.

As I stood with Troylene out the front of Saint Patrick's surrounded by strangers' synthetic sympathy, I was finally approached by family. Gran, Nana and assorted cousins I hadn't seen for years one by one gave me their condolences and I gave them mine. If only they knew the truth.

Then Uncle-Rock-Star-Has-Been Jack appeared with Auntie Elm.

Please no.

'Georgie, darling, we are so sorry about your mother,' he began with furrowed brow, wiping a tear away with his hand.

Wow, maybe today his ego would be absent.

Maybe.

'I want to put on a memorial!' he suddenly gushed. 'A celebration of her life! I will perform, of course, she always did love my voice! Did you know she came to see me perform with Dragon? Did I tell you I nearly had a hit single but…'

Thank dog Auntie Elm dragged him away before he finished his rant.

Then I noticed someone I did not want to talk to making a bee-line toward me. It was the Quack, decked out in a purple suit with his trademark grey Quack Quiff styled higher than usual. He looked like a 1970s pimp.

Shudder.

'Hello, Georgina,' he said in his usual gruff tone. 'I am sorry for your loss…'

The old fool trailed off as he looked me up and down, clearly not enamoured with my choice of funeral attire: the black hoodie, ripped Levi's and green Converse ensemble again. If only I owned a purple pimp suit, I'm sure that would get his approval.

'Your mother was a very special person...' He cleared his throat before unleashing the clincher. 'Unlike yourself; I hope you will keep her affairs in order, though I doubt it.'

'Fuck off, you idiot!' Troy yelled uncharacteristically, making me burst out laughing while the posers around us gasped.

'Well, I never!' the Quack said in horror whilst fiddling with his purple cravat.

'Leave Georgie alone! She was running the household herself while her mother was unwell, did you know that?! All you ever did was live in that house, sponge off everyone and verbally abuse Georgie. Well, no more. Just fuck off once and for all!'

The Quack did just that. I hugged the life out of Troy while Marlene golf-clapped beside us.

When I finished the hug, I was finally happy to see the people standing before me, for it was my one and only Scoobies.

Prudence; fresh out of rehab and as usual in hot pink, at a funeral too, God bless her. How did I know she was fresh out of rehab? Her pink T-shirt said *Fresh out of rehab*. Leticia; who was looking toned and tanned from her European holiday and wearing all white like the nuns who pretended to be pure. Tits, the Greek goddess/yummy mummy, traditional in a black sleek gown. Mel, her red hair washed and shimmering and munching on a half-eaten Mars Bar. And Shelley, in the lemon gown again and eyeing Troy like a hungry lion, or was that a hungry lemon? These were my peeps. Sure, I liked some a lot more than others, but these were my crazy peeps; we group-hugged while Troylene looked on with a smile. Suddenly, hugging didn't seem that bad.

When we let each other go, I noticed Mrs Tiara, complete with tiara, heading towards me. Her tiara was different though; there were additional jewels and it seemed more regal than usual. Her funeral tiara perhaps?

'I am sorry for your loss, Georgina. Alicia was a fine woman and a great friend of mine. May I ask how she passed away?'

Oh, shit!

Luckily Troy saved the day yet again.

'In her sleep,' he said mournfully.

Well, I guess he was right. She did just fall asleep and never woke up.

Mrs Tiara bowed sadly and limped away.

I realised I would probably never see her again. I felt a little sad for some strange reason.

Goodbye, Mrs Tiara, complete with tiara.

'So sorry about your mum,' Leticia said despondently, grabbing my arm.

Everyone nodded in agreement.

'Thanks,' I said to all of them before turning my attention to Prudence. 'Pru, they let you out.'

'Yeah! Rad, huh?' she said with a massive smile. 'I was doing great, so my folks got me out early and I made this T-shirt to celebrate. Dunno why they don't like it, though.'

We all laughed.

'So, no more E's?'

'No more of anything, Georgie, I'm as sober as a nun!'

More laughter.

'Yep, she is sober,' Leticia said proudly, patting her BFF on the back. 'So next time you need a lock picked, you'll need to ring a locksmith!'

'Well, hopefully those days are over now that Sister Catherine is behind bars, and we sure don't want her lock picked!'

'We know, Georgie, how awesome!' Mel said, before stuffing the rest of her Mars Bar in her mouth.

'Mel, please be careful, I don't want you to choke!' Shelley barked before continuing to give Troy the love eye. Troy looked uneasy and put his arm around Marlene.

I turned my attention to Tits who had been unusually quiet.

'And, how are you?'

'John left me.'

Everyone gasped.

'He was cheating on me with a girl from work with big boobs. They're together now. He moved in with her.'

'Shit and you only just got married!' I said in disbelief.

'I know. Sucks, eh?' Tits said sadly. 'I call John Junior "JJ" now 'cause I can't stand my son having that bastard's name… oh and my mum moved in to our house. She's been great helping me look after him so at least I get a break.'

'As long as she leaves her top on when she vacuums, huh?' I said with a wink.

'That was the only condition I had when she wanted to move in!' Tits laughed.

'Very wise.' I nodded. 'In all honesty though… I always thought John was a sleazy prick.'

'A lot of people did. I guess I just ignored it. But he did give me a son and I'm grateful for that. JJ seems to take after me anyway, thank Jesus, Mary and Joseph!'

'Amen to that.' I smiled.

'So, what do you guys wanna do now?' Leticia asked as she started to file her nails.

'I suggest we indulge in many alcoholic beverages!' Shelley said with a twirl as Mel watched her in shock.

'I don't drink or do drugs or anything anymore, remember?!' Pru protested.

'You can drive us, then,' Leticia said.

'I'm still on the wagon too, guys,' I piped up, giving Troy a reassuring smile. 'So, I'm happy to drive some of you as well.'

So off I went to watch the Scoobies get drunk and then Prudence and I drove them home.

# CHAPTER FORTY-FIVE

The time had come to meet with Mother's lawyer to read her last will and testament.

Oh, joy.

Dad, Andy and I met out front of Robert English's office. Strangely we all seemed to arrive at the same time, even though we all came separately. No doubt Mother's influence from the other side. She never did like tardiness.

Dad gave me a warm smile accompanied by a big hug and said, 'Hope you're holding up okay, kiddo.'

Smile.

Andy gave me a smart-arse smirk accompanied by crossed arms and said, 'I better get the house.'

Scowl.

After our love/hate greeting, we walked single-file into Robert English's office and stood behind three chairs placed in front of his desk. His office had a 1970s vibe. Brown and orange furniture complete with a weird psychedelic light that would look right at home in Greg Brady's room that used to be his dad's den. A hint of musk aftershave lingered in the room. I breathed deeply. The smell of musk always calmed my nerves and was more enjoyable than NPP's stench of Old Spice.

I'd met Robert English before. He was a suave, fifty-odd gent with a slick of black hair and a sharp James Bond suit. He smiled perfect white teeth that I swear glistened as he gestured for us to sit down.

'Thank you for coming in today. I just wanted to start by saying I'm extremely sorry for your loss. Alicia and I go back a long time, and I'm also saddened by her passing.'

'Thank you, Robert,' Dad said.

'All right then,' Robert continued as he opened a folder. 'Shall we start?'

We all nodded.

Robert cleared his throat.

'I, Alicia Anne Appleby, being of sound mind, declare this to be my last will and testament. To Judith Holmes, better known by her nickname *Cook,* I leave one million dollars to start the restaurant she always wanted…'

'What?!' Andy yelled, standing. 'A million to Cook?! There's no way Mother was of sound mind! She must have been drunk!'

'Please sit, Andrew,' Robert ordered. 'I am witness to the fact your mother was of sound mind when she revised her will recently, and I am also witness to the fact your mother was sober at the time.'

'Sit down, Andy, and shut up,' Dad said angrily. I smiled into my hand as my arsehole brother did just that.

'Now if I am able to continue…'

'Please do, Robert. My son will remain quiet from now on.'

'To Marlene Anderson, my loyal maid, I leave two million dollars so she will never have to work as a maid again, and in fact be able to hire her own maid.'

Dad shot a look at Andy who, luckily for him, bit his tongue.

'To my dear friend Ainsley Harriet, who has no need for money, I leave all my jewellery and selected antiques listed below that she has always admired.'

Dad must have noticed my confused expression as he soon leant over and whispered 'Mrs Tiara' into my ear. So that was her name!

'To my son Andrew, whose inheritance was already given to him when he turned twenty-one, I leave five million dollars and the house in Lorne.'

'Five million and that crap house in Lorne?!' Andy yelled, standing again.

Dad stood too this time, grabbing Andy's shoulders and pushing him back into his chair. 'One more word and I'll contest this will and make sure you get nothing!'

Robert cleared his throat and continued.

'To my daughter Georgina, I leave ten million dollars, the family home in Toorak with everything in it, apart from what has been allocated to Ainsley, and the family cars to make up for the loss of her inheritance.'

'Bullshit!' Andy was gone but no one cared.

I was in shock.

'And lastly, to Chocky and Saint Teresa, I leave a lifetime supply of dog food and free vet care.'

My jaw dropped so far it hit the brown shag pile carpet.

Dad and I thanked Robert and left, deciding to go to a nearby café to digest what we had just heard.

'Dad, I got Purgatory Palace. I was sure Andy would get it. I can't believe it!'

'Well, you better believe it,' Dad said seriously. 'Your mother spoke to me when she revised her will recently. She wanted to take Hubert

Peters off. She felt terrible about him stealing your inheritance, so she made sure you got more than Andy.'

'But what about you? You didn't get anything!'

'I didn't want anything,' he said softly as he took his glasses off to clean them. 'I have enough, I have the company... I have money. It was important for you kids to have something, especially you, and she loved Ainsley, Marlene and Cook, she just didn't know how to express how she felt. She even loved the dogs.'

He was suddenly quiet as he stared at his glasses before putting them back on.

'And of course, now that we know the hidden secret she had been carrying around for so long, well, that changes everything.'

He was finally ready to speak of it.

'That's why you left the funeral?'

Dad nodded.

'It was hard to hear people say how amazing your mother was after finding out she had killed Ben.'

'I know... I told Troy. He was shocked. How was Josh when you told him?'

'He was shocked too, of course. I mean, we were all shocked, apart from Andy. I don't know what's going on in his head.'

'Yeah, right? Weirdo.'

'He probably just needs time. This whole thing is difficult, as your mother and I hadn't been on the best of terms. Things went downhill after she found out about Josh.'

'I was wondering if she knew! Well, her homophobia doesn't surprise me. She was besties with Sister Catherine, after all. I never told her I was bi.'

'You're bi?!' Dad said, sounding impressed. 'Good on you, kiddo! Who are you seeing at the moment?'

'I'm seeing the twinkle in your eye.' I grinned.

'Well, I'm sure you'll find someone soon, Georgie, don't you worry about that.'

If only he knew I had found not one but two people and lost them both.

Sigh.

'Anyway, back to your mother,' he continued. 'She did cover her tracks in typical well-thought-out fashion, though. Fixing the car then going on that retreat.'

'Yeah, not that it helped. She just became more of an alco. I just can't believe no one saw her do it. For the last three years I've been cursing that arsehole who ran over him, and it was her!'

'You and me both.' Dad sighed. 'But I guess we just have to accept what happened and move on. Ben's not coming back and now neither is your mother.'

I nodded.

After our coffees, we parted ways with our usual bear hug. Dad had to head back to Sydney with Josh and I was left to contemplate my ten million dollars and fully-stocked Toorak mansion complete with limo, 1967 Jag and assorted BMWs and Mercedes.

And I knew exactly what I was going to do with it all.

# CHAPTER FORTY-SIX

Ten months later, my dream came true when Purgatory Palace became Thank Dog Animal Rescue. It took a lot of money, time, effort and council approval but we got there. Upstairs stayed the same, apart from Mother's room, which I got the builders to make a kitchen out of. There were too many bad memories to keep it as a guest bedroom and we had enough of those already.

Downstairs became the rescue. I had a separate entrance made to the upper level so Purgatory Palace was basically split in two, like *The Chateau*. I soundproofed the ceiling and floor so any noise like music wouldn't bother the animals downstairs. I also rearranged the lounge room, which was now reception, and took pride in burning my Debutante photo with Ugly Guy. Never again would someone say, 'I didn't know you were married!' Lastly, I turned NPP's golf course into a dog park so the rescue pups could get walkies, but decided to leave a small section of the course for us all to play mini-golf.

Mrs Tiara had sent her butler to pick up the items Mother had promised her, which I was thankful for. I don't think I could have stomached another forced conversation with that old lady. I'd also caught up with Mary from SMAR, who was ecstatic about my news and wished me success with my new rescue. We'd still be seeing each other anyway, as we worked in the same industry, which was great.

Thank Dog mainly rescued dogs and cats as well as the occasional rabbit. The best thing was the Scoobies were all working there, not volunteering. I was able to pay them due to my new-found wealth, which made me all sorts of happy, especially in regards to Troy who, unlike the rest of us, didn't have very much to his name. I also knew Troy wasn't the type of person to live off his newly rich girlfriend. He needed to work for himself, so he decided to become the property's new gardener, spending his days on the ride-on mower, which he absolutely adored. Leticia was the receptionist and also in charge of our website and social media. It was the best job for her as all she used to do before was talk on the phone and check social media and now she got paid to do it. She wasn't really into animals anyway as 'they smelt worse than puke'. Prudence walked the dogs and cleaned up the never-ending poo, which surprised me, but she said she didn't mind as long as I got her a Thank Dog Animal Rescue T-shirt in pink. Of course, I obliged. Tits and JJ looked after the cats and did a stellar job. JJ was in charge of kitten hugs. Mel transported the animals from the pound to the vet to us add infinity. She was amazing but she *was* Hayley's sister so it obviously ran in the genes. As long as I put petrol and a never-ending supply of Mars Bars in the BMW it was all systems go. Marlene handled admin after doing a short course and was quite skilled at it. (Remember, Marlene was a millionaire now so she didn't have to do shit.) Even Shelley was loitering around trying to start up a rescue of her own. Shelley's Sheep Rescue. I kid you not. Still did not know whether it was her mother or father who had had sex with a sheep. Oh, and Cook popped in once a week with food for us all, including the animals. She had her own seafood restaurant now, By Hook or By Cook, thanks to Mother, and was making a killing.

Thank Dog was starting to make a name for itself and getting busier when one particular week a few things happened that made me lose my shit big time.

'Hi,' a soft voice said. I looked up from reception, which I had been looking after while Leticia was on lunch, straight into the icy blue eyes of Cute Guy and promptly fell off my stool backwards, just like in science class at the Prison Camp but this time it wasn't intentional.

'Are you okay?' he asked as he tried to help me up.

'I'm fine,' I said, standing quickly and picking up the stool in embarrassment.

Then he smiled and I, you guessed it, did what my famous cheese and tomato toasted sandwich does under the grill.

There was something about him that was different though. His hair was a little bit longer but it wasn't that. He seemed a little stockier, like he had been working out. It suited him.

'Justin,' I said, attempting a smile. 'It's been a while.'

'I know. I hope you don't mind me popping in like this but I heard you'd transformed your house into an animal rescue…'

'Let me guess, Mary-Louise told you?'

'Yes! How did you know?'

'Well, I dunno, isn't that what always happens? Mary-Louise tells Emily Mears who tells you…'

'Oh no.' Cute Guy suddenly got serious as that kissable mouth formed a pout. Oh shit. Stop it, thoughts. Stop it. 'Emily and I are over, for good. She's back in Europe. I actually bumped into Mary-Louise at the supermarket…'

'And you're together now,' I interjected.

'Oh no! Mary-Louise is gay! Didn't you know that?'

What?! So, did the hottest girl from school have a crush on me? Shit's getting weird.

'No, I didn't know that.'

Silence and then, 'So, do you wanna grab a bite to eat?'

'I'd love to but I have to look after reception while Leticia's on lunch.'

Cue phone ringing.

'Oh okay, I can see you're busy. I'll come by again soon. I just wanted to catch up with you, maybe go on a date again sometime, if you're still available?' he asked.

'I'm not sure I am… I have to get the phone,' I said robotically and did just that.

That night I dreamt Justin and I got married. We lived in a country house with a white picket fence and adopted four storm troopers who would play scrabble with us every night while we drank hot chocolate by an open fireplace.

Then three days later this happened.

'Georgie!' Leticia yelled. 'There's someone on the phone who isn't happy with their adoption and they wanna talk to you!'

'Oh dog.'

Leticia handed me the phone and ran off for a nail-filing break.

'Hello.'

'Well, it's about time. This is Maude Pyke. I got a Jack Russell off you a while back and I don't want it anymore! All it does is bark and bite! It bit my hand right off, it did!' yelled a crusty old woman.

'What, um, I don't remember you. Are you sure you have the right animal rescue?'

'Yessss, I do missy! I'm bringing in this Jack Russell right now!'

'Please, um…'

Hang up.

Oh shit.

'Leticia! Are your nails ready to get back to work?' I yelled then noticed someone was standing in front of me, someone gorgeous who I hadn't seen for a long time. That someone was Hayley.

'Hey, Appleby.' She smiled. *'Now about that Jack Russell!'* she said in the crusty old woman voice.

'Oh fuck,' I said before I burst out laughing; typical Hayley.

'How's tricks? I see you're copying me by having an animal rescue now.'

I took that moment to take her in. Her hair was still short and white-blonde, her smile was still to die for, she still dressed in that semi-dishevelled way I adored. Tick every box.

'Hey um, sorry about your mum. Mel told me.'

'Thanks... so what brings you to Melbourne?'

'Oh, I'm back here for good. Didn't Mel tell you?'

Mel actually hadn't been telling me anything about her sister lately and for that I was grateful.

'No.'

'I left the Adelaide rescue a few months ago. I needed a change. Mary got someone else to run it.'

'Mel did tell me you had a boyfriend, the love of your life...'

Hayley blushed, something I didn't see very often.

'Yeah, maybe for a while, but then I realised I'd already lost the love of my life.'

Was she talking about me? Or Kylie?

'And who's that?'

Before she had time to answer, Leticia was back from her nail-filing break.

'I'll call you. We should catch up,' Hayley said as she walked out the door but before she was gone, she turned around and said, 'By the way, it's you.'

'I doubt that!' I called after her.

That night I dreamt Hayley and I got married and adopted a baby goat that turned into a human baby who would yell at us every day to take out the garbage. Animals were everywhere. Some even did the dishes.

So, they were both back and they were both interested and I was still interested in both of them. Or was I? Hayley and I had that intense attraction and the quick wit and sarcastic back-and-forth that I adored but would I eventually tire of her? And Cute Guy had that shy, sweetness that just killed me and made me want to wrap him up in a blanket and smother him, in a good way, but would I eventually get bored? Hopefully they would both decide to leave me alone, as I didn't think I would ever be able to choose between either of them.

# CHAPTER FORTY-SEVEN

I turned twenty-one on a Saturday so a party was inevitable and the perfect location was Purgatory Palace's ballroom. Mother had hosted many a pompous shindig there before Ben's death. After he passed away, she had the ballroom boarded up. No one was allowed to step foot in there again. We never knew why but figured there must have been some memories of Ben within that grandiose room that she didn't want to revisit.

I'd recently un-boarded the ballroom, had it cleaned by professionals due to the dust and cobwebs that had become inseparable and we gave it a cool paint job, making it more of an arty, alternative space, as opposed to a plastic, posh, poser space. I added a new sound system, which included a record player as I loved my vinyl. I also extended the bar to include pretty much every alcoholic bevvy you could imagine. I'd started drinking a little by then but was actually able to stop before I went overboard. Quite an achievement.

The ballroom was magnificent. It was like having my own personal Espy Gershwin Room. There was room to dance, room to sit, room to drink and, when it all became too much and you needed air or a chewy, it opened onto a majestic balcony with black iron tables and chairs and a view of the grounds.

Posh, I know.

Sorry.

This time I was in charge of the invitations so no one I disliked was invited, except for Uncle-Rock-Star-Has-Been Jack as he was family that I was never able to get away from, but most importantly there was no Noxious Nun Choir.

The opposite of shudder.

As amazing as this party was going to be, I did still miss Mother. I wasn't a complete heartless bastard. Not a day went by when I didn't see her shimmying across Purgatory Palace in my mind's eye before she'd had too much champagne and would start staggering. I wished we could have been kinder to each other and I especially wish she hadn't ended her life the way she did, but I was grateful for what she gave me and my loved ones, bar Andy, so in a way I felt closer to her in death then I ever did in life. At least that was something.

I really made an effort with my appearance to celebrate becoming an adult. I wore a gorgeous black velvet suit that one of Dad's fashion designers had made especially for me. You thought I'd be wearing ripped clothes again, didn't you? The suit was my twenty-first gift from Dad. So cool. Chocky and Saint Teresa were dolled up too, wearing their Thank Dog Animal Rescue bandanas and we were all freshly bathed and deodorised.

I already had a few drinks and was in a festive mood by the time my guests started arriving. I'd requested no presents and instead instructed everyone to donate money to another animal rescue as there were heaps in Melbourne and throughout Australia that weren't lucky enough to have the funds Thank Dog did. Twenty-first gifts weren't important as I had everything I needed – well, in a material sense, at least.

All the usual suspects were present: Troylene, Troy's mum Mrs J, Tits, Mel, Shelley (I know!), Leticia, Prudence, Dad (could not believe he made it) and Josh, Cook and Mr Cook, Mary, Uncle Rock-Star-Has-Been Jack and Auntie Elm (it was way past Gran and Nan's bedtime), and some cool girls from other rescues I'd made friends with and their plus ones. It ended up being a good group of around thirty or so and everyone was having a great time. I didn't invite Cute Guy or Hayley and Mel hadn't mentioned anything about her sister wanting to come. I hadn't heard from either of them since they'd both arrived to declare their lust for me in the same week. I figured they'd cooled off due to my lack of interest, which is what I'd hoped for. I never got my hopes up anymore; in fact, my hopes were always down these days when it came to *relationshits*. But you already knew that.

Uncle Rock-Star-Has-Been Jack accosted me early, sporting his gold *lame* suit and freshly flossed dentures while Auntie Elm as usual looked bored beside him.

'Happy birthday, Georgie Appleby,' he beamed, hugging me so tightly I stopped breathing. 'You know what I'm gonna do?'

No, and I didn't want to know.

'I'm gonna open a dog rescue, too. It'll be the biggest and most amazing dog rescue ever! Actually no, it's gonna be a doggie spa, day-care spa, what do you think? The pooches can get pampered and get their nails done, have a bowl of kibble while they wait, ha-ha! I can sing to them and play guitar and they can howl along! I've still got it, you know? Thinking of getting the band back together – well, they want me back of course! Anyway, back to my idea, then when the pooches are all pampered and have listened to my divine music, they can get rescued. It's gonna be the biggest doggie spa and rescue in Melbourne – no, Victoria... no, Australia... no, the world... no, the universe! So sorry, honey, I might end up putting you out of business. Well, if it's the biggest doggie spa and rescue in the universe, I will probably be putting you out of business! I don't do things by halves, you know! I just have this natural talent in well... pretty much everything!'

'SHUT. THE. FUCK. UP!!!'

No, that wasn't me. It was Auntie Elm. I wasn't even aware of the fact she was able to speak. I guess she'd had enough. After having to listen to this idiot's ego for so many years I'm not surprised she cracked. Good on her.

After her outburst, she cleared her throat and turned her attention to me.

'Happy birthday, darling. I've given an animal rescue some money, like you asked.'

And off she went. My uncle followed with his rock star tail between his legs.

Utterly amazing.

My party rocked. Marlene was DJ and played heaps of Nirvana, which would always clear the dancefloor, but that's when Troy and I would get funky with it. Cook and Mr Cook, Uncle-Rock-Star-Has-Been Jack and Auntie Elm and Mary bonded being of similar age and similar dorkiness and boogied the night away, although they requested a tad too many songs from the 70s for my liking, but whatever, they were having fun. Mrs J, who would fit their demographic, wasn't seen dead with them.

The first gate-crashers arrived early in the form of Andy and Barbie.

Oh, joy.

'What are you doing here?' I asked in annoyance.

'Don't be like that, little sis, or Deb will get offended!' Andy whined.

I glanced at Barbie. She was as usual chewing gum with her mouth open while inspecting her nails and had headphones on, so she'd heard nothing.

'If you're here to cause trouble, you can piss off right now!' I yelled.

'I come in peace, sis! Scout's honour,' he said, holding up the appropriate fingers.

Hmmm, maybe it was time to give him a chance.

Maybe.

'So, how's the house in Lorne going?' I asked, remembering how angry he had been about Mother giving him the Ludicrous Lorne Lodge.

'It's great. Deb and I spend every weekend there, but God it was a mess. Someone had a big party there. You don't know anything about it, do ya?'

'Nope,' I said sharply, starting to leave.

'Hang on, hang on,' he said, grabbing me by my velvet lapel. 'Don't you want your present?'

'I said no presents! Donate to an animal –'

'Yeah, I know, even though we weren't invited, we knew that's what you wanted but we don't like animals unless we're eating them, so we got you a present instead.'

I almost vomited in my mouth after *that* sentence.

He nudged Barbie who promptly took her headphones off.

'Happy twenty-first, Georgina. We hope you like it!'

She handed me a girly gift bag.

Oh God, another push-up bra? One isn't enough?

Troy came and stood beside me, eager for a laugh.

I opened the bag and pulled out what looked like a small dildo.

'It's not what it looks like!' Barbie blabbered. 'It's from America! You put it between your boobs while you sleep and it prevents sagging and wrinkles!'

'Why are you so fucking obsessed with my boobs?!' I screamed, making everyone's head turn.

Barbie was taken aback before whimpering, 'I just care, that's all!' before running off.

'Good one!' Andy yelled as Troy stepped a little closer in case things got more heated. 'You don't deserve this.'

He grabbed the dildo from my hand and ran after Barbie.

I glanced at Troy incredulously.

'At least they're gone and took the saggy boob preventer with them,' he said in a baby voice.

Troy made me laugh as always but there was one more thing I needed to discuss with my arsehole brother before he made his getaway.

I caught up to him and Barbie as they were about to leave the house.

'I wanna talk to you alone,' I said, pushing him out the door and closing it on Barbie's face.

'About what?!'

'I wanna know what you think about Mother killing Ben?'

He said nothing, just stood there, fish-mouthed with his stupid Tom Cruise haircut and expensive suit.

'Well?'

'She made a mistake. I forgive her,' he finally said.

'Well, I don't!'

'Of course you don't! You always hated her. You only loved Ben, but I loved Mum – more than anyone else in this world and now the reason she's dead is because she killed Ben. This whole thing is a total mindfuck none of us will ever get over!'

'You know Ben adored you, even though you treated him like shit.'

'He was annoying! What did you expect from me?! You always judge everyone and think you're perfect. Well, maybe you're not.'

'I never said I was!'

'There was so much pressure on me from Mum to make something of myself after high school, I couldn't disappoint her, so I went to Uni, worked hard, had no life, just studied and then started my own business which wasn't easy, y'know! Sure, I had support and money but I needed to succeed to make Mum proud, which I did! Then Ben died and you were such a disappointment to Mum with all your rebellion bullshit, she gave up on you getting anywhere, which wasn't fair 'cause she was always on my back to make something of myself!'

'I rebelled 'cause Ben died! He was my best friend!' I yelled, feeling the tears start to well.

Andy's expression instantaneously changed to a heartbreaking sadness I had never seen before. I was embraced by his hug and then he was gone and I was left speechless.

After Andy and Barbie left, Troy, Mrs J and I started doing shots, lots of shots; lots and lots of shots. I decided as it was my twenty-first I could exceed my limit, just for tonight, but as I had been out of practice, I couldn't hold my alcohol the way I used to.

'Come on, Georgie, keep up!' Mrs J yelled as she sculled another Jager. That woman was insane. How she did it at her age, I didn't know. I was sure by the time I was late-forties I'd be rocking back and forth in an old folks' home somewhere. I soon started feeling woozy like I was about to pass out, so I left Troy and Mrs J to it and went and sat down on the couch for a while.

*** 

Then came Troy's speech. He had everyone in hysterics recounting our adventures, which included my black eye courtesy of that stupid bitch from the mail room. Good times.

Then came my speech. I had to steady myself as I was pretty drunk by then.

'Thank you for coming to my twenty-first,' I said in a puffed-up voice.

I heard a weird metallic screeching noise that seemed to be coming from the ceiling but, ignoring it, I continued to talk.

'Life has been pretty shit but now that my dream has come true and I've been blessed with my own animal rescue, I know I'm finally on the right path.'

I heard the noise again and looked up, noticing a metal bucket hoisted way above my head that was attached to a rope that had been pulled by someone and before I could yell, '*Carrie!*' a waterfall of blood poured on top of me and trickled into every nerve ending.

The room gasped. Troy ran over and started to wipe my face with a serviette. I just stood there in shock thinking, who could have done this? Who is pretending to be my friend here? Why does stupid shit like this keep happening to me?!

Then I tried to summon my telekinesis but remembered I had none.

\*\*\*

'Georgie! Georgie! Wake up! Are you okay?'

I woke to find Dad and Josh standing above me. I jumped upright and inspected my arms and body. No blood. I sighed heavily as I remembered I'd told Troy and Mrs J I was going to sit down. I must have passed out on the couch and dreamt the whole thing.

*THOSE DAMN SHOTS!*

'Are you all right, Georgie?' Dad asked.

'Yeah, I'm fine. I just had a bad dream.'

'All right, as long as you're okay, because Josh and I have to go. You know I can't be around my brother for long periods of time.'

Uncle-Rock-Star-Has-Been Jack strikes again.

'That's okay, thanks for coming. It was great to see you guys,' I said as we had a group hug. 'Oh, and Dad,' I said, pulling him aside. 'Andy and I talked about Mother and Ben. It was okay, ended in a hug.'

'That's great, Georgie. Fill me in later,' Dad said as they started to leave. 'And by the way, that suit looks amazing on you.'

'Thanks,' I said, beaming.

After Dad and Josh left, I went onto the balcony for some fresh air, finding the Scooby Gang sitting around a table.

'Are you all right Georgie? You look like you've seen a nun!' Tits said jokingly, joint in hand as usual.

'It was worse,' I said before explaining my dream to them.

'Oh Jesus,' Leticia said in disgust.

'What's *Carrie*?' I don't need to tell you who asked that.

'Tits, you wanna give Prudence a puff?' I said with a wink.

'Oh no! I'm sober now remember, Georgie! I don't wanna die AGAIN!' Pru yelled before scurrying away in a blur of hot pink.

'Damn, I liked her better the other way.' I sighed as I took Pru's chair.

'I know, Georgie, but at least she's sticking to it. Better to not say things like that anymore,' Leticia lectured before running off to find Prudence.

Yes, Mother.

'So, you're probably freaking out that scene from *Carrie* is gonna happen when you're doing your speech, right?' Mel asked with a smile and a Mars Bar close at hand.

I glanced at Mel through blurry eyes. My head started spinning and I felt sick. Then I noticed Shelley lurking beside me wearing a puffy white dress that made her look like a sheep dressed as a snowman, but her dress didn't stay white for long. Soon it was vomit-coloured.

Uh oh.

As Shelley screamed psychotically for ten whole minutes, I managed to push her into my bedroom where she got changed into my Debutante ball gown which she insisted on wearing, even though the zip at the back didn't do up.

A sheep in a wedding gown.

Such a surprise she chose that monstrosity. I really should have thrown it out by now, or burnt it with that photo of Ugly Guy.

After I cleaned myself up (luckily my spew had missed my velvet suit), I started to feel better. Damn exceeding my drinking limit, what a stupid idea. Never again, Georgie. Never again.

Then Mel suddenly ran into my room hysterically.

'Georgie!'

'What is it?! Is Prudence on the roof?!'

'No! Justin's here...'

'Damn that Mary-Louise!'

'...with Mary Louise!'

'Oh shit, what's she doing here?'

'Maybe they're going out?'

'No, Mary Louise is gay!'

'She is?!' Mel asked in surprise. 'Well, maybe she's here for you then!' She laughed before leaving.

'Oh God,' I moaned, throwing myself on my bed. Chocky and Saint Teresa joined me and soon gave snoring accompaniment to Shelley as she continued to twirl in front of the mirror, oblivious to the world around her.

I eventually forced myself back to the ballroom and was soon greeted by my latest gate-crashers.

'Hi, Georgie! Happy birthday!' Cute Guy beamed as he leaned forward and gave me a kiss on the cheek. His lips were soft and for a moment my mind recalled the fact we actually had sex but before I let myself be carried away, I did what I do best and snapped out of it.

'Hey, Justin,' I said before glancing at Mary-Louise nervously. She was as usual sun-kissed and stunning but her look did nothing for me and never had. Contrary to popular belief, people who are also attracted to their own sex don't have the hots for every person on the planet. I was worried she liked me though, but maybe she didn't. I mean, why would she? Surely, she would be into her own type and not be interested in a weirdo like me.

'Happy birthday, Georgie,' Mary-Louise said, giving me an awkward hug. It wasn't reciprocated. She wasn't on my hugs list.

'I hope you don't mind us crashing your party,' Cute Guy continued.

Why would I mind? He crashed every party I had. So did Hayley. I'm sure she was on her way.

'Of course, I don't mind,' I lied.

'We actually have a present for you,' Mary-Louise said with a wink.

Oh Jesus. She did like me. Or did she? I hoped not and I hoped the present wasn't something for my boobs and anyway, I said no presents!

'I'll go get it,' Cute Guy announced, jogging off.

'Justin and I bumped into each other at the supermarket,' Mary-Louise began.

'Yeah, he told me.'

'We've been hanging out. We're just friends though, because I'm not into guys...'

'He told me that too.'

'We have that in common.'

'Actually, no we don't,' I said, stepping back.

The disappointment on her face was immediate.

'Oh okay,' she eventually said.

We stood there in uncomfortable silence until Cute Guy returned holding a large cardboard box with holes cut out of the top.

'What's that?' I asked, worried, as presents and I usually didn't mix.

'You'll see,' he said eagerly, handing it to me.

I took the box, put it on the floor carefully and slowly opened it.

I got the shock of my life.

# CHAPTER FORTY-EIGHT

Looking up at me whilst sitting on a blue towel was a familiar furry face that I loved so much.

'I Dunno!' I said in excitement, lifting her out of the box so I could cradle her in my arms. 'How did you guys get her?'

'I had to go to the Prison Camp last week to get a reference from Mrs Frankenstein,' Mary-Louise began. 'She said they were looking to rehome I Dunno as one of the new nuns didn't like the convent cat pooing in the rose garden...'

'New nuns? God, they're breeding,' I said under my breath.

'Then Justin told me you'd taken Sister Catherine's dog and had opened an animal rescue so we thought you might take I Dunno.'

'Hell yes!' I yelled as I Dunno showed her ownership of me by rubbing the top of her soft head on my right cheek.

Soon the Scoobies were huddled around me, bar Leticia, taking turns to hug the feline as she purred so loudly it sounded like the popcorn she was making was well and truly ready.

I left my party momentarily and raced downstairs to the rescue to grab a litterbox, kitty litter, cat food and a couple of bowls, then I took I Dunno to my room. I noticed Shelley had managed to pull herself away from the mirror and was gone. Chocky and Saint Teresa woke up and were happy with their new fur guest, although they were a tad too boisterous for I Dunno so I thought it best to lock her in my ensuite bathroom for the time being. As I poured rocks into her litterbox, she ate a bowl of cat food and drank a little water then curled up in the bathroom dog bed, so I knew she would be fine until my shindig was over.

But when I went back to my party, all hell had broken lose.

Shelley and Marlene were mid-screaming-match, with Troy standing between them like a referee as the bemused guests looked on.

'What happened?' I yelled, running over.

'I need your friend to *leave*, Georgie!' Marlene roared. I'd never seen her so angry.

'Why?'

'Because she just proposed to Troy, that's why!'

I hid my smile with my hand as I glanced at my best friend, who shrugged innocently as he held the two girls apart. Then I glanced at Shelley, who had a psychotic longing in her eyes that scared me. Mel was standing beside her, looking worried.

'Shelley had a bit too much to drink and just snapped,' Mel explained. 'She grabbed Marlene's microphone and asked Troy to marry her.'

'Darling, Troy, you know we are meant to be together,' Shelley purred. 'I caught the bouquet at Titania's wedding! That was a sign from the Lord Jesus Christ! Now I'm in my wedding gown, another sign!'

'Looks like you need a hand,' a familiar voice said beside me. It was Hayley. About time she gate-crashed. 'I do have a little experience with calming psychopaths,' she said with a grin.

'Be my guest.'

'Shelley!' Hayley screamed, clapping her hands to get her attention. 'Troy is with Marlene. Do you understand that? He is Marlene's partner. He doesn't want to be with you! Get over it and move on!'

A tad harsh I thought but it worked. Shelley burst out crying and ran off with Mel in hot pursuit.

'Thanks, Hayley,' Troy said softly, as he led Marlene away.

'So, Appleby,' Hayley said, turning to face me. 'I hear you're old now. Twenty-one, is that right?'

I nodded, taking in her sexy black shirt with one too many buttons undone. Obviously for my benefit, or was she here with someone? I bet she was here with someone.

'I was gonna get you one of those walking frames but they don't come in black,' she said with a smirk.

'Hey! You're older than me!' I protested.

'I know! My walking frame is over there.'

I looked to where she was pointing, seeing a walking frame with no owner.

'Whose is that?'

'It's mine!' Hayley said, starting to laugh.

I looked over at it again, seeing the gran of a rescue girl I knew, walk slowly toward it.

'You're an idiot! Why are you even here?'

'I wouldn't miss this night for the world!' she said in mock excitement. 'Nice suit, by the way. I think this is the first time I've ever seen you wearing something without holes in it.'

We stood there in silence for a moment just staring at each other until Cute Guy and Mary-Louise came up to us. As I watched Justin and Hayley greet each other I realised there I was again, standing between them, this never-ending back and forth that went nowhere. Add to the mix Mary-Louise, who just stood there giving me the love eye, and I seriously wondered whether this was a sign I should just give up and join the convent.

It was at that precise moment I finally decided I didn't want either of them. As Kelly from *90210* said, 'I choose me.'

I left my three admirers and found Mel, who said she had put Shelley in a cab back to her parents' house. That would be an expensive cab ride seeing as Shelley lived in country Victoria but I was glad she was gone. Her parents can deal with her lunacy and she could have that bloody Debutante dress too, I never wanted to see it again.

Things began to settle down when Marlene went back to DJ-ing and soon the dance floor was packed. As everyone got more and more drunk, even the remaining Scoobies were shaking all they had. The twenty-first cake was rolled out and the speeches came and went and were non-eventful. All I did was look above me for a metal bucket. Then Cook and Mr Cook, Mary and even Mrs J left as it was getting pretty late. Mary gave Mrs J a ride home as she was plastered.

As Uncle-Rock-Star-Has-Been Jack and Auntie Elm were leaving I wished him luck with his doggie spa and rescue to which he replied, 'Nah, not doing that anymore. Elm and I are going on a cruise instead!'

As I watched Auntie Elm uncharacteristically smile, I remembered the power in calling out someone's behaviour, no matter how long it takes.

Then all of a sudden *Time After Time* came on. Marlene put it on. God, I loved her. Troy and I immediately spotted each other from different corners of the room and started our *Romy and Michelle* dance as the floor cleared around us. Then just as I was about to do my first ballet move, the song stopped abruptly and *The Lord's Prayer* began.

Deja freaking vu.

I shuddered to the bone.

This wasn't a very funny joke Marlene was playing. I turned to look at her but she didn't smile. She just stood there frozen like she had just seen a ghost.

Then everything went black.

People started to scream. I heard someone yelling for everyone to calm down, that it was just a blackout, but what was really creepy was *The Lord's Prayer* kept playing, which made me think it wasn't a black out, someone had just turned the lights off.

Then a minute later the lights came back on. I turned around and noticed a nun in a black habit standing at the entrance of the ballroom by the double doors.

It was her, my nun-nemesis, it was Sister Catherine.

She stood there smirking wearing her ridiculous Coke bottle glasses and held up a new voodoo doll that was my spitting image. This one wasn't wearing a green school uniform, though. It wore all black. Then she threw her head back in laughter before exiting through the doors.

I tried to calm everyone down but the guests were creeped out and soon left. Hayley ran outside to see if she could find my nun-nemesis while Troylene, myself, Cute Guy, Mary-Louise and the remaining Scoobies searched Purgatory Palace and the rescue in case Sister C was hiding somewhere. I also checked on Saint Teresa, hoping the crazed nun hadn't taken her dog back, but I was happy to find Saint T fast asleep next to Chocky. After we found no sign of Sister C, we reconvened in the living room, bar Hayley, and sat down to digest what had just happened.

'I can't believe she's back,' I said in shock.

'And she has a new Georgie voodoo doll!' Prudence cried. 'I'd be worried if I was *you*!'

'Thanks, Prudence.'

'How was she able to put *The Lord's Prayer* on and turn the lights off at the same time?' Cute Guy asked, glancing at Marlene, who was being comforted by Troy.

'She had an accomplice,' Troy said seriously.

Marlene nodded.

Everyone gasped.

'Marlene didn't see who it was,' Troy went on. 'They held a gun to her back and made her play the song before Sister Catherine turned the lights out.'

Poor Marlene was not having a good night.

'Oh my god,' Mel said, shivering.

'Who's her bloody accomplice?' Tits cried.

'Sister Virgilius?' Leticia asked.

'No,' I said. 'I didn't see her. There weren't that many people at the party, I would have seen her. Plus, she's like 120 years old and can barely walk.'

'Maybe she was in disguise, I wouldn't trust her no matter how old and frail she is,' Tits said.

Maybe, or maybe it was NPP in disguise? Or was it someone who was at the party the whole time, one of the rescue girls or their plus ones? Or was it someone I was actually related to or friends with. Was it someone in this room? Jesus!

'I thought Sister Catherine was in jail? When did she get out?' Mary-Louise asked matter-of-factly as she flicked her blonde hair.

'Who knows? She probably escaped,' I said, defeated.

'I hope Hayley's okay, she's not back yet,' Mel muttered.

Just then Hayley burst through the living room door, scaring the hell out of all of us.

'What happened? Did you find her?' Leticia asked in anticipation.

'No, did you?' Hayley puffed.

'No, she's not in the house... we hope,' Tits said with a shudder.

We all shot a look of complete and utter dread at Tits and decided we had to search Purgatory Palace again, including the rescue, just to make sure that my nun-nemesis was definitely nowhere in the vicinity. I had already decided I would sleep with the light on tonight and make sure my bedroom door was locked, which I didn't usually do but what if Sister C was hiding in my bedroom? No, she wasn't, she wasn't!

After our second fruitless search, we returned to our positions in the living room.

'Hayley, did you know Sister C had an accomplice?' Troy asked.

'No, who is it?'

'We don't know.' I sighed, slumping deeper into the armchair.

'I'm not a hundred percent sure but I thought I saw Bird Girl tonight,' Hayley said slowly.

'Bird Girl?!' Leticia shrieked. 'Do you think it was her?'

'I dunno, Bird Girl was blonde and this chick's hair was dark, but that beak...' Hayley continued. 'Did anyone else see her?'

Everyone shook their heads.

'Her beak is one in a billion though,' Mel piped up.

'I wouldn't be surprised if it was her,' Tits said. 'She always hated us.'

'I feel sick,' Prudence whined.

So, she was back. My nun-nemesis was back and she had a brand new twenty-one-year-old Georgie voodoo doll to torment me with, along with an unknown accomplice that could be Bird Girl. So typical, just when my life was on the up, it turned to shit yet again.

'I need a drink,' Hayley announced, heading toward the bar on the mantelpiece. As I sat staring at the carpet deep in thought, I didn't notice her grab the large fancy champagne bottle that was decked out in a black studded leather jacket. I glanced over just as she put the bottle to her lips and took a swig.

'You're drinking my mother,' I deadpanned.

Hayley frantically spat out a mouthful of ashes and wiped her mouth on her sleeve.

'Jesus! Why is your mother in a champagne bottle?!'

'It's what she would have wanted.'

***

But who was Sister Catherine's accomplice?

Why wasn't she in jail?

And what was she going to do with my new voodoo doll?

The plot solidifies...

Shawline Publishing Group Pty Ltd
www.shawlinepublishing.com.au

SHAWLINE
PUBLISHING
GROUP

Milton Keynes UK
Ingram Content Group UK Ltd.
UKHW020738220224
438207UK00006B/45